Necessary Lies

NECESSARY
LIES

Eva Stachniak

SIMON & PIERRE
A MEMBER OF THE DUNDURN GROUP
TORONTO · OXFORD

Editor: Marc Côté
Proofreader: Julian Walker
Design: Jennifer Scott
Printer: Transcontinental Printing, Inc.

Canadian Cataloguing in Publication Data

Stachniak, Eva, 1952-
   Necessary lies

ISBN 0-88924-295-X

I. Title.

PS8587.T234N42 2000   C813'.54   C00-931770-8
PR9199.3.S683N42 2000

Canadä

ONTARIO ARTS COUNCIL

THE CANADA COUNCIL FOR THE ARTS SINCE 1957 | LE CONSEIL DES ARTS DU CANADA DEPUIS 1957

CONSEIL DES ARTS DE L'ONTARIO

We acknowledge the support of the **Canada Council for the Arts** and the **Ontario Arts Council** for our publishing program. We also acknowledge the financial support of the **Government of Canada** through the **Book Publishing Industry Development Program**, **The Association for the Export of Canadian Books**, and the **Government of Ontario** through the **Ontario Book Publishers Tax Credit** program.

www.dundurn.com

Dundurn Press
8 Market Street
Suite 200
Toronto, Ontario, Canada
M5E 1M6

Dundurn Press
73 Lime Walk
Headington, Oxford,
England
OX3 7AD

Dundurn Press
2250 Military Road
Tonawanda NY
U.S.A. 14150

*To the memory of my father, Jerzy Jerzmański,
and to my mother, Anna Jerzmańska.*

PART I

Montreal 1981

Piotr would say that she was betraying Poland already.

He wouldn't mean that Anna had become besotted by Canadian comfort, by supermarkets overflowing with food, by the glittering lights of Montreal office towers she described for him in such detail in her letters. He wouldn't even mean the ease with which she showered her praises over the smallest things. Strangers smiling at her. Cars stopping to let her cross the street, mowed lawns moistened by humming sprinklers, a man on Sherbrooke Street bending to scoop up after his dog.

Piotr would tell her that the signs of her betrayal were far deeper and far more troubling. He would say that she had let fear creep into her heart. He would be right.

September of 1981. The time Poland was on everybody's lips.

After the unrepentant strike of 1980 in the Lenin Shipyards of Gdańsk, *Solidarność* grew stronger in defiance. The whole world was flooded with images of the grim, determined faces of the striking workers in blue overalls, crossing themselves and kneeling at the feet of makeshift altars; above them hovered the concerned smile of the Polish Pope. Books on the Polish August, on the first independent labour union in Eastern Europe — or rather, as certain commentators knowingly stressed, **Central** Europe — piled up in store-windows. The triumphant smile of Lech Wałęsa, his hand holding a giant cross and a red pen with the Black Madonna of Częstochowa, followed Anna as she walked the Montreal streets. A thirty-seven-year-old unemployed electrician, the papers glowed, had defied the Kremlin. "We want to show the world that we exist," he said at a conference in Geneva, and then stood patiently when hundreds of labour delegates lined up to shake his hand.

That Anna was in Montreal at all was a miracle. In Poland she taught literature in the Department of English at the University of Wroclaw. She had applied for a scholarship to England to research emigré writers, but was told to wait for her turn. The Canadian scholarship was one of these unexpected offerings from fate. "You would have to leave in August," the Dean's secretary said when she called Anna at home late in the evening, "*they* start *their* academic year in September."

Piotr was looking at her from his armchair, eyebrows raised. She pointed at the ceiling in a gesture of bewilderment.

"Someone screwed up," she heard in the receiver. "As usual. They just called us from the Embassy. They need someone from humanities, right away. Are you going?"

"Yes," she answered. "I'm going."

Six months in a good library was a long time. "Any good library," she said to Piotr as he pulled her toward him, his fingers making tunnels in her thick hair, caressing the nape of her neck. She was piling up her reasons. She was already twenty-eight and had never even been to the West. Even if she saved a hundred dollars from her stipend, at the black market prices it would mean twenty times their salary. And she, too, needed a break, a few months of respite from the line-ups, the constant strikes and protests. Anyway, by February, when the winter semester started at the Wroclaw University, she would be back, wouldn't she?

He was mouthing her name, whispering it into her ear. "Go," she could hear him say. She felt the edge of the armchair against her hip. His lips tickled her, made her laugh. He would just miss her, that's all.

"Couldn't you go with me?" she asked him then, even if she already knew the answer. Now? When all was being decided? When the fate of Poland was on the line?

Anna piled up her daily portion of newspapers and magazines on a table in the reading room of the McLennan Library at McGill. *The Gazette, The New York Times, Newsweek, Time.* It was an oak table with metal legs, its edges polished by generations of wrists and elbows. Long commentaries in *Newsweek* and *Time* calmly analysed Polish chances, printed diagrams describing the position of Russian tanks and East German troops, and included colourful tables that listed all previous attempts to shake off Communist rule: East Berlin, the Hungarian Uprising, the Prague Spring, the Polish revolts of 1956, 68, 70, 76. All of them in vain.

She didn't have to be reminded of that.

Yet another bloodshed? Letters quivered in front of her eyes, and she looked away. The fingers of the young man across from her who was reading *Le Devoir* were blackened with ink. In his last letter Piotr reminded her once again that the Communists could not arrest ten million people. That the prisons would burst at the seams.

The man, his young, square face tanned the colour of sunset, must have seen her look at his hands, for he took a crumpled tissue from his pocket and began wiping off the ink. She blushed as he smiled at her, embarrassed by the depth of her curiosity that made her stare at people here as if they were not quite real and wouldn't mind.

"*The New York Times* is even worse," he said. "You need gloves to read it."

It was evening already, but on this side of the Iron Curtain, cities did not surrender to darkness. Even from where she was Anna could spot the glow of the store-windows on Sherbrooke Street. On her last day in Wrocław, Piotr took her out for a drink. They parked their tiny Polish Fiat near the Town Hall and walked in darkness to the wine bar they used to go to when they were students. *Piwnica – Świdnicka, –* Świdnicka Cellar. They sat at a table, its top sticky with spills, the ashtray overflowing with cigarette stubs. A waitress came by, carrying bottles of beer in a wicker basket. There was no wine. The beer was warm.

Piotr demanded she clean their table first.

"I have no cloth with me," she snarled.

"Then go and get one," he said.

That was Piotr all over. Left to herself, Anna would have shrugged her shoulders and wiped the table. Emptied the ashtray onto the dirty plates stacked on the table next to them.

Why bother? Now, the waitress would only make them wait. But Piotr never thought of consequences. There was no selection to his battles, she often thought. In streetcars he demanded to see the identification of the ticket inspector before producing his crumpled ticket. For years he wrote endless letters of complaint to the *administracja*, the elusive owner of the building in which they bought the permission to convert a part of the loft into an apartment. Complained about the crushed vodka bottles in the hallway. Stolen milk from outside their door. Low water pressure. Missing light bulbs in the corridors.

She admired it in him, really, thought it a far superior quality of character than her own willingness to ignore what bothered her. This tenacity, this refusal to give up when she would have waved her hand and went about her own affairs.

When she met Piotr, she was barely seventeen.

After classes, in the school washroom, she lengthened her eyelashes with black mascara, and spread a touch of lipstick on her cheeks to make them look flushed. Her flaxen hair, always unruly, tangled when she brushed it. She unpinned the school badge from her arm. Her friends were already waiting for her on the Partisans' Hill, where they always met to talk and smoke, looking out for teachers who would have liked to catch them transgressing. Report them to their parents. Lower their behaviour mark.

Piotr Nowicki came to meet them on Partisans' Hill. He was a friend of a friend, Daniel said with an air of mystery about him, a law student with "political connections." He was "to sound them out. Make sure they could be trusted." It was January of 1968. The students were beginning to stir.

Partisans' Hill was right by the city moult. A park with a cream-coloured pavilion and empty old fountains with rusted pipes blocked by slime. The boys bragged of knowing where the entrance was to the underground bunkers. Even claimed to have broken the chained lock once and gone in, but Anna did not believe them. On Partisans' Hill, in 1945, when Wrocław was still German and was called Breslau, the Nazi defence had its headquarters. When the Red Army came too close, General Niehoff moved to the basement of the University library. *Festung* Breslau — that fanatical Nazi stronghold, Anna was to be reminded every 6th of May — defended itself longer than Berlin itself.

It was a cold January afternoon, the air misty and damp; they were huddling under the pillared roof, six of them — Daniel, Basia, Andrzej, Hanka, and her, Anna — smoking, waiting for Piotr. She spotted him first, walking in the wet, melting snow, past the empty fountain, his dark blond hair clinging to his forehead and to his pale cheeks. He walked slowly, hands in his pockets, whistling softly to himself. She wanted to brush the dripping curls off his face, kiss the rain off his lips. He didn't see them yet, or maybe just pretended not to see. With the corner of her eye she saw him stop, raise his face to the sky and open his mouth to catch the falling flakes.

It was an awkward meeting. Hands were shaken, promises exchanged. He thought them all mere schoolchildren, babies with mothers' milk smeared over their faces, playing at danger. The cigarettes were silly, he said. So was the make-up, the lipstick. "Why draw attention to yourselves over such trifles?" he asked. "How is that supposed to help?"

Daniel was the first to drop his cigarette to the ground and step on it. It sank into a melting snow. Andrzej followed suit. Hanka wiped the lipstick from her lips with a handkerchief. It didn't quite come off. It left a red stain behind.

Piotr told them that all the Polish students wanted were the rights guaranteed in the Polish constitution, confirmed by international treaties. "For what we now have is a mockery," he told them, in a feverish whisper, "A pyramid of lies."

She thought: He isn't looking at me. He doesn't care for anything but politics.

"We have enough," he continued. In Warsaw, the Communists closed the performance of *Dziady*, in the National Theatre and the *milicja* attacked the students who placed flowers in front of the monument of its author, Adam Mickiewicz, proving that in this "new and just Poland" even the greatest Polish romantic poet was not immune from persecution! Soon, there would be protest everywhere. Dormitories were stocking up on food and candles. Underground presses were printing leaflets that someone had to distribute. There were proofs of harassment to publish. Of unlawful arrests. Of deaths.

"These are difficult times," he also said, his voice turning grave as if he were their teacher admonishing a warning. "There will be provocations. You have to keep your heads clear, watch out for informers. It's not a joke."

She thought: He will go away now, and I won't see him again. She watched his lips as he spoke, pale from the cold.

One by one they were sworn to secrecy. Anna saw Piotr was impatient to go, looking at his watch. They were small fry, not much help could be expected of them. This meeting was more a sign of good will than real action. A groundwork for the future.

"Right," Piotr said turning to Daniel. "I've got your number. I'll contact you when I need help."

"Wouldn't it be safer if you called me?" she said in a moment of inspiration on which she was to congratulate herself for years afterwards. "You could pretend you were asking me for a date."

He turned to her before she had finished the sentence and smiled for the first time. It was a funny sort of smile, the smile one gives to a child's antics.

"Sure," he said. "Why didn't I think of that?"

She gave him her telephone number, scribbled it on a page torn from her notebook. She went home thinking: He will call me. She wanted to sing it, to chant it as she skipped on the granite tiles of the pavement. At home she pinned her hair up and took off her glasses. Her profile, she decided, was not her strong feature. There was a slight backbite to her jaw that she did not like. She looked far better with her hair loose, curling along her cheeks.

She kissed the mirror. She baked a plum cake.

"What's the occasion?" her father asked.

"Oh, nothing," she said. "I had a good day at school."

Piotr called her that same evening, far less sure of himself than he was on Partisans' Hill. All he wanted to do, he fumbled, was to check if the number was right.

14

"Yes, it is," she said and waited.

To check, he continued, if perhaps, she wouldn't mind seeing him. To discuss things, procedures, in case there was an emergency. For a coffee, perhaps. She liked the hesitation in his voice, the hint of insecurity. Delighted at her own power, she was not going to make it any easier for him.

"What if one of my teachers sees me," she asked, her voice as casual as she could make it. "You know we are forbidden to go to cafés. Wouldn't it be *drawing unnecessary attention* to myself?"

"No," he said. "Yes. It doesn't have to be a café," he said.

She pressed her lips to the receiver before she put it down. Then she blew him a kiss, in the direction of the window, Central Station, the Town Hall.

For two long months they met in various places, on Partisans' Hill, down by the statue of Cupid on a brass horse, by the milk bar in – Świerczewskiego street. Piotr brought her books to read, handed them to her like treasures, like bouquets of flowers. *The Plague, Caligula, The Trial*, tyranny and evil exposed, observed, stripped of its disguises. Then he gave her the Parisian edition of Arthur Koestler's *Memoirs* and Czesław Miłosz's *The Captive Mind*, so that she would understand the power of propaganda, the temptations of betrayal.

He fumed about Sartre then, angered at the blindness of a great mind. The gravest disappointment was when intelligence did not suffice. How could a philosopher be so blind, he asked, a man who saw so much elsewhere? How could he defend Stalinism, dismiss reports of terror and the Gulags, turn a blind eye to so much suffering?!

"Because it was happening to someone else," she offered her explanation. "Because it was far away?"

He was not convinced. "It's too simple, *maleńka*, my little one," he said, frowning. "There must have been other reasons."

She may have wanted to kiss that frown away from his forehead, but she knew how to wait.

He insisted on walking her home, on taking her upstairs, to the doors of her parents' apartment. When they reached the second floor landing, he made her ring the bell right away, pressing her hand to the brass button.

She thought: Why don't you kiss me? What are you afraid of? She waited.

He kissed her a month later. Two months later they were lovers. "This is," he whispered, his face buried in her hair, "what I was afraid of."

She was not afraid. For weeks she walked with a knowing smile on her lips, shrugged her shoulders when boys shot her looks at the vaulted school corridors covered with layers of beige paint. "Puppies," she thought, her lips pouting. What was happening to her was serious. It was real love.

She had to sneak by the concierge at his dormitory, bending to pass underneath the counter, his hand tousling her hair. His three roommates would leave, obligingly, leaving their smell behind them. The sour smell of cigarette smoke, spilled beer, and something else, a strong smell of young men, restless, far away from home. All they had was two hours. Two hours to be alone, two hours for the world to shrink into a narrow bed covered with a rough grey blanket and their naked bodies. Two hours of nothing but love.

She was intoxicated with the daring that grew in her. "What's happening to you?" her mother asked. "You should be studying. I need your help around the house." *Babcia*, her grandmother, was no longer alive, there was no one to stand in lines for food, to cook and to clean. They all had to contribute now. There were no excuses.

When *Dziadek*, her grandfather, died, *Babcia* took his body to the Powązki cemetery on the outskirts of Warsaw. "That's where I want to rest, too," she had said. Wrocław she didn't trust. It felt too German to her. Too transient. Land that had changed hands could be changed again. "Who knows how long before the Germans come back to take it all away?" That's where she was buried, too, next to her husband. In Polish soil.

Anna hurried with the dishes, whirling through the kitchen like a fury, impatient with all that could stop her. She hovered over the telephone, determined to be the first one to answer it. From time to time her father gave her a knowing smile, but she knew he would never tease or embarrass her. If at any time it was he who answered the phone, he would never ask who Piotr Nowicki was the way her mother would.

"A friend," was all she was prepared to say. She would tell them more when she was ready. But only then.

In March, Piotr was given leaflets to take to the students at the *Politechnika*. This was the real beginning, he said, when Anna came to see him at the dorm. This time they hurried; there was no time but for a kiss. The leaflets were in two bundles. An explanation of the need for action, a call for peaceful protests and for a Poland-wide student strike if necessary. He put the bundles into his shoulder bag.

"Give them to me," she said. "They won't search a schoolgirl."

He hesitated.

"Come on," she said. "Give them to me."

She washed all traces of mascara from her eyes and tied her hair into a ponytail, a thick flaxen curl between her shoulder blades. Pinned the school badge to her left arm, smoothed the sleeves of her uniform. Let her glasses slide down her nose. She could look fourteen when she wanted, innocence itself.

"Give them to me."

He didn't look at her when she took the bundles from his bag and pushed them into her school satchel. For the first time it occurred to her that he might be scared, but she dismissed the thought at once. Not Piotr, not him.

At the last moment she put a jar of jam and a loaf of bread into his bag. And then she rolled the newspapers that were lying on the table and added them.

"Just keep cool," he whispered into her ear and offered her a shot of vodka. She drank it and felt nothing but warmth, not even a turn in her head. He had two shots, one after another and gave her a mint candy to disguise the smell.

The first time the *milicja* patrol approached them she did keep cool. They had discussed the best tactics before and Piotr was now doing his part, leaning on her shoulder, his body heavy and limp. She gave the men a helpless smile, a smile of a woman left to carry her burden, an old dance of the sexes. They had counted on that. On their laughter at his mumbling voice.

"Just don't be angry with me, little sister," Piotr pleaded with drunken insistence. "Can a man not have a drink in this country anymore without a woman screaming at him?"

"Wait till Mother sees you," she yelled and gave his body a shove. "She will teach you a lesson." That's when the *milicja* men laughed.

Later, far from their sight, Piotr heaved his body straight. "Bastards," he said and she watched his upper lip tremble. "Bloody pigs."

The second time they were stopped, the two men in blue uniforms with set jaws in their pale faces emerged from around the corner before they had time to do anything.

"Documents!" they barked and then stood, feet apart and looked at them as they fumbled for their I.D.s. Anna handed hers first, to the shorter one. Slowly his eyes travelled from her face to the photograph in her school identification. Piotr, she had noted, handed his internal passport, not his university I.D. "What's in this bag?" the taller one asked, pointing at Piotr's shoulder.

"Nothing," Piotr said. "Groceries. We've just done some shopping."

"Open it up!"

The bag slid onto the pavement. Piotr kneeled to open it and took out the jam, the bread. The newspapers.

"Student?" The shorter one was taking over.

"Yes."

"Where are your books then, Mr. Student? Aren't we supposed to be learning? Aren't we supposed to study hard?"

"At the dorm," he said. "I left them at the dorm."

"Is that so, Mr. Student? Or maybe we needed some room to carry other things than books?"

Anna stood motionless, staring at them, watching their every move. Think, she told herself. They are going to beat him up. Think! If she didn't clear her throat, she would choke.

"A nice girlfriend. A lucky bastard, too!" the taller was looking at her now. The shorter one spit on the pavement, the white blob landing at Piotr's feet. Glass cracked. Kicked, Piotr's bag landed a few feet away. The *milicja* men laughed. Their knuckles tensed on the handles of the white night-sticks. "Let's see how lucky you really are!"

She could see, with a corner of her eye, that the sinews in Piotr's neck were tensing up. He would say something now, she knew it, say something that would make the men strike. Call them pigs. Moscow lackeys. Quote his constitutional rights. Then they would be arrested, searched. She had to stop it, right away. Now.

"Him!" It was the contempt in her voice that caught their attention. "He's no longer my boyfriend. And he is no longer a student. He failed his exams."

"Third time," she said and laughed. "Failed for the third time."

She was counting on the power of their contempt, on the slight chance that they might dismiss Piotr as not worthy of their effort. She was not taking into account the simple fact that she was humiliating Piotr. Such deliberations required time. She felt the men's eyes slide up and down her face, her breasts, her belly. She was waiting, a soft smile on her lips. Anything that might tip the scales in Piotr's favour.

The shorter man, who was holding her ID in his hands, had been staring at her picture for some time now, but did not write anything down. A golden ring on his finger glimmered in the sun.

"Shouldn't you be at school right now?" the taller man finally said, and she knew that she had won. He was returning her school I.D.

"That's where I'm going," she said, taking it and putting it in her pocket. Her school was, indeed, a few streets away. "Only now I'll be late."

"Scram, you piece of shit!" the taller *milicja* man said to Piotr. "And don't let me catch your ass around here again."

She was so proud of herself, so relieved that it was all over, that she never noticed his silence. As soon as they turned around the corner he took her bag from her and told her to go to school right away. She tried to protest, but he said he had no time for any nonsense. It was only when he didn't call her that evening that she realized the enormity of her defeat.

You fool, she said to herself. You damn fool. What have you done?

Anna went to Piotr's dorm a few times, left messages with the three roommates who swore to tell Piotr she had come by. She cried so much that in the morning she had to put cold compresses on her eyes before she could face her mother, but even that did not help much. "It's all that reading," she lied. "Studying for the exams."

A few days later, Daniel brought her a note, slipped it to her in the math textbook. The note was from Piotr. In Warsaw, during a protest against repressions, the students were beaten up by the *milicja*, right in front of the University. That was the spark they were all waiting for. Now, Piotr was inside the *Politechnika*. The Wrocław students demanded to be heard. He was not going to call her, for all calls were monitored and he didn't want to put her in danger. She was to wait and trust him. He knew what had to be done.

In the school bathroom where she went to read Piotr's note she burst into tears. She cried again, on Partisans' Hill where Daniel patted her on the shoulders and kept saying that Piotr would be all right. But she was not crying from fear. She was crying from happiness. Piotr had forgiven her. She had not destroyed his love.

Soon it became clear that the student revolt had turned into one more defeat, a handy excuse for the government to start another internal purge. The Communist Party had no trouble convincing the workers that the spoiled "brats" from universities were forgetting who was the ruling class in Poland. Whose sweat was paying for their education? As to their demands and criticisms — some were justified. It was not the Communist Party, however, that was at fault, but the Jews. Weren't they responsible for the Stalinist rule? Weren't they infiltrating the party ranks? The Jews who never truly supported Poland, never cared for her? If only they would leave, all would be better off. Poland was for true Poles only. The students were misguided at best.

When the strikes and protests were over, the interrogations began. "Why did you do it? Who told you to start it? When? Give us names, more names. That's your only chance." Piotr knew the questions by heart, prepared himself with answers. Rehearsed them with Anna, debated the merits of giving the names of known informers or perhaps not mentioning any names at all. Many of their friends were kicked out of the university, barred from all but the most menial jobs, and most of their Jewish friends had already been told to leave.

Newspaper columns filled with code words, *foreign element, cosmopolitanism, internationalism.* Suspicious words, alien, not Polish. "No one is keeping you here," the commentaries declared. "Leave. Go to Israel. Isn't it what you always wanted?" Piotr was interrogated and arrested. Taken from his dormitory room in hand-cuffs. Daniel called. He told Anna to write to Piotr's father in Kraków.

This is when Anna learned Piotr's father was not just a doctor, but a well-known heart surgeon whose skills had a price beyond money.

"Please," he said and his voice when he called her sounded just like Piotr's. "I have to know everything before I start asking for favours. It is absolutely essential to establish how much they know."

She agreed to meet him. Her own parents still knew nothing of Piotr. She wanted no comments from her mother that she was still before her *matura* and university entrance exams, that there were eight candidates for each place at the Department of English. That if she didn't do well, very well, her whole future would suffer.

Dr. Nowicki waited for her in the Monopol Hotel, in –Świdnicka street. He won her over at once, with his resemblance to Piotr in spite of the grey in his hair, with his concern for his "foolish" son, a concern, she decided, mixed with admiration.

"He is just like me," he said, smiling, holding her hand up and kissing it. There was a smell of Old Spice aftershave around him. She knew it; her father used it, too. In her best olive green dress and with her glasses hidden in her purse, she was worthy of his son.

"Please forgive me for imposing myself on you. Piotr should have brought you to Kraków, to introduce us properly. Now, circumstances make their own demands."

She wished she had not taken off her glasses. As he sat across from her at the table, she could not see the fine details of his face.

This was not the first time he had to come to his son's rescue, Dr. Nowicki began. But he was not blaming Piotr. Far from it. It was all Communism's fault, he said.

"Bullshit," she would hear Piotr say later. "Of course he blamed me. His methods, of course, are so much more superior to mine, right? All he has to do is to cut open a few party bosses and then ask for a small favour in return."

But that was to come later. Then, at the Monopol Hotel, Dr. Nowicki was still investigating the situation that he admitted was very unpleasant and delicate. "You see, *Pani Aniu*," he said, "This is not the first time I'm doing it."

"I know," she said.

She did know. Why would anyone, she once wondered, come to live in Wrocław? Come here from Kraków, of all places, that rare Polish city untouched by the war, saved by a miracle that, depending on who was describing it, involved a German art-lover, a Russian marshal, or wet and sabotaged explosives. Leave a city where generations of Polish kings lay buried in the vaults of the Wawel Castle, where in St. Mary's church a trumpeter stopped his bugle-call in mid note in memory of a Tartar arrow that pierced the throat of his predecessor, centuries ago. Leave to come here, to Wrocław, this city without a past, where history ended with the desperate Nazi defence of *Festung* Breslau.

Her own parents came to Wrocław because Warsaw was bombed and destroyed. They stayed because this is where they got their jobs. There always had to be reasons, reasons to come here and ever better reasons to stay.

"I got into trouble," Piotr said. He told her how, with his two friends, he went to the country and bought a pig. "Then," he said, leaning toward her, his eyes still sparkling at the thought, "we painted it red and let it out. During the May First parade. Right underneath the tribune, all their fat party leaders standing at attention."

"You did what?" she asked. She couldn't stop laughing. He watched her, smiling, pleased with himself, so very much pleased.

"Wasn't easy, you know. We had to bribe the peasant with a bottle of vodka to sell it. He said we didn't look like the types who would know what to do with a pig. Then we had to bring the beast to Kraków, in Father's old car. But, ah, it was worth it. The looks on people's faces! You should have seen it!"

She wished she had. It was a story she loved to hear, the picture filling out with each retelling. The pig squeaking, running in circles. The stinking car that had to be washed and aired for days. The red faces of the "pompous fools" on the tribune.

"How did they find out it was you?"

"Someone squealed," he said, winking at her. Someone saw them, heard the noise. The police found the paint in his room. They were blacklisted, thrown out of Jagiellonian University.

"My father had to pull a few strings to get me to school here," he said, shrugging his shoulders.

That's what attracted her then, this recklessness that seemed to know no fear. "As if there were no tomorrow," her grandmother would have said, with a sigh.

Now, Piotr's father was telling her of his vigil in front of the Party secretary's office. Of his pleas to let his son continue with his studies. Of biting his tongue when he was lectured on how badly he had brought him up.

She told Piotr's father all she knew. About Daniel. About the leaflets. About the nights spent at the *Politechnika*. Dr. Nowicki listened and nodded. Sometimes he asked questions. He asked, for instance, if Daniel was likely to testify.

"Daniel is all right," she said. "Nobody interrogated him."

"Are you sure?" he asked.

No, she wasn't sure, but Daniel never said anything about any interrogation. Never seemed worried or upset at school.

"Good," Piotr's father seemed relieved, too. He asked for Daniel's phone number, though, and she gave it to him. That, too, would later make Piotr very angry. She had no right. She broke the first rule of conspiracy. "I gave it to your father, Piotr," she said.

"You shouldn't have," he said. "Not even to my father."

The results of Dr. Nowicki's visit were visible within a few days. Piotr was interrogated, but he was never beaten. His file was quietly shelved. A plain clothes policeman gave him a stern lecture on his responsibilities toward his fatherland, a warning not to get mixed up again with the wrong crowd.

"Fuck you, Pig," Piotr said.

The policeman chose not to hear him. "Kiss your father's hand when you see him," he said. "To thank him that your mouth is still on your face."

That was his second humiliation. It was the one that almost killed their love.

After his release, Piotr went to Kraków for a few weeks, then returned. When she called him he said that he had no time. She was already a first-year student when he came up to her in the *Uniwersytecka* library. He looked pale and gaunt. She could smell vodka on his breath. When he whispered her name, tears welled up in her eyes.

That's when he told her this joke: "Two friends meet. You know what, Maniek, one asks. Something terrible is gonna happen. – What do you mean? Maniek asks. Another war? – No! – Germans will invade again? – No! – The world will end? – No! – So what will happen? – Nothing! We will always live the way we live!"

They walked together, slowly, along Szewska Street, to the Town Hall. Piotr talked incessantly. Of new proofs of callousness, stupidity, and vicious lies. Of Polish troops in Prague, helping to extinguish the Prague Spring. "Welcomed with flowers by the grateful citizens of Czechoslovakia," the papers wrote, "helping to preserve freedom." Of corruption, sloth, pilfering. Of the viciousness of anti-Semitic attacks that were making Poland a laughing stock of the civilized world.

"I still love you, Piotr," she said. "There is no one else."

She did love him. There was no one else. She never thought there could be.

He asked her to marry him. Right there, by the monument of Alexander Fredro that had been lugged here all the way from Lvov to replace Frederick Wilhelm III. Plucking a flower from the flower bed, shaking off the earth from its roots. His eyes shining with joy. With love. With hope.

At the McGill library the man with ink-stained hands rose to leave. He asked Anna if she cared for his paper or if he should take it back to the rack.

"Please leave it," she said. "And thank you."

"You are welcome," he said.

Solidarity gets tougher. It defies Moscow with a call for free unions in the Eastern Bloc and free Polish elections, she read. The newspaper columns grew more and more alarming. Military hospitals were being put up on the Soviet-Polish border. Troops were kept on standby alert, guns were loaded and routes to the Polish border were mapped out. The Warsaw Pact started its military exercises, *Zapad 81* — West 81 — in the Gulf of Gdańsk. The deafening noise of a few hundred thousand soldiers, of tens of thousands of tanks, aircraft, and ships was heard for miles. The commentaries pointed out that Brezhnev's words, *We will not leave Poland alone to suffer,* left no illusions as to the Soviet intentions. The Polish situation was threatening to the Warsaw Pact. *Newsweek* printed pictures of workers gathered around Wałęsa, their raised fingers forming the sign of a V; on the opposite page there was a photograph of Russian missiles, pointed west.

Refugee camps in Germany, Italy, Spain, Greece and Austria were filling up. Every day more Poles jumped ship, defected, extended their holidays abroad. Tens, hundreds of cars with Polish license plates arrived at the entrances to the camps, whole families poured out and pushed through the gates, terrified that there wouldn't be enough space, that they would be turned out, told to go back. Inside, photographed and fingerprinted, they surrendered their passports for a room, food rations, and immigration interviews. Until the day when their names would appear on the list for a flight to the United States, Canada, or Australia they would wander the streets, looking hungrily at shop windows, at supermarket shelves, at colourful stalls filled with oranges, watermelons, peaches, and grapes.

Piotr would say that the West was merely panicking. That stories like that were exactly what the Communists wanted to frighten everyone into submission. That all the West really cared for was their fat asses, their precious market shares and interest on Eastern European loans. Haven't they betrayed Poland in 1939, and then again at Yalta? She must not lose heart. Not now. Not when victory was so close at hand. When they finally, finally, had a fighting chance for a normal country.

"You are not thinking we could leave, are you? Like these cowards who beg the Austrians or the Italians to take them?"

"Are you?"

For Piotr, Anna composed her little descriptions of Montreal, the grey stone buildings of McGill, the beam of light travelling across the sky, rotating under greying clouds. Everything she saw excited her. By the time each day ended, its beginning was already a far-away memory. Transformed by the sounds of English and French, nothing around her was ordinary. Not even a simple walk along Sherbrooke Street, past chic Victorian townhouses with their art galleries and boutiques where the prices — mentally exchanged into Polish *zlotys* — multiplied into unreal, unattainable sums. Her eyes took it all in — the red brick façades, the bay windows with black frames, the stores she didn't dare to enter.

Along St. Catherine Street she felt more courageous. The carpeted interiors welcomed her with music, and she fingered the soft cotton of Indian summer dresses, asked to try on thick-soled brown leather sandals, wrapped a muslin shawl around her neck and then returned everything, guiltily, apologetic at not having the strength to curb her desires. Only on the Main, dizzied by the bargains of St. Laurent, where signs *Two for a dollar* were scribbled in black marker, did she really let her hands dive into the cardboard boxes spilling into the street, fishing out the splashes of colour, the promising shapes from which she concocted her new look.

That's where she bought white, green, and yellow beads which, in the morning, she carefully braided into her long hair. That's where she found the mauve cotton dress and black leather sandals with steel studs. Wire glasses, a round, grandmotherly type, gave her what she liked to think of as an artistic appearance. It suited her. It drew looks.

You would not believe it, darling, she wrote. *It's a world straight from pre-war Poland I thought I would never see. I heard haggling over prices, in Yiddish, and Polish. They still sell pickled herring, here, from barrels, wrapped in old newspapers! Measure out fabric with wooden rulers! Yesterday I saw Hassids in black coats and hats, their beards untouched by scissors and it was as if I were transported right into my grandmother's Warsaw. They walked with their eyes cast down, to avoid temptations.*

She rented an apartment on the corner of De Maisonneuve and Rue de la Montagne, right above a Hungarian restaurant that served spicy goulash and *spätzle.* Marie pointed out to her that the location was perfect. Anna could walk to McGill. Across the corner was a small Czech patisserie where she could have her morning coffee. Didn't she just love the sweet pastries displayed on paper doilies, folded over glass shelves? The Czechs were Marie's friends; she had interviewed them once for one of her radio programs. The owner defected in 1968, after the Russians invaded Prague and was now dividing his time between Montreal, the Laurentians, and Florida. To Marie he confessed that he no longer needed to bear the cold nor the humidity. Let the next generation sweat it out. He could afford his escapes.

Anna's apartment consisted of a tiny kitchen, a bathroom, and two small rooms, furnished with an old sofa-bed, a dresser, a couple of bookshelves, and a grey Formica table with two plastic-covered chairs. In the closet Anna found a cardboard box with a rusted frying pan, a few books in Arabic with pages swollen from dampness, and a small coin with a square hole in it. The first day she made the mistake of leaving an opened cereal box on the counter, and found it swarming with cockroaches. This was a detail she did not include in her letters home.

In the fall of 1981, out of all her Montreal friends, Marie Chanterelle was already the closest. A journalist with Radio-Canada, equally comfortable in English and in French, Marie had been to Poland and to Czechoslovakia. She had smuggled manuscripts from Prague to Vienna, interviewed Michnik and Havel. "Trying to find out what gives them the strength to go on," she told Anna. "Where do they get the courage not to grow bitter."

With Marie, Anna could discuss the futility of hope, the overwhelming evidence of Eastern European helplessness. Together they listed the reasons. The bleeding Budapest of 1956 and Kadar's show trials. Dubček's pale face when he was called to Moscow to account for the fever in the streets, and his tears when he gave his first speech after Soviet tanks entered Prague. The unmarked graves of the workers killed in Poznań, Gdańsk and Szczecin in 1956 and 1970. With Marie, Anna could pore over the maps of Poland marked with thick black arrows, the possible routes of another invasion.

"Piotr," she told Marie then, "doesn't want to leave Poland. Ever."

"Are you afraid?" Marie asked her.

Anna *was* afraid. In spite of what Piotr might tell her, she was afraid of Russian tanks, of Piotr being killed, or even arrested, sentenced to years in prison. Of his father, now her father-in-law, not being able to help next time.

Marie squeezed her hand. For weeks she had been interviewing refugees from Poland. She got Anna's number from a McGill friend and phoned to ask her how Polish women survived the chronic shortages, how they managed without toilet paper and sanitary napkins, how they kept clean without shampoos and toothpaste. "Can I come over to speak to you?" she had asked. "Don't worry. I won't use your name. No one will know."

Anna told Marie of hours spent in line-ups, of the constant lookout for things that could be traded, of hair washed with egg yolk and teeth brushed with baking soda. It was all terrible, humiliating, she said. Nothing worked, nothing was available. Marie did not agree. Her own parents still remembered the Great Depression in St. Emile. There was nothing humiliating about resilience, she said. Nothing to be ashamed of.

From their long talk that first day, just a few clips were used in a collage of voices Marie summoned to express the feeling of the impending catastrophe among Polish refugees. In her documentary, politicians warned of military retaliation, crowds in front of the Soviet embassy in Ottawa chanted their demands for freedom. "Nothing would make me go back, now," a man's voice declared. "There is no hope." Then came Anna's voice, describing the life of shortages. High-pitched, she thought, and strained. And then a young woman's voice, shaky, bordering on tears, "I have a three-year-old son and a husband who are trying to leave before the doors close. I'm praying every day that they make it."

The McGill library was getting hot and stuffy. Anna shifted in her chair, her back muscles begging for relief.

Round two in Poland, she read. *Warsaw puts military patrols in the streets as Solidarity resumes its rebellious national congress.* Military officials were being deployed in every Polish village, amidst uneasy explanations that their sole purpose was to combat corruption. General Jaruzelski, whose hollow face and dark glasses she now saw regularly alongside Solidarity leaders, announced the formation of a Committee of National Salvation. Hopeful stories were recalled of his family estate confiscated by the Soviets in their 1939 invasion of Poland, of his family deported to Siberia, of his youth spent in Soviet camps where his eyelids cracked from burning sun, of slave labour that injured his back and took the life of his father. Was the man in dark glasses, she read, a faithful servant of a powerful master, or a man waiting for his chance?

No, Piotr would never think of leaving. No matter how long the line-ups for food, however easily whatever freedoms they still had would be crushed. Oh, yes, he would agree with her that their lives were outrageous, would fume at the necessity of nights spent sitting on folded chairs in front of stores to secure a place in a line-up for a car battery, a refrigerator, a bed. But shortages, he argued, were nothing more but another proof that Communism had failed, gone bankrupt, and would have to go.

Their last evening in Wrocław, they drank the warm beer in *Świdnicka Cellar* and held hands across the table, the top now smelling of the rotting rag with which the waitress had wiped it. Piotr chose to ignore the foul smell and the obvious resistance of the waitress.

"I'll miss you, darling," he whispered. "Why am I letting you go? Come back soon!"

They had been married for ten years. They had never parted for long.

"I will."

She stopped herself from saying anything else. In the car his hand was already making its way inside her blouse, brushing her breast. She could feel her nipples stiffen, making their delicious pulsating promise.

If anyone had told her that this was the time she might fall in love with another man, she would have laughed. Friends she would make, of course, that she knew. But love?

Newcomers to McGill were all invited to an afternoon at the Faculty Club, and Anna arrived there slightly resentful of having to waste the whole afternoon she could have spent in the library. She never liked big parties and now when Canadian writers were beginning to intrigue her, she felt she had so little time left. From Poland, Canada seemed like a vast, blank sheet of prosperity. Only with its writers did the whiteness take on the first shades of colour. She read, mesmerised by what was emerging before her, the sharpening contours, the hues.

Marie l'Incarnation dreamed of walking into a vast, silent landscape of precipitous mountains, valleys and fog until she came to a small marble church. The Virgin with Jesus sat on its roof, talking about Marie and about Canada. Then the Virgin smiled and kissed her three times. It was a sign, the French nun wrote, to come here and make a house for Jesus and Mary, among the Hurons.

Anna read stories of forced conversions, of New World blankets harbouring the killer germs, decimating the Huron villages. Of French farmers clinging to their language and religion amidst a sea of English. Of being told one was only good to carry water and serve one's betters. Of the revenge of the cradles and the Quiet Revolution. Of the miracles, shrines, and protests. Of martial law and fervent, thwarted hopes for independence.

"Isn't it just like in Poland, now," Marie's friends often said. Anna liked them a lot, these men with bushy long hair, chain smoking Gitanes, and the women who, hearing she just came from Poland, hugged and kissed her, assuring her the Polish people were *marveilleuse* and *formidable*. They made her admit that *Le Devoir* had far more coverage of the crisis in Poland than *The Montreal Gazette*.

"You should understand us so well, Anna! We, too, are struggling for our independence, here. For our way of life! Our very survival is at stake!"

"No, it isn't like Poland," she kept telling them. But only Marie would agree with her.

At the entrance to the wood-panelled hall she was given a name tag to stick to her dress. It said, *Anna Nowicka, Poland. Visiting scholar. Department of English.* Her resentment evaporated. She was charmed by the ease with which conversations started. "I just thought I would come up and say hello," was all that was needed.

"No, my husband couldn't come with me," she tried to explain if anyone asked. Passports were not easily given to families, and, besides, Piotr couldn't really just leave. He was teaching civil law at Wrocław University, he was a legal adviser to a local Solidarity chapter. No, of course it wasn't the best of solutions, but what else could they do.

"A girl from Breslau!" That was William's voice, raised in amazement. "Where are you from in Poland?" he had asked,

31

and she said, "Wroclaw," prepared for the need to explain once again the shifting borders of post-war Europe, the story of the territories gained and lost in which a German city became part of Poland. But he did not ask her for explanations.

"A girl from Breslau!" he repeated. "What a coincidence!"

"Wrocław," her mother would protest, each syllable a distinct, resonant beat. **Vro tswav!** That's how she would say it, **Vro tswav,** her face locked in a tense grimace of mistrust.

William's eyes narrowed with pleasure as he smiled at Anna. He was wearing a black turtleneck under an open shirt — yellow and red patches twirling on the fabric as if spun by a juggler's hand. His beard, trimmed short, made her think of the plumage of some rare silver bird. He had brought her a glass of wine, and she was holding it so tightly that the shape of the stem imprinted itself on the palm of her hand.

She knew he liked her, felt it in his eyes, in his smile, in the growing intensity with which his blue eyes took in the curls of her hair, the movements of her head. As if, with every move, with each simple gesture, she was accomplishing something truly extraordinary, something no one else, ever, could have done.

"So you *do* know where it is?" she asked him, brushing her hair back, away from her face.

The days were still warm and she was wearing a loose Indian dress she had bought in a store on St. Laurent. It was a black cotton dress with purple patches, the shape of falling leaves.

"Are you surprised?"

"Yes."

"I was born there," he said. "When it was still Breslau, that is. So we are really from the same place."

She was playing with the beads in her hair, turning them with her fingers and then letting them go, thinking of an old photograph she had of herself, a tiny figurine, a white dress, a halo of curly hair.

In the black and white picture, she is holding her mother's hand. Behind her are the ruins: piles of rubble spilling into the streets, clusters of red bricks, some still paired together with mortar, slabs of concrete and granite. A sea of ruins, surrounding small islands of still-standing buildings. Bent pieces of wire stuck out of cement blocks, ripped from the foundations. Underneath the crumbling plaster of what used to be walls of apartments, a wicker lattice revealed itself like a web of veins under the skin. Some of the houses were cut in half, gutted, with discoloured patches on the walls where balconies had fallen off. Where rooms had been — living rooms, bedrooms, studies — the walls betrayed the decorating tastes of their now departed inhabitants, mosaics of greens and blues, walls papered or painted. Streets, too, had been ripped apart by explosions; big craters cut through stones and sand, through the granite blocks of pavements. Some of the streets led to neighbourhoods that no longer existed, deserted valleys in between mountains of debris. Smooth, steel tramway tracks still cut through them, ending in the piles of rubble, disappearing in grass and weeds.

"That's nothing," her parents told her. In 1945, when they arrived, it frightened them to walk past the abandoned shells of walls, of houses gutted and burnt. The city was empty, so terribly empty that for months after they would fight tears at the sight of a child in the street, the first, fragile promise of permanence. By the time Anna was born, the Baroque houses of the Old Market Square had been restored, their façades painted white, beige and pale yellow. By the time her parents took her for walks by the Gothic Town Hall with its brightly painted sundial or the majestic towers of the Cathedral on the Oder Island, it was almost possible to believe that the war had passed them by.

"When did you leave Breslau?" she asked William that evening.

"In 1945, in January," he said. "I was five. But we came to Canada before I turned seven."

The walnut panelled room of the Faculty Club was beginning to grow too noisy and too hot. Anna could feel people pushing her from behind, murmuring their apologies and moving on. She had to strain her ears to separate his voice from the noise around her.

The thought that he was German, even if his German childhood might be nothing more than a few memories of the war, cautioned her to be careful of the things she said. She didn't want him to think she was expecting expressions of guilt, feelings of contrition for the crimes of another generation. But in truth she was. She needed to put him in a safe zone, for she was already aware of how much he could mean to her.

"I don't really remember much," he said.

Later she was to learn that it wasn't true. All she had to do was to discover the right question. But at that time she didn't know about Käthe, did not know that she should have asked him about his mother.

And yet, even then, he did remember something. In his Breslau street, as in the Wrocław street she grew up on, there was a row of acacia trees, covered in pale white flowers. In the spring the whole street looked as if it were sprinkled with creamy snow. When he sucked the tips of the flowers they gave up a faint taste of sweetness and wilted under his fingers.

"Nothing else?" she asked. He must have heard the disappointment in her voice for he told her of the long wait for the train that was to take his mother and him out of the city, the smell of heavy coats, of sweat, the suffocating feeling of having nowhere to escape to. "I've never been so afraid in my life," he said. "And I don't think I ever will be again."

He had calmed himself by staring at the spirals and mazes of cracks on the ivory tiles lining the tunnel of Breslau *Hauptbahnhof*. Every single one of them different. He had traced these cracks with his finger, the little cells and cobwebs made by the frost and the pounding pressure of heavy trains passing above.

"Have you ever gone back?" Her throat was dry and her voice came out trembling, losing its self-assurance.

In 1975 or 76, he wasn't quite sure of the year, he had toured Poland with the McGill student choir and Wrocław was one of the stops. *Wratislavia Cantans*, he remembered the name of the festival. Had had a beer near the Wrocław Town Hall and watched the crowds. The women were gorgeous. He liked the way they walked, their bodies swaying in a rhythm almost forgotten on this side of the Atlantic. And the city? Didn't care about how German it looked. Never liked Germany much. His family was not Nazi, thank God. His grandfather was executed in Berlin on Hitler's orders, but he didn't take much comfort in that. German acts of defiance didn't amount to much, after all, did they?

He must have seen her relief.

"You might have passed me by," he laughed, suddenly taken with the thought.

"Were you alone?" Anna asked. She was already trying to feel her way around. He wasn't wearing a ring. She looked at his hand. And she knew he had noticed hers.

"Yes. Marilyn, ex-Mrs. Herzman, didn't much like to rough it with the students. She was into mud spas, then. Excellent for her nerves, she said. Would *you* have been alone then?" he asked.

"No," she said. "I wouldn't."

No, not then. They were not from the same place. His Breslau was no longer there and in her Wrocław he could only be a visitor from the West on an exotic trip to a deprived land, marvelling at how the locals could live among such squalor.

"You must have thought us all very shabby," she said, regretting her remark at once. It wasn't pity she wanted from him.

But he protested. It was a fascinating world, far more exciting than anything else he had seen in years, but not because of its German past. He did notice that the old German buildings were run down, but he couldn't make himself care. The past was not worth getting excited about, he said; it only diverted your energy from more important things. It was the present that fascinated him, the defiance of the people, their resilience, their courage.

Anna knew this was not all together true. For wasn't it the past, so drab and deprived in her memory, that was now making her somehow better in his eyes? Better than if she had been born here, in Montreal.

Later that evening when a tall, pretty woman threw her arms around William and kissed him on both cheeks, Anna slipped out of the Faculty Club. "Darling, you are impossible!" she could still hear the woman's sugary voice. "Where have you been hiding these days?"

Anna walked home slowly, a short walk down McTavish

Street, to Sherbrooke, turn right, past the glittering veranda of the Ritz Hotel, past the crowded restaurants on Rue de la Montagne. In one of them she saw a couple, a gaunt man and a petite woman in a red dress, toasting each other at a small round table. The woman gave her a quick look and burst out laughing, tossing her head backwards. In the store windows, chic mannequins posed in thick, winter coats lined with fur — men and women, frozen in half step, elegant and poised. Carefree.

Anna could still hear William's voice. She half-imagined him next to her, his arm touching hers. "That's nothing," she kept thinking. "Someone I could've become friends with. Someone I'll never see again." The wind was cool, and Anna was feeling its bite. Was it already the first sign of winter? Canadian winter she had been warned to fear, as if no Polish winter could match it.

At McGill Anna signed up for courses in literary theory, in which she discussed the futility of making any valid and objective statements about literary texts. Thoughts of words upon words that redouble and multiply meanings as they are read excited her. "I have so much catching up to do," she wrote in her letters to Piotr. She wrote to him about the trappings of deconstruction, the stripping of layers of ideology from literary texts, revealing biases, contexts, underlying interests. "Nothing is innocent," she repeated. "Nothing without its negation."

Piotr's letters arrived in shabby blue envelopes, with her name in a big uneven script. *Lies, lies, nothing but damn lies,* he wrote ignoring the censors. He was angry. Angry at the betrayals, the blank pages of Polish history that, now, finally, could be brought to light. What was the true extent of repressions after the 1968 student revolt? Who started the anti-Jewish campaign and why? Who signed the orders to shoot at the workers in Gdynia in 1970? Who had connived with Stalin at the show trials? *We have to find the whole truth,* he wrote. *Uncover every treachery. Otherwise there will be no new beginning.* She put his letters back in their envelopes and placed them on the night table, next to the photograph of the two of them, on a hike in the Tatra Mountains. In that photograph Piotr was making a V sign with his hand, and she was resting her head on his arm.

William called her two days later. She thought he might and prayed he wouldn't.

"Anna? William here. William Herzman."

She had forgotten how warm his voice was. There was music in the background, the soft chords of a piano concerto, coming from another room.

"Where did you hide? I turned my back and you disappeared. The clock hadn't even struck midnight!"

He had looked for her, she thought. He had found out where she lived.

"I had to beg the Chairman of English to give me your phone number. Made a complete fool of myself!"

With her fingers she was straightening the black coils of the telephone cord, trying to disentangle them.

"There is so much I want to show you here. You must let me take you around Montreal."

Infatuation, that's what she called it then. Harmless, she told herself. Less than love, fleeting, ephemeral, easy to forget. If she didn't stir, it would pass by.

Each morning, her hand trembled slightly as she blackened her eyelashes and drew a thin line along her eyelids. She imagined running into William at the library or in the campus bookstore. "What a coincidence!" he would say, smiling, "Would you care for a cup of coffee?" and she would smile back and say yes, and they would go across the street to a small bistro and she would sip her coffee slowly, hoping it would never end. A thought like that could make her laugh aloud; she could imagine him next to her, his arm around her shoulder, and then she would stop and tell herself not to be silly. "Utterly silly, insane," she would say, and her hands would touch the spines of books on outdoor stands, the rough surfaces of the walls.

It was the time when she began her long walks through Montreal. She couldn't stay in one place then, too impatient, too eager to know what would happen next. Something would have to happen and only time itself had to be pushed forward. Faster, faster, she hurried past the tree-lined campus, past the white townhouses of Milton Street, and then up Avenue du Parc, onto the Mountain.

On one such walk, at a fruit stall, she bought a handful of red cherries and as she walked she took them out of a plastic bag, pairs of fruit joined together at the stems. If she were little she would wear them like earrings, carry them with her for a long time, before she would allow herself to taste such a treat. But now, laughing, she pushed a whole handful into her mouth and greedily chewed the red sweet flesh until only the smooth stones remained.

"Oh, my God! What am I doing?" she would ask herself when she stopped, out of breath, her heart pounding.

"I can't be in love," she repeated to herself, smiling, already pleased with the thought. "It's impossible. It can't be."

"All about you," he said. "I want to know all about you."

She laughed. "You want to know all my secrets?"

"Yes. All your secrets."

She wanted to bury her face in his chest.

He took her for a drive to the Laurentians. The summer had been dry and the fall colours were already beginning to show. Browns and golds of oaks and maples, flaming red leaves of the sumacs. He took so many pictures of her that afternoon, by the fallen tree, in front of a red barn, waving to him from the edge of the lake, petting a country cat, its speckled eyes narrowing with pleasure. "Smile," he kept saying. "We are all very unthreatening here."

She thought: Then why am I so scared?

The country roads were almost empty of traffic. "What's that?" Like a child she pointed to things she had not seen before, farm silos, communication towers flashing their mysterious lights. She wanted to know so much about him, but she promised herself she wouldn't ask, so she was watching him instead, his hands gripping the steering wheel a little too tight. On his black sweater she saw the glimmer of silver, the hairs shed from his beard that she had an urge to pick.

Only later, when they were crossing the bridge back to the city, she broke her own promise.

"Didn't your parents want to go back with you?" she asked. "To Breslau," she added, as if he could doubt what she meant.

"To Wroclaw?"

It pleased her that he observed the politics of geography. He paused, as if the question required his thought.

"Yes."

"I've never known my father," he said, slowing the car down and she thought that he, too, began counting the minutes before they would have to part, "and my mother never wanted to see Breslau again."

Montreal spread before them. Among the warm fall colours of the Mountain the green dome of St. Joseph's Oratory was almost invisible. She was thinking that in his voice she could hear some old, recurring arguments.

He had no patience with nostalgia, he told her then. He was tired of old Breslauers he sometimes met, suspicious of their stories. All this talk of the perfect city, prosperous, safe, well planned! Bourgeois heaven!

"Youthful amnesia, that's what they all claim now," he said, his lips pouting, "but in these border towns they all voted for the Nazis. These glorious defenders of the German soul!"

Didn't she, too, find it was always so? he had asked her as he drove off the sun-lit highway, into the downtown streets filled with strolling crowds. Wasn't the past always presented that way? As better? More mysterious? More meaningful? Even the worst, most guilty past, he added, and his shoulders rose in a shrug. It seemed to her then that he was reading her thoughts, anticipating her questions, answering them before she was even aware they were there.

They were two blocks away from her apartment. One more turn and she will be alone again.

"Did you see your old house?" she didn't want him to stop talking. This city she had left with so little regret, where she never felt at home — Wrocław — had now begun to intrigue her. "Is it still there?"

"Yes," he said. "It's still there."

"Did you get in?"

"No."

He had driven past it in a taxi. He hadn't even asked the driver to stop, just to slow down, so that he could take a quick look without drawing anybody's attention. As the car passed by, he remembered that his *Oma* had buried a box with family silver in the back yard, right before leaving for Berlin. Under the hazel bush.

"And you never even tried to get it back?" she asked.

There was never any parking space on Rue de la Montagne. He had to stop in mid-traffic to let her out.

"No," he said as she freed herself from the seatbelts. "Of course not. Why disturb the new owners, remind them of the old hatreds, stir up the past?"

She had to agree with him. Why, indeed?

"A new friend of mine," Anna told Marie, then, "a composer from McGill." She had the overpowering need to speak of William, then, to confirm his existence.

"What's his name?"

"William. William Herzman."

"Never heard of him," Marie said. "What has he written?"

In the music library Anna had found a recording of William's oratorio, *Dimensions of Love and Time*. On the back of the record was a photograph of William from fifteen years before. He was sitting in an empty room, on a carved antique armchair, looking away from the camera. His face was longer, she thought, with a touch of austerity about it she had never noticed. It must have been the absence of beard, she thought.

William Herzman is one of the most promising Canadian composers of the decade. His music draws its inspiration from the act of questioning. It rings with the profound distrust of the sacred. It allows for no comfort, no escape; it demands the suspension of emotional involvement as we seek to understand the essence of the human experience.

She ran her finger along the contours of his face.

"Anything else?" Marie asked. "Has he written anything else?"

Anna said she didn't know. "It doesn't matter, anyway," she said, lightly. "I just thought you might have heard of him. At Radio-Canada. That's all."

A week later, he was waiting for her in front of the Arts Building on the McGill campus, sitting on the stone ledge, looking at the city below. She could see him from afar, motionless, hands folded on his lap, in his beige coat and a brown felt hat. A fedora. In her grandmother's stories of pre-war Warsaw, men wore fedoras and foulards, they lifted their hats to greet women. He looked at his watch. She was late, but not too late yet, not beyond hope.

"I can still turn away," she thought, "There is still time." It was getting dark already, and the beam of light circled the sky over the downtown office towers. "We can be friends," she kept telling herself. "Just friends."

There was nothing wrong in seeing him, she decided. They liked to talk, that's all. They liked the same books, the same movies. For hours they talked of Elias Cannetti, Günter Grass, Apollinaire. "You absolutely have to see it," he would say and take her to all his favourite films. In the red velvet seats of the Seville Repertory Cinema she laughed at *The Life of Brian*. With amazement she watched the rituals of the *Rocky Horror Picture Show*, when at the clue from the screen the audience threw rice, lit cigarette lighters or squirted water. William took her for evening drives up the Mountain to show her the lights of the city. They lined up for hot bagels on St. Viateur, had late dinners in restaurants along Prince Arthur. When they walked, they were still careful to keep a distance between their bodies, conscious of every swerve that could bring them closer together. All that time he never asked her about Piotr.

He smiled when he saw her approaching, a smile of relief.

"Dinner?" he asked.

41

She loved these long, unhurried dinners, with dishes arriving one by one, filling her with delicate flavours. For the first time in her life she tasted escargots, black bean soup, the pink flesh of grilled salmon, green flowers of broccoli. She was insatiable, always looking hungrily at the colourful plates, eating far too much, as if to make up for lost years.

She nodded. If there was already something irreversible about this evening, something that made it different from all the others, she was trying not to think about it.

"So," he asked when they sat down, the flame of a candle wavering between them. The day before she had promised to tell him why she was so fascinated by her emigré writers, stories scattered in emigré papers, thin volumes of poems printed by the small presses of London, Chicago, Montreal. As if the mere act of leaving anointed people with some mystical, unexplainable superiority. As if they could see more.

"Isn't it a prisoner's dream?" he asked.

The question troubled her. In Poland she would never think of the need to defend the importance of these exiled voices from abroad. Her interests might be declared suspect or embarrassing to her department, dangerous perhaps, but they would never be questioned like that.

"Dangerous?"

"Of course! After all," she said, "they defected." He waited for her to continue.

"And yet," she added, "for us they were never absent."

If they pined after Poland as they were scrubbing capitalist floors or committed suicide by jumping from their New York windows, she told William, then such writers could count on scraps of official memory. They were of use to the Communist government; their failure scored points against the West, poisoned the illusions, proved that happiness on the other side of the Wall was a mirage. If they denounced the crimes of the post-war years, kept alive the memory of Stalin's betrayals, their words were smuggled into the country in the pockets of travellers and reprinted in the underground presses.

"In Poland it wasn't easy to get to them," she said.

She had to get letters of recommendation from her research supervisor and a special permit from the censor before she was allowed to open yellowed copies of emigré newspapers in the Wrocław library. Provided she did not make photocopies of the material that the old wrinkled librarian grudgingly placed on her table.

But, there, in Poland it was all a ruse. An excuse to get facts for Piotr's bulletins. In the 1930s ten million Ukrainian peasants were starved to death on Stalin's orders. In the Soviet Gulag, before the guards could stop them, prisoners devoured the frozen meat of a mammoth. In orphanages, the children of dissidents were taught to worship the great Stalin, their true and only father. Near Katyń, Charkov, and Pver, the Soviet NKVD executed fifteen thousand Polish officers, prisoners of war, and, when in 1943 the mass graves were discovered, blamed the crime on the Germans.

Here, in Montreal, she sank into the descriptions of the lost Eastern lands, the sandy banks of the Niemen river and the depths of the Lithuanian forests. It was a forced exodus. When the post-war borders moved westward, the Polish inhabitants of Vilnius and Lvov had to leave or become Soviet citizens. She read of the trek of the displaced that ended in the former German lands, in Wrocław and Szczecin, in the villages of Lower Silesia and Pomerania. A flood of people, tired, defeated, humiliated, mourning their dead, remembering the minute details of houses left behind, the creaking floors, the holy pictures. These people whose towns and villages were cut off by the borders of barbed wire and ploughed fields became her Wrocław neighbours. "Where are you really from?" they began all conversations, "How did you get here?"

"I was lucky," *Babcia* would say. She had left Tarnopol, a small town east of Lvov, in the 20s. Her parents were still buried there. On All Souls Day there was no one to light candles on their graves.

Her *immigrant scribblers*, William used to call her emigré writers, tending their marble graves. "Have you noticed," he kept asking Anna, "that whether written in London, Toronto, Sydney or Geneva, the tunes of lament are always the same?

43

Is there nothing out there but what you've known before?"

That's what Anna tried to explain to William that night. "They are remembering the forbidden," she said. "That's what I am trying to do, too."

"What if nothing is forbidden?" he asked. "What then?"

She thought about it, sipping her wine, making little circles on the tablecloth with her fingernails.

"I can't imagine it yet," she said.

The wine was beginning to soften her tense muscles. She took a bite of bruschetta the waitress placed between them on the white tablecloth.

"You do love your husband, don't you?" William asked her.

She saw that William looked away when he said it. So she, too, only permitted herself to stare at his hands. Tanned, slim hands, long fingers softly folding a dinner napkin, or tracing the shape of his beard. She was playing with the strands of wax dripping from the candle. She must have shivered then, for he put his hand over hers, and, quickly took it away.

"I'm starving," she said and took another bite of bruschetta. The piece of tomato slid from the bread and fell on the tablecloth. She picked it up and tried to soak the stain with her napkin.

"Don't worry about it," he said and poured more wine into her glass.

When the world whirled in front of her eyes, she tried to stop it by staring in one direction only. She took a sip of water. In the morning she had passed by his McGill office in the Music Building. Second floor, third door to the right. The corridor was empty and the floorboards creaked under her feet. Quickly she touched the brass knob of his door and walked away before anyone could see her. She thought about borders. The dangers of crossing them. Of finding herself on this other, forbidden side. Of the point, still hidden to her, from which there would be no turning back.

"You are changing, Anna," she heard William say, his voice so warm, so full of concern for her. "Your new needs are as real as your old ones."

"Are they, really?" she asked, thinking of Piotr, trying to remember the touch of his lips.

44

William drove Anna back home. There was no place to park the car, and, as soon as he stopped in front of her apartment, she released the latch of the seatbelt, ready to flee.

"I've fallen in love with you," he said then. Blood rushed to her cheeks. "You know that, don't you?" The car behind them honked. The driver leaned out of the window. "Hurry up," he motioned to them and flashed his headlights.

She opened the door and dashed out. She didn't even turn around to look at him. Inside her apartment she didn't switch on the light. She sat on the floor, back to the wall, and held her knees. She rocked her body, until the phone rang.

"I'm sorry," William's voice on the phone was quiet, almost shy. "I shouldn't have said it. You have enough problems without me."

She was sobbing into the black receiver.

"Anna," she heard. "Anna. My darling. Are you all right? Am I hurting you?"

She didn't answer.

"If you tell me to go away, I will. Tell me to go away."

"I love you," she whispered, and then waited in the dark, tears and laughter mixing together. She heard the soft knock at the door and let him in, his face white and drawn. He bent to kiss her, and she stood there, still crying, feeling his soft lips on hers, both happy and terrified of what she had done.

"I'll go mad," she kept saying. "I'll go mad. I'm so happy I want to die."

In the bedroom she watched him kneel on the floor and kiss her hands, and bury his face in them. She felt her skirt lift, rise above her knees. She was shedding her clothes like skin, like another, inferior version of herself. She no longer wanted to resist. That she allowed herself to be so besotted was a sign in itself. This love was like a new life, too strong to oppose.

"Anna," he whispered, "my darling." She knew then that she would never go back to Poland, to Piotr, but the thought didn't hurt yet. Gently she licked the tips of his fingers as they moved over her lips. His hand slid down her neck onto her naked breasts, down between her legs. "Oh my God, please don't punish me. I'll be better, I promise. With him, I'll be better, I'll understand more," she prayed, closing her eyes.

She repeated the words he whispered to her, the English words his voice gave new meanings to, "My precious darling, my love."

"I don't want an affair," she said. "I won't lie about you."

And then, her eyes still closed, with the pores of her skin she felt the warmth of his lips.

"I'm thirsty," she said.

He walked barefooted to the kitchen and poured her a glass of cold water. She was shaking when she drank it all, gulp after gulp, a cold snake entering her, filling her insides. He kissed the glass, licked the drops of water from her chin. They laughed. Through the window they watched the roofs of houses, the lights of lampposts, of passing cars. Across, in the distance, was the giant cross on the Mountain, erected by a city grateful for being spared from a flood, now long forgotten. He pulled her toward him again, her hair tangled, her body ready for him. It occurred to her that she should check the balance of desire. That it was dangerous to love too much, to be that insatiable. Before she had completely formed the thought, she was ashamed of it.

There was moonlight in the room where they lay, entangled, still hungry for each other. The furniture was grey — all shadows, dark, indistinguishable. There were layers to their bodies, whole territories to explore. The soft outer layer of his skin wrinkled when she pushed it. The veins were like underground tunnels criss-crossing the body. She breathed in the smell of his hair, a vague scent of wood smoke and the wind. "Are you making sure I'm real?" he had asked, capturing her hand, and she laughed in response. A teasing laugh, a challenge.

Her first dream of him must have been a nightmare. She woke up in the middle of the night and found her flat, narrow pillow wet with tears. She could not remember the dream, just the feeling that he had been there in it, the centre of everything, and that she, in some dreamy, bodiless form, was being dragged away from him. The emptiness that descended on her took away her will to live.

Still crying, she sat up in bed. She embraced her legs, drew them tighter and rested her chin on her knees. The room was cold, and she was shivering. The air coming from the open window was thick with the smells of cooking, stale food and last night's garbage, the smell of downtown alleys, wet from the rain.

In the apartment on Rue de la Montagne Anna could spot Piotr's letters in her mailbox before she had opened it, blue envelopes showing through the brass slits. They all had blurred ink stamps on them — *EKSPRES* — underneath her address, an attempt to speed them up.

She walked slowly upstairs with his letter in hand. She examined the stamp, an aeroplane rising over the newly reconstructed Warsaw castle, the last, missing part of the Old Town, rebuilt from pre-war records, paintings, and photographs. She let the letter lie, unopened, on the table while she was rearranging bottles of creams on the bathroom shelf, wiping off specks of dust. Upstairs someone was moving furniture, scraping the floor. In this building the apartments did not keep their tenants for long. There was no lease to sign; all the landlord asked for was a deposit and a month's notice.

She pulled on the flap of Piotr's letter. It came off at once; the glue on Polish envelopes did not resist. Inside, on an onionskin sheet of paper, rows of uneven, small letters. She would have to read them slowly, word by word, for Piotr had used both sides of the paper and the writing showed through, like an inverted echo.

Darling! The word startled her. She had already begun to read his letters as if they were meant for someone else, as if she were eavesdropping on intimacies that could only embarrass her. Piotr was thanking her for a postcard of St. Joseph's Oratory, asking what else she had seen, complaining that her letters took too long, that they arrived sealed in a plastic bag with a stamp, THE LETTER ARRIVED DAMAGED, a telltale sign of censorship.

It was pointless, she thought. There was no sequence to their writing, no order. When a letter finally reached her she would find him answering questions she had already stopped asking. The express postage must have helped this time, for this letter had been mailed only a week before, on the 25th of November, 1981. *We don't much plan for the future, here, or speculate what might or might not happen. Or calculate our chances,* he had written. *We cannot all leave and let the Communists take over, we cannot let them win. Someone has to stop the madness, this perverted lie. Besides, is there enough space on earth to take in the whole nation? Or would you rather I said, "to hell with the whole nation, I'm interested in myself alone."*

She tossed the letter away. "It doesn't matter anymore," she said aloud. She had already given the landlord her notice, taken down the photographs from the wall.

I have read and reread your last letter many times. Darling! I don't understand what you are trying to say. What has Polish ethnocentrism to do with anything? Who is self-centred, unable to see beyond the horizon? And what about this "inability to forgive" you are so worried about? You are very cryptic in your letters, which must make the censors as bewildered as I am. Not that I care much about the censors! Forgive whom? For what?

His life consisted of meetings, evenings spent alone, frustrated, angry. There was a package of Earl Grey tea he got from some smart British guy who interviewed him for the BBC and knew what they really needed. This cup of tea, some cheddar cheese and some crackers was his definition of luxury. He had reminded her of the evenings they spent together, of the poems by Herbert he read to her. *Remember Mr. Cogito's message?* he had asked: *Do not forgive in the name of those who were betrayed at dawn.* She read on, unable to stop, but no longer listening.

I know you would agree with me. That you agree with me now. You wrote that you have changed, but surely change does not have to mean that you have forgotten what we both believed in? For if it does, darling, maybe this is the time to stop changing.

Carefully she folded the thin sheet and put it back into the envelope. To Marie, over a soft peak of cappuccino sprinkled with chocolate, she said later, "Damned country. You can't even leave your husband without feeling that you've betrayed your fatherland. Nothing is private there. Not even my damned letters to him. Nothing."

There were more letters from Wroclaw. Her mother wrote of empty stores, of growing line-ups for meat. There was no bread, no flour. *Try to see as much as you can and eat well. Don't worry about saving any money. Who knows how long we will be allowed to travel, when you will have such a chance again.* William helped her make food parcels, filled with corn flour, flour, raisins, almonds, baking powder, gelatine, boxes of cereal, and, together, they took it all to the post-office. Her Christmas present, she thought.

There was nothing she could say that would make them understand what she was about to do.

In a liquor store she picked up cardboard boxes and began packing her things. Books, notes, copies of articles on her emigré writers. She folded her new dresses, a pair of jeans, loose cotton shirts. Five cardboard boxes joined the suitcase with which she had flown into Mirabel "Is that all, darling?" William said. "My, you do travel light." He helped her carry them to his car; all of her possessions fit into his trunk.

In William's place, which Anna slowly learned to describe as "our Westmount townhouse," she was still like a rare and distinguished visitor. He told her he had bought it for nothing, half of its real value when, at the time of the Quebec referendum the real estate prices collapsed. That's how it was here, he said, in spite of what she might have heard from her crazy French friends. The French Canadians kept a knife at Canada's throat and nothing would satisfy them but the breakup of the country. For now, it may all seem settled, but he wouldn't hold his breath for the future.

Anna loved the house, its red brick walls, oak woodwork. There were stained glass transoms over the doors and a bay window in the living room. She moved through the rooms carefully, listening to the creaks in the floors, learning the views from each window. Her own things melted into the house without a trace. Her cheap paperbacks lay unpacked.

Her clothes took just a few hangers in William's closet.

She loved watching William move through the kitchen in his red apron, among the scents of food, adding herbs to the steaming pots, pouring wine into them, setting the timer, turning the roasts, lighting cognac on steaks. Foods had their own chemistry, he said, there was a science of mixing tastes, a sensitivity to the palate that had to be trained and then indulged.

She touched the lids of his musical boxes, with their brass, ebony and mother-of-pearl inlay, turned the brass keys to listen to the tunes of Weber, Mozart, Bellini. He had repaired them all, she learned, big and small, fascinated by the simplicity of their mechanisms. All that was necessary was a spring, a cylinder with steel pins that would lift and suddenly release the tuned steel teeth, and a brake of sorts. "Mechanical music, a challenge for the human mind. Clarionas, multiphones, hexaphones, Violano-Virtuosos." His eyes sparkled when he showed her his treasures, opened the boxes to point to the perforated paper roll, the Geneva stop-work that prevented the springs from overwinding. These air brakes as he called them had parts with funny names, the governor, the butterfly, the flyer, the worm.

"Play them for me," she asked and he walked around the room winding them for her. The bells, the chimes, the soft tunes filled the room, and she laughed and clapped her hands, delighted. When he was away, she would open his violin and touch the strings, the black pegs, the smooth black hollow where he rested his chin. He had told her that violins remember, that when they were played with mastery for a long time the wood captured the exquisite sounds within itself, kept them for the future. "Nothing else matters, nothing but love," she whispered into the resonance holes and laughed.

In the evenings, lying in bed, hands behind his head, William watched her as she moved around the bedroom in her ivory lace nightgown, one of the many presents he gave her. "You are so beautiful," he murmured and she felt a pulsating, throbbing warmth rising inside her, crouching between her legs. After they made love, when his muscles tensed and when his head fell against her neck, she listened to his breath, shortened and raspy, broken by the sighs of pleasure, and then she listened to the beating of his heart.

"It will hurt," William told her. "It always does. But we will be all right, won't we?"

"Yes," she said. "We'll be all right."

She did not think of it much until then, the pain of parting with Piotr, breaking up her marriage. With William beside her she was happy, blissfully happy.

In the first week of December she dictated Piotr's number to the operator. By the time he picked up the phone her heart stopped a million times, a torrent of little deaths. Her palm was sweaty, and she gripped the receiver too hard. She was to remember this for a long time afterwards, the spasm, the tingling of her hand.

Piotr didn't understand. "You've met someone? You are not coming back?" he asked, as if she were talking of something entirely impossible, ridiculous even.

She had to repeat, for the connection was poor, the buzz of static overwhelming, and then there was the echo that made her hear her words as if they were spoken into a vacuum, returned to her before she had finished speaking. It humiliated her that he didn't understand. In her mind she had already altered the past, made him expect her desertion, and his surprise was an affront, a slap on the cheek. How could he not understand? How could he not see it coming? Did she pretend so well? Feign her happiness with him, her love? For she must have feigned it. If she truly loved Piotr, she would not be in love with William now. Would she?

Marie, of course, did not think so. "You are not the first woman, darling, to discover you can love two men at the same time." But Anna could not believe it.

Now, with Piotr at the other end of the receiver, Anna did not know how to find words sharp enough, words that would make him hear, that would make him understand.

"Please. Try to forgive me," she said. "I didn't think it would happen, and I can't explain it. It's all my fault. I'm sorry."

William was in the other room when she made the call. They were still unsure of their territories, still learning to judge what could be demanded and what should be left unsaid. He paced the living room floor. He could hear her speak, but he could not understand what she was saying. Her voice, he would tell her later, seemed to him all consonants, sharp, whistling, a shiver.

Piotr must have understood finally, for he told her to suit herself. "I haven't really known you, have I?" he asked, and then she heard a muted curse and a slam of the receiver.

She wept the whole evening. She let William rock her to sleep, give her a tall glass with gin and tonic. She drank hastily. Sleep was an escape, long, deep, incoherent, filled with the images of the world disconnected, hands, knees, the warmth of someone's skin. Wetness. The pillow was wet when she woke up, in the middle of the night, alert.

She slipped out of the bedroom, quietly not to wake William up. In the credenza drawer there was an old packet of cigarettes she had spotted a few days before, a leftover from an old, discarded habit. The window in the living room had a stained glass panel, and she sat in the wicker armchair, legs curled up, staring at the grey patterns of squares and circles. The taste of smoke surprised her; she had not smoked since that day, thirteen years ago when she met Piotr on Partisans' Hill. It hit her lungs with a force she had forgotten. Her brain swirled. She inhaled the smoke deeply and let it out. Another long drag, the glowing tip sparkling and fading in the dark. She sat like that for a long time. Cars passed, the lights made patterns on the ceiling, flashes of light, one chasing another. She did not move. In the morning William found her with her head resting on her arm. Asleep.

On December 12, 1981, they gave their first party to celebrate their coming together. Marie brought Anna a bouquet of red roses and hugged her for a long time before she let her go. "Just take care of yourself," she whispered in her ear. William's friends came with good wishes and curious glances. "Long time, no see," she heard voices in the hall as William greeted them, "You lucky man. How do you do it?" Her extended hand was squeezed and shaken as William introduced her to his colleagues, former students, their wives and girlfriends.

She was asked how she liked Montreal, if she had already been to *Place des Arts*, to the Laurentians. "William is a great guy," she was told in conspicuous whispers. She was nodding her head, smiling, recounting all the trips they had already taken. No one asked her about Poland any more; she was no longer a visitor, and it was now tactless to mention what she had left behind.

By degrees the living room became too warm, too smoky, and she found herself drifting off, unable to fend off the thoughts of her mother who must, by then, have learned about her and Piotr. In her big, dark Wrocław apartment, among the mismatched pieces of furniture and threadbare carpets her mother and father were getting ready for Christmas. There would be tears at Christmas Eve supper, and an empty plate at the table where she would have sat.

"Are you all right?" William asked. "You look pale."

"It's nothing, love," she said. "I'm fine." It pleased her so much to call him *love,* to hear the concern in his voice. To exchange little smiles of understanding across the room. She thought she should hide her pain from him, keep the old life away from the new.

There were too many people she didn't know to make her feel comfortable. Marie was busy talking to a tall, handsome man who was sitting cross-legged on the floor. She was kneeling opposite him, making large circles in the air with her hand. The black strap of her silk blouse kept falling off her shoulder. From where she stood, Anna could hear Marie's laughter, see her thick, black hair tossed back. She did not want to interrupt.

Anna walked to the window to open it a bit more, to let in fresh, cold, wintry air. Outside, the world was covered in a white snowy blanket. Thick caps formed over street lamps, fire hydrants, parked cars. Enormous white flakes danced in the light. She wanted the party to end, to stop the growing noise, the laughter, the stories of events that had no resonance for her yet, memories of the lost referendum, absurdities of the French language policy, upcoming constitutional wrangles.

Eva Stachniak

"Lévesque was stabbed in the back," she heard a fierce whisper. "Once again!" Someone hummed a few notes of a song. "Oh, come on!" she heard. "Stop it!" By candlelight the faces of the guests looked long and lean. No, not frightening, but strangely distant.

Piotr she dismissed when he appeared to her then. It was not an easy decision, but she had the right to make it. Even if she did go back, she told herself, how long would it be before she started to blame him for every day that went wrong. How long before she would make his life miserable. It all made perfect sense. She could betray either him or herself; there were no other choices to make.

On the morning of December 13, Anna woke up in what she still, in her mind, called William's bed. In his light pine bed, on a thick, springy mattress, between his smooth white sheets. He was quite conservative that way, she had discovered, linen, towels, tablecloths had to be white, snow white, without a blemish.

She thought she should get up and start cleaning up after the party. They had both been too tired to do it in the evening. A pile of dirty dishes had been left soaking in the sink. Even in the bedroom, with the window opened a crack, there was the faint smell of cigarette smoke and wine.

William was still asleep beside her, snoring. She smiled. She wanted to shake him gently, to make him turn on his side, but knew she would only wake him up. It moved her to discover these little things about him, to learn of his habits. Piotr wouldn't have woken up even if she switched on the radio or talked to him. She didn't feel like getting up, not yet. The alarm clock was set for nine o'clock. There were still a few minutes left.

This is the CBC news. Our top story. Last night Polish troops took over control of the country. General Jaruzelski went on national television and announced the imposition of martial law. There are unconfirmed reports that the Solidarity leader, Lech Wałęsa, was arrested last night, together with the entire leadership of the First Independent Trade Unions.

"Shit!" William said and sat up, wide awake at once.

"What?" it was Anna who kept asking, as if the words she had heard made no sense to her. "What's happened?"

"Martial law," William said. "Oh, God. Bastards!"

The first images on the ABC morning news showed the Polish TV screen. General Jaruzelski, his eyes hidden behind his dark sunglasses, was sitting at his desk, behind him a huge Polish flag. "Citizens of the Polish People's Republic!" he was saying in a strained but steady voice. "I turn to you as a soldier and the chief of government! Our fatherland is on the verge of an abyss!" When the speech ended, and before it was repeated, the screens showed pictures of flowery meadows, still background for the music of Chopin.

The state of war was declared at night. The declarations posted on street corners were printed in the Soviet Union — American and Canadian commentators stressed — to preserve the secrecy of the operation. Poles were informed that all schools, theatres, movie theatres were closed, that public gatherings of any kind were forbidden, that no one could leave his place of residence without official authorisation.

Anna kept switching the channels, hoping to learn more. By midday came the first shots of grey tanks slowly rolling in the Polish streets. One shot, in particular, appeared over and over again, at every television station, the neon signs of the Moscow cinema in Warsaw announcing "Apocalypse Now." The tank that stood by the entrance had its turret aimed at the street.

Anna walked around the room, in circles, avoiding the stacks of plates, leftovers of the party. She noticed that someone had spilled beer on the beautiful art book William kept opened on the coffee table, and now the pages were swollen with dampness. A feeling of panic, so strong that she had to stop herself from rushing somewhere, anywhere, spread all over her body. Her hands were cold and she had to sit down to catch her breath. William followed her into the living room, silent, picking up the plates, emptying ashtrays, taking them all to the kitchen, grateful to have something to do. He had run to the store and brought her papers, *The Gazette*, *The New York Times*, *Le Devoir*, but the news seemed all the same to her.

"It's still too early," he tried to calm her down. "We'll have to wait." He brought her a glass of water and a piece of toast, but she only shook her head. Then he began making coffee, and she shuddered at the grinding noise of the coffee mill. The phone rang. "Yes," William said. "I will. You can imagine how she feels. Yes. Thank you. I will."

She dialled the operator.

"Sorry, Ma'am. All lines to Poland are cut off. I'm really sorry. Please try again later."

In the evening, exhausted from crying, her mind unable to sift through reports that called the events in Poland everything from *utter betrayal* to *the choice of a lesser evil*, she let William take her out to dinner. She was silent the whole evening, staring beyond him, her eyes aimlessly recording the shapes of wainscotting, the maze of squares on the wallpaper. He looked at her, and then looked away. "I don't know what to say," he said.

She didn't say anything. William's face seemed to her too sharp, too finely chiselled, the way the world looked on the days in her childhood when a fever hit her. Trees had sharp, spiky branches, clouds stood out from the blue of the sky, the stocky, dark houses had sharp roof tops and red wavy tiles. Now it was William's face she saw as if cut out of paper; the edges, if she ran her fingers over them, capable of slashing her finger, a thin shallow wound painful to heal.

"Don't cut me off like that," he pleaded.

It was her own body she concentrated upon, following the trajectory of each shiver, hands folded, pressing against her thighs. The food she had forced herself to swallow lodged itself against the walls of her stomach, a hard, sour lump, refusing to dissolve. She was trying to steady another surge of panic, the urge to stand up and run, blindly, fast, the fastest she could. She took a long breath and drank the wine William placed in front of her. She thought that the force of her pain disappointed him; the resurgence of old ties diminished the new. She didn't care.

He ate fast, watching her all the time. He tried to reason with her, to plead for her patience, for time. "It won't be too bad. At least it's not the Soviets, Anna. Communists won't dare to do anything too drastic. They can't afford it." She nodded but did not listen. "Tell me what you are afraid of," he asked, but she only shook her head. How could she tell him about shame? About blaming herself for her selfishness. In the last four months she had come to believe that she had the right to think of herself. Thought herself brave, even. Until the moment when she saw the images of tanks in Polish streets, telling her that what she did had nothing to do with her new freedom. *It wasn't courage*, she thought, *it was betrayal*. "I haven't really known you, have I?" Piotr had asked.

"You cannot change anything, darling," William kept repeating. "Would you rather be there now? How would that help?"

"I want to go home," she said, and rushed out of the restaurant. The door swung behind her. William's car was parked nearby, but she kept walking through the streets, her feet slipping on the frozen pavement. She didn't even turn back to check if he followed.

The news flew fast. There were accounts of massive arrests of Solidarity activists; the lists, rumours had it, had been prepared months ahead. There were reports of strikes, of tanks crushing the entrance gate of the Lenin Shipyard in Gdańsk. Striking miners were dying in the *Wujek* coal mine, in a losing battle with the ZOMO forces. The arrests of Wałęsa, Kuroń, Michnik were confirmed; Frasyniuk was reported to be on the run. On the walls, defiant graffiti, "Winter may be yours, but spring will be ours."

It was not hard to imagine how it would go: Loud knocks at the door. The old, worn platitudes. *You're under arrest. Don't try any tricks.* Piotr would flash his defiant smirk, lips folding as if he were getting ready to spit in their faces. Would she love him more for it had she stayed? Would nothing else matter to her, too? Anna didn't know any more. She had lost the certainty of her judgments. She was floating in between worlds, unanchored, weightless. Could it be that her love for William was nothing but an infatuation after all? Love misplaced, uncertain, already tainted by her shameless desire for peace, for comfort. What had she done then?

William, she thought at times, was getting tired of her tears. She could hear him slip out of the house in the morning. "Do what you want," she whispered to herself, "Why would I care?"

She spent her days waiting for news, flipping through TV channels, listening to short wave broadcasts. Her eyes were permanently swollen; there were red, sore patches on her nose and face. At night she turned her back to William and stayed close to the edge of the bed. She watched him with suspicion, collecting all signs of his indifference. He frowned when he looked at her. He locked himself in his study for the whole afternoon. He put a record on too loud, to drown the static of the short waves. She was provoking him, too. She left him to do the dishes, shopping, laundry. "You go," she said when they were invited over to Christmas parties. And all the time, she watched what he would do. He waited.

The Christmas cards that arrived a few days later, forwarded to her from Rue de la Montagne, had been mailed before her call to Piotr. *We wish you a Happy Christmas, your first so far away from us. We love you and think of you all the time,* her mother wrote. Words that by now, she was sure, would have been taken away. Piotr scribbled his wishes in rows of small letters. *I miss you. It will be a sad Christmas, and the last one apart. I shouldn't have let you go. From now on it is either together or not at all, right? I'll be thinking of you on the 24th. Love you, Piotr.*

She sat down on the living room sofa and let the cards fall on the floor. William was away that morning, and the only sound that reached her was a distant noise of a passing plane. She examined the veins on her wrists, running her fingers along them, absorbed in the realisation of how delicate, how thin were these outer reaches of her body. William must have walked into the house then, but she hadn't even heard him.

"You still love him, don't you," he asked. "If you tell me to go away, I will."

Startled, she looked up and saw that there were tears in his eyes, swelling, rolling down his cheeks, one transparent drop chasing another. He didn't try to hide them, to wipe them off.

He just stood there, looking at her, letting the tears fill his eyes and flow. It was with these tears that he won her again.

She did love him; it was not an illusion. She stood up and threw her arms around him. His lips touched hers, whispering her name, between kisses. "Anna," she heard, "Oh, Anna," and he buried his wet face between her breasts. Running her fingers through his soft, silver hair, she felt his tears soak through her blouse. His hair smelled of the winter air, crisp and fresh.

The repressions were not as bad as they could have been. The worst — those who managed to leave Poland stressed — was the overwhelming sense of hopelessness. William helped Anna make more parcels. She packed the food into cardboard boxes, and he wrapped them up in brown paper, tied them tightly with string and carried them to the post office. It was a good sign, he stressed, that the post still accepted parcels, for this was all she could do to make her parents' lives easier.

When the first letter from Poland came in, two months later, it had the word CENSORED stamped across it. *Dear Daughter,* her mother wrote. She must have hesitated for a long time what to call her. Piotr was in Warsaw on the night of the 13th, and that's when he was arrested. He was now in an internment camp in Bialolęka. Her brother was fine, and so was her father. Yes, her parcels arrived, and they all thanked her, but asked her not to bother again. They would survive as they had survived before. *Distance,* her mother wrote in her even, round letters, *blurs the real picture. We all hope that you will find happiness and peace.*

PART II

Sometimes, in Anna's dreams, William is still alive and he laughs at her red, puffy eyes and tears that leave salty trails on her cheeks. "I'm still here, darling," he tells her in the voice she is beginning to forget. "Can't you see?" And then he laughs, a hollow laugh that echoes through empty rooms. "Not a thing has changed," he says, and she touches his hands and laughs, too, cautiously at first, but then louder and louder, until the sound of her own laughter wakes her up.

William's grave is a block of black granite with nothing on it but his name and the two dates in brass letters: William Herzman, 1940-1991. There is space on the lower half of the stone for other names. "Mine," Käthe said, when Anna brought her here a few days ago. In the nursing home William's mother is silent and tense; for hours she can stare out of the window but then, Anna is told, she walks around the room and has to be given a sedative to keep her from exerting herself.

Her bones are brittle; she may fall.

Anna recalls the deep hole of the grave, and the coffin slowly lowered into it. A pile of soil, half covered with flowers, lined the site. Someone handed her a trowel, an ordinary garden trowel like the one she had used to transplant flowers in her garden, and she let a clump of soil fall on the coffin. There was a soft, dull thump when it fell.

"I'm a widow now," she thinks. *Wdowa*, the Polish word echoes, an ugly, black word she would like to recoil from. On All Souls Day in her childhood, flickering candles lit the sky over the Warsaw cemetery where her grandfather was buried, and she would spot this luminous orange glow from far away, growing brighter with each step she took. The cold November air was filled with the smell of paraffin. By the graves, women in heavy black coats muttered the prayers for the dead. They polished the headstones, fussed over the chrysanthemums in terra-cotta pots, pulled the weeds from the graves. "It's the loneliness that gets you," they would say. Her grandmother never protested. "Doesn't get any easier," she would add. "Ever."

Spring is late in Montreal. The ground is still frozen, and the wind makes Anna shiver. William has been dead for thirty-six days and she has felt the weight of every single one of them. At his grave she crosses herself, just as she crossed herself at the hospital. *Wieczne odpoczywanie racz mu dać Panie*, she whispers — grant him eternal rest, Oh Lord — the only prayer she remembers for the rest of the soul.

"But he was always so strong!" He played tennis, he swam, he lifted weights. She hadn't imagined all that. There were proofs, indisputable, solid. His tennis rackets in the closet, his exercise bike still standing in their bedroom.

"There was nothing we could do. It was a quick, merciful death," the doctor said. "Like a stroke of lightning . . . Believe me, I know." He was a young man, nervous, unsure of how to talk to her, where to look. He couldn't have done that sort of thing too many times, she thought, not enough to develop a procedure, to detach himself from death. "Please, believe me."

She wished it for William, such an absence of pain. In a private hospital room on the first floor, she had leaned over his body hidden under white sheets and a blue blanket, trying not to look at the livid tips of his fingers, the purple frames around his nails. These were the signs of struggle, and she wanted to remember the peaceful stillness in his face.

Death made him look older. It must be the lips, she thought, frozen into a rueful smile, so cold when she kissed them. "Why have you done it, baby?" she murmured her reproach, smoothing his silver hair, half-hoping for a reply, for his eyes to open and wink at her, delighted at the success of this incomprehensible joke.

When the doctor took hold of her wrist, to check her pulse, she just kept staring at the assortment of objects in his little office. A jar with cotton pads, another full of tongue depressors, a box of latex gloves with one half pulled, a model of a human ear with the red and blue cords representing veins and arteries. She registered it all, but hazily, as if an invisible cottony gauze was thrown between her and the world. Outside the narrow window of the doctor's office, a woman in a pink dress walked by, her head crowned with an unruly mop of dreadlocks, a folded cardigan over her arm. Stopping, she looked around as if deciding where to go, her soft, overweight body wobbling on the pointed heels of her black shoes.

"I didn't know," Anna said. "I didn't notice anything was wrong."

She had missed the signs of danger. On their last evening together she let her mind drift away, her eyes grow heavy. What was she thinking of? Laundry. The croissants she would buy in the morning. Student essays she would have to mark. She could have looked at him, instead, at his chin pressing the violin to his neck, at his right hand so perfectly in tune with the vibrations of the strings. His fingers, she often thought, possessed their own intelligence, quite separate from him, inexplicably fast, free of false moves. It wasn't just the violin; he was like that with everything he touched. Rolling up phyllo pastry, fixing the cylinder pins and vibrating teeth of the musical boxes he brought home from auctions to restore. "Little miracles," she used to think, but even miracles wane and pale with time.

She liked the piece he played that night, Bach's *Chaconne in D Minor*, an ancient dance, its slow and solemn melody transformed each time it is repeated. But, unlike his, her mind could never stay long with the sequence of sounds alone. It was slipping away, unaware of what was already taking place. For there was still time to get him to hospital, to keep him with her. If only for a few more years, months, or even days.

"Are you all right?" the doctor asked.

She nodded.

"He flinched as he was getting up in the morning," Anna's voice cracked when she started to speak and she swallowed to soften the lump in her throat. "Then he rubbed his left shoulder." The numbness that started around her heart began to spread. It crawled down her spine, to the soles of her feet. Like fear, it made her shudder.

"It's nothing," William had said, annoyed by the concern in her voice. She didn't have to mother him all the time. He could take care of himself.

"It'll go away."

She believed him. He was so proud of his own strength. He had never had the flu in his life, never knew what back pain was. He could still beat younger men at tennis. She went out to do the shopping, took her time chatting with Pauline, her neighbour, who was shovelling snow next door, her morning exercise, she said, her cheeks rosy from the cold.

Back home she didn't suspect anything. The kitchen smelled of cinnamon and baked apples, and she thought that William got tired of waiting for her and must have warmed a slice of pie in the microwave. She opened it and the pie was there, forgotten, enveloped in a shroud of plastic wrap. This by itself was not unusual. When he was composing, William would often leave things mid-way. He didn't like to be interrupted. "By anyone," he had told her once and she had learned to deflect telephone calls, avoid stepping on a squeaking board.

The kettle was still hot. His mug was beside it with a tea bag steeping inside. She put a brown paper bag filled with groceries on the kitchen counter and only then she noticed that the door to his study was half opened. That was unusual. "William?" she asked softly, half expecting an angry grunt of warning, but he didn't answer. "Your tea is getting cold, Darling," she said softly, and started unpacking the brown paper bag as quietly as she could. Cold cuts and cheeses went on the top shelf of the refrigerator, red peppers on the bottom. She was still in her coat, her purse over her arm. He would laugh, if he saw her like that. "Why can't you ever finish one thing before starting another?" he would ask, and help her take off her coat.

It was only when she had placed the warm croissants on a wooden tray by the toaster, that the silence began to bother her. "William?" she asked again, and then, only then, she did push the door to his study open and saw him, on the floor, face buried in his hands as if he were hiding from her in some childish game.

She could feel her purse slide off her arm as she knelt beside him, its contents spilling on the almond boards of the floor. Her keys, her wallet, a compact powder fell out, a lipstick tube rolled under the desk and stopped. William's face when she touched it was still warm, but a chill was already setting in, as if he had just returned from a brisk walk in the cold. Her hands shaking, she called the ambulance, cried into the receiver, begged the woman at the other end to hurry, to please hurry, for God's sake. "Oh, my God," she prayed, "Please, please, don't punish me."

"This pain in the shoulder area," the doctor said, kindly, "could've been the first sign." He gave Anna a quick look as she was getting up from the examination table, dizzied, her feet cautious and unsure, testing the firmness of the ground. "But you can't blame yourself. It was easy to miss."

He gave her a sedative that made her head swim, a small, white, oblong tablet.

"It couldn't have been the first one," he said. "There was scar tissue on his heart. For all we know it could have been hereditary."

"What?" she asked, uncomprehending.

"Heart failure that strikes like that. It often runs in the family. How did your husband's father die?"

"I don't know. I don't think anybody knows for sure. He died in the war," she said, slowly. It seemed to her that the lining of her mouth had lost all its moisture and something bitter in her throat was crawling toward the tip of her tongue.

At five in the morning the bedroom in the Westmount townhouse is still dark. Anna wakes up and lies motionless, terrified by the thought that the borderline between what is still possible and what is already lost is so thin, so easy to cross.

Once she had awakened to murmurs reaching her from his study; a low hum of his voice, breaking through her sleep. She kept her eyes closed, waiting for William to come back to bed.

She heard him tiptoe through the room, freezing with a hiss as he tripped, trying not to wake her up. And he, thinking her asleep, sat down beside her. "I love you," he whispered, his hand gently smoothing the curls of her hair. She held her breath, as he bent over to kiss her cheek.

Now she closes her eyes and imagines that he is still with her, lying flat on his back, staring at the ceiling, and she can almost hear the rhythm of his breath. Imagines he has just woken up, and rolls over toward her, his eyes heavy with sleep, and she extends her hand to smooth the hair on his chest. He locks her hand in his, and kisses the tips of her fingers. Shaking his head he smiles at her, a cheeky smile that softens his handsome, weather-beaten face. At fifty-one his grey hair is no longer a statement.

"You dyed it? Why?" she asked him, once, just a few months after they met.

"To look older than my age?" he tried to laugh it off. "To make pretty women wonder?" His voice teased her, made her laugh with delight. "You do like it, don't you?"

"Come on, seriously," she wasn't going to give up.

"Do all Polish women always have to know everything or is it just you?"

"Just me," she said. They were walking up the Mountain, past the trees covered with ice, bending under its weight. He stopped. His eyebrows rose, deepening the lines of the forehead.

"Let's say I'm not too partial to the Aryan look."

She squeezed his hand and pulled him forward, and then she felt a surge of blood rising to her face.

In her mind she lets her eyes wander to the mound of ashen curls between his legs. "Hi there, sunshine," he murmurs, and begins to hum as he swings his legs to the rug. *L'amour est un oiseau rebelle . . .* she hears the phantom words. He is in the bathroom now, leaving the door half-open, vanishing into the vapours of a hot shower, emerging from the mist with a towel across his shoulders and she watches him directing an imaginary orchestra, bending over the green marble counter, stopping to inspect his face, to trim unruly hairs from his nostrils, and then, his voice rising to a crescendo of the finale, bending in a deep bow, waiting for her applause.

The feeling that death is an illusion, that nothing ever ends overwhelms her. Her heart begins to race. The soles of her feet tingle. If she hurries she can still catch him, bent over his desk, a steaming mug of coffee in his hand. In her father's stories elves and fairies could be caught like that. All that was needed was to surprise them, to snatch something they cherished, without which they couldn't remain invisible.

But death is no illusion. On her kitchen calendar January 26, 1991, is circled with a thick black marker. "At noon," she wrote that day in her diary. It is already the first week of April. A few hours later, on the front lawn Anna will spot the first, shy patches of melting snow, revealing yellowed grass, last year's uncut growth.

In the nursing home, Käthe's room is painted pale blue. In certain light this is the colour of her eyes.

Käthe's hands are gnarled, spotted, her skin is pale and wrinkled, folds of it gathering around her mouth. She raises her head and frowns. She is wearing a black dress with a white lace collar; her grey hair is taken back, braided tightly and woven around her head like a crown.

So often for the last ten years Anna has tried to find the connection between William and this small drying body, the pursed, thin lips, the mouth set back into the skull. William whom, in her blindness, she has thought so strong. Indestructible. There was little resemblance, she has decided, almost none. Perhaps a shadow, in his lips, in the shape of his fingers.

There is a patch of sun on the lawn, in front of Käthe's window. Dappled, swaying in the wind, moved by the branches of an old oak tree. "Victory oak," Käthe had said when they brought her here for the first time. "Like the ones in Breslau."

Anna remembers them too, old, gnarled trees commemorating the Prussian victories of the last century. Black bark, leaves smaller than on Canadian oaks. One of them stood on the First of May Square in Wrocław, with its twin monuments of Fight and Victory, on the left a naked man wrestling a lion, on the right, the same man, now triumphant, straddling the conquered beast. The oak tree was cut down in the seventies, sliced into slabs the size of a table to make room for a pedestrian crossing underneath the intersection, linking the city core with newly constructed districts. Wroclaw was bursting at the seams then, its narrow streets crowded with cars, the *Jugendstil* buildings blackening from the soot and diesel fumes, dissolving in acid rain. The streets paved with pre-war, smooth grey stones were slippery, treacherous, but the back asphalt with which some of them were covered was not much of an improvement. As it melted in the sun, it took in the shapes of car tires and stiletto heels, its black, sticky surface releasing the sickly smell of tar.

"The tree wouldn't have survived in this air," Anna has heard, but now she doubts such explanations. Because of something William once said, she went to the library and found out that, deprived of the means to stand up and leave, trees have developed formidable defences. Oak trees step up seed production every few years to support the extra population of mice that would feed on gypsy moth larvae. When attacked by fungi, some conifers can subdivide themselves into compartments, walling the infection in. Trees may seem slow, she read, insentient, brooding, but they have simply exchanged drastic and immediate responses to danger for a subtler strategy of survival.

"It's cold here," Käthe murmurs, and Anna spreads a brown chequered rug over Käthe's knees. The nurse has dressed her in two pairs of thick stockings and a pink angora sweater. When she walks, Käthe's feet shuffle, slowly, one after another, on the vinyl floor of her room. She knows she can no longer have rugs, for she can trip over them. The wires have to be neatly tucked against the walls and fastened with silver tape. She has to take precautions against falling. Her bones are thin and brittle, refusing to take any unexpected pressure, to bend more than absolutely necessary. She has broken her hip once already, and even her shuffle is unsteady, heavier on the "good side."

Käthe turns to the window and watches a squirrel, his thin, scrawny body shaking as he digs a hole in the lawn.

"The squirrels are cheeky, here," she says. "Black, not red. I could never believe that there were no red squirrels in Canada. When I came here, with Willi, after the war, he thought they were rats, and he was scared."

It was William's decision to bring Käthe here, after that November afternoon, a year ago, when Anna spotted her mother-in-law on her knees, climbing the steep flight of stairs to St. Joseph's Oratory. She had never told William her own reason for going there. It was not a secret, just an omission. Her little Polish ritual, like slipping a layer of hay underneath the tablecloth on Christmas Eve or crossing herself every time she boarded a plane, quickly so that no one would notice. William would only tease her at times like that, say something about the bloodlines that ran that deep. It was the anniversary of her grandmother's death and she lit a candle for her and prayed for her soul.

She had just come out of the Oratory, when a lonely woman pilgrim on the stairs caught her eyes. At first she only saw a loose, black coat, then she could make out the shape of the wobbly figure. Curious, she came nearer; the middle stairs were to be climbed on the knees, but Anna had never actually seen anyone doing it. In her black coat and hat, the woman looked like a giant ant surveying an unfamiliar path, probing the air in front of her before making the next step.

The sky was grey. Anna felt a drop of rain on her face and it was then that she recognized that the kneeling pilgrim was her mother-in-law. "She shouldn't be here in this weather," she thought. "She's had such a bad year."

Käthe had had a bad year. Her once strong body, which could withstand 36-hour shifts of nursing, was giving in. She'd had pneumonia in the spring. In late September, a fever that wouldn't go away, painting the tops of her sunken cheeks with reddish hue. Anna visited her often, then, helped her around the house, stocked her fridge with groceries.

They got along fine, without William around. A thought like that was a sore spot, and Anna tried to ignore it. Käthe's stories of her nursing days was what kept their conversations going.

Homo homini lupus, Käthe liked to begin, her lips twitching slightly, a grimace of disgust. People were like wolves to each other. A pack of predators, ruthless in pursuit. They left their traces behind, the trail of the hunters imprinted in the flesh of their prey. Bruises, torn muscles, broken bones.

Once she summoned a surgeon back to the hospital, dragged him from his New Year's Eve party, because she didn't like the paleness of her patient's cheeks. "She was only a young girl, *ya?*" she would tell Anna in her thick German accent. "I knew she was bleeding to death." The doctor tried to reason with her, but Käthe stood her ground. "What's with you," she asked, shaking with anger. Wasn't it his duty? His sacred duty he swore to uphold? She had been right. The girl did have an internal haemorrhage and she, Käthe, had saved her life.

"*Ya, ya,*" she was like that, she would tell Anna. "The Iron Kate."

That November afternoon Anna rushed back to the lobby of St. Joseph's Oratory in search of a payphone. William said he would be right there, would have to miss a faculty meeting, but would come. "Watch her," he snapped. "It's going too far," and Anna immediately regretted having called him at all. She should've tried to get Käthe into a taxi, call William only when she was safely home. But it was too late.

Fifteen minutes later she saw him in the courtyard, below. No hat, no scarf, his grey hair tousled by the wind. His black coat opened. He left the car parked by the curb, lights flashing.

"Where is she?" he had motioned to Anna from below, throwing his arms up, but then he noticed Käthe himself, the only pilgrim on the stairs. She had already climbed the first few steps of the second landing and was now motionless, her head bent.

"Mother!"

Käthe did not acknowledge William's presence. She lifted her knees awkwardly to the next step, steadying herself with her hands and then stopping again to clasp her palms and pray. Anna thought that the boards must be hard, and that her knees must hurt her by now, but Käthe kept praying, her eyes fixed on the ground. William ran up the side flight of stairs and stood on the second landing, watching her from above, motioning to Anna to come and help him. Only when Käthe reached the landing did she open her eyes.

"Mother. How could you!"

There was no surprise in her eyes. But she did not protest when William took her firmly by the shoulders and led her down to the car.

The nursing home room is too small to let Käthe keep much from her old apartment. Most of her things are in Anna's basement. The enamelled wineglasses and beer steins are carefully wrapped in layers of white tissue and placed in cardboard boxes marked, "For Julia." So are her books and her embroidered linen. Out of all Käthe's furniture William took one piece only, a rosewood curio cabinet with a crystal glass Käthe had bought years ago at an auction. He said he liked it when he was a boy, and that it would be just great for his music boxes. The bed and two night stands have been brought here, to the nursing home. The rest of the furniture, William decided, was not worth anyone's trouble.

On the night stand to the left there are the photographs of William, Julia, and Marilyn at the seaside, their skins young, smooth, without a blemish. In the one Anna is looking at now, Julia is not more than three, and William holds her up, above his grey hair, like a trophy.

"Marilyn called," Käthe says. "She will stay in Boston. The library is expanding, and she is now in charge of rare books."

"She didn't come to the funeral," Anna says. It sounds like a complaint and it is.

Anna wrote to Marilyn after William's death. A short note was all she could manage. A few details of how she found him that day. Then, in a moment she has regretted ever since, she added a plea for forgiveness. She could never understand why they couldn't stop hurting each other, after all those years.

"They didn't let me go to the funeral," Käthe says in a cautious whisper, and looks around as if someone might hear her.

In one of the photographs on the wall, William's hair is all blond. This is a Breslau picture, a determined look of a five-year-old, dressed in a velvet suit of a little lord. Anna knows this look. Tainted by impatience. With the photographer, the clothes that on this occasion are festive and uncomfortable. With his mother who, he told Anna many times, was there, too, a cold, watchful figure in the corner, her eyes ordering him to stay still.

"You had a fever, again. The doctor said you had to stay in bed. You were in no shape to go anywhere," Anna says.

What a mess it all is Anna thinks, what a tangled mess. She is covering Käthe's arms with a warm woollen sweater, light blue with white trimmings. It is lamb's wool, silky to the touch. She feeds Käthe small morsels of bread with cream cheese and lean turkey. Baby food, she thinks. Käthe eats slowly, chewing each mouthful for a long time.

"Did you sleep well?" she asks and Käthe nods. They don't talk much these days, but the silence is never uncomfortable. Even if there are things Anna finds hard to forget. "Your wife called me," Käthe would say to William, meaning Marilyn. "Anna is my wife, Mother," William would protest. "Is it really so hard to remember?"

When the meal is over Anna gathers the paper plates and places them in a plastic bag she has brought with her. She will throw it out on her way home; she does not want to leave any garbage in Käthe's room. By the time the room is cleaned it would fill with the smells of stale food. She carefully gathers the crumbs from the table.

"Leave it," Käthe says. "They can clean it up, *nein*? That's their job." She always says the same thing, and Anna always nods and keeps cleaning. This is what she has learned long ago, a thing William found so hard to do. "Just nod and do your own thing," she kept telling him, "it's not impossible."

Käthe points to a small lamp by her bed. "Touch it," she says. Anna touches the brass base with her finger. The lamp lights up.

"Julia gave it to me," she says. "It's very convenient. I don't have to look for a switch when I wake up at night."

"It's nice," Anna says. "Very nice."

It was William who has made Anna think of his childhood as lacking. "Deprived" is the word he used. A war, he said, can be an excuse to deny a lot to a child.

74

"There was never enough love," he said, and Anna thought of a little boy pulling at his mother's skirt. He could plead and whine all he wanted and the most Käthe would do was to tell him to stop it, or hand him over to his nanny. He always felt the sting of her stubborn, silent mourning for his father.

Bel ami, bel ami, bel ami! he remembered the song from some afternoon tea-room, in Breslau, his mouth full of poppyseed cake, crumbs falling onto a tiny china plate with little flowers all around it. This was an unusual time, his mother was smiling then, listening to the song. For a moment her face was carefree, and so pretty that he thought her an angel. She was wearing a white dress with a v-shaped collar, with a single pink rose pinned to it. He felt a desire to put his head on her breasts, quickly, to feel the beating of her heart before she had the time to stop him. She was tossing her hair back and then, suddenly, as if she could read his thoughts, her face grew tense, and she sat up straight. "Let's go, Willi," she said, ignoring his protests. He had not even finished his cake.

"Is that all that happened?" Anna asked. It seemed to her strange that he would remember a moment of such little consequence. There could have been so many reasons to hurry.

No, he didn't like it when she said things like that. He didn't want her to find ordinary explanations for what he had felt. His mother was full of them, too. "But it was the war, Willi. Your grandfather was in prison! Those were dangerous times!" Words like these came too late, he said, and only after he had complained of her silence. A belated effort to soften his heart, or maybe just one more call of duty, a little, self-satisfied station on his mother's way of the cross. How could she hope to atone for all the incomprehensible moments of harshness? To make him forget the sharp pulling of his arm, her kisses that brushed his skin lightly without leaving a trace. His mother never raised her voice. He used to dread her calm more than he would dread an outburst, her subtle sighs of resignation echoed by every wall in the room.

This was a dangerous zone Anna was trying to enter, a minefield of hurt feelings. She may have learnt quickly what not to say, but that didn't mean she understood.

William said that his mother had always kept him at arm's length. He liked this expression; it suited what he wanted to convey. Not too far, and not close enough. He was her duty, her responsibility so faithfully fulfilled, but he was not her joy. When Anna objected that there must have been other times, he conceded. Yes, during that terrible winter trek from Breslau. When he thought he would die and she, holding him close to her, promised he wouldn't. She kept me warm, he said. She fed me. Then, there was nothing more important than hot cabbage soup and fur gloves she somehow managed to get. But as soon as they were out of danger she was back to her old ways.

His presence, William would tell Anna, was his mother's punishment, a cross she had to bear with patience and humility. This is what he had really remembered from Breslau. These walks on which she always hurried him home. On which there was never enough time for another swing, an ice-cream. So, in the end, he would hurry, too, home to Gretchen, his beloved nanny, who waited for him at the door.

It was Gretchen who pinched his cheeks, drew his bath and tickled him until he sputtered with laughter and saliva. Gretchen who taught him songs and stories he would remember for a long time after. "Hear this?" she would ask, and he listened to the thunder rolling through the sky. "The Wild Hunt." She told him about Wodan, the king of the gods, leading his frenzied gallop through the sky. Wild, wild horses carrying their masters, the warriors slain in battles, galloping through the darkened sky, in hot pursuit of some fantastic game.

"Good warriors, Gretchen?"

"The bravest. The best. The most valiant. In the heat of battle a beautiful Valkyrie, a maiden on horseback, would appear to the chosen one. 'Get ready,' she would say, 'Get ready, my brave one. For you the great Wodan will open the sacred doors of Valhalla.' And so went the valiant warrior, his eyes still filled with the memories of the fight. He would join Wodan at the last battle, at the twilight of the Gods."

During all these uncomfortable evenings in Käthe's living room, when conversations faltered, or went in circles, or stopped at unpredictable moments, it seemed to Anna that both, mother and son, tried to catch each other at some grave transgression. All they were looking for was one more proof that would finally lay bare what they both knew was there all along.

Anna remembers one such evening, a few years ago. Käthe's sixty-fifth birthday. William bought her an old musical box and restored it himself. It was lovely, Anna thought, with its inlaid pattern of fern-like leaves. Käthe still lived alone, then, on Terrebonne Street, a housing complex for seniors.

Anna had her own worries consuming her then. Marie had just come back from Poland, her first trip after martial law was declared. She talked of dark grey streets, of people walking without a smile in their faces, trying to remain invisible. All telephone conversations were monitored, all letters opened and read. There was no food, no coal for the winter. Police were everywhere.

She had visited Anna's parents. "No one says *martial law* there. They all say *the war*," she said. "Your mother said it was worse than the war because this time it was not the Germans who were pointing the guns at them."

For days afterwards Marie spoke of nothing else but dark, dirty cities, of the Wroclaw Central Station smelling of spilled beer and sour vomit, of people standing in line-ups for hours, motionless, seemingly resigned to what was happening to them. Her visa said three weeks, but she had to leave after two – she couldn't take it any more.

Käthe opened the door wearing a grey dress. Her only piece of jewellery was a golden chain with a small crucifix. They talked for a while, an innocent talk of the winter, the chill of the northerly winds, the slippery pavements, a city forgetful of its pedestrians.

There was a routine to their visits and this was not an exception, in spite of the musical box wrapped in golden wrap, and a card with best wishes of happiness and peace. They brought a cake from the Patisserie Belge in Outremont and a box of Belgian chocolates. Käthe cooked dinner. At that time her arthritis did not bother her that much. The movements of her hands were still quick and precise. Like William's, Anna thought, but of course never said it. The table was set for three, with Käthe's embroidered tablecloth, white damask roses on white linen, the wineglasses enamelled with grapes and vine leaves. The whole apartment smelled of garlic and parsley. And something else. Marjoram.

"Sit down," Käthe said. "Before it all gets cold."

"Doesn't she mind living alone?" she kept asking William. "Shouldn't we ask her to move in with us?" She thought of *Babcia* who came to live with her parents the day *Dziadek* died. But William only laughed.

"Of course not. She lives her own life. I told you she doesn't need anyone else." He was right, Anna thought, in a way. Käthe had her own friends, former nurses like her. At the time when she was less fragile, they went out to concerts, for walks. William recalled the times of her treks to the Rockies, to the Sierra Mountains, to the Grand Canyon, but Anna only saw pictures of these trips, Käthe in shorts and sweatshirt, knee-high woollen socks, a green knapsack on her back, leaning on a walking stick. Behind her were the mountains, the canyons, the springs.

Later, when her arthritis made hiking impossible, Käthe's friends came to play bridge with her, leaving behind them full ashtrays and greasy aluminium trays from store-bought hors-d'oeuvres. "Buy and lie," they called them. Alice Woolth, Bernice Camden, Vicki Norton. Old, wrinkled women, sitting around Käthe's dining room table, smoking, remembering old patients. The woman who called Bernice at four thirty in the morning asking for the result of her pregnancy test from two months before. The man who looked up at Alice as she was wheeling him down the hall to surgery and asked if those three little donuts counted as food.

"Open it, Mother," William urged her. Käthe unwrapped the golden wrap carefully, folding it, putting it away for later. "Come on, play it," he said and she did, listening to the chiming notes of the Viennese waltz as if it were a funeral dirge. These were William's words, said to Anna after they had left, for at the time she thought he was hiding his disappointment so well, navigating the conversation past the usual points of no return.

The first signs of trouble came soon enough. "Have you talked to Jul*chen*?" Käthe asked, and Anna stopped eating, waiting for William's reply.

"No, I haven't heard from her for a while," he said, and she relaxed for his voice was still normal, still ready to take this question as an innocent inquiry about a granddaughter, nothing else.

"You haven't?" Käthe asked, her voice raising slightly, the first sign of a reproach she was still trying to cover. She hurried to the kitchen from which she emerged with a bottle of soya sauce, even though no one asked for it. William shot Anna a telling look, "See," he seemed to be saying, "I told you." But Anna averted her eyes. She was not going to encourage him.

"So what have you been up to, Mother?" William asked when Käthe sat down again. There was this false cheerfulness in his voice, the cheerfulness Anna did not like. It was a sign that he had been hurt and was now putting on a face.

"You should try to see her more often, Willi," Käthe said. "I'm not going to interfere in your affairs, but a child is a child. You have to call her. She needs guidance, *nein*? *Ya, ya*, you will do whatever you want, you always did."

"Lovely soup, Mother," William said, and Anna nodded. "Yes, excellent." On white china plates the broth looked pale, but it was strong and fragrant with herbs.

Käthe gave William a stern look as if he were still a little boy learning his lessons. A fork in the wrong hand, a drop of wine staining the tablecloth were no mere slips; they justified her suspicions that there was more at stake. His character, his entire life.

When they had finished the soup, Anna picked up the plates and carried them to the kitchen. From there, she could hear Käthe's voice asking William what used to be so important that he had to leave Marilyn and Julia for months. "Your wife and child," she said. Wasn't he aware how hard it was for a woman to raise a child alone?

"Anna is my wife," she heard him say. "I don't want to talk about Marilyn."

When Anna came back into the dining room William gave her a telling look. "See," it said. "I *am* trying." He uncorked the bottle slowly, poured a small amount of wine into his glass to taste it and then filled the other two. Anna stared at her glass. The pink enamelled grapes on green stems seemed to quiver every time the table moved.

"To what shall we drink?" he asked. "Family love?"

Käthe took a small sip from her glass. William drank almost half of the wine, as if it were water, and Anna was tempted to do the same.

The pork roast with steamed white cabbage was an excuse for silence. Anna chewed on the meat, poured more sauce on the potatoes, praising the taste of wild mushrooms, the touch of coriander in the steamed cabbage. Then would come the cake, Anna thought, a cup of tea, and they could say good bye for at least another week. But that was not to be.

"Loyalty and duty, Willi," Käthe announced all of a sudden, "set intelligent men apart from the rabble."

"What is that supposed to mean?" William asked.

"Exactly what you've heard," Käthe said. "I'm telling you what I think. But why should you care what I think? I'll die soon. Don't make a face like this, Willi. Lord is merciful and I don't mind going. Not at all."

"I've had enough, Mother," William said, standing up. "We won't take any more of your time."

Käthe didn't even rise from the chair to see them off. They were both so stubborn, so single-minded, Anna thought. Neither one would give in. It made no sense.

Anna followed William to the car, hardly able to catch up with him. He got in and opened the door for her from inside. Silence, Anna had learned by then, was often the best strategy. It was better to let William calm down, not to try anything hasty. After a day or two he would mention Käthe himself, comment on her stubborn character, on the way she always knew how to annoy him, suspected him of the worst. Anna would listen and nod and a few days later she would call Käthe who would invite them for dinner as if nothing had ever happened.

Käthe walks slowly to the window and looks out at the oak tree in the yard.

"Perfect to age cognac in, *nicht wahr*?" she says. "*Vati* always said that only the oaks that grow alone, make good barrels. The wood has to soak up enough sun. If it doesn't, it won't release the taste or the smell."

"Your father said that?" Anna asks, puzzled. It's the first time ever that she has heard Käthe mention her father. But Käthe has already turned back and motions to her to help her lower herself into the armchair. She no longer wants to talk.

Conversations, even that short, mean improvement. When she learned of William's death, Käthe wouldn't speak at all. For days she sat frozen in her wicker armchair, staring at the crucifix on the wall, a wooden cross with Christ's steel coloured body, the wounds of flagellation scattered all over it. "You see, darling," Anna sobbed into the pillow. "You were so wrong about her. She does love you. She always has."

The nursing home doctor, a nice, chubby man with a gentle smile, a favourite of all the residents, said he was watching her closely, but that Anna should let her grieve. Then one day he called. "I think you should come," he said, and Anna could sense relief in his voice. "When I walked into her room, in the morning, your mother-in-law told me to straighten the pictures on the wall and stop grinning like a fool. I think that's a good sign."

That was a month ago, and now Anna has come bringing a bunch of red tulips with her. Käthe asks her to put them on the night table, and then, in a gesture that takes Anna by surprise, she smoothes Anna's cheek with her hand.

"Ann*chen*," she says. "I am praying for him. And for you."

Letters come every day. The screen door opens with a squeak; white envelopes fall through the mail-slot and spill on the floor. Anna picks them up and takes them to the kitchen to read. They move her, these words of sympathy, the memories of old conversations, the friendships of his other life, long before he met her. This one is addressed to Frau Herzmann, with the German double "n" William has dropped from his name in Canada.

The news of your husband's death reached me only a few days ago through Frau Strauss, an old friend of the Herzmann family, from Berlin. I was saddened to hear that it was so unexpected, that he had no time to reflect, to reconcile what may have needed reconciliation. You will forgive me for saying that; we Catholics pray to be spared from a sudden death.

Your husband has often been in my thoughts and in my prayers. I've always considered myself to be his friend, even if we spoke rarely, for it is the depth of conversations that really matter. He came here for the first time in the spring of 1976, to examine some old music we have in our library, here at the monastery. I was asked to assist him. We talked a lot about Germany. He was of the generation touched by the war. Too young to have taken a stand, too old to say it happened before his time. This is a European disease, this mixing together of blood and soil. Pick a handful of it, they say, and you will squeeze blood.

At the time of this conversation, your husband was still shaken after a boat trip on Königssee, not far from here, in the Bavarian Alps. It was an occurrence of the utmost importance, he told me, the essence of what was wrong with us here, the blind worship of the past. He said that from the moment he boarded the wooden boat he was expected to behave as if he were in a church. Nobody on the boat dared to speak a word, he said. Everyone listened to a young guide in his twenties, with blond hair and blue eyes. The guide spoke of the purity of the place, of the mountains where Bavarian kings once hunted, of the sacred trees in these forests, of the lake's crystal waters, the salmon and trout that live there. He stopped the boat and put his finger to his lips. They sat there for a long time, watching the darkness fall. Then, the guide blew his flügelhorn, and they all heard a single, long, haunting note. A moment later, reflected by the mountains, the echo of the horn came back, seven times. Your husband found it disturbing, very disturbing. One couldn't help but notice that he was bitter about Germany that way. He said he never admitted he was German, if he could help it, that he refused to speak German, and looked at me when he said it as if he wanted me to protest. But I said he did what he needed to do. He asked me how I dealt with it. I said that for me it was a mission I had not chosen but could not refuse. He only laughed.

He came here one more time, as a visitor that year, for a retreat. We have a few rooms in the monastery where people come for peace. Perhaps it calmed him to be in a place where we accept the limitations of reason. I said to him then that in the depth of doubt there were always two roads, one of despair and one of hope, and that I always chose hope.

I pray to God that peace and hope comes to you, dear Frau Herzmann. You and your late husband will always be in my prayers. Father Albrecht

Once, at a party in Montreal to which William took her, Anna met a Filipino woman who said she could remember everything that ever happened to her. "Exactly the way it happened," she said firmly, "As if I were watching the same film over again."

Anna remembers feeling incredulous at first, then irritated with the certainty in the woman's voice and then, guilty that her own memories came maimed, malleable, prone to manipulation. "I can close my eyes," she can still hear the woman's slow voice, "and I can see what I saw twenty years ago. Feel the shape of the rope with which we had to tie the house down before the hurricane. Smell the wax on the bamboo floor."

"All of it, right here," she knocked at the side of her head, a soft knock muted by a layer of black, shining hair, "forever." But Anna no longer knows how much of what has happened is already lost.

How she regrets now the wastefulness of the first weeks after William's death. Knits her brows at the recklessness of picking up the small silver scissors with which he trimmed his beard and then putting them back, in their place on the glass shelf in the bathroom. Of breathing in the air trapped in the fibres of William's shirts, opening the book he left unfinished, a book mark pointing to a traveller's account of the journey through the Russian steppes: *The spring is chilly in the steppes. The wind has no barrier, here, no reason to stop.*

How much smarter she is now. She knows that without her efforts William's presence will evaporate from the rooms. Keeping it demands ministrations that rarely repay her with the vividness she craves. In the street she might see a man his size, turning his head in a gesture that is unmistakably William. Then she has to stop herself from running after him, grateful for this momentary sharpness of feeling, which is all she has left.

She has devised some temporary measures. "Stay away," she tells herself. "Save it," she murmurs. "Don't look." She stays away from the black case of his violin, hides William's favourite mug, his navy-blue dressing gown still smelling of sandalwood soap, with some threads pulled out already, breaking the thickness of the terry cloth. These she guards, saves them for the empty time when memories have to be coaxed out, enticed.

She flings the door to his study open and walks in. She brushes her fingers over the surface of the mahogany desk, over the pile of papers, over the drawers with their round brass locks. She opens them, one by one, slides her hand inside, smoothing the things that retain the layer, however faint, of his touch.

"My haven," he called it when he brought her here, for the first time, and she looked at the piles of books and papers lying on the floor, seeing in them a maze of paths that would take her years to unravel. His ex-wife and her inexplicable outbursts of hatred. Julia's angry silence. William was standing right behind her, his arm around her waist, his mouth nuzzling her hair aside and touching her neck. She leaned back and pressed her head to his chest. When she was little she would ask her father to let them walk like that, together, her feet on his. He pretended to wobble as they walked and she laughed at these big steps she was making, the sweeping swings to the left and to the right, the sudden twists broken by a peal of laughter.

I am that which is.

I am everything that is, that was, and that will be. No mortal man has lifted my veil.

He is of himself alone, and it is to his aloneness that all things owe their being.

They frightened her then, these words, so beautifully penned on white parchment paper, in their wooden frame.

"These?" he repeated her question. "These are ancient oracles. Beethoven had them mounted under glass on his working table," he had told her. "You don't think I'm arrogant to do the same?"

"No," she laughed, "I don't."

How relieved she felt then, how light! Borrowed, words somehow became less ominous, easier to tame.

"I'm worried about you," Marie says as she so often does. The touch of her friend's hand is firm and not unpleasant, but Anna withdraws her own hand swiftly. At Stach's, a Polish restaurant in Old Montreal where Marie has taken her for a bowl of goulash and a thick slice of rye bread, Anna separates strands of soft meat with the tip of her spoon. She puts her spoon down, and sips water from a thick, green glass.

"It is this absent look," Marie says, "I can't stand it."

No one, Anna thinks, has told her about the apathy of grief. Of the loathing of the slightest effort, the slightest gesture. Of the long, empty hours spent in bed, curled up, her head covered, hoping that the world has stopped as it should. Of the times, increasingly alarming to her, when she finds herself doing something she does not remember starting, as if, in these blank, missing moments, her mind floated somewhere above and could not be accounted for.

"Can you sleep?" Marie asks.

Anna shakes her head. That has changed, too. At first she could. Right after William's death sleep was an escape, a relief; she could have slept night and day. Now she has to rely on Halcyon, her mind emptying itself in a heavy, dreamless slumber. The pill doesn't help her fall asleep; she takes it for the dawn when, without it, she would have woken up, no matter how dark she has made the bedroom. At five in the morning her mind refuses all consolation.

Every day Marie insists on taking her out, or on coming by, placing food in front of her. For Marie, Anna's appetite is the measure of her mood. If Anna pokes her fork into the leaves of lettuce, Marie pleads for a movie, or a walk. If Anna eats what is in front of her, she can be left alone.

"When will you go back to teaching?"

"I don't know," Anna says. It hasn't been too hard to find a replacement for the two English classes she usually taught at that time of year.

"I don't need the money," she says as if that's what Marie were worrying about.

"But you need something to do," Marie snaps. "You can't cry all day."

In this other life, as Anna sometimes thinks of the time William was still alive, she had so many plans. There was a radio documentary she wanted to work on with Marie, interviews with Polish refugees who could now go back to the new, democratic Poland. "Would they?" Marie wondered.

"He wanted to have a trout pond. And a vineyard," Anna says. She has taken to speaking in short sentences as if words tired her. A thought takes too long when it has to be wrapped up in words. Is this why William turned to music? She would have asked him if he were here.

Marie has heard it before, a list of what is no longer possible.

"Here," she says and hands Anna an envelope with newspaper clippings, William's obituaries she has collected. *Brilliant composer . . . cruel loss . . . he had so much more to give.* Hackneyed, threadbare words come too late, but Anna craves them nevertheless.

His music. In the last years he wrote so little, and what he wrote he tore to bits and threw away in disgust. She had to become an expert on consolation. From old reviews she had memorised whole passages and recited them back to him over the breakfast table. *His music thrives on ambiguity and conflict. It is interested in the decay of sonorities, in patterns that collapse as we become aware of them. In its avoidance of pulse it mocks our need for stability. Change, when it happens, has no purpose; it is time that takes away some things and substitutes them with others...*

"Listen to me, darling!"

Insatiable, seductive, brilliant. William Herzman's music transcends the boundaries of genres. It takes us beyond our selves, shakes off our complacency...

He always listened. Rolled his eyes in mock impatience, but never ever stopped her. Never tired of praises, however stale she feared they'd become.

"What would I do without you!" he would say and, now, when she remembers it, she is awash with tenderness.

Marie orders two shots of *Żubrówka*, bison vodka, fragrant from a blade of sweet grass. The waitress places them in the middle of the table.

"Come on," Marie says. "Together."

They raise the glasses. Anna flinches as she drinks, but the vodka does warm her up.

"How's your Mother?" she asks.

"Fine," Anna says. "They're all fine."

"And Adam?" It's all a deliberate, transparent effort to make her think of her family in Poland, and it works. She has a sister-in-law now, and a nephew. In a twist of fate it was Marie who had met them, and Anna has not. When Marie visited Anna's parents in 1983 Adam was just a toddler with a crooked smile and small plump hands. When Marie was leaving, he gave her a wet kiss. She has had a soft spot for him ever since.

"Adam sent me a card," Anna says. He is but a face she has traced on photographs, recognising the toys and clothes she and William have bought for him.

"I'm going to Prague next week. Why don't you come with me? You could go to Poland, too. See your parents?" Marie says.

"All I ever got were false signs," Anna says, as if she hasn't heard. She is thinking of the times her heart stopped when she looked at the kitchen clock, its black hand moving too fast, advancing into spaces she found increasingly difficult to explain. "He is late," she thought, trying to calm down, "a bit later than usual. He was stopped by a student. He had nowhere to call from." She would pace to the window and back, all the time waiting for the sound of William's car in the driveway, for the cheerful squeak of the storm doors, the sound of a key turning in the lock. When he did come in, ashamed of her fears, she would run to him, throw her arms around his neck, and press her cheek to his chest. "What's that all about?" he would say, laughing. "Another bout of your Slavic soul?"

"Anna," Marie says softly. "You can't blame yourself for not knowing. You shouldn't think of it like that."

"Like what?" Anna asks.

"Like you could have somehow stopped it," Marie says. Her black hair has a slight purple hue to it. It's very becoming, but Anna will not say so. It annoys her that she would even notice a thing like that.

"I've been punished," Anna says. "For coming here. For leaving Piotr. For leaving Poland."

"That's absolute bullshit and you know it," Marie says, frowning. "So don't even start it." She is fixing her eyes on Anna now, her grey almond shaped eyes, clouded with anger and impatience. They have been through this before. Anna knows Marie doesn't like these self-accusations, but she brings them out nevertheless, with blind persistence, like a tongue pushing on a loosened tooth. She longs to hear Marie's protests. "For Goodness sake, Anna! People change, they grow! You had the right to think of yourself, of your own needs! Can't you see that?"

Anna tries to nod, but she breaks into tears, instead. Warm, abundant, like a spring shower.

It was no business of hers to write to Marilyn, but she has always been rash, always trying to mend what wasn't hers to mend in the first place. "I'm sure," she had written, "that in the face of death a lot can be forgiven."

Marilyn wrote "No" across Anna's letter and returned it. Anna still has it in her purse when she is sitting in Julia's living room in N.D.G. This is a new place, just rented. Anna is sitting in a wicker armchair and she is watching her stepdaughter make tea. At the funeral service she was glad to have Julia next to her, to see her swaying gently back and forth, crumpling a white handkerchief in her hand. Through the mesh of Anna's veil, Julia's face seemed darkened, turned into a shadow, but at that time Anna was grateful for the black muslin draped over her own hat, hiding her swollen eyes, dampening the brightness of colours, protecting her grief.

The peace between them is a fragile one. Seven years before, when her stepdaughter stormed out of their Westmount home, Julia was thin and nervous, her long hair tied into a golden ponytail. She always bumped into things, then, bruised her thighs on table corners, cut her fingers when she was slicing bread. Now, at twenty-seven, Anna's stepdaughter moves with confidence, her gestures slow and deliberate. Her hair is cropped short, making her look slightly boyish, in spite of her full lips and her tight dress.

"Still with honey instead of sugar?" Julia asks her. She is placing a pot of herbal tea on a low coffee table with rattan legs. She holds it firmly by the handle.

Anna doesn't really like Julia's new place. It is too noisy, even on a Sunday, and too dark. The furniture is simple. A futon by the coffee table, a pine bookcase, and an armchair. On one of the walls Julia has put the same framed poster she had in her old apartment, the *Expose Yourself to Art* one William had given her, a man opening his coat to a sculpture of a naked woman.

"Yes, please," Anna says to the offer of honey. She has been leaning to the side far too long, and now her right leg has gone to sleep. She lifts herself up and limps toward the window. Julia's windows look right out on Sherbrooke Street.

"I wish I made myself call him," Julia says. Her bottom lip trembles. She chews on it to stop the trembling. "I wish we had one good talk before he died."

For the last few years William didn't even want to speak about Julia. He frowned and shrugged his shoulders, defeated. "I've tried," he said. "You are my witness. We've both tried."

In 1981, when Anna met her, Julia was seventeen. There was a smell of talcum powder around her, then, and something else, something familiar and, at the same time, out of place. "Vanilla," Anna realised a split second later, "a scent of vanilla."

They were all rather nervous that evening. When Julia sat down she took a white paper napkin into her hand and began tearing it into small pieces and then, with her index finger and a thumb she rolled the pieces into little balls, and dropped them on the carpet.

"I hate school," she announced when William asked her how she was doing. She was tall, pale, and very thin. Her lower lip was thrust forward, as if she were sulking, but this, too, could have been a calculated effect, for it gave her the aura of a pretty, spoilt child.

"Wow," she said when Anna brought in an assortment of cheeses, prosciuto with melon, and smoked salmon spread. "How did you know I loved this stuff," she asked.

Anna had hoped to become friends with Julia, then, had images of the two of them meeting for ice cream and coffee, or shopping for clothes. She wanted to smooth some of the lingering harshness in the way Julia spoke to her, some uneasiness, jealousy perhaps.

That evening Julia talked all the time, as if afraid to let them have a word, to contradict her. What did she talk about? Anna still remembers Julia's admiration for some girl who really had class. The friend she so much admired, Marcia, was *lethal.* "You should have seen her, Dad. Swinging her purse. Guys just lose their heads."

Marcia thought it cool to pinch things from stores, a lipstick, a comb, a packet of chewing gum. "There is this older guy, a sick jerk," Julia went on without a pause. "His fat lips quiver when he sees her. Waiting for her after school in his Jag. 'Just to see you, my angel!' Julia's voice rose at the end of each sentence, as if they were all questions, and waited for William to disagree.

"Marcia said he begged her to sit in the car. She sat there and pissed on the seat."

When she laughed, Julia tossed her head backwards and her shoulders shook. She bombarded them with words, unable to stop the staccato of exclamations and forced, jeering laughter. It was a performance, Anna thought, a rehearsal. She came to hear herself speak and to check her own power, to see William's eyes following her.

Julia, it seemed to Anna then, paid no attention to her. It was William she wanted, William with this smile on his face that betrayed him. He was so happy to see his daughter again that he would accept everything she told him, pay any price. Agree with everything she said.

"I wish you could speak to Ma!" Julia said, finally. So that's why she came, Anna thought, to get him to fight her battles. She excused herself and went to the kitchen. From the living room Julia's voice was a long murmur of which Anna could make only a few words. "You are in my house and you are under eighteen. I'm not going to let you ruin your life . . . Tell him to get out of here or I'll call the police . . . She has no right! Hell, I'm not going to tell *her* everything."

In the kitchen, Anna felt her body become heavier, harder to move. It was getting dark, time to switch on the lights. "Now," she urged herself on and arranged a few more slices of poppyseed cake on a platter. When the murmurs in the living room became less intense, she walked in. Julia took a big piece of cake from the plate and winced.

"I'm eating like a pig. God, you must think I'm pregnant or something," Julia laughed, addressing Anna for the first time. William laughed, too. It was a guilty laugh, begging for acceptance.

"Oh, no," Anna said, quickly, and then thought that it was probably a stupid thing to say.

They never knew when Julia would come, when a few angry words from Marilyn would make her pack her bag and arrive on their doorstep. It became a way of life, a sea-saw in which they were only one of the sides — once up, once down. And there was always Käthe with her terse calls to William. "But Willi, she is only a child."

Anna let words slip, betray her resentment. She was not good at sharing William, at changing plans at the last minute because of Julia's arrival. It became harder and harder to pick up damp clothes from the bathroom floor, to remove Julia's long golden hairs from her hairbrush.

"Why do you let her speak to you like that?" she made a mistake of asking William after a long series of "Oh, shut up Dad," and "Lay off, will you!"

"What do you want me to do?" he asked in return.

"Tell her she can't live like that. Tell her *you* don't like it."

He gave her a hurt look, then, as if she disappointed him, turned into someone else, someone he could no longer trust. "Then she won't come here, at all," he said. "Is *that* what you want?"

When Julia turned twenty she moved in with them, taking psychology and music at McGill. William beamed with pride. Anna could hear them, from behind the closed doors of Julia's room, laughing, recalling stories from the past. Some cat with a striped tail making off with Julia's doll. The bitter lettuce leaves from their garden in the country. She couldn't shake off the feeling that they were talking about her, laughing at her behind her back.

Her own questions Julia answered with quick *yes* or *no*, flashing Anna a smile with her braced teeth, their conversations ending before they could begin. Anna thought herself only good enough for picking up the trail of crumbled tissue, dirty dishes on the floor, on the sofa, socks rolled into sweaty balls that had to be turned inside out and soaked before washing.

If only she and William could have a child, she thought, it would be all different. She wouldn't mind it so much. But no matter how much they wanted it, she couldn't get pregnant. Her doctor urged her not to despair. There was no medical reason why she couldn't conceive, he said. It may be just a matter of time. She was not the only one, either. It happened so often in his practice.

The trip to Italy was to be an escape, a rest from the tensions of the last months. Two weeks alone with William, long walks though the streets of Florence, Tuscan meals at trattorias, his voice whispering in her ear how well-dressed people seemed there, how open about their bodies. "Look at the ease and grace with which they move," he kept telling her, his eyes following the young women who passed them by. They went to see *David* at the Academia, and then sat looking at Michelangelo's *Bacchus* in the Bargello, at the rounded belly and the lecherous half smile of the marble god, suspicious of the boundaries of virtue. When they sat there, a blind man in dark glasses walked in. He was holding a thin white cane, and a young boy who held his arm described to him, in a soft, humming voice, what sculptures they were passing by. When they reached *Bacchus*, the blind man leaned forward and slowly ran his fingers along the marble skin.

Something wasn't right. She knew that as soon as the taxi brought them from the airport. Julia was standing behind the screen doors waiting for them, her hair gathered into a tight pony tail, her pale face covered with red blotches. "I'm sorry, Dad," she said, biting her lips. "Could I talk to you . . . alone?"

"Go ahead," Anna said. "I'll wait." She paid the driver, an elderly Sikh in a freshly ironed blue shirt, and asked him to leave the suitcases in the driveway. "The children, Ma'am," he said with sympathy. "With them, there is always trouble. But without them, there is no life." Anna nodded and waved to him as the taxi backed and left.

The lawn, she noticed at once, was a mess. Cigarette butts were scattered among drying, trampled grass, and broken beer bottles glittered in the sun. Someone had dug out deep square holes in the middle of the lawn. A splash of silver by the window turned out to be one of the junipers, sprayed with paint, its branches imprisoned in a shining amour.

Anna waited outside for a few more minutes, registering more broken flowers, spots where grass was painted red, blue, and yellow. Someone had pushed a tire into the flowerbed. She was growing anxious. "William!" she called. Nobody answered. "William! Julia! May I come in?"

She stood in the hall listening, but heard nothing. In the living room Julia was standing by the fireplace, leaning over the mantel. William was sitting on the sofa, his face hidden in his hands.

"No, I have nothing to admit," Julia was saying when she Anna came in. "And I don't have to take this shit, especially not from you!"

The sour smell of vomit, cigarette smoke and spilled beer filled the air. The walls and ceiling were covered with drying red flesh of tomatoes, yellowish seeds still clinging to the pulp.

More broken glass; among the shards were fragments of William's crystal wine decanter. Anna stepped on something soft that squiggled under her foot. Bending down, she saw it was a used condom.

"What has happened," she asked. It was hard to believe that what she saw had a cause, a beginning, an intention.

When William didn't answer, Anna walked up to him, took his hands and pulled them off his face. He was crying. The cigarette burns in the soft brown leather of the sofa formed a big, crooked star.

"Do you think I've been punished enough?" he asked.

Julia was moving fast behind the doors of her bedroom. When she emerged, she had her rucksack on, a red bandanna across her forehead. The doors closed and the storm doors followed with a thud.

"She threw a party," William said.

"A party? What kind of a party?"

"The neighbours called the police," he said. "Someone broke the window in the bedroom. A tire was lit up in the backyard. But they didn't come fast enough to catch anyone."

He brought a package of black garbage bags, and Anna opened the windows to get rid of some of the smell. "Don't touch anything with your hands," he said handing her a pair of latex gloves. With these rubbery fingers they picked up sticky condoms, crumpled paper towels, tablecloths and sheets glued together with dried vomit. Turning her head away, Anna pushed the soiled cloth into the black bags. William announced a list of damages: beer spilled into his violin case, the toilet seat broken, CDs missing, a handle torn from the door, black scratches on the living room floor. Flour and sugar dumped into the washing machine.

For days everything they touched seemed sticky, defiled. There were tomato seeds still hiding between telephone buttons; a slice of pizza was rotting behind the bookcase. It scared her to think of the destructive rage that must have fuelled it all.

The neighbours were forgiving. "You are not the first ones," Pauline said. "A Canadian right of passage, a crashed party." John and Louise apologised for not intervening earlier, but, they stressed, Julia seemed always so mature. She must have had a bit to drink, missed the tipping point beyond which there is no control. "Poor kid, who needs an experience like this? She must feel awful, now."

Anna thought: Poor Julia? What about me? What about her father?

If she did regret what had passed, Julia kept such feelings to herself. She didn't call, didn't write. Not even a postcard with an apology. It's just as well, Anna thought then. She needed time. She needed time not to feel a tinge of pleasure when William said that he didn't want to speak of Julia at all. Ever.

The beige metal shelves in William's office at McGill are full of papers, books, and records. Some of the books have white library stickers on them. Valerie, the secretary in the Music Department gives Anna a few empty cardboard boxes. One of them is marked, "Return."

"This is for library books if you find any," she says and sighs. Her red jacket is open at the front. "Take your time. There is no rush. We are all so sorry. He was still so young."

This is not the worst, Anna thinks. At least she is not offered a spiritual lecture about the ebb and flow of life, the need to accept death. Or told, with an uneasy smile that she will get over it, with time.

"Fifty-one," Anna says, "Only fifty-one," and her heart shrinks, for words like these reduce William's life to a number, a score.

There are two photographs on his desk in brown leather frames, one of her and another of Julia, her hair still long, her now straight white teeth exposed in a wide, cover-girl smile. Anna is glad to have the picture here. Julia called her in the morning and suggested they have dinner together. "Do you want me to come and help?" she asked, but Anna said she would rather go through it on her own.

EVA STACHNIAK

That was in the morning. Now, overwhelmed by the inevitability of the task before her, Anna escapes to the washroom and stands motionless in front of the bathroom mirror, leaning over an orange Formica counter. Swallowing is hard, painful. She touches the purple shadows under her eyes. Her face has turned alien in grief, bird-like, she thinks, revealing the first short lines cutting into her lips, almost invisible, but already there.

Back in William's office she goes through his things, slowly, refusing to part with any traces of his presence. A thought that he won't, ever, touch anything else is what prompts her. At home, she hugs his dressing gown hanging on the door hook, kisses the rim of the collar, touches the polished tips of his shoes, still in the shoetrees to preserve their shape. Here, she is sifting through what has remained.

The papers on the upper shelves turn out to be students' unclaimed assignments, dusty and yellowed. These the department can have. They can also have the music journals, some of them still in their plastic covers, unopened, unread, as well as the files in the drawers, minutes from committee meetings, grant proposals, students' petitions asking for his recommendations.

A thick manila envelope is in the file marked personal. It is sealed and when Anna tears the flap to get inside, letters, postcards, and photographs spill on the desk. In these photographs, taken within moments of each other, William's face is moving from his pensive frown to laughter. He is wearing the black turtleneck and the brown tweed jacket she always liked so much, leaning forward as if trying to convince someone of something very important. In the last picture the lock of his silver hair is falling over his forehead, just before the moment he would brush it away.

A postcard from Baden-Baden — an old, sugar-sweet postcard, flowery wreaths and bells ring merrily, musical notes spilling out. The handwriting is hard to decipher, the letters are tall and tight. It takes Anna a while to see a pattern in these edgy lines, to make out the words. *L'absence est à l'amour ce qu'est au feu le vent, il éteant le petit il allume le grand.* It is signed: *Ursula.*

Anna opens a small blue envelope, and takes out a folded piece of paper. Her heart stops for a few seconds and begins again to pump blood, rushing it to her face. The paper shakes as she holds it. *Darling, It is so empty here without you. The rooms echo my steps, and your voice is still around me. I'm pretending that you've just stepped out for a moment and that you will be back, soon, a good husband, away on a short trip. I feel married to you in the most profound sense of the word. Why would we need anything more? Ursula*

Another sheet, folded in four, rustles as she unfolds it. No date. *Got home late, and the apartment was dark and cold; I had turned the thermostat down before I left. My old Prussian hatred of waste, the miserly me. I crawled into bed thinking of you. Today, I don't want to talk to anyone, for then I would forget your voice. Urs.*

London, then. We will have late dinner at Durrants Hotel and then walk on George Street and kiss. I want to be courted. Please, buy me a ribbon and a comb and take me to the wax museum, and we will laugh in the still faces. We will make love and drink horribly strong tea (milk first), and be as British as only Germans long to be.

Anna sits down, legs unable to support her. Something has snuck up behind her, is touching her shoulder. She turns her head and looks at the bookshelves she has just emptied. Nothing there but specks of dust. It's not what you think, she says to herself. It can't be.

"It's just for a few days," she remembers him saying. "I need to be alone. You do understand, don't you?" She stood in the doorway and watched him pack his brown leather suitcase. Round balls of socks went to their place on the right, his beige corduroy pants lay flat on the bottom, Shetland sweaters were folded into even squares, empty sleeves tucked neatly inside. He closed the zipper of a brown leather sachet with its scent of sandalwood.

"Be together but not too close together, like two pillars of a temple," he had said. A line from *The Prophet*, one of his presents for her, the maxims of the sixties. She didn't drive him to the airport; he hated that. It was better to say goodbye here,

97

at home, and she was careful not to hold him for too long, faking impatience to cover up the pain. Anger she couldn't afford. It could simmer in her, but she would not let it boil over. "Thank God you are not like Marilyn," he said once, and she remembered everything he had said about his first marriage. "You don't have her vindictiveness."

William was already anticipating his own return, slipping his hand under her sweater, around her waist and pulling her toward him. "I'll call," he murmured into her ear.

He did. From Frankfurt, Berlin, Munich, his voice cheerful, concerned. "Do you miss me, love?" he asked and she laughed. "You do understand, don't you?" But she thought he just wanted to be alone for a while. Did he really believe she was allowing him to betray her? Not him. Not William. She must be wrong, of course she is. She has no right to suspect him.

Finished "The Faces of Women" today. All shots are black and white. Colour spoils the deadly transformations I want. You don't have to be alarmed, William, my obsessions are not too easy to spot. The Nazi women are there in spirit only, in the looks of submission, fanaticism, and self-annihilation. I didn't have to go too far for looks like that. A few night tours of Berlin bars sufficed. Lothar didn't say anything, but gave me a bear hug. That was the best review I got. Walked along Ku-damm, still watching. Disco music pours out of the stores. Young women are wearing tight blouses and jeans and balance their bodies on platform shoes. Schoolgirls have loud voices and bold looks. Of course, I'm emptied and sore. Way too concerned with trivia, distracted by moments of inconsequence.

Anna takes off her glasses and closes her eyes. Her eyelids feel as if there were tiny cracks in them, itching and sore. She knows the only way to conquer the itch is to stop rubbing the eyelids, to wait through the surge of pain, but she rubs them until tears appear and torn eyelashes stick to her wet fingers. When she opens her eyes, the edges of the room look softer. Books on the shelves turn into patches of colour; the ceiling is a stretch of white, without a blemish.

Darling, No! No regrets. None! I wake up at night, watch the lights of Berlin and pretend that you are here with me. What I

want is the sea — green, cold, smelling of seaweed and wet wood.
Some escape from this constant fever. You tell me I've forgotten
that there is something worthwhile beyond ecstasy and despair. I
do listen. Sometimes,U.

Anna's cheeks are flushed, and she presses her hands to hot
skin. She waits for something to happen now, some necessary
sequence to this discovery, something that would explain it,
make it go away. From a distance she hears doors open and
close, someone's voice outside is rising then falling sharply,
silenced, cut short. "Yes, yes of course," she hears, "I'm sorry." It
occurs to her that Valerie must have placed all these letters into
William's mailbox; for years she must have watched as he
picked them up and hurried to his room to read them.

She stands up and takes a few steps away from the desk. It's
not fair, she keeps thinking. Not now. Not when he is dead,
when he cannot explain. She sits down again.

Darling, Your voice sounded rather sad and whiny, and I'm
sorry I was so rushed. You caught me in the middle of a session.
Tried to call you back, but you were out already. No, it's not easier
on me. Just because I was the one to say it, doesn't mean it's solely
my decision. There is historical evidence that we would end at each
other's throat, and that we would burn in this hatred, so don't try
to change my resolve. I might be in Montreal next month, to
photograph the faces in your Canadian national parades, the
progress of the Referendum, so don't sulk for too long. Rather, tell
me what will your wonderful, innocent country do if it splits. "Je
me souviens?" Isn't that what your license plates say?

Quebec Referendum. Before she came to Canada. Of course!
These letters were written before she even met William. They are
from the time she has no rights to. She reasons with her own
uneasiness: William had a love affair when he was married to
Marilyn. He didn't tell her about it. He didn't want her to think
him unfaithful, capable of betrayal. Such reticence is
disappointing, but understandable. It may even be thought of as
discretion. She didn't tell him that much about Piotr, either.

October, 1979. Blackness is like poison, a drain of colour, and
I succumb slowly. First goes hope, then energy seeps out. I sit and
stare at the walls of my room and wait until it goes away. I wait

*until, by some divine intervention, a new beginning will grab me,
and I will rise to start again.*

There are magazine articles attached to some of the letters,
folded, yellowed at the edges. In German, in English. Anna
pushes them aside, impatient. There will be plenty of time to
read them later. Now she needs to be reassured. *January 1980.
No, it wasn't too bad. Just a skirmish between creativity and
despair. You needn't be concerned. I plunge into such days
willingly and emerge fortified. The sky is sapphire-blue and the
wind penetrates the skin. I slipped into a small church, round the
corner from here, smelled the whiff of camphor from the furs, and
listened to the pastor with a golden tooth and a slight lisp. "As it
was in the beginning, is now, and ever shall be, world without
end." Not much hope, then, for change, nicht wahr? Today I woke
up full of resolutions. Like a prisoner I may have nothing but a
teaspoon to dig a tunnel with, but I will go on. As chance presents
itself, I'll dispose of the soil, sand, and stones.*

*March 1980. I went to touch the Wall today. The doors and
windows of the apartments facing the Wall in the East are sealed.
This is a divided city, after all; German metaphors are solid,
made of reinforced concrete. The guards on the other side will
shoot to kill. Yet the brave ones dig their tunnels, scale the Wall,
run for their lives. If they manage to get here, I see them,
sometimes, drinking themselves into oblivion in West German
bars, throwing their accusations in our faces. To them we are
cold, callous, and naive. We don't understand anything.*

It is the dates Anna is checking now. Date stamps, for many
of the notes are not dated at all. She remembers that William
kept a magnifying glass in one of his drawers. It is still there, in
its black leather case. She examines these smudged dates,
carefully. 1980, 1977. Some months are missing, or so it seems
to her, but then they appear, merely misplaced, overlooked.
William has known Ursula for a long time.

"A Berlin photographer I know," he said to her once. For
months there was no name attached to this phrase, and she
didn't ask.

In another conversation, she remembers hearing Ursula's name. Someone mentioned it, Malcolm perhaps, asked him about his photographer-friend from Berlin. "Ursula?" William said and Anna asked, "Who?" and he said, "Ursula, you know, the German friend I told you about."

From the tinge in his voice she knew that it gave him pleasure to hear her name spoken.

"Quite mad," he also said, "doesn't believe in sparing herself."

Many of the notes are hand-written and these Anna has to decipher slowly, match the shapes of letters, guess their meaning. *Life is too short for pettiness,* she reads. *You are too impatient, but I do love you.* She skims over them waiting for the change of tone. Hopes for the signs of love fading, turning into friendship.

September 1981, What's wrong with our love, William? It weakens me; it makes me mellow. I walk through the day with a self-satisfied grin on my face and see your smile everywhere. I catch myself whispering your words. I hum, I skip as I walk. Don't be too pleased with yourself, though, this is a pitiful sight! This is why I'm asking you to stay away. Please don't be angry, you won't lose me, ever. You'll just let me breathe, and for this I will love you even more.

October 1981, It's our souls, darling; they cannot stand letting go of the other lives they could have led. It scares me to think how much we have to cast off in order to choose.

October 1981, A Polish woman and a refugee, William? Isn't she another one of your atonements?

Her lip hurts, but it takes a few second before Anna realises that her teeth have sunk deep into it, cutting the skin. There is blood on her finger when she runs it over her lip, and she stares at the red smudge before wiping it off. She has run out of excuses. "Fool," she says aloud, "fool." Her mother's voice is with her now. "What were you expecting, Anna, *from a German*?"

Each date now is like the lash of the whip. "Until the end," she murmurs in disbelief, "until the very end."

May, 1987. I've never promised I'll be faithful, and I don't ask for your exclusive interest. Oh, I know, you will never admit that you are jealous! You will just sulk and try to punish me with your silly little games. How sordid of me! Sorry! Am I hurting your sensitivity? Poor Willi. I don't believe in secrecy, and I don't hide you from anyone else in my life. You are the one who pretends that the past and the present can be kept apart and I let you, so, please spare me your little sermons.

March, 1989. Don't sulk! I woke up in my darkest mood, today, despairing. I looked at the last shots and they were all wrong. False, contorted, smug. Too light, too clean. What rot! A good photograph is like a prediction, isn't it? It captures something about the future, but you have to hurry before time turns it into a cliché. So I hurry, rush, follow my hunches.

January, 1990. When I was coming back to Berlin I saw the dawn. It stretched, pink and red, and golden. "A ribbon at a time," Darling. Remember? Maybe you are right, maybe I'm not that tough. I telephoned Lothar, and he came and let me speak of you. He made me some tea and we finished off the brandy you left behind. I couldn't drink it alone.

November, 1990. So it's next week. In Munich. I have a map of the world and put red tags for every city where we have been together. The spots of love. The map is pretty red, by now. Three days and three nights. I'm waiting already.

In some of the envelopes Anna finds dried wildflowers, which now crumble under her fingers, shreds of cloth, splinters of grey wood. Short notes give way to longer letters, to more newspaper clippings, pages with passages highlighted and peppered with exclamation marks. She opens the envelopes, blue, white, pink, unfolds the pages. Most of the letters have been mailed in Germany, *Mit Luftpost*, the blue sticker informs, by *Deutsche Bundespost*, but there are notes scribbled on grey stationery from Hôtel Intercontinental Genève with its bilingual warning that, *L'expéditeur de cette lettre n'engage pas la responsabilité de l'hôtel.* The sender of this letter does not entail the hotel. By now Anna has abandoned all search for order, picks the letters at random, little snitches of the love William hid from her so well.

Mutti came for a few days, and she said I had to let her remodel my bathroom. The faucets were leaking and she gasped in her funny way. "My poor darling!" Her daughter is impractical, erratic, irresponsible. Smokes and drinks too much. Loves too much. Places no limits on herself, gives herself away. I said she could do whatever she wanted to the bathroom, a bloody mistake. I left for a few days for Paris, and when I came back I found this pink(!!!) heaven. The basin and the tub are two inverted shells. I have a mirror across the wall and pink tiles with white shells on every sixteenth one. I counted them, so I know. The floor is white — a damn nuisance, for every fallen hair stands out. She has also bought me a pile of pink and white towels, thick and fleecy. Only the taps are decent, a kind of Bauhaus style, brass, quite nice to the touch, you will like them. She went away, pleased with herself and I, quite sinfully, poured her strawberry bubbles into this shell and soaked in the water until my skin resembled prunes. I tried to call you, but you were already at home so I imagined you instead.

Dearest, We love each other so much because we are far away and we save for each other only what is best in us. We meet, full of longing, we part before we are filled, before impatience sets in. When I come back here, I thank the gods for you and hold my breath not to spoil anything, but you, you try to imagine the limits of what we could be for each other, what life together could mean. I'm not that brave. Urs.

Anna stands up so fast that she overturns the oak swivel chair. Valerie, William's secretary, must have heard the noise for she is now knocking on the door. "Are you all right?" she is asking, her voice filled with concern.

"I'm fine," Anna says. "It's just the chair. I ... it fell down." She opens the door and even manages a faint smile. "It's nothing."

"I'm right here, if you need me," Valerie says, smiling gently, and Anna can see that she is relieved.

"Yes. Thank you," Anna closes the door and waits until the steps fade away, before settling down to work. Time is rushing forward, and she is trying to catch up with it. The first thing she needs is to be back home. Here, she is too much aware of the presence of other people: Valerie, William's colleagues. Malcolm's office is right next door. If she screamed, he might come running.

The boxes are lying on the floor. With a thick black marker smelling of paint thinner she quickly writes "discard" on the side. First she empties the contents of the top drawers, removing everything from them in scoops. Paper clips, pens and pencils hit the cardboard bottom. Thumb tacks, scissors, rolls of tape. Then she opens the side drawers and yanks the papers out. She throws them into the boxes, handful after handful, until the boxes are filled.

Soon the only things left on William's desk are the two photographs and Ursula's letters. Anna stuffs the letters and Julia's picture back into the manila envelope and into her handbag. Her own face on the other photograph annoys her with its smug grin of contentment.

She remembers that they made love here once, in this office, right behind the door. A few weeks after their wedding, after their Barbados trip where she had seen palm trees for the first time, where she tasted glistening, moist slices of papaya. She came running in to see him, her face flushed, her voice bubbling with excitement. "Darling, I want to show you something." She doesn't even remember what it was. What she recalls with the sharpness that hurts so much now is how he stood up and locked the door behind them. "And I want you," he said and kissed her, and ran his hand down her spine. He pushed her against the door, pressed her back against it. For a moment, before she closed her eyes, she saw her own face, in that photograph, watching them, smiling, amused. Was he thinking of Ursula then?

Anna removes the cardboard from the back of the frame and takes the picture out. She tears it in half, then in half again, into smaller and smaller pieces that she throws into the box.

The door to William's office closes with a piercing squeak. Anna waves to Valerie from the corridor, walks quickly down the stairs, hoping she won't meet anyone who might want to stop her and talk. By the statue of Queen Victoria, she turns around for another look at the soot-covered walls. She is holding her purse close to her body as she walks. On the bus, she sits in the back and watches the lanterns along Sherbrooke Street light up, the whole row of them, still decorated with tinsel and evergreen wreaths, in memory of another passing year.

At home she disconnects the phone and puts the letters on the dining room table, on the white tablecloth she no longer bothers to take off. She leaves them lying there and goes to the kitchen to get a glass of water. It is something she can concentrate on, letting the water run from the tap, filling the glass, swallowing. Her hands are unsteady and she has spilled some water on the kitchen counter. She wipes it off with a yellow j-cloth.

Back in the dining room, she arranges the letters in even rows on the table, like cards in the game of solitaire. The proofs that for ten years her husband has been in love with another woman. All these years he has lied to her, laughed at her behind her back. She has never suspected anything. There is some grim satisfaction in these thoughts, some dark pleasure in laughing at her pathetic love, her own smugness. She used to think Marie was too suspicious of men, too cautious. She used to think that of many women.

You can write it all down, now, she tells herself. The wisdom of Anna Herzman, the biggest fool of them all.

The water has helped. She is no longer feverish; her heart has hardened. The letters in front of her are her evidence. She will read them slowly, carefully, one by one. Nothing will be skipped, nothing overlooked.

A Polish woman and a refugee, Willi? No, I'm not jealous and, yes, I'm quite cynical about atonements. But love becomes you, darling, it always has. You are not doomed, like I am. You will learn to live on a leash, if it is not too short, and she will learn to be happy with you if she is anything close to what I imagine. Perhaps what you are doing is the only intelligent thing to do, so don't take it as criticism. I do pray for you at times like that, so I'm not that bad.

Dearest, I have just finished speaking to you on the phone. You said I knew you so well. I wonder what is it that I know. I merely watch you, I have watched you for years, and I take what I see. And you, you mistake this resignation for knowledge. The truth is that you never cease to amaze me. Urs

Jealousy is a smuggler's prop. It has secret compartments and hidden bottoms that appear when Anna thinks she has reached its limits. False pockets to confuse her, revealing layers of bitterness, more and more of them, crumpled, entangled, choking her now, cutting off the passage of air.

She can imagine William and Ursula together, in this house, perhaps. In the same bed in which she sleeps now, alone. She can see their legs, arms, entangled, their bodies pressed against each other. Heaving, pulsating, inseparable. Was he also moaning into Ursula's ear when he came? Nuzzling her neck, after they have made love, making her laugh with his stories? Telling her of his doctor friend who, seeing a stripper spread her legs, thought. "I could cauterize this." Was Ursula laughing as much as she had?

It is the vividness of such thoughts that breaks her. The whisper in her heart that when he came home from his love trips she would be the one to unpack his bags and wash his dirty clothes. Take the brown tweed jacket to the dry cleaner. Put the laundered socks and underwear back on the shelves, slide the folded shirts into drawers.

Her heart is hardening, she can feel that. From the darkest corners of her memory come the thoughts she has never allowed herself to think. What was it that Hitler thought of all Slavs? An inferior race of slaves? The dirt of history, a mere notch above the Jews. Slated for death to make living space in the East for the master race. *Drang nach Osten. Lebensraum.* Hasn't she been warned so many times? Hasn't she seen the evidence, the ruins, the graves? But she wouldn't listen, would she?

Lebenslüge, she says, remembering the German word William once used telling her of his marriage. The word Marilyn liked to throw back at him so many times. *Lebenslüge.* The lie that transforms your life.

I'm sorry I was difficult, darling. I wasn't really, you were. You were jealous, and cranky, and you sulked. Perhaps it is time you stopped blaming me for who I am. It's a bit as if you asked me to change the colour of my eyes. But, then, your letter was beautiful, and I had to forgive. Love. U.

Dearest, The exhibition went very well, but I won't quote the reviews. They only distract me, make me chase phantoms. The evening was rather quiet. I saw Fassbinder's "The Marriage of Maria Brown," another variation on his obsessions. Love for sale and the corruption of innocence. Incredibly bitter and quite brilliant, as he often is. He made me think of us, all of us, locked together in these little, deceitful transactions, of the secret agreements between submission and power, the craftiness of innocence! This is my obsession, too, as you have noticed so many times. Yes, I believe we, Germans, have a duty to expose self-delusions. Keep checking the collective pulse. We, of all people, cannot be caught filming another "Triumph of the Will."

I went to dinner with a rather too willing and confused friend of Rainer who got drunk and made a few passes at me, at first rather to my amusement and then much to my growing boredom. I've heard the first nightingale this spring, right in the Tiergarten, and you will be happy to know that I slept alone.

Dearest, I know what I'm talking about. Once you said that with you I would change, but I know I would only bury it all, and I would hate you for it. Perhaps I'm not that different from Marilyn, after all. We would have turned love into hate, and I don't want hate, not here, not in this country. You can be both guilty and wronged, Willi, nicht wahr? U.

She shouldn't be going through this alone, Anna thinks. But Marie is in Prague. Marie, who would put a bottle of wine on the table, fetch the glasses, put a fresh box of Kleenex in front of Anna, and start her interrogation. "So who is she? How long did he know her? How often did they meet? Where?" Sharp, pointed questions, tracing the logistics of betrayal. But Anna wouldn't know what to say.

In William's study, books take up the whole wall. These are mostly hardcover; he hated cheap editions that would fall apart before he finished reading them.

"I hate jealousy," he kept telling her. "It's not the way to live." How convenient, she tells him now. How very convenient for you. I hate to be lied to, does *this* matter?

She starts by opening the desk drawers, one by one, yanking the papers out. She holds the white sheets to the window as if they could contain some hidden marks, some traces of invisible ink. Why would Ursula be the only one? Why not other women? Students? Colleagues? Friends? She looks for hiding places, empties each file. She opens books, upsets the even rows on the shelves, leafs through the pages in search of evidence. When she finds a folded sheet, she pounces on it, heart fluttering. On one there are a few musical notes. On another Julia's childhood drawings of giant smiling heads on spidery legs, with arms sprouting from the ears. The books land on the carpet, one by one, and when she walks back to the desk she trips over them.

She has found a whole stack of last year's birthday cards, *Happy 50th Birthday, Many Happy Returns of the Day.* She is surprised William kept them. She had needed to hoard keepsakes, theatre programs, tickets, old calendars. Stash them away "like a hamster" he laughed, but now even this discovery hurts. What else did he keep away from her? She deciphers all the signatures. Malcolm, Jerry Dryden, Leanore. Old friends, everyone beyond suspicion. "Support the arts, kiss a musician," Malcolm's card says, letters dancing over a figure of a bass player, surrounded by floating notes. No card from Julia, the lingering disappointment of that otherwise splendid day.

The computer starts with a hum of the hard drive, the beeps of files loading. Anna stares at the screen, viewing the content of each file. Official letters, "On behalf of the editorial board of the *Musical Quarterly*...," an unfinished article on the German performances of Beethoven's Ninth in the last one hundred and fifty years, grant proposals, reports.

Nothing. Not that she really hoped she would find anything. He wouldn't keep things here, not where she could've stumbled onto something by chance. Even now she has a feeling that William has prepared himself for this invasion, that he has foreseen her moves. Everything in this room is in order, everything can be accounted for.

"Liar!"

She pounces on the pile of telephone bills: Germany 20 minutes, Germany 10 minutes. Among his calls to London, Amsterdam, Moscow always the same Berlin number. The last call was on New Year's Eve, only weeks before he died. Two minutes, enough for a short message on the answering machine. Ursula wasn't home?

At night Anna wakes every hour, but manages to fall asleep again and again. The dreams are shallow and jittery, impossible to connect. She is walking through a field of grass and flowers, so high that they reach her face. She has to spread the grass with her arms, but even then each step is a struggle. Her legs get tangled in the roots, the blades of grass beat her face.

Ursula, her voice multiplied by echoes, shouts something to her from a long maze of tunnels. Someone laughs at Anna from afar, the laughter coming closer and closer. At dawn, William appears. He is standing over the bed telling her that nothing has really happened, that it is all just a bad dream from which she will soon wake. "I promise," he says and when she does wake up, for a split second she believes him again, until her hand touches the empty space in her bed. Then she begins to sob, pounding the bed with her fists until she has no strength left.

In the morning, at William's desk, Anna takes out a clean sheet of paper. *How could you....* she starts and crosses it out, *Why couldn't he.... You owe me an explanation..... Can you even try to explain why.....* She crumples the sheets into balls and throws them on the floor.

I have found your letters to my husband, she finally writes. *I know he was your lover. If he were alive I would ask him why he lied to me, but now I have to ask you.* She catches the glint of her wedding ring as she writes. She slides it off her finger and throws it into an open drawer.

She licks the long white envelope, and the glue leaves a bitter taste on her tongue. She copies the Berlin address, and takes the letter to the mailbox across the street. Only when the envelope drops inside she wonders if Ursula knows of William's death. If she does, who has told her.

Her conversation with Julia is a short one. "I've found Ursula's letters," Anna says. The silence on the phone is already a sign.

"Where were they?" Julia asks. She is not surprised but her voice is lower, deeper than a minute before.

"What does it matter where they were?" Anna snaps. "Why didn't you tell me?"

"Where did you find them?"

"In his office. Why didn't you tell me?"

It is the tone of Julia's voice that maddens her. Slow, deliberate, calm. The voice of the social worker her stepdaughter has become. "It's not so simple. You have to understand my position." A voice so different from the sobs she treated William to, the late night calls for help.

"No, I don't have to," Anna says to that voice. "I don't have to do anything I don't want to. Isn't that what you always believed in?"

"I've paid my price," Julia says.

"You were not the only one. But why am I saying it? You never cared for anyone but yourself."

Why should she let Julia forget the silence, the unanswered letters, the years of absence from their lives.

"That's not true," Julia says, still calm, still sure of herself. "You know it's not true."

"You told her he was dead, too. I shouldn't be surprised, should I? You are *his* daughter, after all."

Anna slams the receiver, silencing Julia's protests. This may be just a small substitute for revenge, but it gives her pleasure.

The phone rings for a long time afterwards, but Anna doesn't pick it up. *Sorry, we are not available to take your call. Please leave your name and number or call us again,* she hears her own voice, calm, carefree. She has forgotten that the answering machine switches itself on if one waited long enough.

"Anna . . . Anna, please . . . I have to talk to you," she hears Julia's voice. "You can't cut me off like that."

PART III

WARSAW 1991

Marie arrives from Prague with the most recent instalments of the Eastern European drama. "Central European," she corrects herself. "I keep getting corrected, but they are right. Vienna *is* east of Prague."

"I'm so glad to see you," she murmurs, giving Anna a hug. Her eyes slide over Anna's rusty red shirt, her brown jacket. Anna has not worn black since the day she found Ursula's letters.

"You look better," Marie says, fingering the silk of the shirt. "I like it."

They are standing in front of the Roddick Gates, the entrance to McGill, on Sherbrooke Street.

"You should've gone with me, Anna," Marie squeezes Anna's hand.

Anna thinks that with her black hair tied back into a bun Marie's face seems thinner, lighter. Her days in Prague have made her stop at the street curbs and look with suspicion at the drivers. She says she has seen people scurry in fright at pedestrian crossings.

"Walk at your own peril," she remarks, "anywhere east of the Oder." In Prague she helped an elderly woman get on a subway escalator. Held her hand and steadied her as the speeding stairs pushed them off, into the platform. "Why do they make them go so fast, Anna," she still marvels. "It's not a damn roller coaster, is it?" Her Czech friends only laughed at her bewilderment. For them it was yet another lingering proof that Communism was designed for able-bodied workers. "If you were old, or frail — tough luck."

They cross the street and walk east, past the verandah of the Ritz Hotel.

"Isn't it incredible, though?" Marie asks. "It's not just Poland and Czechoslovakia, Anna. The Russian Empire has already begun to crumble. In Vilnus the KGB crushed a peaceful demonstration with tanks. Concrete walls have been erected to protect the parliament buildings in Talinn and Riga. The Kremlin panics."

She reminds Anna that only two years ago the demonstrators who gathered on Prague's Wenceslas Square placed lit candles on the ground were attacked and beaten by the police. The whole country shook in outrage. After a few dazed, smoke-filled days of strikes and protests, Václav Havel, the king of Czech dissidents, was brought to the Hradcany Castle.

This has only been a beginning, now almost forgotten. Marie is still shaken by what her Czech friends have told her of the *lustrace*, the national hunt for former Communist collaborators. Lists of suspected security agents have been published in Prague papers, often without proof. "It is not Communism but our old habits that are our greatest enemy," Havel has warned his countrymen, but no one is listening. A rumour or an informer's report is enough for a condemnation. "They are all going mad," Marie says, "This is a hysteria of vengeance."

She is uneasy about revenge, however well founded, Marie says. Her Czech friends, former dissidents themselves, are also terrified and appalled. There is no way to defend oneself, they have told her, even a record of persecution, years spent in prison, the courage it took to sign petitions when no one else dared to, do not guarantee forgiveness. Rudolf Zukal is rumoured to have spied on American students in Vienna in the 60s and this is enough to make him an "ideological collaborator," and drive him out of Parliament in disgrace.

Is that enough, Marie asks, to condemn Zukal? The man whose full name and address appeared on every petition since the Prague Spring, with carbon copy to the government? The man who lost his job as a University vice rector just because he refused to endorse the Soviet invasion? Who went to work as a bulldozer driver for twenty years? Lived in trailers, was crippled by industrial accidents, had three heart attacks? Whose children were denied higher education?

The man who, in the files of the Secret police, was listed as Czechoslovakia's 265th most wanted dissident? Is there no forgiveness for youthful fervour, for an old mistake tenfold repaid?

Those who judge him now, Marie says, are the same people who didn't dare to protest. Who went home to their families after work, drank their beer and congratulated themselves on their caution and common sense. Who said there was no point in becoming a martyr.

All of it is happening right now, in beautiful Prague, with tourists descending on the newly discovered jewel, a forgotten city. Marie has seen whole groups of Western teenagers treading through *Václavské namestí*, the Old Town, *Karluv most*. Feeding the swans on the *Vltava*, dropping coins into the upturned hats of street musicians, smoking marijuana and singing about wearing flowers in their hair.

"Why?" she asks Anna as they turn south, down Rue de la Montagne, past Anna's first Montreal apartment. The Hungarian restaurant has since closed. There is a new restaurant there now, Terra Mare, a seafood place. The windows of her old apartment are opened, but the curtains are drawn. The mustard coloured curtains, with frayed edges have not been replaced. Anna's mind drifts to the past, to the time when William stopped the car to tell her that he loved her.

"I thought people had decided to start a new life," Marie's voice breaks through her memories. "After all, no one was without sin."

"What do you expect?" Anna asks. There is irritation in her voice for which she has no excuse. Marie is right, and yet Anna goes on. "That they all instantly forget? Just like that?"

Marie gives her a cautious look.

"I mean amnesty, not amnesia, Anna," she says, taken aback. "I'm not saying it is easy."

Quickly, before she loses courage again or can change her mind, Anna opens her purse and takes out the envelope with Ursula's letters.

"Here," she says. "I've found them in William's office."

"What?" Marie asks, stopping abruptly, making the young couple behind them swerve to avoid bumping into them.

"Letters," Anna says. "From William's lover."

"From *whom*?" Marie fixes her eyes on Anna's face, not sure she has heard right.

"From William's lover," Anna repeats and swallows to ease the burning feeling in her throat.

They find a café to sit. There is only one table free, plastic plates piled up on it. Marie throws them into the garbage bin. The table is still littered with croissant flakes.

"I found letters from his lover," Anna says. With her left hand she is gathering up flakes on the table surface, neatly, into a pile. Small and compact. When the pile is perfect, she scatters it all up and begins again. Her voice is slow, subdued, still calm, but Anna knows how precarious that calm is, and she hurries. "William had a lover in Berlin."

"When did you find out?" Marie asks.

"Right after you left. When I started clearing his office."

"How long did it go on?"

"They met when he was still married to Marilyn. But they've always been lovers. Until he died."

"Are you sure?" Marie asks.

Anna nods. The envelope is lying on the table. Unopened.

"What a jerk," Marie says, frowning. "I could've wrung his neck. Men are all like that. They think they can tramp on you if it suits them." Her black hair falls over her eyes as she shakes her head. "Oh, God, Anna. How could he do it to you?"

"I didn't see anything," Anna says. "I was blind." She doesn't like the sound of her voice, it's too plaintive, too hurt.

Marie is calculating something in her head, putting together what she has just heard.

"Does she know he is dead?"

"Yes," Anna says. "Julia phoned her. They all knew it, for years. Marilyn and Julia. I was the dumb one." Her voice hardens when she says Julia's name, when she tells Marie about her last conversation with her stepdaughter. She might as well say everything that bothers her. Get it over with. She wants to hear she has the right to feel the way she does.

"Oh, God, Anna. You have to understand her, too," Marie's voice quivers when Anna has finished her confession. "What else could she have done?"

"I don't *want* to understand," Anna says with such force, pulling at the sleeves of her jacket, that Marie lets the matter drop.

"All I want to know is why he did it. It's the deceit I mind." Anna's voice is breaking down, "the lies."

Marie remains silent.

"That's all there is to it," Anna says, regretting her outburst already. She was hoping she could talk about her own feelings with more detachment. She really would like to know what Marie thinks. But now she has pushed herself into a rut, begging to be consoled. "I was his second-best," she says.

"I don't think so," Marie says softly and holds her hand across the table. "William knew how to be a complete asshole at times, but I saw the way he looked at you."

Anna's eyes well up with tears. "I could do with a coffee," she says.

Marie stands up and goes to the counter. She returns with two cheesecakes and two cups of coffee. The cakes, rich and soft, have a mound of whipped cream and a chocolate stick on a layer of breadcrumbs. Marie takes a bite of hers. "Shit," she says, stirring her coffee with a white plastic spoon, swallowing. "What a mess! What a bloody mess!"

The comfort Marie offers is not too elaborate, a touch of her hand, a sweet bite of the cake, and Anna is again filled with gratitude.

"Ursula," Anna says. "Her name is Ursula Herrlich. I wrote to her and she wrote back. Said I should go to Berlin, to see her."

There is nothing wrong with being consoled. That's what she has longed for, hasn't she?

"Will you go?" Marie asks.

"Why?" Anna answers with a question. She doesn't want to admit how many times she has imagined picking up the phone and dialling the Berlin number. "Ursula Herrlich," she would hear from the other end. "Anna Herzman" she would say, but then her imagination fails her. What would Ursula say then? How could she reply?

117

"Are you afraid to see her?" Marie asks.

"No," Anna says. "I'm not afraid." But this is a lie. Of course she is afraid.

"So why don't you go to Berlin?"

"Why should I?"

"To see things as they really are," Marie says. "To stop thinking of her all the time."

"I don't," Anna says. "I'll go to Poland. To see my parents," she says. "I have to see Piotr, but I don't have to see her."

"All right," Marie says. "You'll do what you want."

Anna can tell her friend is not convinced. She will try to keep calm, Anna tells Marie. Go through what she has to go through and then, maybe, she will know what to do next. Travelling is good that way, lets one see things in a different way. She will see her family, and come back to Montreal. Forget the past. Forget her humiliation. Forget her defeat. There will be a new life. There always is.

With that Marie agrees.

Since her discovery of Ursula's letters Anna has lived in a frenzy. She has invented chores, filling her days up to the last minute until the evening when she falls asleep too tired to think. In this frenzy she took William's suits off the racks, folded his sweaters and shirts, his beige coat she had helped him choose. She put all of his clothes into garbage bags and dropped them off at the Salvation Army. Then she spread her own clothes on the rack to fill the empty space. She called Malcolm and asked if he would take William's exercise bike and his tennis rackets. "I don't care what you do with them," she said, shielding herself from his surprise, "I want them out of here." She cleared the pantry of anything that might go bad. She had her hair cut and had ash-blond highlights put in. She made a list of presents she wanted to buy. Some were easy, like the ones for her brother and his new family she was yet to meet. But she kept returning what she had bought for her mother — a silk scarf was too dark, she decided, a mohair sweater too small. She didn't like the picture frame, either.

Finally she settled for an angora shawl, salmon pink. For her father she bought the most expensive wallet she could find.

Now she is pushing the thoughts of William away from her. He betrayed her and he doesn't deserve her pain, she tells herself. But Ursula is another matter. She cannot be silenced, her letters are always close by, speaking to a William Anna will never know. Echoes of old quarrels, reproaches, rebukes. In this exchange William is the silent one.

OK my farsighted lover! So I am vain, egotistical, self-serving. I get on my high moral horse, as you have so nicely put it, and have a solution to all your problems. I have no right to sound so damn superior. What else? There is another me, without illusions that I have any other way of getting at this world. That's all there is, and that's who I am. But you know where we differ? To me the world is incredibly beautiful. Visually beautiful, even in its pain. And I have given myself the right to disregard everything else. So I'll pay my price, whatever it is going to be. I don't bite anyone else if I hurt.

Darling, If you were here, with me, you would see that I'm wearing a black dress with a white lace collar and white cuffs and I'm in my nunnish mood. I'm fasting, too, to get back some of the tastes I have dulled. Sometimes this works much better than indulgence.

You want to block the past, William. You want to forget. When payment is demanded, you sulk or fly into a rage. You want to be cuddled, nursed through your moods. You know what? You might just manage, but you will ultimately not feel enough. And if you keep doing it, your music will never be any good. So don't ever tell me that you are not involved, that you are above it all! Oh, damn it, Willi, why do I have to tell you that?

Have I ever told you of Hitler's bunkers? We were taken there during the air raids, in the last months of the war. We were given food and a place on bunk beds, and told that our Führer loved all the German children. Once a woman who looked after us brought us some soup to eat, cabbage and carrots in greyish, greasy water. Nobody liked it, but we were too scared to refuse. It was really awful, and I said I wasn't going to finish it. "You will eat it" the woman screamed, "or no one will go to sleep until you do." I can still remember her face, red with fury. She seemed so big to me. I was four-years-old, and I really thought it was her scream that made the lamp swing. So I finished the soup, but I couldn't hold it and vomited it all over the plate. She made me eat the same soup again, to teach me a lesson, she said. I guess I'd learnt it, because when I vomited again, I did so all over her, and no one went to sleep that night.

It's the middle of April, still cold and bare in Montreal, but in Poland, Anna's father said on the phone, the forsythia is already in bloom. A few hot summerlike days, and then snow flurries, typical April weather. *Kwiecień-plecień*, the month of rapid changes, braiding summer and winter days. "Don't forget to take some warm clothes."

In one of Anna's oldest memories, her mother is sitting by the window, her auburn hair lit up by the dusty rays of the sun coming through the lace curtain. She is feeding Anna's little brother. The baby is cuddled in her arms, pink and wrinkled, his eyes closed, and Anna can see the shape of her mother's breast, bulging, full. There is a little black mole on it, a little button she would like to press. Sometimes, when her brother stops sucking, she can see the pink nipple, swollen and long, slipping out of his tiny lips, but then the hungry mouth snaps at it again, and she hears his soft, whimpering sounds of contentment.

This is when Anna picks up a pair of big steel scissors lying on the lowest bookshelf in front of her. The metal blades, heavy and sharp, feel cold in her hand, and with all the force she can muster, she hits the edge of the table. Bang!

"Mother of God! Anna!" Her mother's scream pierces her ears and makes her jump, as if Anna hasn't expected it. The baby has bitten her mother's nipple, and is now crying, too, his little face red and wrinkled, locked in the recurring spasms of anger and fear.

"How could you?" her mother asks.

"You wicked, wicked child," she says, and Anna watches her mother's face change into a grimace.

120

"My own daughter?" she asks in that voice of hers Anna hates the most, raised, shaking, admitting to helplessness, to resignation. "No. That I can't understand. I can't!"

Her mother shakes her head again, and this is when Anna breaks into tears. She is too big to behave this way, she is told. How can she torture them all with her outbursts of blind, suffocating anger, her wailing cries, her constant checking, even in the middle of the most absorbing play, if her mother still has her slippers on. Afraid of new babies coming home, Anna watches her mother like a hawk.

Sometimes her vigilance works. Her mother stays home, plays with her, shows her how to change the baby, how to tickle his little pink heels, how to laugh at the monkey faces he makes.

"See, he likes you," she says, "Look, he is smiling at you," and Anna begins to believe her. But most often her mother says, "I have to go to work, to the Institute," and Anna begins to cry so loudly that she has to be held back by her nanny, for this is still before the time when her grandmother moved in with them. Her nanny murmurs, "Shame on you, such a big girl!" and leaves her alone in the room.

Her nose pressed to the cold windowpane, Anna watches her mother from above, walking quickly across the street until she disappears. If her nanny let her, she would stay right there, for the whole day, on the wide window sill, staring at the same spot where her mother has vanished so swiftly around the corner, waiting for the moment when her slightly bent, familiar figure would appear again. But her nanny will not let her. She has to eat or, rather, sit in front of a full plate, with food in her mouth, filling her up, gagging her. Then she has to go for a walk, her hand holding the baby's carriage, and listen to what the neighbours have to say. Her morning "concert" is described in detail to anyone who wants to listen, and stout, ruddy women lean over to tell her that she is too big for such silliness. "Shame on you! Your mother has to go to work," they say, and her nanny nods, hoping that all these sensible comments will make Anna see the foolishness of her crying, of her eyes, locked into the spot where her mother's figure disappeared behind the corner.

"You had a nanny?" William had asked. "In Communist Poland?"

"Yes," she said, slightly piqued at his amazement. It was the time when she was not yet sure what she wanted, to be part of the world in which nannies were possible, or to be pitied for the deprivations, the drabness of her past.

She could always amaze him with the vestiges of the proper middle-class existence her family managed to pull off. That's what he said, "pull-off," as if it were all a magic trick, an elaborate cheating game in which Anna had her summer holidays in the country, her first communion in a long white dress, her English lessons, her nannies, her long hours at the piano practising scales. All of it happening among the ruins, right under the nose of a Communist government with its five-year plans, parades of iron-fisted workers, holding the portraits of Marx, Engels, Lenin, and right behind them, the portraits of their current successors.

"Oh, but that was *their* life," she said, lightly. "We lived our own. You must have heard that Poles are notoriously hard to occupy."

"I've heard that," he said, smiling.

But that's not what she wanted. She wanted him to be moved by her stories. Promise her that now, when she had escaped such drabness, he would show her the world, take her with him to Paris, to London, to Rome — all place names she pronounced with such religious fervour, as if they were not real cities but fairy lands. Hug her and tell her that he was her reward, that he would make things right for her, make up for the ruins, the squalor, and the fears.

A fool!

Anna must have fallen asleep, for when the sounds of applause for the smooth landing wake her up, the plane has already touched down. She has missed the approach to Warsaw, the slow descent through the milky clouds. She has not expected to be this nervous. Her stomach is now pushing against her ribs, a sour lump burning inside. "Your parents will be so happy to see you, Anna," Marie kept telling her. "Nothing else will matter. I know that."

Perhaps they will; Anna would like to believe it. Her parents never visited her in Montreal. It was her mother that always came up with excuses. But tragedy and loss, Anna thinks, is the surest way to buy compassion, a semblance of forgiveness. If nothing else works, she can always count on that.

As soon as the plane slows down, the passengers rise to pick up their luggage. The stewardesses on the LOT flight are all young and pretty, their skin still immune to the scarcity of sleep. One of them now points to the signs that the seatbelts are to be fastened, that the plane is still in motion, that standing up at this time is dangerous, but no one is listening. Angered, the stewardess stares at the man in front of her, who is trying to get his bag from the compartment above. "Sit down," she tells him. "Sit down this minute." The man looks around, shrugs his shoulders to indicate that she will never get anyone's attention now, but he sits down and watches, amused, as she turns to someone else, a lost battle, for the plane is already coming to a stop.

On the bus, which ferries Anna from the plane to the airport, the level of excitement rises even more. Most of the passengers speak Polish; Anna listens to the strained jokes, the excited whispers comparing the lengths of absence. Ten, fifteen, twenty years have passed since they left, and, now, allowed to come back, they will see for themselves how much their country has changed. The mood is sceptical, weary. "First they kill the fish," the short man to her right announces, "and now they drop it back into the water, hoping it'll learn to swim. How can it ever work?"

Anna registers muted, uneasy laughter, and a few unconvincing protests. "Stranger things have happened," someone says and waits for a response.

The passengers line up at passport control, which goes briskly. The passports they hold in their hands testify that they are American, Canadian, Australian, British. The woman officer who checks these passports makes an effort to smile. It is a strained smile; her muscles have yet to become accustomed to such expressions of civility.

The tiny, single terminal is filled with families and friends, necks craned above the crowd, hands waving, bouquets of flowers wrapped up in cellophane. "Anna!" someone screams, and she turns toward that scream only to see an elderly woman hugging a younger one, perhaps her daughter. There are tears, smiles of anticipation, relief.

The thoughts of Piotr are hard to hide from; his pale, handsome face, as she remembers it last — a bit worried, unsure. Looking at his watch because he had to catch the Odra express train to Wrocław if he were to make it for the next day's meetings. She had urged him to go, to leave her, but he wouldn't. He wanted to wait until the very last moment, send her off with his kiss on her lips. She still remembers his hand waving a white handkerchief as she was passing by security, right here.

For years she has kept her memories of him wrapped up in layers of resentment and doubt, but she no longer can. In the last weeks there have been terse requests for the sorting out of affairs. Of course she will see him, she wrote back. This is the least she can do.

From her mother's letters she knows that he married Hanka a month after he was released from the internment camp. Hanka whom Anna can vaguely remember, tall and slim, with dark bangs and a warm, bewildered smile. There is a child, too, a daughter. "Very beautiful," her mother wrote, "with hair just like yours when you were little." Piotr made a shrewd career move; he became an expert in environmental law. He is a parliamentary advisor now, negotiating community and business rights. No one else, her mother wrote, can understand the post-communist legal mess as well as he does. Big German and American companies have already approached him for his legal expertise. In her mother's letters there are hints of money and travels: Berlin, New York, Brussels.

In spite of her nap Anna is beginning to feel the effects of a sleepless night. The waiting area seems hot and cold in turn, and she pushes though the crowd, avoiding eye contact with short, stocky men who hope to sell her a taxi ride or a hotel room. "Look for a radio-taxi or call one," her brother told her on the phone. "This is a regular Mafia, the guys at the airport. Watch out." He insisted that he would come to Warsaw to pick her up, but she refused. "I'm not a child," she said, and even managed a little laugh. "I'll call for a radio-taxi. I'll be all right."

"They'll still charge you three times what they would charge me," he said.

"That's all right. Lots of airports are like that. It's not just Warsaw. I'll be careful."

Outside of the terminal building she spots a radio-taxi that has just deposited a man in a light trench coat, with a black leather briefcase. Yes, the radio-taxi is available and she gets into it with relief, not lost on the driver who gives her a reassuring look. The driver is fat and jovial. He picks up her two suitcases, as if they were filled with feathers. Inside, the black interior of the taxi is pasted up with photographs of pin-up beauties in scanty bikinis, a collage of breasts and smooth bums. Wound around the rear-view mirror is a black rosary, a tin cross dangling from one end. The driver, who has just finished placing her suitcases in the trunk, sits in front, a lit cigarette in his mouth.

"From Canada?" he asks in a friendly voice. He must have noticed the red maple leaf of old Air Canada tags on her canvas bag. A mistake, she thinks, she should have replaced it with LOT ones. Cigarette smoke fills the inside of the car and makes her dizzy.

"Yes," Anna says. Her brother would have given her a nudge, here. She is already breaching security, making herself vulnerable. And yet, with all the warnings, she doesn't feel threatened at all.

"I have a brother in Toronto," the driver says. "Drives a taxi, too."

"Have you been to visit?" Anna asks, determined to keep up the conversation. She considers briefly if she should ask the driver not to smoke, but decides against it. She rolls down the window, instead, and looks at the streets.

"No, not yet," the driver says wistfully. "But I'd like to. I want to see Niagara Falls."

"You will," Anna says, and sees that the driver smiles with satisfaction. He takes her words as if they were a prediction, as if she had the power to make his dreams possible. Is it her proximity that suddenly makes Canada so close or the arrival of capitalism, awaited with so much fervour?

"Everything is still falling apart," the driver informs her. "The Commies have just painted themselves over; now they are capitalists." Later he will tell her the latest joke: If General Jaruzelski ever gets together with Electrician Wałęsa, they will form General Electric.

"Nothing has changed," he says.

But that's not quite true. The city is changing, in spite of the pervasiveness of grey. As they approach the centre, Anna sees makeshift stands everywhere, on street corners, along passageways. Stands made of camping tables, folded beds, on which colourful packages pile up. Passers-by crowd around them, peer over each other's shoulders.

"Oh, that's nothing," the driver laughs, seeing her curious looks. He has forgotten his pessimism of a moment ago, and is now eager to point out the newly freed penchant for trading. "You should see what's happening around the Palace."

That's *Palace of Culture and Science*, Stalin's gift to Warsaw, a giant monument to the superiority of the Soviet system. All over Poland children learned about it at school, about its thirty floors and 3288 rooms, about its exhibition halls, theatres, cinemas, a swimming pool, and a Congress Hall. Around it, the architects left concrete space, an enormous empty square designed to accommodate endless parades, prescribed displays of power. "Where do you get the best view of Warsaw?" the joke went. "From the thirtieth floor of the Palace! —Why? —Because you can't see it from there!"

It is where, the driver informs her with glee, Warsaw's greatest bazaar takes place.

"Uncle Joseph must be spinning in his grave," he chuckles. Anna smiles with him. "*Ruscy* have their stands there, too," he says. He'll not call them Russians, as if the word was too good for the people who brought Communism here.

"You should see what these *lords of the earth* sell," the taxi-driver pouts his lips in contempt. "The junk of the Empire."

A few hours later, Anna walks near the grey palace, with its sculptures of muscled workers. This is her first walk from the Marriott hotel where she is staying. She has chosen the hotel deliberately; its international anonymity promises to be a refuge, if memories prove too much.

In April 1991 Warsaw is damp and chilly. The taxi driver was right; it is a true bazaar, a maze of stands overflowing with Turkish leather, silk blouses from Hong Kong, electronics from Taiwan. Young men in jean jackets guard packages of American cigarettes, French perfume, German soaps and shampoos. The prices are ridiculously low. Cigarettes go for a dollar per pack, for ten dollars she can have a bottle of *Channel # 5* or Yves St. Laurent's *Rive Gauche*.

Anna holds her purse tightly under her arm as she passes by the stalls. "Come on, have a look," the sellers call to her. She walks to the edges of the square, to the Russian stands. Two middle-aged men with broad, tired faces lean against a tree, chain-smoking. The cigarette smoke has a sour, thick smell to it, the lingering smell of cheap tobacco. The sight of their missing teeth, the nicotine stained fingers, and the ill-fitting clothes, crumpled from the long cross-border journey chokes her throat.

She is sorry for them. That's all she feels.

The Russians have spread their wares on a grey blanket. A teaspoon, a thermos flask, a camera, a kitchen mixer, which, although brand new and still in its original packaging, looks as if it were straight from the sixties, with its turquoise colour and *faux* leather case. No one seems to be interested in the offerings, even at the prices made possible by the rates of exchange. The mixer would go for an equivalent of fifty cents, a thermos flask for ten. Only the older man in the corner, in a tight blue cardigan with missing buttons, seems to be doing some business. He is selling penknives and auto parts. Three young men are squatting next to his blanket, weighing a shiny pump and a coil of wires.

All she can feel is sorrow for this city, this country, all these people. But that's not right. No one here needs her tears. She wouldn't have needed them, either, if she lived here.

"You want to run away and hide," she recalls Piotr's old arguments. The irritation in his voice. Impatience with her pleas.

"I don't want to live like that."

"Then let's change it."

"Nothing will ever change, here, Piotr. Not in our lifetime. We have tried. You know that."

"Do you really think that people in the West are better? That they are any different from us? That they care about our problems? Come on, Anna. Don't be so naïve!"

"Is leaving really such a betrayal?" she kept asking him. "Don't we also have a right to a normal life?"

But then, for Piotr, these were meaningless questions. Mere excuses to make *her* feel better.

She quickens her step, pushes through the throngs of pedestrians, past more stalls, camping tables, old cardboard boxes. She has never seen Warsaw so dirty, but promises herself not to mind. She is only a visitor here, she tells herself, she has no right to judge. Crushed pop cans, plastic bottles, cigarette butts, and mounds of soggy boxes lie in the corners of the underground passage. The sour smell of urine is everywhere. "Garbage collectors are on strike, Madam," the concierge at the hotel has explained, adding, "We are truly sorry for the inconvenience," with an apologetic, embarrassed smile. The Marriott staff has kept the marble slabs around the hotel shiny and spotless, and it is easy to see the line where the hotel property ends. Beyond it, the pavement is covered with a sticky film of dirt.

In the underground passage that leads from Central Station to the Marriott, new stores have taken over the once-uniform interiors. In front of them, a Gypsy child in a torn cotton dress is kneeling on a folded piece of cardboard, a hand-written note on her chest. *Please help poor girl. I am mute. Please give money for hospital operation and I will pray for you to Blessed Virgin Mary. She give you what you want most of all.* Seeing that Anna has stopped, a young Gypsy woman with long black braids quickly moves toward her and adds her whining voice to the child's mute plea, pulling at Anna's skirt, muttering something so fast that the words drown and lose meaning.

"Just look at her," Anna hears a hiss right behind her. "So young and only interested in begging."

"How can they live like that," an elderly man in a brown hat joins in. There is anger in his voice, mixed with contempt. "These poor, dirty children. What do they teach them?"

"They drug them, you know," a woman's voice adds. "That's why they can stay still like that, for hours."

"Go back to Romania!"

"Thieves!"

She should keep on walking, Anna thinks, but instead she opens her purse and takes out a few Polish bills. "Don't give them anything," the elderly man snaps at her. "You only make things worse."

Anna drops the money into a tin can, which has a few bills in it, already. The Gypsy woman gives the crowd a defiant look, bows her head down, and loudly asks Our Lady to bless the kind *Pani*, to give her happiness, to take care of her in her time of sorrows.

Back in the hotel Anna calls her parents to tell them she has arrived safely.

"How do you feel?" her father asks. He picks up the phone as soon as Anna has finished dialling the Wroclaw number. He must have been waiting by the phone.

"Fine," she says, but she knows he wants to hear more than that.

"So how do you like Warsaw now?" he asks.

"It has changed," Anna says. She cannot think of anything else to say. "I like it very much."

"Have you seen the bazaar?" he keeps asking. "The shop windows?" He urges her to acknowledge at least some sense of surprise, and she humours him.

"Yes, I have. It's hard to believe!"

"I never thought I would live to see it," he says.

"I never thought I would, either," she echoes.

"We are all waiting for you," her father says. He wants to finish this conversation. It's a long-distance call and he is conscious of every minute that passes. "It doesn't matter," Anna has tried to tell him so many times before. "I have enough money. It's not really that much." But for her father there is never enough. *Scarcity is a state of mind*, Marie likes to say. Her parents were like that, too, having grown up during the Great Depression. Wouldn't take a taxi even if they had to crawl home.

"We'll talk more when you come here. We are both waiting, *Mama* and I."

"I'm coming. It's only two more days now." It seems to her that she can hear her mother's sobs, in the background. Tomorrow Anna will visits her grandparents' graves and the following day she will take a morning train to Wroclaw.

"Good bye." He puts down the receiver so fast that she hears the click of the disconnecting line.

For a short while Anna sits motionless on the double bed. Then she switches on the television. On Warsaw One, she catches the beginning of a discussion on the Warsaw Uprising of 1944. Three panellists, two men and a woman, are sitting around a low table. Forty-seven years have passed since that August afternoon of 1944. The cost was staggering: the whole city destroyed, hundreds of thousands dead or deported. Now, when Warsaw is finally free, there is no better time to ask the fundamental question: Was it worth it?

"Look at Prague, now," the younger of the two men begins. He is in his late thirties, and he waves his hands as he speaks. "The Czechs were right to just wait the war through. It is more important to protect the fabric of the nation than to spill blood."

"How can you say things like that!" the older man interrupts. He is breathing hard, his face is red with anger. "Without the Uprising you would've been born in the Soviet Republic of Poland."

"With the Uprising Hitler was able to finish off the Home Army, which was exactly what Stalin wanted," the younger man doesn't give up. "Let me remind you that the Russians watched the slaughter from the other side of the river. They got Hitler to do their dirty job for them."

The third panellist, a tall bony woman in her sixties, is listening in silence. The moderator has introduced her as an American professor of Slavic Studies from California. When she begins to speak the men quiet down. In her muted, halting voice she tells them how, in 1944, pregnant with her daughter, she saw her twenty-one-year-old husband for the last time, as he turned back to wave to her. In this Uprising she lost her husband, her brother, and two cousins. After the war she was arrested by the Communists on drummed up charges and spent seven years in prison, one in solitary confinement, while her daughter was placed in an orphanage and told her mother was "an enemy of the people." Her daughter is a doctor now, in Boston, and has three children. They all speak Polish, but they are American.

"We lost the best people then," she says, quietly. "I think we'll never know if we paid too much." The camera closes on her face. Her blue eyes are dry. All that Anna can see in them is loneliness.

In the bathroom, Anna pours herself a glass of water from a bottle of Vittel. "Marriott tap water has been filtered and it is safe to drink," she reads a printed note. "But for those of our guests who would rather drink bottled water we are happy to provide it." The note is in English. The water is lukewarm and tasteless, but it does soothe her throat.

Ursula's letters are now spread on the Marriott bed. On the one side Anna puts all the evidence of betrayal, love letters read and reread until Ursula's words have been etched into her memory and cannot fade. These she ties up and hides at the bottom of her suitcase, underneath the sweaters. On the other side she puts the articles, book reviews, accounts of Ursula's travels. In Montreal she has just skimmed through them, impatient with anything she decided did not concern her. Now, she is no longer sure.

She opens one of these articles and begins to read.

Unity Valkyrie Mitford, a real golden-haired lady, was the fourth daughter of Lord David Bertram Ogilvy Freeman-Mitford. "I don't believe in your God," she said to her religion teacher at

St. Marie School, and on the blackboard she drew a naked pair in a passionate embrace. She was expelled. In 1933 she went to Nuremberg. Among cheering crowds, men in brown shirts marched at night in the light of torches. Beams of light shot into the sky. Swastika banners billowed in the wind. "I want to meet him," she said to her sister Diana after she had heard the Führer speak. "There is no one else I can be with."

In Munich, day after day, Unity sat at a table in Osteria Bavaria, watching Hitler dine with his companions, order his favourite vegetarian dishes. Since he did not approve of makeup and smoking, she wore no lipstick. On the 9th of February, 1935, a miracle happened. The Führer noticed her unfailing presence; his eyes paused on her blue, lively eyes, her shiny blond hair.

"It was the most beautiful day of my life," Unity Mitford wrote to her father. "His aide-de-camp came up to me. 'Madam, the Führer wants to speak with you.' When I approached His table He rose and shook my hand and asked me to sit next to Him. I told Him He should come to England, and He said, 'I would be afraid to, for I could start a revolution.' Then, Rosa, the waitress, came to ask if I wanted a postcard for Him to sign, and I said yes. Not that I approve of American customs, but He asked for my name and signed the postcard for me, and invited me to Bayreuth. He told me that we should not allow international Jewry to divide two Aryan nations, and I said that, soon, we will be allies, fighting the same war. I am so happy. I must be the happiest girl on earth. There is nothing left for me now but to die of happiness."

To her mother, she wrote: "What really struck me was His great simplicity. He was so natural that my shyness evaporated. It is a true miracle that this most powerful man on earth is so humble and straightforward."

She followed him everywhere. Into the flap of her black suit she pinned a swastika with his signature underneath. Hitler's aides called her Mitfahrt, a fellow traveller, always at his side when he wanted to see her, in Munich, Bayreuth, Berlin, Nuremberg, Breslau. She sat on the marble dais at party rallies and at the Olympic Games, rushed for breakfasts at his hotels, tea and walks at the Berghof."I have two fatherlands," she said.

*"Germany and England. And I love them both." In 1939, she
wrote in the Daily Mirror that Hitler would never make England
his enemy. She could guarantee that.*

*When on the 3ʳᵈ of September 1939, England declared war on
Germany, Unity Valkyrie took her most cherished presents, the
Führer's portrait in a silver frame and a swastika with his
signature, wrapped them up and returned them with a letter. "I
cannot bear the thought of war between Germany and England. I
choose suicide." In the Englischer Garten she shot herself in the
head. She didn't die, but the bullet was too firmly lodged in her
head to be removed. Paralysed, she lay in a private clinic, waiting
for death. When the Führer came to visit, he brought her a bouquet
of red roses. Her suicide attempt did not surprise him. Wasn't she
only a woman? Influenced by an emotional longing for a force that
would complement her nature? "I want to go back to England,"
Unity said, looking at him. The roses, dried, went with her.*

*In England she refused to see anyone. Alone, half-alive,
unable to move, she waited for the news of German victory. She
died on May 28, 1948.*

Hunger wakes Anna in the morning, a painful, gnawing knot in
her stomach. Breakfast is served in a room called *Lila Weneda*, the
only Polish name she has seen anywhere in this sterile, glittering
hotel. She can vaguely remember the Polish romantic play from
which the name is taken, its pure-hearted peaceful people and
their vicious invaders. A curious choice of a name, the thought
has crossed her mind, a play by a poet who chastised Poland for
being *the peacock and parrot* of other nations.

As she rides downstairs to the breakfast room, Anna
watches herself in the elevator mirrors, her face multiplied by
smokey panels, surrounding her on all sides. Two American
men enter the elevator on the third floor. Clean-shaven faces,
black, freshly pressed suits.

"Gee, these cats here are tough," one of them says. "They
sure know what they want." He bends down and pulls up his
socks. "Free market. That's what it was all about, wasn't it?"

"That's right," the other man answers and they laugh.

133

In *Lila Weneda*, under stainless steel domes there are scrambled eggs, pancakes, sausages and bacon. On the opposite side an arrangement of cheeses, fruit, cold cuts, small jars of marmalade and jams. Anna piles slices of smoked salmon on her plate, adds a few capers, a spoonful of cottage cheese. She eats slowly, glancing out of the window at the grey square building of Central Station. She has slept the whole night through, in spite of the time lag. It must be the low pressure, she thinks; outside wet snowflakes are getting thicker. Her father was right. *Kwiecień-plecień*, the braiding winter and summer.

A young waitress avoids Anna's eyes, flashing her a smile of fearful submission. When Anna tries to open the lid of a coffee thermos jar, she rushes forward and does it for her. "Allow me, Madam," she says in English.

In one of Anna's old dreams of return they would have come here together, with William, for a concert tour. William would be given an enthusiastic reception. Every evening, she would watch him bow to the cheering audience, and then look at her. She shrugs her shoulders and takes another sip of coffee. Today she will take another look at Warsaw, and tomorrow she will be on the way to Wrocław, on her way home.

"Es gibt keinen jüdischen Wohnbezirk—in Warschau mehr! The Jewish district in Warsaw is no more," wrote Herr Kommandant in his official report, in 1943. Burnt down, blown to pieces, with its mazes of bunkers and hiding places, the sewers and corridors, booby-trapped bunkers, killing German soldiers long after those inside took their own lives. "So damn clever," Herr Stroop marvelled, "who would have thought? These sub-humans?" The glorious victory of Grossaktion. He described the behaviour of entire families, first throwing out their bedding in the street and then jumping from the roofs of burning buildings. "Paratroopers" Herr Kommandant laughed, and urged his men to take aim at the moving targets. "How they hated us," he said, "these lean catlike men," jumping back into the scorching buildings, with a blob of spit at Herr Stroop, arms jerking in a last gesture of contempt. The women, "these young witches, with smooth skin

and wild black eyes," who aimed their last shots at SS officers from pistols smuggled on their snow white bodies.

The world, Herr Kommandant wrote in his reports, has entered the luminous, prosperous era of strength and order when all that is weak and imperfect will be eliminated. After the victory, on this scorched land, German architects would build a district of spacious villas and well-tended gardens. There would be red tiled roofs and green shutters, fountains, oak trees, rose bushes and wide, elegant streets. The biggest of them, charted by Himmler himself, would be named Jürgen-Stroop-Allee.

Jürgen Stroop was arrested by the Polish army, tried, and executed for war crimes. But in the post-war settling of accounts something incredible had happened. The Communist authorities put Jürgen Stroop in one cell with Kazimierz Moczarski, a Polish partisan from the Home Army arrested as part of post-war repressions for backing up the London government. The outcome of this nightmarish encounter is Moczarskis's book **Conversations with the Executioner.**

For nine months, in between interrogations, a Polish partisan listened to his cell mate talk about his childhood, the war, the destruction of the Ghetto. His Aleja Róż apartment of ten rooms, so close to the Łazienki palace that Herr Stroop could ride his horse there. His terry robe in SS colours, white and black. Marches in the glory of standards, swastikas and eagles. An encounter with a Polish owl that had attacked him in his open car on a night journey to Posen. The owl he had ordered tied to a tree and shot.

He spoke of Otto Dehmke, his SS friend, killed by the Jews in the ghetto when he tried to remove the flags of defiance. Polish black and white and Jewish white and blue. Of the long letter he wrote that night to his bereaved mother. Of the day he himself pressed the button on the electrical unit that triggered the explosion of the Great Synagogue in Tłomackie Street. Of his tired but happy soldiers and officers who watched these fantastic fireworks of triumph.

"No, I wasn't able to forgive," Moczarski wrote, "but I still wanted to understand."

The sky in Warsaw is overcast, but it isn't raining anymore and the morning snow has left no trace.

"You don't need his absolution," Marie told her back in Montreal, meaning Piotr. "Get a lawyer to talk to him," and Anna registered the thought, briefly, without conviction. It was a joke between them now, this North American need for resolutions. A habit of thought, they laughed. Here, on this side of the world, problems were to be suffered through; you proved your strength through endurance.

She takes a white Marriott taxi to the Powązki cemetery where her grandparents lie buried. The taxi takes her past the new apartment houses, built on the ruins of pre-war Warsaw. Somewhere, in one of these non-existent streets, her grand-parents had their grocery store.

A group of children runs out of one of the apartment houses, an ugly concrete block covered with grey stains, slamming the door behind them. They are dressed in jeans and T-shirts with the emblems of New York Rangers, California Angels, Chicago Bulls. One of the boys has a soccer ball, and he kicks it ahead of him, past the rows of cars parked everywhere, along the street, on the sidewalks, filling up even the smallest of space.

In front of the cemetery gate Anna buys two wreaths of fir branches braided with white calla lilies and two candles in glass containers. The containers have perforated metal caps that will allow them to hold the flame, in spite of the gusts of wind.

Her grandparents are buried at the edge of the newer part of Powązki, far from its distinguished quarters. Their grave is a square of black marble with space for flowers along both edges, the earth neatly raked and ready for spring planting. Someone is taking care of it, a successor of the old crippled man who took care of the grave when only *Dziadek* was buried there. The small bench *Babcia* had put in beside it is still there, with its storage bin, cleverly built into it. Inside there was always a vase for cut flowers. A simple one, made of a milk bottle, for anything better would have been stolen in no time.

"This is what happens," *Babcia* had said every time they came here for All Souls day, "when you live so far away. If you cannot come and check things for yourself."

But when Anna asked her why she had to bring *Dziadek*'s body here, why she did not bury him in Wrocław, *Babcia* would only scowl at her. That was one of these questions, Anna shouldn't have asked. *Babcia* did not trust Wrocław. It was enough to have her own parents lie in a village cemetery near Tarnopol, now in Ukraine, where she could never go. Why tempt fate? No, he was her husband after all, and he would rest in Polish soil. And so will she when her time comes.

Quickly, Anna lays the wreaths on the marble slate and lights her candles. Then, kneeling on the marble ledge at the graveside, she says her prayers for the dead. From the two oval photographs on the headstone her grandparents look at her. Time has paled their sepia faces, lighted their contours. She tries to remember them the way they were, but all she can think of are the two black spots on her grandmother's lower lip. When she was little, she watched *Babcia* cover them up with lipstick. Two layers, always two layers, so they wouldn't show.

In September 1939, after the first German bombs fell on Warsaw, *Babcia* packed two of her most sturdy suitcases and decided to go back east, to her parents. She took her daughter with her. *Dziadek* refused to leave the store. The *Prezydent* of Warsaw was appealing to everyone for calm, he kept saying. Britain and France had declared war against Hitler.

Babcia did not want to listen. Her daughter was only eleven, she said, too young to die. They were in a column of refugees when a German *Messerschmidt* dived right over them and this was when *Babcia* bit her lip. She said the plane dived so low that she could see the pilot's face. His square jaw, the shining buckle on his leather cap. Then she heard the sounds of machine-gun fire and saw people fall down dead. With bullet holes digging into their chests, exploding inside their heads.

"We were nothing to them but prey," she said. "You can't forget that, Anna."

Babcia had been sent to Warsaw, in 1922, to live with a distant aunt who, after much coaxing, agreed to look after her.

Her parents did not trust the new world order. True, Poland had just been made free after 123 years of partitions, but the Germans called it the "Seasonal State," and for the Russians it was "the bastard of Versailles," a "persecutor of the working class." Borderlands were never safe. Such calculations were always important, here: the constant reassessment of which territories had a chance to survive and which would most likely succumb. *Babcia* was 23 years old, with long auburn hair and almond-shaped eyes. Her parents thought she would be better off in the capital.

In Warsaw, in her Aunt's house, for seven long months *Babcia* waited for a husband. She imagined herself charming a handsome army officer, or one of the young lawyers in her Uncle's chambers. Her Aunt laughed at the dreams of a poor relation, really no better than a servant. "Sausage is not for the dogs," she had said, "a pretty face is not enough." Time was running out. Picky women were left alone in the world, stale buns on the shelf.

Dziadek owned a small corner store in Podlaska street and above it, on the first floor, he rented a three-room apartment. He liked the shy, pretty woman he saw praying in church, pressing a lace handkerchief to her full red lips. Liked her enough to make inquiries about her position and prospects through one of her Aunt's servants. Enough to pursue her for weeks, to send her flowers, cakes, a pair of kid gloves. She tried to return the gloves, but they came back accompanied by another bouquet of red roses. Her Aunt smiled approvingly, called *Dziadek* a respectable young man and asked him to come and have tea in the best parlour. He sat there stiffly, playing with a silver teaspoon, elaborating on the prospects of his colonial store and his need for a woman who would not be afraid of work. One afternoon, when *Babcia* was in church, praying for deliverance, he proposed. It was the Aunt who was given the mission of persuading *Babcia* to accept him, hinting at the hardships of having another mouth to feed. "And you, my dear, are not getting any younger."

They were married three months later. To Anna, *Babcia* often said that she knew of a wife's duties. Of the vale of tears this life was supposed to be. She knew of all her sins for which she deserved her lot in life. But one thing she couldn't do. She couldn't learn to love the man who ignored her pleas to leave her alone.

To Anna the existence of *Dziadek's* grocery store has always been something of a mystery. "A colonial store," *Babcia* said, and the word had something delicious about it, but also hard to imagine. For it was hard to believe that the pre-war customers could choose between brands of produce, have their shopping delivered to their homes. No line-ups, no shortages, no pushing and shoving. It was in the rented apartment above this grocery store, after three miscarriages and a baby boy who died a few days short of his first birthday, that Anna's mother was born.

"They always quarrelled," *Mama* said about her parents. "Something was always wrong."

A beloved daughter, the apple of her father's eye. Spoilt with the gift of a gold watch for her First Communion, Belgian lace for her dress. Visits to Blikle café, carefully hidden from her mother, where she was allowed to order and eat as many cakes as she wanted. When they came home, giggling and swearing to keep it all their secret, she would be served her supper and she would not be able to eat it. It was then, after expert questioning, that the truth would be revealed, and her parents would quarrel again. Over her, over the sweets, over the future of a daughter brought up in such indulgent manner. The same daughter whose freedom *Babcia* would one day buy from the Gestapo when, arrested in a street *lapanka*, Anna's mother would be taken with other passers-by to witness a street execution and told she would be sent to Germany for forced labour.

Mama recalled bars of chocolate on the counter of the store, oranges and lemons wrapped in delicate tissue paper with pictures on them, the smell of cinnamon, nutmeg and cloves, the scent of soap, the taste of exotic teas. But she also remembered how the children at school teased her, a shopkeeper's daughter. Once on their way to Łazienki Palace she pointed out the second floor windows of an apartment in *Aleja Róż* to Anna.

"Your Great-Uncle," she said. "Lived there once. He was a pre-war lawyer."

The colonial store was hit by a German bomb in August 1944, in the first days of the Warsaw Uprising. "What's gone is gone," *Dziadek* said and refused to see it, but *Babcia* went to take one last look, right before they were marched out of Warsaw by the Nazis. "I shouldn't have," she said. Broken glass and shards of wood cracked under her feet. She thought she would take something with her, something to remember, but there was nothing to take.

During the Uprising, her grandparents hid in the cellar, the city above them burning to cinders. For years *Babcia* was to remember the damp mattress on which she lay day and night. *Forgive us our sins, as we forgive those who sinned against us. Now and in the hour of our death*, she prayed. She had heard the cries of people burnt alive in the church of the Sisters of the Visitation.

People crowded in these cellars, listening to the sounds of planes, the howl of falling bombs, the explosions. A few blocks away. Next door. The end was easy to imagine. The cellar doors could open at any time. The last thing you would hear in this life was the blast of grenades. When children wailed, mothers said, "Don't cry, you will die soon."

"What a human soul will endure!" *Babcia* would tell Anna.

Yet there were miracles, too. In one of them, *Babcia* said, they were reunited with *Mama*, in a relocation camp after the war. Their daughter who had turned into a Home Army soldier, who had cut her hair short, and who refused to talk of what she had done or seen.

It was then that *Dziadek* decided they should all go to Wrocław, to the newly *regained* territories, Stalin's consolation prize for the lands lost in the east. The Germans were fleeing west, leaving their homes and businesses behind. There, forever an optimist, he was sure they would be able to find an abandoned store. Soon they would be back on their feet again. When *Babcia* objected, he asked if she had other ideas on how they might survive. If she knew of anyone in the world willing to take them in. Feed and clothe them. Educate their daughter. Make sure she would have a chance in life.

In Wrocław, *Dziadek* found a corner store with the name of the German owner strewn with bullets. Cigarettes and food gone, the store was in a good shape, nevertheless, with solid wooden shelves in the back, cherry wood counter, marble floor, and some inventory. In the boxes stacked in the back of the store *Dziadek* discovered carved pipes and bundles of pipe cleaners. In the ruins he found boxes of buttons and sewing needles, a good supply of candles and matches. Not much, but something to start with.

In the back of the store, there was a small apartment. From the destroyed store next door *Dziadek* salvaged some sturdy iron bars that he installed in all the windows. At night, he and *Babcia* pushed the heavy oak table against the front door. Every night they heard gunshots and screams. When someone pounded on the door, to be let in, they would hold their breath and wait until the pounding stopped. There were so many stories about this city that curdled their blood, stories they read about in the papers. A man had his eyes slashed with razor blades for a pair of shoes. A woman traveller stepped into a factory to ask her way to a friend's house; one by one the workers raped her and then pushed her out of the second storey window to the concrete pavement, below. That's what the war did to people, *Babcia* said. Freed the worst in them.

For the next two years, the Wroclaw store prospered. Soon *Babcia* was wearing a fur coat, wrapping a fox collar around her neck. She still had a good figure, she would catch herself thinking. At forty-five she could still turn heads in the street. Make men smile with pleasure when they raised her gloved hand to their lips. Her daughter was in a private school, catching up with her schoolwork, getting ready for university.

"I might still know what happiness is," she liked to think then.

In 1947 a man in a trench coat came to the Wroclaw store and asked *Dziadek* for two hundred grams of chocolates. *Dziadek* rolled a bag for him from a square piece of brown paper and weighed the sweets. The man paid and left. Half an hour later he was back with a policeman, accusing *Dziadek* of overcharging him. *Dziadek* was arrested on the spot, and the store was sealed. "Bloodsucking capitalists," *Babcia* was told, "had to be stopped form cheating the working class." In a judge's verdict a few months later the store was declared state property and *Dziadek* was sentenced to six months of hard labour and socialist reeducation. Released, he was ordered to work in his old store, as an assistant, for a state salary. "The Communist Battle for Trade" was won.

For years, *Dziadek* spent all afternoons with his ear plastered to the radio speaker, sifting through the jamming noises to hear the daily news from Radio Free Europe and Voice of America. The same Radio Free Europe *Tata* switched off when he gathered enough courage to ask for *Mama*'s hand. "I had to," he laughed. "Otherwise, he wouldn't have heard what I had to say."

Dziadek died a few years after his granddaughter, Anna, was born, quietly, after a routine hernia operation that went wrong. "He liked his vodka," the doctor said to explain the internal haemorrhage noticed too late. "There was nothing we could do."

Babcia did not say anything. Wife or widow, she had stopped expecting anything from life.

There are no radio-taxis outside the cemetery gate so Anna hails an ordinary taxi and asks to be taken to the Old Town. She will walk from there to the Marriott, she decides.

This taxi-driver is silent and pensive. When the ride is over he asks her for the equivalent of fifty dollars. When she protests that a radio-taxi would cost her no more than five, he shrugs his shoulders and tells her she should have made sure of the price before getting inside. He is an independent taxi-owner. This is capitalism, in case she hasn't noticed. He charges what he pleases.

"Are you going to pay or do you want me to call the police," he asks her.

"Don't bother," Anna snaps and gives him what he wants. He takes the thick wad of Polish currency with a broad smile of a winner.

She slams the door of the taxi so hard that flakes of rust fall off. The driver honks and drives off, leaving a puff of black smoke behind him.

The winding streets of the Old Town are paved with cobblestones. Anna walks slowly, stopping at the displays of jewellery stores, trying to restore her calm. The incident with the taxi-driver has made her hands shake. This, too, is an old feeling from here, she recalls, the impotent rage at such small acts of cruelty. At being cheated, pushed, told to go to hell, not to put on airs and expect God knows what. She wants to forget such feelings. She would rather remember the heroic resistance of which there are so many reminders. Flowers against the walls still mark the spots of street executions. The best and the brightest, her mother would say.

"Thirty-four," she reads as she passes. "Thirty-four Poles died at this spot, executed by the Germans." The flowers, red and white carnations, are wilted. The letter P with its base turned into an anchor, the symbol of resistance, is made of brass. Her brother wrote to her once that hours after martial law was declared, these signs appeared on the walls in every Polish city.

In one of the stores in the Old Town Anna buys an amber necklace and a pair of earrings for Marie. Two drops of amber on long silver rods.

"Do they really look the same way as they looked before the war?" she had asked her mother once about these reconstructed façades, the winding streets and cobblestones.

"Yes," her mother said, her voice hardening already, warning her not to doubt her conviction. "They do."

Flashes of afternoon light manage to break through low clouds, shed beams of warmth onto the walls of buildings. Anna is on Krakowskie Przedmieście now and these are yellow walls with a shade of pink. Nuns walk out of the Church of the Visitation, in long black robes and white wimples. They walk in groups, slowly, whispering among themselves, bending their white, pensive faces. Anna takes out her camera. The flash goes off; so there is not enough light, after all.

Nothing here, she thinks, is like it was. Every reconstructed building in this city is a defiant cry to the people beyond the Oder. Nothing happens here without being tied in the most profound and visceral way to this other presence, the presence of Germany. These buildings stand here because Germans said they wouldn't. There is no forgiveness.

In the Marriott room, the light cream bedspread with green flowers has been turned down to reveal snow-white sheets. There is a Sweet Dreams chocolate in a black envelope on her pillow. In the bathroom, Anna lowers herself into scalding water, slowly, inch by inch, until her skin absorbs the heat and allows her to go deeper, taking away some of the tension that is still mounting in her.

It must have been a Christmas present. The bag of sweets, she remembers, was tied with a red ribbon; the entire room smelled of spruce and resin. Chocolate acorns were wrapped in golden foil, which, later, she would smooth carefully with her fingernail into a thin leaf and hide between the pages of her books. There were bonbons with dark, wet interiors that spilled onto her tongue, covering it with the bittersweet taste of coffee. Crispy wafers with rich hazelnut filling. There were two of these bags, one for her and one for her brother.

"*Poczęstuj nas,*" her mother reminded her of her duty to share whatever it is she has, and she held the bag to them and expected that, as always, they would take one small piece each, or even decline the treat with a smile and the words she has been waiting for. "No, that's all for you, love. Chocolates are for the children." But this time something was wrong. *Mama* took the whole chocolate bar with round hazelnuts buried in it. *Tata* picked another bar. *Babcia* said, "I think I would like a few of these acorns," and she took a whole handful. Anna held back her tears, not knowing what to say. She had made her offering, and it had been accepted. How could she complain? Why would she want to cry?

A few minutes later, even though to her it seemed that hours had passed, she heard her mother's voice. "I think that's enough," she said, her voice solemn and quiet, and they all nodded and said that they agreed. Yes, this was enough. "Good girl!" she heard. "What a brave little girl you are!" They were proud of her. "We are so very proud of you. You have passed the test."

Through tears she watched how the sweets, untouched, were returned to her bag, how all was restored. She felt her father's hand on the top of her head, heavy and warm. "Our sweet girl. Wasn't she brave! Tears in her eyes, but she kept going." Slowly the heaviness in her chest began to lift and she smiled, too, convinced of her own courage, the generosity of her heart. Her lips closed on a chocolate acorn and she waited for the moment in which the warmth of her tongue would melt the chocolate and release the soft, nutty filling inside.

The curtains of her hotel room are drawn. Through a narrow slit she can glimpse the lights of Warsaw. She closes the curtains tight, and pretends she is suspended in the air, nowhere in particular.

PART IV

"He is German," Anna recalls her mother's voice, a phone conversation from long ago she would like so very much to forget. "So what did his father do in the war?"

"I don't know, Mother. William doesn't know, either. He has never even seen his father."

"That's what they all say, now."

"I don't care, Mother. I love him."

"But I care, Anna. And so should you."

Anna reads another of Ursula's articles: *The summer of 1938 moved fast. Magda Goebbels watched her husband change his cream coloured silk shirts twice a day, dress in white suits, soft rimmed hats and go on the prowl. "Thirty-six actresses, a number of secretaries and wives of lesser officials" Karl Hanke said. "Bock von Babelsberg. A ram of the film city. It used to be that an actress had to sleep with Jewish producers to get parts in films. Is the Minister of Propaganda no better than a Jew? Are we really no different from them, Frau Goebbels?"*

She listened.

"He says he is in love and he wants to leave you, the children, and the Führer. Leave Germany for a Czech actress with Slavic cheekbones and a swooning voice. Leave his German wife, for this Lidushka, the woman he shamelessly parades with everywhere. At the Nuremberg party rally, he kissed her just before it was time to go to the marble dais on the Zeppelin field, and she had to wipe her lipstick from his lips. 'Look at me,' he said. 'I'll be speaking to you only.' She sat in the front row, below the stage, watching him turn toward her and bring her handkerchief to his lips.

"Here it is, Frau Goebbels, all the evidence. Copies of his letters, bills for flowers, a stack of love notes. A complete list of all his liaisons. "I cannot look at how your husband treats you and not rage.

"This Czech whore, Frau Goebbels. Every day she is in the street, in front of the ministry, so that he may see her when he looks out of the window. He is at her apartment every evening.

"You, a woman of such beauty, such distinction. The woman I love."

Karl Hanke, her husband's aide, his state secretary.

"He is my husband's vassal," she thought at first, embarrassed by his love. "Awkward. Unpolished," she said to her friends. "He thinks I need to be saved! Imagines himself to be some kind of a knight." Then she asked the Führer for divorce.

"Give your husband one year," Hitler said. "One more year. If you ask me again, I'll agree."

Ordered by his Führer to mend his ways, Joseph Goebbels set out to work. There were no more actresses and no more lady friends. Or, if there were, even Hanke could not find the slightest evidence of their presence. There were flowers for Magda. Gifts for the children. "Hanke is not the man for you, my dear Magda," Goebbels said to her once, across the dinner table. "You don't need me to tell you that. We belong together, don't we?"

The reconciliation agreement was drawn up in detail and approved by both sides. Among Magda's conditions was the future of Karl Hanke, her disappointed knight. He was to become the Gauleiter of Silesia and take up residence at the Castle of Breslau.

She saw him once more, in 1944, when she came to a Breslau clinic for an operation. She was driven along the boulevards of the city. "We are safe here, working hard for the Reich," Hanke said, proudly, pointing to new factories attracted by the calm of the hinterland. But the refugees from the east were already swelling the streets, crowding in Breslau apartments, waiting. "This city has sworn its loyalty to the Führer," Hanke whispered to her. "If the Russians ever come here, they will find nothing but a heap of smouldering ruins."

In the Führer's headquarters the radio carried the last speech of Gauleiter Hanke from besieged Festung Breslau. "We who have promised to die for our Führer will not back away from our promise. We shall turn our fortress into a mass grave for the Soviet hordes." Even Dr. Goebbels was generous with applause: "If all our Gauleiters in the East were like this and acted like

Hanke, we should be in better shape than we are," he wrote in his diary. But the greatest reward came in the Führer's last will; Gauleiter Karl Hanke replaced Himmler as the Reichsführer-SS, and Chef der Deutschen Polizei.

"Our glorious ideals of Nazism have been destroyed and with them everything in my life that has been beautiful, admirable, noble and good," Magda Goebbels wrote in her last letter to her oldest son, a prisoner of war in far away Canada. "Yesterday evening, the Führer unpinned his gold Party badge and fastened it to my jacket. I am proud and happy. May God give me the strength to do my last, most difficult duty. . . . The world that will come after the Führer and the defeat of National Socialism is not worth living in. That's why I am taking the children with me. They are too good for the coming world, and God will understand me, when I bring them their deliverance. . . . . Harold, my dear child, I bequeath to you the best thing that I ever learned from life — be true, true to yourself, true to others, true to your own country, in every way, always, in everything."

Of the children only Helga suspected something and did not want to drink the tea. She alone had bruises on her body, the only signs of struggle. The other children went to sleep peacefully, and Magda poured cyanide into their throats, emerging out of the bedroom after each death to take a deep breath and a drag of a cigarette. A few hours later, pale but composed she walked with her husband to the yard of the Chancellery and swallowed her own "capsule of happiness." Her body, doused with petrol, smouldered for a while, but the swastika in her lapel was not touched by the flames.

The names of the children all started with H. Hedda, Heide, Helga, Helmut, Hilda, Holde.

On May 6th 1945, a single engine plane left the newly constructed airstrip behind the Kaiserbrücke in Breslau, the city below exploding, street by street. Karl Hanke, reports say, was killed by Czech partisans a few weeks later.

The train from Warsaw to Wrocław is slowing down again. It was in no hurry to begin with, the wheels hitting the rails leisurely, moaning when the train-cars were pulled out of their inertia, forced into movement. Perhaps, if she closed her eyes, the rattling of metal against metal would quiet her thoughts, put her into a shallow sleep. *What a moving story of motherly love!* Ursula has scribbled across the margins. *And all these Breslau touches! Perfect for you, my love, as you wallow in self-pity, isn't it? Should give you some consolation.*

The day is sunny and quite warm but there is a cool draught of air coming through the door that won't close. Anna picks up a sweater and covers her shoulders. This is not the way to return, alone, unsure of forgiveness, chased by the words of another woman. The train picks up speed only to slow down again.

Anna travelled in such trains many times in her childhood. Long train journeys marked the beginnings and ends of all her summers, two leisurely months spent in a rented room at the seaside, away from the hot and dusty city. "To breathe in iodine from the sea," *Babcia* said, hoping that this year, unlike all the previous ones, the cure will work and Anna will not fall sick. Anna remembers staring at the plume of smoke from the steam engine and the loud, long whistles cutting into the sleepy rattle of wheels, making her sit up and ask for a drink out of a red thermos bottle full of sweet, lemony tea.

There were always people around, pushing, coughing, clearing their throats, swearing. The throngs of people at the stations, storming the trains, rushing in to grab their seats. Young men with hard suitcases rammed their way through the crowds. "Taken," they yelled, when *Mama* pushed Anna and her brother past closed compartments where those who managed to get in spread their hands on the empty seats, saving them for their own families.

There was never enough room, but *Mama* always managed to get a seat for them, always found the way, spotting young, strong soldiers travelling alone, smiling at their clean-shaven faces long before the train rolled into the platform, holding Anna and Yan up, their plump innocence and her flattery securing their protection. What words she used Anna does not remember, but she remembers being lifted up into the air and carried — "like a princess" her mother would later say — right above the heads of the crowd into a seat by the window. She remembers the touch of green woollen fabric of the soldier's uniform against her cheek, rough and prickly, and her mother settling comfortably right next to her, her face beaming. *Babcia* is slowly crossing herself, muttering a short prayer to the Virgin Mary to take care of them on this journey. Pulling out sandwiches from her big shoulder bag, hard-boiled eggs, red apples peeled and cut into thin wedges. Giving Anna a brown paper bag full of sweet cookies and asking, in a whisper, to offer them first to these nice young men who helped them, and then to everyone else.

Among all this, there is never a memory of her father who stayed behind in the city, and who, as always, would join them later when they were already settled in their one-room lodgings in a seaside village, Ustka or Łeba, where *Babcia* would make a shade out of an old newspaper to cover a naked bulb, and where Anna and Yan would sleep in one bed, on a prickly straw mattress, smelling of the fields.

Now Anna is grateful for the unhurried pace of the wheels, grateful for the few hours of time. The train is almost empty and, in Warsaw, she passed a number of compartments before choosing this one. When she called her brother from Warsaw and told him she would take a train, Yan asked her to make sure not to be alone in a compartment. It was not even a warning, just a reminder, necessary only because she was coming from her soft and protected life in Canada.

On the train no one speaks to her, no one shows any interest in her affairs. After a short "good morning" followed by a quick look at her black leather coat, the young woman opposite her, whose pale and narrow face is carefully made up, resumes reading colourful magazines. *Your Style, Success —* Anna can make out the glossy titles.

The woman has taken off her high heels and has put on a pair of fuzzy, pink slippers. The two young men, who, without being asked, briskly helped Anna put her bag and suitcases on the metal shelf above their heads, do not start a conversation either. They both wear grey sweaters and corduroy pants, are slightly overweight and pale, and talk about business in low, quiet voices. "Someone dunked a lot of money in sugar," Anna hears. Someone else had great plans but sank in the Russian markets. The KGB is into business debt collecting now. For a mere five percent. The idioms are easy to figure out, but they no longer sound familiar. Anna is glad they do not pay attention to her. She would rather be invisible.

The conductor who comes by to check their tickets assures her that the train will be in Wroclaw on time. Anna half-expects him to say something like, "Thank you and have a nice journey," but this is asking for too much, too soon. She should be satisfied with a smile.

Wroclaw, Breslau. When Anna was growing up just pronouncing the word Breslau made the children uneasy, as if recalling a secret, silenced but still dangerous. A Polish city without the past. A Polish city filled with German ruins.

Footpaths led into these ruins, she remembers. Paths weaving like trails through mountains, up and down, over precipices and valleys, through the mysterious caverns of half-buried cellars and low concrete bunkers, smelling of rot and wet, crumbling plaster. They played there, all the children in the street, and she remembers the tightening of muscles, a contraction between her legs, the anticipation of the unexpected. They were warned that people could still vanish here, told that not so long ago a walk in these streets after dark was a death sentence. That the nights in Wroclaw belonged to prowlers, hot on the trail of anything that could be stolen or robbed. That in the mornings, corpses stripped of clothes were found among broken bricks.

The children who went into the ruins alone were asking for trouble; among the debris, no one would hear their screams. Warned so often, they walked alert, ready to run away. "Vampires" and "werewolves," they whispered in the dark, recalling their parents' words. The boys knew the routes to old bunkers and cellars. In the dark they whispered about German spies they had seen, and one of them would always try to frighten the rest with a scream. Sniffing the moist, mouldy air of the bunkers, they searched for German *schmeissers* or Russian *kalashnikovs,* for steel bullets that could be polished with a piece of cloth until they shone.

It was from these trips that they brought back German coins, lapels with SS runes, blue, red and purple stamps with swastikas or Hitler's moustached face, rusted helmets filled with slime and rotting leaves. In the evening dusk, they hit the granite pavements with steel bayonets setting off blue sparks, or plunged the sharp steel tips between the stones, lifting the granite cubes from sidewalks and rolling them down the street.

Anna remembers standing by the living room window, counting the huge trucks, roaring below in the street, carrying the rubble away. Sometimes twenty or thirty passed in the morning. "Good riddance," *Mama* sighed with relief, thinking of mines, of unexploded bombs.

Yes, her mother was pleased when the burnt out façades of the buildings were pulled down. Pleased when the giant statue of Frederick Wilhelm I was pulled from his horse and smashed to the ground. When Frederick Wilhelm III gave room to the Polish playwright, Alexander Fredro. When *Strasse der SA* became the Street of Silesian Resistance Fighters, and *Kaiserbrücke,* the Grunwaldski Bridge. When the bricks from German ruins, cleaned and sorted, were taken away to rebuild Stalingrad and then the Old Town in the heart of burnt-out Warsaw.

Returned to motherland, the slogans of her childhood said in big red letters. Slogans spread on thick, concrete pillars, on white billboards. Slogans perched on the roofs of houses, on the bays of bridges, their red and white background flashing in store windows. *We haven't come here, we have returned.* Returned to the ancient Piast capital of Lower Silesia which, too, was a Polish province. To think otherwise would have been a betrayal.

Yet, even when the last of the rubble was cleared and carried away on trucks, children found something — flattened toys, bent silver spoons, broken knives, forks with missing tines, pieces of green and blue glass, shards of white and blue porcelain, black gothic German lettering still intact.

If William were here with her on the train, he would look out of the window and, as with all their journeys together, he would draw her attention to the strange assortment of objects lying in people's backyards: old bathtubs, piles of rusting pipes, concrete blocks, old buckets. He would point to dogs chained to little wooden doghouses. He would notice how square the houses were, like shoeboxes perched in the middle of muddy roads, with no lawns or flower gardens, but with useful rows of vegetable plots and fruit trees. He would point to women riding black, old-fashioned bicycles, their heads wrapped in big, woollen kerchiefs. To village children standing at the railway crossings and waving at the passing trains. To groups of men in quilted work jackets and dark blue berets, drinking beer under a tree. Or he would say that forests here have only two kinds of trees, birches and pines.

Ursula's words hover over her, *It's our souls, darling. They cannot stand letting go of the other lives they could have led.* Words like a flock of birds over ploughed fields. What troubles her is their accuracy. She would rather they could be dismissed.

"You have to think about yourself," Marie told her before they parted. "You are only thirty-eight. You have a whole life in front of you. You cannot change what has happened." No, Anna thinks, but what has happened changes you, pushes you where you would never go. And over that you have no control.

The train approaches Wrocław slowly, in the dusk of a late afternoon. The carriages shake and tremble in the rhythm of cluttering wheels. Cigarette smoke drifts through the doors; it is everywhere. It has already penetrated the fibres of her clothes, it has lodged itself in the pores of her skin. For a long time, Anna stands in the corridor, outside her compartment where the two men have dozed off, their heads bent backwards.

The Polish city and its German double. Filled with shadows. Hers and William's:

"What's your name, lad?"

"Willi."

"Come here, Willi. Take a look. Take a good look. This is the end of your *Heimat*."

He hadn't liked to talk about Breslau, but some memories came in spite of this reluctance. Death fascinated him, he told her once. The absolute, motionless stillness he could not comprehend. His mother could have covered his eyes with her hand when they passed deserters hanging in the trees, but he would wiggle away from her grip. Later, at home he would lie down on the carpet, close his eyes, and wait for something to happen.

Führer befiehl, wir folgen. Order us and we shall follow.

"Where is my father," he asked his mother one day.

It was a harsh winter day, and he had to wear a fur cap with flaps that covered his cheeks and that he hated with a passion. He wiggled away from Käthe when she tried to put it on. That's when he heard the sound of muted drumbeats, and a man's voice, high, serious, rising over the static of the radio. *The battle of Stalingrad has come to an end.* Then came the music, sweet, tender sounds of cellos, the *Andante con moto* of Beethoven's Fifth.

"Your father fell in the war," his mother told him. "At Stalingrad, Willi. Your father died at Stalingrad."

He kept looking at her, but he didn't hear what she was telling him. He was listening to the music.

As the train rolls through the outskirts of Wroclaw, Anna watches the city with suspicion. Old pre-war German houses are easy to spot, big, grey, solid, in spite of the forty-five years that have passed from the day the war ended. Old German working class districts with their red brick, soot-covered façades and tile roofs. She can tell where the ruins have been for that's where the post-war slab houses stand now, the ugly concrete constructions of Communist Poland, like scars. Whole blocks of them, sinister, beginning to crumble the day they were built.

Warm and *kalt,* she can still remember black Gothic letters on round, white bathroom taps in the house she lived in. *Briefe* on the heavy brass flap through which the postman dropped blue envelopes and faded yellowish postcards with workers saluting their leaders on the First of May parade. Underneath the thick, yellow wallpaper she helped her father strip, the walls were pasted with German newspapers, their black, incomprehensible squiggles forming yet another layer that had to be removed and washed away.

She ran with other children through the ruins, wielding stick guns, yelling at the top of her voice, in the heat of play.

How many German words they knew then, already! *Raus, Hände hoch, schneller schneller*. Get out, hands up, faster, faster. *Polnische Schweine*. Polish pigs.

Ta ta ta ta ta taaaaaa! Deutschland Deutschland über alles, Hei li hei la! Hei li Hei la!

Drang nach Osten. Lebensraum.

She remembers a boy holding a piece of white chalk and drawing the spidery arms of a swastika on a grey, bullet-riddled wall. Then, slowly, as if to test their endurance, filling in the spaces between the lines, turning the upturned cross into four innocent little squares.

Hitler kaput!

"The Wild West," her father said. "It was like the Wild West." But all Anna remembers is how terrified he was to walk through the streets.

"The Recovered Territories!" he had read. "The land of opportunity." Newspapers painted pictures of opulent villas abandoned by fleeing Germans, houses fully furnished, equipped, businesses waiting for Polish settlers, new pioneers, as if this land had no past and had to be reclaimed from nature. "Go!" he read. "Tomorrow may be too late."

In June 1945 her father was alone and had nowhere else to go. "It took one bomb," he said. Anna thought of the incredible luck that made him miss the last tramway home before curfew and stay with his friends. From his distant relatives who had survived the war, he had collected small pale photographs of his family — men, women and children with hard-to-make-out faces. "This here is your *Dziadek* Stanislaw. Your *Babcia* Helena." Everyone in these pictures was someone's son, daughter, brother or sister, and everyone's fate had already been sealed. The web of relationships between the pale sepia figures seemed absolute to him, and he was always surprised when Anna and Yan mixed them up.

"How can you forget?" he asked them, ready to explain once again, but all they wanted to hear about was the story of the missed tramway, a mattress on the floor in his friend's room that had made their own existence possible.

Tata had come to Wroclaw in a crowded train, with a

leaking roof and a broken window, sitting on the cardboard suitcase he had tied up with a leather belt. The train arrived late in the evening and he had to wait in the station until morning. He heard gunshots, screams, a wave of rattling noises, spoons and ladles hitting tin buckets and iron pans, a warning to the looters, he was told, a show of support. The city was under curfew. He was cold and wet. At dawn, he climbed into a tramway in which all the windows were broken and seats torn out and he rode a few stops along empty avenues of this strange, abandoned city, past rows of unsteady houses, still smouldering, still hot. In streets covered with red dust and littered with broken furniture, German and Russian helmets, and bundles of rags, only the rats moved without fear.

He told Anna and Yan how he had crept past fallen trees, entered emptied buildings looking for a safe place to stay. He described the motionless bodies in the streets, the overturned trams, barricades made of broken tables, chairs, credenzas and beds, the stink of the ruins — of burnt flesh. Terrified of the emptiness of the suburbs, he found a room in a sort of boarding house near the station, a bed infested with bugs. His meals came from a barrel of pickled meat with an off-smell that made his stomach turn. "I'll go back," he thought, unable to admit that he could ever live here for long. "Soon," he promised himself, "to Poland."

That's what he had said: "To Poland." For in his mind then Lower Silesia was no man's land, a magical robbers' den for the dispossessed, a haven for marauders, a chance for the politically suspect. One could disappear here, *Tata* said, but one could also die from a stray bullet or a knife in the back.

"Why? You ask me why? For the oldest of reasons, Anna. Revenge, greed, despair."

The trains leaving the Wrocław Central Station every day were filled with would-be settlers, one-day pioneers who took away with them whatever they could find, rob, or trade from those Germans who had not yet fled. Furs, jewellery, pots, sewing machines, lamps, typewriters, layers of white embroidered sheets, silk lingerie and dresses of Westphalian linen. Jars with *Pfeffer, Salz, Zucker* on them, Rosenthal cups, Meissen porcelain, earthenware beer *Seidels* with tin or silver lids that could be lifted with a thumb. But the contents of these bags, bundles, and suitcases were just a drop in the general exodus of things. The Red Army, waiting for Stalin's decision on what to do with these lands, was securing its share of the spoils. Trucks leaving Silesian towns and villages for the Soviet Union were filled to the brim with the best of furniture, farm equipment, the insides of entire factories. Settlers spoke of copper wires torn out of the walls, kilometres of railroad tracks removed, buildings with holes in the concrete floor from which the machines had been torn out, where not a screw was left in place.

When he enrolled in the Department of Geology at the Polish University of Wroclaw, *Tata* was given a shovel to help clear the rubble from the classrooms. In teams, the students removed the debris from lecture halls, sorted out bricks and masonry, replaced broken glass. At night, the buildings they helped to clear had to be guarded; it was no secret that the lizards, snakes, frogs, turtles, human foetuses and organs, lining the shelves at the Natural Science Museum, were floating in precious alcohol. Before the windows of the first floor were walled up and armed guards stationed at the only entrance, night brought swarms of marauders who rummaged through the museum rooms, leaving broken jars and dried out specimens as the only evidence of their nocturnal presence.

Tata had told Anna and Yan how, with other student guards, he was sent to bring whatever could still be salvaged from the houses of departed German professors. The abandoned suburban villas stood silent behind junipers and pines. Anna and Yan could imagine him, nervously eyeing the road behind him, in his hand a piece of paper with addresses he got from university archives. They could hear his footsteps on a gravel path. He was hoping to arrive there before the looters. Everything was priceless then, he said, microscopes, scales, sets of encyclopaedias, typewriters, supplies of paper and ink. Anything that could enrich the museum collection — rocks, fossils. But the most precious, he said, were the geological maps of Lower Silesia. The new Polish land had to be assessed for deposits and drilled.

"It was dangerous," he said, his voice still uneasy. "One never knew then." He had heard stories of Nazi treasures buried in the old mineshafts, in the web of underground passages where whole trains with Breslau gold had vanished without a trace. He had heard stories of *Werewolf* executions, swift death for those who saw or heard too much, of being in the wrong place at the wrong time. He fumbled with the locks of these solid German doors, giving them the final push, before they gave and let him into the smell of floor wax and dust. He pulled at the drawers of rosewood desks, oak secretaries; he emptied old bookcases and picked up rocks from shelves, wrapping them carefully in old German newspapers that stained his hands black. Other students helped him as he loaded these treasures on wooden carts, excited at each find, pointing their fingers at the brass instruments, at polished glass, laughing nervously as they walked. Triumphant, they brought their finds to the Polish University of Wroclaw, relieved that no one had stopped them on the way.

"And then," Father said, as if it were a miracle he still couldn't quite understand, "I met your mother." That's when they moved into this mutilated street, between the long prisms of ruins, into the apartment where, Anna can still remember, in each of the three rooms thick wooden poles supported the ceiling. "The structure had been shaken," Father said, and after that, every so often, she would stop in the middle of what she was doing, stand still and watch for the first signs of tremors.

He knew about such things, she thought. He showed her the rocks he had brought from his trips to the Sudeten Mountains, rocks that looked as if someone had broken them into halves, and then put the halves back together, but not exactly at the same place. "This is a fault from here," he said. "Look how old it is, how small. Frozen, but it can still tell you what was here before."

She looked at the piece of rock with suspicion, ran her fingers over the rough surface. Took the rock in her hand and gave it back to him, to be put back, high on the shelf. "That's what I'm trying to do," he told her, then. "Find out how it all happened."

"How can you tell?" she asked.

It wasn't easy, he conceded. What was visible was deceiving. Important parts of these rocks could be missing, eroded, crumbled to dust. That's why he had to drill deep into the earth's crust, to find out.

"You can have it if you want," he said, offering her a grey cylinder, a drilling sample. But Anna preferred the rocks that came from far away lands. The volcanic glass with its shiny black surface, the white plates of celestite, or the green, red, and blue hexagons of quartz.

The first thing her father did in the Wroc aw apartment was to install thick metal bars in the windows and three long bolts with which they barred the door every evening. The bars are still there, as if her parents never felt safe enough to remove them.

When they found it, the apartment was almost empty, save for a heap of broken glass in the living room, a pile of books, and a few photographs of a man with a swastika on his arm. The photographs were pierced with a knife. The place was filthy. Rotting rags stuck to the floorboards, the large wooden table was split in half with an axe, the walls were smeared with excrement, a jar of marmalade was emptied over a pile of books. Her father thought that soldiers must have camped there. "Maybe," he said, "that's why the apartment was still empty."

It took her parents a whole week to wash the walls and scrub the floors clean. They slept on the floor in the big room to the right, and in the morning carried down the rubble they had cleared and left it by the curb of the street.

The bombs had left parts of the houses intact, and from these teetering caverns her parents rescued the bright yellow curtains now hanging in the big front room, and the little rosewood table with a marble top that stands in the study. They took whatever they could find, the round table they ate on, oak chairs with leather seats, white iron beds, white china plates, a mahogany clock with an eagle perched on top, and Anna's favourite, a *Scherenschnitt*, a paper cut-out still hanging on the kitchen wall in her parents' apartment. How she loved to stare at the black silhouettes of a man with an umbrella, of two little boys, and of a dog struggling with wind and rain. One of the boys in the picture watched how his umbrella turned over, another ran after a blown off cap. Only the dog plodded along, pretending not to mind.

Babcia did not like the curtains, the table, the brown leather armchairs with head-rests. She would have preferred her daughter to have the family furniture, if only she could have it back. "These are so heavy," she complained, "so German." She did not mind when they gathered chips and bruises, and shrugged her shoulders when Yan and Anna jumped up and down on the beds, until the springs moaned.

"I didn't want to come here," she said. "This is not where my grandchildren should have been born." The world Anna and Yan were supposed to inherit, like the Warsaw store, was destroyed, and now they were destined to live their lives among someone else's things, in this poor substitute for real Poland. "Robbed and betrayed," she said, her face locked in a grimace.

There were so many things her grandchildren should never forget. The frozen Siberian fields in Kolyma, where prisoners' bodies were so well preserved that when the time came, even hundreds of years from now, future generations would be able to see the last expressions on their faces. Gulag-bound ships where the smallest sign of discontent brought swift death, decks with protesters flooded by water and left to freeze into one solid block of ice. Those who had returned never said a word about the past but stared at the world with wide, empty eyes.

"Yes, Anna, it was better not to know."

Those who started this most terrible of wars, she would say, the Germans, laugh at them now from their new, opulent homes in West Germany, rebuilt with American money, laugh at them, caught behind the Iron Curtain, lining up for scraps of meat and loaves of stale bread.

Anna did not like when *Babcia* spoke like that, for her voice rose, tensed and then dissolved into sobs. Nothing Anna could say would bring any comfort. It was better to stay silent, to look down, and to wait until the wave of bitterness passed.

"What kind of life is it, I ask you!"

"What's the use, *Mama*. Thank God we are all alive," the

pleading voice of Anna's mother was meant to soothe. She, too, was made uneasy by so much pain.

It is the smell of perfume that Anna remembers now. *Soir de Paris*, a soft, luxurious smell mixed with the scent of face powder wafting into her nostrils when her mother leaned over her bed to place a soft kiss on her cheek. *Soir de Paris*, Anna whispered long afterwards, evening in Paris, thinking of the small bottle the colour of a ripe plum with a chrome cap. It kept the soft memory of the scent long after the perfume was gone.

Her mother was leaving for a New Year's ball. Her high heels clicked on the floor as she hurried around the room in her new taffeta dress, in which golden threads intertwined with brown and beige. The dress had a full skirt and a strapless bodice from which her mother's soft arms emerged like a statue trying to free itself from the tight embrace of stone. Her hair was pinned high, held in place with a wooden clasp. Father, dressed in his best black suit, was standing in the corner, his eyes following her with the amazement that Anna understood so well. For once again her mother had transformed herself in front of them; she was so confident and so beautiful, laughing at their muffled gasps, turning around to give them one more look before she covered her arms with a shawl. Soon she would put on the beige gloves that reached up to her elbows, slip her arms into the long furcoat Father was holding for her, and pick up a small purse. "Bedtime is at nine," she would chime. "No moaning." With her gloved fingers she would blow them the last kiss before closing the door, and they would hear the clicks of her heels descending the stairs.

Babcia had made the dress herself. For weeks the three of them had eyed the newspapers and magazines for the slightest hints of changing fashions. With a magnifying glass they had examined snapshots of actresses and diplomats' wives from small, unfocused photographs that sometimes appeared in magazines. They had noted the cuts of dresses, the shapes of heels. *Babcia* didn't need much else. She could copy any dress they set their mind on. The taffeta ball gown had a Marilyn Monroe feel to it, quite unusual, for *Mama* had an eye for simple but dramatic patterns, contrasting fabrics, lines that made the most of her narrow waist and shapely legs. *Soir de Paris*? Over

Babcia's protests they had made a trip to the hard currency store filled with Max Factor face creams, Colgate toothpaste, French perfume, and American cigarettes, whisky and blue jeans.

"What if something happens?" *Babcia* had said, angered by such extravagance, "What if you have no food to give the children?"

"A little bit of luxury," *Mama* had whispered into Anna's ear, as if to excuse herself, having extracted green dollar bills from a leather pouch she kept hidden somewhere in the study. *Dziadek* gave it to her before he died, the result of some transactions he had hung on to. "Buy yourself something nice with it," he had said. "You only live once."

Anna loved to watch her mother on evenings like this. *Babcia* eyeing her creation, spotting a hanging thread or a forgotten pin, pulling the dress on one side, making *Mama* stand still for just one second to make sure the hem was even. In her student days, *Mama* told them, nothing would stop her from dancing. Once when her heel snapped off one shoe, she slipped off her shoes and stockings and danced barefoot. When the dance was over, she snapped off the other heel and wobbled home.

These were the kinds of stories Anna liked best, but she had to ask for them, plead against her mother's preoccupied silence. Sometimes, when Anna asked often enough and when they were away, on vacation perhaps, far away from her mother's work, she might even hear of her parents' courtship — the most favourite story of them all — for it foreshadowed her own existence, involving her in such a wondrous way. That's when her mother would smile this half-smile, poised between pride and joy and say, "I never even noticed him, at first. I always had so many friends, but he had already been watching me for months."

It was in these stories that Anna's father emerged from the crowd of *Mama's* admirers slowly, winning her by his steadfast patience and determination. He would slip funny notes in between the pages of her books, wait in line to get a dance with her. Once, he brought her a cluster of gypsum roses, white crystalline balls closing like rosebuds in a tight bouquet. This he bought at the *szaberplatz,* the black market of Breslau treasures. It must have come from the geological museum, he would later say, for that was not an ordinary find. He skipped dinners for a whole week to afford it, but *Mama* wouldn't know that for months. "How beautiful," she had said simply when he placed the rocky flowers into her hands. The gypsum roses are still standing on the shelf of her parents' study and have to be dusted very carefully not to break the delicate petal-like formations.

"He was so funny, then," *Mama* would say at times like that, smiling. *Tata* only blushed when she talked to him and stammered some silly apologies, as if unprepared for such luck.

In the photographs from that time *Tata* is tall and handsome with a high forehead and round wire glasses. Anna has his curly hair, his smile, shy but winning, and his quiet persistence. That's what her mother always said, "Daddy's daughter."

How attracted he must have been by her mother's boundless energy, Anna thinks now, by her mercurial spirit. By the tenacity with which *Mama* refused to be weighed down by the ruins, the lost store. That wasn't enough to stop her, not more than a broken heel of her dancing shoe. Alone in the world, Father needed that kind of strength, his only hope for permanence. Soon her mother could not imagine an evening of dancing without his quiet presence, his patient waiting for her, when tired and so very happy she needed to lean on his shoulder and let him escort her through the dangerous Wroc aw streets to her student room. "I had nothing but my hamnler," *Tata* would sometimes add to these stories, the same pointed hammer with which he split the rocks.

There was one reason why *Mama* had little time for them, why the best of stories came rarely and had to be begged for, why dressing up for the ball seemed such a wondrous transformation for them all. Her work. She was a chemist. At that time she was completing her PhD research, her mind absorbed by her experiments in surface tension, which Anna understood only vaguely. It had something to do with particles of minerals suspended in water, rising to the surface by bubbles of air. Her mother was trying to separate the ones she wanted, find ways of recovering them. The laboratory smelled of solvents and burning gas, and on the shelves Anna could spot jars labelled with human skulls and crossed bones. "Don't touch anything," *Mama* would warn her. This wasn't the place for children, she would say, ushering Anna outside, quickly, anxious to get back to her work.

Babcia did not approve of her daughter's occupation. "Not a job for a woman," she would say to Anna as they sat in the kitchen peeling potatoes for dinner, her lips pouting with disgust. "She will blow herself up or drag some poison home." *Babcia* was dubious of her daughter's ability to keep the family safe. She would make sure *Mama* changed her clothes as soon as she came home and would wash them separately, rinsing them a few more times than she would anything else.

"Her place is here, with you. What is she going to do when I die?" she would ask Anna and Yan, pleased that they had no answer for her.

The train enters the giant glass-and-steel hangar of Central Station. There is a smell here Anna remembers, soot mixed with steam, the smell of a railway. How German it still looks, Anna thinks. Forty-five years later the German *genius loci* is in the shape of metal columns that support the roof, in the classical ornaments, the pale ivory tiles on the walls. What has changed, to her, is the size of it. The station seems smaller than she remembers it, and later, she will have to fight the persistent feeling that the whole city has shrunk in her absence. Her throat is dry, as if all moisture has evaporated, leaving her cracked open, like parched, barren ground.

Her brother waits on the platform, by the little round kiosk, to the right. Anna knows it is him long before he has recognised her. His eyes scan the train, trying to spot her. In some ways he has not changed at all. He is still large, with wide shoulders and a head that seems too small for his body. "He is stooping," Anna thinks, "I don't remember him stooping so much." When he notices her, he throws his arms up and shakes his head, taken aback. It must be her black leather coat, Anna thinks; her brother does not remember her dressing like this. Before she left Poland, she had a preference for loose, flowery dresses of cheesecloth — the hippie style. She feels his arms around her, squeezing her, pulling her toward him.

"Anna," he says, "Anna. Good Lord! Good to have you here." He does not mention William. He does not know how.

"Yes," she murmurs. "Good to be back. I haven't thought I ever would."

He leans back, his hands still on her shoulders.

"You look swell," he says looking at the cut of her hair, the ash-blond highlights. "American!"

She doesn't, really. She avoids mirrors for her face is still pale and drawn, aged by sadness, but now she smiles and is pleased by her brother's words.

"Thank you," she says, and realises that this is not what he expects her to say. If anything he would expect her to protest, to say how tired she is from the journey, how crumpled her clothes are, and then he, too, would protest, complimenting her even more. So now, puzzled, he watches her closely, looking for other clues how the years away must have changed her. They were not too good at corresponding. Her letters were short and general, and often left unanswered for months. She tried to call him, but these were just excuses to hear his voice, for she knew her brother well enough. He was no expert at hurried conversations.

Under martial law her brother joined an underground dissident cell, delivering leaflets, preparing safe houses, carrying messages, lecturing clandestine groups on the legal means of active opposition. In Canada she knew little of these activities, except for vague hints in the letters smuggled out of the country and mailed outside the reach of censors. Her mother did not write about him, either.

"How is Basia," she asks. "And Adam?"

"Oh, fine. They will come to see you later." His wife and son, her sister-in-law and nephew, new family she has only seen in snapshots. Adam in the clothes she has sent from Montreal, sitting on a soccer ball, eyes rising to the ceiling in a gesture of exasperation. Basia, her long auburn hair plaited in an old-fashioned braid.

Yan lifts Anna's suitcases up, and leads her to his car, the interior of which smells of gasoline and plastic seats. This is another childhood smell, Anna thinks, the smell of rare trips in a taxi, the now-forgotten curved line of the first Polish car, *Warszawa*, when she fought nausea for the sake of this tiny bit of luxury, a ride through the streets of the city, then almost empty of traffic. "My wheels," Yan says with pride. "A bit on the old side, but still in good shape." The car starts with a clutter and a shake, but takes off fast.

"Remember?" he asks.

"Sure," she says, terrified of the proximity of other cars on the road, her brother's overly aggressive manoeuvres. Marie was right when she said that drivers in this part of the world accelerate and brake, as if speed or full stop were the only alternatives. But Yan laughs at his sister when she holds on to the seat.

"Relax," he says. "I won't kill you."

"How are they?" she asks about their parents.

"Grumpy," he says. "They never go anywhere. *Mama* doesn't let *Tata* do anything. He cannot drink, and cannot smoke without her making a fuss. You know how he is. He'll never say boo to her. Never could."

"But how is he?" Anna asks.

"You'll see for yourself."

Yes, her brother looks tired; his face is sunken and grey. Partly it is the haircut, Anna thinks, too short for him, but partly it must be the life here. Too much vodka, too many cigarettes, and no desire to camouflage the passage of time. "Men do not live long in this country," he tells her, as if he could read her thoughts. "We keel over before we are sixty-five." He tells her this in a casual tone, as if it were gossip, something funny to tell a visitor from so far away. He uses a term that makes her shiver, "over-mortality of men," and, all the time, gives her quick looks out of the corner of his eye.

"Listen, I'm so sorry about William."

"Yeah," she says, and suddenly, overcome by bitterness and loss, she chokes with sobs. Yan stops the car and lets her cry, waiting patiently until she calms down. He makes no attempt to quiet her, to comfort her sorrow, to reason with her. With all her smug talk about the habits of the land, this is something she has forgotten, the overwhelming acceptance of pain. Her brother knows she has to go through it, and there is nothing she can do but wait for the wave to pass. When she stops crying and dries her eyes, he drives off, cautioning her about the dark stretches of the streets.

"It's no longer a safe city," she hears. "Don't carry any big money in your purse." He is worried that with the way she looks now, she will stand out in the crowd. "Blend," he seems to be telling her. "Don't draw attention to yourself." A game of survival, she thinks, and promises to try her best to become one with the crowd.

The stairs seem lower than she remembers, winding past closed, silent doors of the neighbours. Walls and doors are painted light grey, the paint unevenly spread, with drops dried midway down, like thick, frozen trails. On the first landing Anna peeks through the window into the back yard where someone has left a pile of broken boards, bricks, and chunks of concrete. A rusted bucket sits on top of the pile, splattered with remnants of white paint, and next to it lies a broken ladder, three rungs missing. A few children run across the yard, playing tag. "Got you," cries a girl with a ponytail so light that it seems white. "Did not," chants the other, smaller girl. "Did not!"

Anna can still remember a thick crystal glass panel with snowflake patterns in the front doors, smooth green tiles in the hall with brown outlines of chestnut leaves, carved wooden staircases, the shine of brown linoleum on the steps. The crystal panel was smashed on one of the Saturday nights when the hallway always smelled of urine and when she could hear feet pounding the ceiling above her bedroom, screams, dull thumps, things falling on the floor and rolling until they stopped. The panel was replaced first by an ordinary glass pane and subsequently by a piece of plywood. One by one, carved railings disappeared. The banister was held in place by roughly hewn pieces of wood.

In the backyard she used to play with other girls, hiding secrets in the grassy meadows, filling shallow holes with flower petals, beads, coins and then covering them up, first with a piece of glass and then with earth, promising never to tell. In this backyard, crabapple trees yield thick, pink blossoms in the spring and small, tart red apples at the end of the summer. *Rajskie jabłuszka*, the little apples of paradise was the Polish for them, and when she bit into the white flesh, it made her tongue tingle. Every spring, the children broke off thick, blooming branches and carried them home to their mothers. Every fall, the boys climbed the trees, cracked more branches under their feet, shook the trunks for the shower of crab apples, cut their initials deep into the trunks.

Tata stands in the open doors to what was once Anna's home. His hair has thinned and there is an uneasy seriousness on his face, a mixture of apprehension and joy. He clears his throat and shuffles toward her. Anna moves forward to embrace him. He murmurs his greetings in a hoarse whisper. His breath is shallow and uneven. From their telephone conversations Anna knows that he has given up scouring the countryside in an old army jeep, drilling for deposits. The doctors were adamant in their warnings; "It's this or two metres under," one of them said, pointing to the ground. "Make your choice." In the last years he has been slowly finishing his geological maps of Lower Silesia, completing the webs of lines and marking levels of elevation with different colours.

"Come inside," he says. "*Mama* is waiting." He lets her go first and she can hear the heaviness of his breath as he follows. Her brother takes her suitcases and carries them inside.

Anna walks cautiously, listening to still-familiar sounds. The crackling of the floorboards, squeaking in exactly the same places. The gas stove in the kitchen clicking as it used to, when her brother puts the kettle on. A whiff of a sickening, sweet odour of gas. Her legs remember the elevated threshold between the rooms, the one guests always tripped over. Her hands remember the shape and feel of the brass door handles.

Mama is standing by the living room window.

"How thin she is," Anna thinks when she sees her, as if with each year her mother has contrived to take up less and less space. It is her face that Anna watches, searching for signs

171

of forgiveness. Tears flow along the deep lines on her cheeks.

"She has came back," *Tata* says, taking *Mama*'s hand in his. "I told you she would."

"You sit down," *Mama* says firmly to him. "He won't listen to the doctors," she says to no one in particular as he lowers himself to a sofa covered by a thin red blanket, "He won't stop smoking. So stubborn." She gives Anna an exasperated look and makes a face her father does not see, a face of stern resignation. "Now it's your turn. You convince him."

There is a moment of awkward silence as they sit, everybody waiting, fumbling for words.

"Some days he can't breathe at all," *Mama* resumes her complaints, breaking the silence.

Anna sees drops of sweat gathering on her father's forehead. He wipes them off with a chequered handkerchief and listens to his wife's denunciations with a mischievous smile on his lips as if it were all a prank, a good joke he was playing on her.

"Doctors," he says. "What do they know?" He winks at Anna.

Yan comes from the kitchen and looks at her. They all watch her. They try to guess what she feels. They want to check how much she can recognise, how much she remembers.

Anna notices new things in the room: a brass flowerpot, a leather covered pillow, a round sewing basket covered with an embroidered cloth. The palm tree by the window has grown so much that it now almost reaches the ceiling, its spiky leaves spreading like a green, dusty canopy. Her presents from Montreal, so carefully chosen, now annoy her with their uncalled-for sleekness. They stand out in the shabbiness of the room: an art deco photograph frame with her picture in it, a set of paper boxes with flowery lids, potpourri in a crystal jar with a silver lid. These are the only things that remind her of William.

"Are you tired?" her mother asks, her voice still uneasy.

"No, no. I'm fine," she says, quickly.

She gives them all their presents and they open the packages and thank her. Her mother wraps the shawl across her shoulders, her father smells the leather of the wallet.

From the kitchen, her brother brings in platters of food. The table, Anna notices, is covered by what has always been

Mama's best tablecloth, freshly ironed, white linen with red cherries embroidered along the edges. The cherries have brown stems and pairs of green leaves. She knows that the colours at one side of the cloth are markedly different, the stems of the cherries are black and the leaves are of paler green. This is where *Babcia* ran out of yarn and couldn't buy more of the same colour. "You only notice it when you know," she would say hopefully. They always agreed. The table is set with white porcelain plates, cups with wreaths of blue flowers, and silver cutlery. Platters with slices of ham, salami, roast pork take the whole centre of the table, beside a bowl of potato salad, bowls of dill pickles — marinated mushrooms, onions, herring. A basket of rye bread, thinly sliced. Slices of cheesecake and poppyseed cake, arranged on an oblong crystal platter in alternating rows wait on the side.

Anna sits at the table and lets them offer her food, taking a bit of everything. Her plate looks full, and she knows she will never be able to eat that much. They watch as she cuts a slice of ham into little bits, chews and swallows. One by one they are asking if she has missed the old tastes, if the food is good, if all is as she remembers it. "Yes," she says. "It's excellent. It really is."

The tea is weak and served with lemon and sugar. A glass pot with two teabags still in it sits on the table, and her mother pours the tea into the cups. Half-slices of lemon are arranged on a crystal plate. *Mama* is the only one to drink her tea in a glass, the Russian way. "It tastes better," she says and stirs the pale liquid vigorously with a spoon, heavy, solid silver that was always kept for most important visitors.

"So many people left the country," *Mama* says and sighs. "Young people. Another generation decimated. How long can Poland withstand this constant loss of blood."

In Montreal, for the last ten years, Anna opened her mother's letters with growing uneasiness. At first they were short, very short. Reports on her father's deteriorating health, on Basia whose good humour won everyone's heart, even if she so obviously "lacked ambition" and dropped out of university.

But then her mother began remembering the war. Anna could almost see her, writing, bent over the paper, smoking a Carmen cigarette from which she has torn off the filter. That peculiar, scented smell was what always struck her as she opened the lined white pages filled with stories she refused to tell Anna for years, stories that made her voice break.

She wrote to Anna about *Babcia* finding ways to buy back her daughter's freedom from forced labour, thankful for someone's penchant for good whisky, for her daughter's innocent looks, her ability to recite the poems of Goethe in German that amazed someone important enough. She wrote of the Warsaw Uprising, of daily descents to the sewage canals to carry orders from one unit to the other. She recalled how she helped carry a wounded soldier on her back, her legs immersed in sewage up to her knees. The soldier was crying. He was thirsty, hurting, but he clung to her neck. He begged her to give him a drink. *I don't have any water*, she said, and he tried to lower himself to drink the water from the sewage, but she wouldn't let him. All she had was a sugar cube, so she gave it to him, and he quieted down and only moaned and grew hotter and hotter on her back. When they got out, he was taken away on a stretcher. *I don't even know what happened to him,* she wrote.

Inside the underground tunnels explosions were dulled, muted. She remembered the texture of the red bricks and concrete ledges on both sides where she saw blankets, rucksacks, jars with lard — all abandoned in desperation. The feeling of something soft getting entangled around her feet. *Funny*, she wrote, *how I don't remember the smell*. Their noses must have given up in those days, dulled by the burning smoke, the rotting flesh of the city. As they walked, they kept an eye on open manholes, in front of which they crouched and waited in absolute silence. *That's where*, she wrote, *the SS threw grenades to get to us. That's how we were meant to die.*

How hard it was, she wrote, with regained sense of smell, to wash away the stink of the sewers. She threw away all her clothes, then, soaked her hands in hot soapy water until she thought the skin would peel off. *My hair was the worst*, she wrote. *Sticky. Nothing helped. I had to cut all of it, and I had nothing but a pair of blunt scissors.*

When the Uprising fell, the survivors were marched in long columns out of Warsaw, on a warm, sunny October day. The columns took the whole width of the street. *The Germans were surprised that so many of us survived.*

Why did Anna have to cut herself off from Poland, her mother asked. Had she not thought of funerals? She may not need her parents, but her parents were not immortal; they may have need of her. *Give me a reason*, her even, rounded handwriting insisted. *Give me one good reason why.*

Anna was thinking of a glass case with a mummy of a small girl she saw in a museum once, wads of greyish bandage hiding the body. It was better that way. Better not to see what's inside. To her mother she wrote of her health, of Montreal, of Canadian weather. There was no telling what would be unearthed if they let themselves go.

"Tell us," her father says. "Tell us about Canada."

But it is they who talk, who tell her what happened when she was away, in Montreal. About the cut off phones, Chopin's music on all radio stations, tanks in the streets. About a prison guard who confiscated Piotr's Bible with its dedication *So that Truth will always be victorious.*

"A Russian invasion we would have understood, yes, but not the coup. Not our own people," her father says. "This was the hardest to accept."

"On TV," Yan joins in, "the announcers had military uniforms. They read lists of offences punishable by death."

"We had curfew," her father adds, "couldn't go anywhere without permissions. But just a few days later you could get permissions by the dozen. Stolen from the offices, already stamped."

They want her to know that even at the height of martial law the spirit of the nation was not doused. It strikes her that they are explaining all of this as if she had never lived here. They use phrases like "geopolitical situation," "general conditions," "historical position," talking all at once, talking as if she never stood in line-ups with them, as if she never huddled in front of the radio, waiting for the news, tuning in to Radio Free Europe, listening past the buzzing noises and whistles of the jamming towers. "I was away for ten years, only" she says, and they nod as if this only confirmed the need for such explanations.

The doorbell rings with a shrill, piercing sound. "Here they are," Yan says and rushes to open the door. For the last half an hour, he has been checking his watch anxiously. "It's all because of Basia's mother," he explained. "She has asked them to come and help her." This, he wants Anna to know, is the only reason why his wife and son are not here yet to greet her.

"That's all right," Anna responded. The apologies seem to her excessive. What is there to explain?

She can hear her brother's reproaches and a woman's soft, humming voice. "I couldn't . . . you know how she is . . . she wants my attention." And then Anna hears a child's voice. "I can?" and the sound of footsteps.

Adam is standing at the door, his eyes fixed on Anna. His smooth, oval face looks serious, concentrated on what is about to happen, but he stops at the threshold, motionless, and looks back to see if his parents are behind.

"Go in," Yan says, "She doesn't bite."

Anna doesn't wait for Adam to come in. She rises from her chair and comes closer. She squats so that their eyes meet.

"Do you know who I am?" she asks.

"You are *Ciocia* Anna, from Canada," Adam answers. His voice is clear and pure, like a chime. "You have sent me all these neat toys and clothes. I have your picture in my room. *Tata* gave me."

Anna's eyes mist with tears as she embraces Adam, feeling his thin arms cling to hers. Basia laughs, pleased at this display of affection. There is no sight of the old-fashioned braid. Her hair is now short, styled in waves over her cheeks. "You have to watch out," she says to Anna, "now he won't leave you alone."

Anna stands up to say hello to her sister-in-law, who embraces her warmly and, from her quilted shoulder bag, takes out a small bundle. Inside a white linen cloth there is a piece of bread and a small jar of salt. "Old custom," Basia says, "to say how glad we are you've returned."

Anna takes a piece of bread, dips it in salt, and puts it in her mouth. The bread is thick and heavy, and she chews it slowly, the salt crystals dissolving in her mouth. They are all moved, fighting tears, inventing chores to cover up the emotions. "Come on, sit down, the tea is growing cold," her mother says, and offers them more food. Adam, who has unwrapped his presents — a memory game, a truck, and a box of Lego blocks and tucked them safely inside his mother's bag — insists that he wants to sit between his *Dziadek* and *Ciocia* Anna. His plate is moved and they all make space for him. As soon as he is settled, he begins telling Anna of his new aquarium, of the fish he bought, of the new pump and filter he still needs. He interrupts his story only to watch what food is being placed on his plate. "You know I don't like ham," he protests, and Anna watches his smooth face, his straight blond hair, dark eyes. "Did you know that there are vacuum fish, not really vacuum, but I call them vacuum, and they clean the floor of the aquarium for me. And I will have baby fish..."

"That's enough, Adam," Basia says. "Let *Ciocia* talk to us."

"We will go out together," Anna promises Adam. "Tomorrow. Then you will tell me all you want. OK?"

"What time tomorrow?" Adam asks. "I have to know," he adds, hesitating as he watches a frown on his father's forehead.

"Ten o'clock," Anna says, looking straight into Adam's serious eyes. "Just the two of us. I'll pick you up and we'll go for a pizza and ice cream. Will you remember?"

"I will," Adam says, nodding, and takes hold of her hand.

Basia praises the food, asks questions. There is a pleasant warmth about her, a need to smooth what can be smoothed. She has praised the dress *Mama* is wearing, the flowery pattern, the softness of cotton. She has read of some home remedies for respiratory problems and has cut out the article for her parents-in-law to read.

Tata has brought out a bottle of *jarzębiak*, a fragrant Polish brandy and is pouring it into small narrow glasses. Adam gets a glass of juice. "Now you can get any juice you want. Apple, orange, grape," *Mama* says. "So why did we have to scrounge for forty-five years?"

They all nod.

"Your health," *Tata* says, and Anna drinks slowly. The brandy stings her throat but the warmth that comes releases some of the tension in her neck. The muscles let go slowly, one by one, as she leans back in her chair.

"That's more than asthma," Basia says when an hour later Anna helps her wash the dishes in her parents' kitchen. "We've been trying to find a really good doctor. Piotr's father gave us a few good contacts. Perhaps then we'll know more."

"That's nice of him," Anna says, uneasy at Piotr's implied presence. She will write to her former father-in-law, she thinks, with thanks.

Basia dips the plates in soapy water, Anna rinses them and stacks them on a plastic rack. They can hear Adam's voice in the dining room explaining something, insisting that he knows what he is talking about.

"He's always been like that," Basia says. "Just like Yan. He has to have his way."

For over four years Anna's old apartment, where her brother lives now, was a safe house for Solidarity activists. Equipped with high-frequency radio equipment to monitor police cruisers, a bag full of false identity cards. Sometimes "visitors" stayed for a few days, sometimes for a few months, sleeping on the living room sofa, staying away from the windows so that the neighbours wouldn't know too much. At night strangers knocked at the door to take dispatches and to bring supplies.

Anna asks Basia about that time. "How did you manage?" she asks. "With a baby?" Basia, Yan said once, smuggled underground leaflets in Adam's pram.

Basia laughs. Adam, she says, was instructed not to tell anyone of the "uncles" who stayed with them, and he was very good. Once only, in a crowded store, when he was four-years-old, he pointed to the Most Wanted poster with a familiar face in it. "*Mama*, look! This is Uncle Karol."

"I froze," Basia says. "Someone in the store just started to laugh. They thought it was funny. So I laughed, too. But my legs were so soft I could hardly walk."

The dishes are done, dried and stacked in piles. "We'll leave the rest to *Mama*," Basia says. "She has her own way of putting them away. Don't even try to mess it up."

Anna nods and they both laugh.

"How did I manage?" Basia returns to Anna's question. Anna will remember her like this for a long time, recall this moment over others. Basia, her hands alongside her body, her face turned to Anna, pensive, serious, just like Adam's.

"You know, I'd just look at my son. At his tiny lips, opening up to me, so totally dependent on what I would do. I've brought this baby to the world, I thought. I'm responsible. All these police vans all over the city, troops throwing canisters of tear gas, tearing our posters from the walls, painting them over. It all seemed so ludicrous, so utterly insane. I knew it couldn't last. I wanted to do something to change it."

Anna watches as Basia waves her hand in a dismissive gesture. "Nothing, really," she adds. "I'm much more confused now, with all the politics. Everybody is quarrelling. Everyone accuses everyone else of betrayal, of taking bribes. It frightens me to listen to the kind of Poland some of our own friends want now. You know, Poland for Poles only, for Catholics... Sometimes our old enemies make more sense than they do. I don't even know who I support."

They sit down on the rickety stools in the kitchen. Basia has poured some mineral water into small glasses.

"What are you going to do, now?" she asks Anna. "Will you stay with us for a while?"

Anna takes a sip of water, the tiny bubbles rising to the surface, exploding into mist. She shakes her head.

"I'll be all right," she says and manages a reassuring smile. It is not a lie.

Shrieks of laughter reach them from the living room, Adam is having a good time. Anna would like to sit like this for a little while longer. Basia must feel the same, for she makes no effort to stand up and leave the kitchen. It's Yan who finds them there, silent and content.

When Yan and Basia leave, taking Adam with them — Adam who reminds Anna of their promised trip in the morning — it is hard to fill the emptiness that is left. *Mama* sighs and goes to the kitchen to put the plates away. *Tata* gathers the cards he took out of the desk drawer to show Adam some tricks. As in Anna's childhood, they ended up playing her once-favourite game, scattering cards on the table, building a house on them and trying to remove the cards from the base without making the house collapse. She was always too impatient with it, pulled too hard, too fast. Her father remembers that, too.

"You always wanted to play it," he says. "Every evening."

"I know" Anna says, smiling at the memory. The cards are now in their separate boxes, and Anna puts them where they've always been, in the second drawer of her father's desk.

"But you didn't like to lose. You'd cry for the whole evening, if you did. You'd bite your lip and cry," her father says, gently. "So I always tried to let you win."

Mama comes into the room, quietly, and listens. The whites of her eyes are bloodshot from exertion. She can't have been getting enough sleep.

"How is your friend?" she asks about Marie.

"Fine," Anna says. "She sends her greetings. Still remembers her visit here. During martial law."

Her mother nods her head. She liked Marie's warm enthusiasm, her compassion. She recalls how Anna's friend sat right here, on the red sofa, clenching her fists. There was a store she saw that afternoon, a store full of nothing but sugar at the time when their ration cards allowed them a kilogram per month. She thought it cruel, blatantly cruel.

"But for us it seemed normal," *Mama* says, and then, adds her old, well-tried explanation. "*Takie były czasy.* "Such were the times."

At night, even with the door to her room closed, Anna can still hear the once-familiar noises. *Swish* goes the water, flowing down the pipes from the apartment upstairs. The boards squeak, the refrigerator in the kitchen switches on and off. Distant trains go by, and at times Anna can hear the echo of the announcements from the speakers at Central Station.

She hears whispers in the kitchen, louder now for her parents are hard of hearing. She hears Piotr's name mentioned, and then William's. She cannot make more out of it, just the grave tone, the murmurs, the concern. The room is chilly. The thick solid German walls take long to warm up.

When she was little, she lay in this room listening to *Mama's* steps, her hushed voice. "Sh . . . you will wake up the children," and the low whispers that followed. What were they talking about, she wondered. Another war? *Babcia* lived through two world wars, *Mama* through one, why would Anna think she might be spared?

She assessed her chances of survival. Wardrobes were treacherous, she thought. Bottom boards could squeak and reveal her presence. Dogs could sniff her out. The walls of the pantry could crumble, and suffocating smoke would find its way through the layers of goose down covers. She remembers knowing that her mother was the only person in the whole world who could save her at a time like that. Her mother's strength was her only chance.

Only with William beside her, her hand in his, could she laugh at such an addiction to catastrophe, such persistent expectations of the worst. To him only could she speak mockingly of Eastern-European fatalism, perennial pessimism, this Slavic melancholy of the soul that has touched her forever, made her fearful of the future, doubtful, suspicious of good fortune. He would laugh, and she, the traitor, would laugh with him.

In the photographs of Breslau that Anna has found in Ursula's letters the towers of the Cathedral on the Oder Island have metal roofs on them. Shop signs display the names of their German owners, Eduard Littauer, Gerson Fränkel, Brothers Barasch.

In one of the photographs, an SA parade marches along Schweidnitzer Strasse. The street is packed with people, cheering, saluting the men on horseback and the marching troops. Anna would like to look at their faces, but they are too small. All she can see are outstretched hands. William's mother, Käthe, could be standing there, waving to the men. Houses are covered with bunting, adorned with swastikas and wreaths. On the other side of the photograph Ursula has scribbled: *Did you know that there are mazes of underground tunnels underneath your Breslau, some still flooded by water? Who knows what's still buried there! The pot of diamonds Göring's servant carried behind the Field Marshal, lest he had a sudden urge to dip his fingers in the stones?*

In the next days, when she walks along Wroclaw's streets, Anna carries these pictures with her, noting the changes. The convex art nouveau windows have been replaced by flat panes of glass, the spires of St. Mary Magdalene's church have gone. In the antique stores of the Old Town, German artifacts still dominate the shelves, fill the insides of curio cabinets in Biedermeier style. Miniatures of Prussian officers with reddish beards and sideburns, buttons sparkling on their uniforms, pale glass lamps, oak coffee mills with wrought iron handles. Meissen china plates and cups, calfskin gloves, velour top hats, cigarette cases. "No export," a note pinned to the red velvet cloth reminds buyers that no object produced before 1945 can be taken out of the country. *To protect national heritage.* The note is translated into German and English.

"Käthe never speaks about Breslau," she tells her brother who meets her one afternoon for coffee. "I've tried to ask her about life here, but she won't say anything. Must be too hard for her."

Her brother shrugs his shoulders and downs his espresso. There is a hint of impatience in their conversations these days, and it is growing. She has ordered a bottle of mineral water with her coffee, and she sips it slowly. "Whatever . . ." he says and looks away. Stories of Breslau do not interest him. He thinks that maybe Canada or William's influence has made Anna too soft, too accepting, that she is forgetting the facts, the evidence of the past. "German skinheads with chains on their fists are waiting for our tourists," he likes to remind her. "Right across the border. So don't get carried away." He has already chastised her for noticing the shabbiness of the streets, uncut lawns, uneven pavements. Mocked her sensitivity, which he considers newly-found, a frill.

"People could at least wash the windows and cut the grass," she has defended herself, pointing to a withering rosebush fighting for space among tall weeds. "Or is this also the Communists' fault?"

"I'd rather have this than police raids on uncut lawns, like they had in East Germany when the neighbours snitched," he has said. "Face it, Anna. A Pole will never run around with a mop. Life is too short."

He could have also told her that in Russia it would be even worse, and she wonders which answer would annoy her more. She has promised herself not to judge, but she has already broken her promise.

Dearest William, Stalingrad, of course, is now called Volgograd. I was allowed to walk around, to visit what the military maps indicated as "Höhe 102," the sight of the fiercest of battles. At the hotel I was told that in the spring of 1943, as the winter receded, the hill was pink from the blood of the dead. The people were friendly and helpful, even though they knew I was German. The roads are still muddy, and the fields are covered with sun-bleached bones, hundreds, thousands, tens of thousands, scattered for as far as I could see. Your father, if he is here, is just one of these skeletons. The contours of the trenches and dirt bunkers are still visible in the parched earth. I took pictures of the heaps of bones, arms, legs, pelvic bones or ribs, jaws with teeth. Skeletons with identity tags still attached, lying next to a rusted machine gun. A pair of hobnailed boots, still standing upright, even in decay.

A young Russian man, Boris, quite wonderful, with ruddy cheeks and short, blond hair was my guide. Thanks to his

*ingenuity and a bottle of Johnny Walker, red label, we had an old
jeep to travel through the fields. You would've liked Boris. Short,
rugged looking, in black rubber boots, a soft smile on his lips. He
pocketed a carton of cigarettes, a roll of American dollars, and a
bottle of whisky with style! When I placed the flowers on the
Mamai Mound, Boris unscrewed a bottle of Stolichnaya, and we
drank straight from the bottle. He told me about a farmer he
knows who still has a sack full of German skulls in his barn, and
about how he, Boris, played in the bone fields when he was a boy.*

*Thanks to Glasnost, there will be burials. The Organisation
for the Care of German War Graves will bury the bones and
restore the cemeteries that the Sixth Army used until the final
defeat. In the first months of the battle, the graves were still
marked with an iron cross and a soldier's helmet, but by now they
have all vanished and will have to be searched for and uncovered.
Boris told me that one such site has become a garbage dump and
a landfill, another a patchwork of garden plots where the local
citizens have erected wooden shacks and lattice fences.*

*It is the grave robbers, now, who come here. It's good
business. An identity tag brings five to ten dollars, an Iron Cross
fifty dollars, a Ritterkreuz as much as a hundred. Even a rusted
helmet will fetch twenty dollars, which is more than a worker
here can earn in two weeks. Before I left, I shelled out more
American cigarettes for Boris. Boris gave me the buttons from the
army coats, for me and for you. I refused to touch the Iron Cross
and the daggers, but the buttons we can keep, nicht wahr? Ursula*

"I'd like to see Käthe's old house," Anna says. It is so much easier
to think of William here, a little boy, so far away in the past.
Gretchen, his nanny, a thick, greying braid wound around her
head like a crown, pouring hot water into a washbasin, laughing
and tickling him. *Bei Mir Bist Du Schön.* . . he remembered her
singing, under her breath, her throaty voice lulling him to sleep.
Or *Bel ami, bel ami, bel ami.*

Gretchen had treasures, wonderful things he was allowed
to see. Postcards on which little kittens played with balls of
wool. Handkerchiefs with tiny pink and blue flowers in the

corners. Things she brought from places far far away, from village fairs around Breslau where clowns did somersaults, doves flew out of top hats, balls appeared and disappeared in pockets, sleeves, and boxes that, only a moment ago, were empty. Where Gretchen saw a monster woman with a black moustache, and a long white beard.

William's *Oma* always had maids, country girls from around Breslau who arrived by cart, with a basket covered by chequered cloth, smelling of buttermilk. Frieda, Helga, Elsa. William liked their cheerful whistling. They washed the floor on their knees, until the skin of their legs became red and the shape of the floorboards left deep white tracks in it. They laughed when they saw him, and their buttocks swayed as they moved backwards on their knees, like giant crabs, wet floor in front of them shining in the sun.

His *Oma* he recalled had boxes filled with hats. The hats came from Schurz. Some of the hats made her look stern and mysterious. In others she looked distant and very elegant, like an old queen.

He also remembered his mother's fox collar, smelling of perfume, a faint fragrance of jasmine petals. The same smell that lingered inside the wardrobe, among his mother's furs, among her dresses and coats. Before she left the house Käthe wound the fox around her neck, its limp paws with their black claws hanging loose, the fox's mouth snapping at its tail, to hold it in place. The mouth had a spring hidden inside and he liked to play with it, snapping at the maids, pretending the fox was alive.

The maids, he recalled, always talked of the premonition of some end, of something terrible lurking in the dark, waiting to destroy them all. There were signs, they said, whispering among themselves. Bad signs. In Gross Wilkau a calf was born with two heads, foxes were no longer afraid of humans and killed the chickens in broad daylight. Frieda dreamed of fires and floods and teeth falling out. But then they remembered how bad things were, before Hitler. "Riots," he had heard, "red menace, havoc." Men in crumpled suits standing on street corners, giving them evil looks, shouting after them, asking how they liked emptying the chamber pots of the rich. Long, loud whistles, invading eardrums, making the membranes rattle.

Besser ein Ende mit Schrecken als ein Schrecken ohne Ende. Better an end with terror than terror without end.

There was a poem he learned, then, from the neighbour's children. So insidious that he couldn't stop chanting it for days. Käthe scolded him all the time, then, but never said it was the poem she minded. His voice, she said, was a problem. It went right through her skull. Gave her headaches. She would complain that he couldn't sit still, ran up and down the stairs, fidgeted at the table, spilled his drinks.

In the poem a spider caught a fly, a sparrow caught a spider, a hawk caught the sparrow, and the chain went on until, at the end of it, a hunter caught a wolf. William could still remember the refrain:

> *'Please' begged the victim, 'let me go,*
> *For I am such a little foe.'*
> *'No,' said the victor, 'not at all,*
> *For I am big and you are small!'*

"Do you still think we have come from the same place?" she asked him then. He laughed, admitting defeat. No, of course not. Her Wrocław had little to do with his Breslau.

The house is a short tram ride away, in Karlowice, but Yan insists on driving her there. Anna doesn't know her brother that well anymore, but she can still guess what he must be thinking. This, at least, is a concrete request he can understand, better than these constant comments she makes about how the buildings around them have been modified or transformed. He scowls when she takes out these German photographs to show him the missing globe and the *fin-de-siecle* windows that once decorated the department store of the Barasch Brothers, Breslau's pride. The building still houses a department store, Phoenix; it is shabby inside, with makeshift shelves and crowded, haphazard displays. Right before she left for Canada, Anna lined up there for four hours, at the butcher's. When she reached the counter she could only buy half a kilogram of fat beef with crushed pieces of bone sticking to it. She was close to tears when she left the store, clutching the bleeding brown paper package, holding it away from her not to stain her clothes.

"Put them away," her brother says, pointing to the photographs in her hand. There is an embarrassed smile on his face, the one she has seen many times already. He smiles like that whenever she makes what he considers unreasonable or outlandish demands, like refusing to put an unwrapped loaf of bread into the wire basket in a grocery store, or looking for tongs to pick up rolls for supper. She puts the photographs away wondering if her interest in German Breslau is unreasonable or merely outlandish to him.

As they drive, Yan is pointing to street vendors, to streetcars covered with colourful ads, to a new restaurant that has just opened. "Just give us a few years, and you won't recognise the place," he says. Anna is thinking of Adam's smiling eyes as he ate his pizza, flat and thin but smothered with mushrooms and melted cheese. In his clear, chime-like voice he warned her not to break her leg on the potholes in the pavement.

"So when did they run away?" Yan asks about Käthe and William. Underneath the bridge they drive along, the Oder river is slow and muddy.

"January 1945," she says. "When Karl Hanke ordered all women and children to leave."

She would like to tell him more, but Yan changes the subject. He is thinking of opening his own law office, going private. It's impossible to survive on the salary he is making. Adam is growing up; he deserves a better life.

"What do you think?" he asks her, and Anna says it is a great idea.

Karłowice, *Karlovitz*, Anna almost says but stops herself just in time, is a quiet district that escaped the siege of Breslau largely unscathed. Yan parks the car and they walk along the street, past thick, overgrown gardens, in which houses hide behind tall chestnuts and acacias, behind junipers and boxwood hedges. All

Anna can see from the street are tiny towers with metal flags, tiled turrets, white and black triangles of half-timbered walls, the steep red roofs with half circles of windows. The villas are surrounded by wrought iron fences, overgrown with vines.

She is armed with the name of the street and a few photographs she has found among William's things. Three maids in the dining room, holding big Meissen platters. Standing by a long table set with porcelain and family silver, their blouses buttoned up, white aprons starched, stiff, and immaculate. On these platters, William said, were his grandfather's favourite dishes. Veal with mashed potatoes and cauliflower in brown butter, roasted geese stuffed with dried fruit, bowls of sauerkraut and *Eisbein, Wiener Schnitzels*, and vanilla pudding for dessert. Käthe, in front of the house, wearing a long dark coat, a fox collar around her neck. In another picture she is holding William's hand, bending over him, as if listening to a secret. Yan glances at the photographs and hands them back to her without a word.

Anna is trying to remember all William has ever told her about this house. Frau Knorr with her sweet smile and her daughters, Moni and Bibi. Little Jutta with her freckles and reddish locks, playing hopscotch on the pavement. "My first love," he said, recalling polka dot dresses, and heavy coats with a herringbone pattern. Maids tied kerchiefs at the top of their heads to keep the dust out of their hair as they beat the carpets, rising clouds of grey particles that drifted with the wind. Most of all, he said, he remembered his mother's face, always tense, impatient with him, and her angry voice, "Willi! Williiiiiii! Stop it. Stop it at once!"

That's what has always happened, Anna thinks. He started telling her about Breslau, but the story always swerved and returned to his mother, to the old stubborn feelings of being watched, judged, and found wanting.

Anna is first to spot the house on Gerhart Hauptmann Weg, now Maria Konopnicka Street — a German writer giving way to a Polish one. It is a corner house, covered with ivy, with a wrought iron fence, grey columns and a narrow path that leads to the front door.

William remembered a stained glass picture hanging against

the windowpane, with a country girl climbing a rock, high in the mountains, her right hand reaching into an eagle's nest. The glass frame was made of red, yellow and aquamarine squares, and when the sun shone the glass glittered. But of course it's no longer there. Whoever walked into this house in 1945 must have found Käthe's books, clothes, photographs, preserves in the cellar, the mahogany box with William's toys. Perhaps some of these things are still here, Anna thinks, perhaps all she has to do is to be let in and she will see the carved furniture, the bookcases. Maybe even old pictures are here, hidden in the attic where the new owners have put them, thinking that maybe other people's memories should be spared. She has heard things like that happen. Refugees from the East, driven from their homes by Stalin, were not as hostile to the Silesian Germans as the Poles from Central Poland. They were known to preserve old family keepsakes and return them when asked.

The front door of the house opens and a woman appears. She is in her late thirties, wearing a tight pink dress and white clogs. She must have seen them through the window and now she is curious, wants to establish her presence. Anna feels her gaze, not unfriendly, she thinks, but cautious and she remembers the first West German cars of her childhood, slowly coming to a stop on their street. They followed these visitors like shadows, guiltily accepting handfuls of chewing gum and candy, hiding the sweet treasures from their parents. One man Anna remembers particularly well, because of the shining gold of his glasses and his bluish grey suit. He was invited inside by *Pani* Walczakowa, offered coffee and a slice of plum cake. Later she heard *Pani* Walczakowa describe how the German asked to be left alone in one of the rooms, and through the keyhole they all watched him sit there without moving.

"Why don't you ask her to let us in?" Yan says, curious, wondering what will happen. "Maybe she won't mind." The woman waits, motionless, watching them. When Anna gathers her courage, the woman does not seem at all surprised at her story. "Your husband was born in this house?" she repeats, nodding. "Moved all the way to Canada?" She seems impressed by these words. "Come in," she says. "Please. Come in."

"I'm Magda Olejniczak," she says. Her hand is soft and limp.

"Anna Herzman," Anna says, and smiles with gratitude.

Inside, Magda points to a few pieces of furniture that, she says, have been here for as long as she remembers. "This side table," she says, "and the grandfather clock." She doesn't know if they were here in 1945, as she is not the first owner of the house. In fact it is her parents' house and soon they might be forced to sell it. Taxes are rising and jobs are no longer secure, she says. Her father had a good, steady job, she doesn't say where, but now he is threatened with cutbacks. Also some people don't like the fact that he didn't join Solidarity from the start. As if he did something wrong, she says, by being cautious.

"Does your husband speak Polish?" she asks, looking at Yan who stands in the door, hesitating.

"Oh, no," Anna says. "This is my brother. My husband died. In January."

"I'm so sorry," Magda says, embarrassed by her mistake. "But I thought . . . I am sorry. I didn't mean . . . "

"That's all right," Anna says.

The rooms have been painted many times over, and are now the colour of green peas. The pictures on the wall are cheap reproductions of Polish paintings, a young peasant woman stretched on a meadow, an old peasant and a young boy watching a pair of flying storks.

Anna asks if there is anything else left that could have belonged to Käthe's family.

"No," Magda says, there is nothing in the attic. There used to be some clothes she remembers, coats with fur trim, boxes with hats, but moths got into them and her mother had to throw them away. She remembers the clothes because when she was little she used to dress up in them, pretend she was a lady.

Anna takes out a photograph of Käthe and William and shows it to Magda who examines it. The evergreens around the house, she says, are so small. The giant fir in front is no larger than a Christmas tree.

In the backyard, underneath the hazel bush the breadbox with family silver may still be buried. Käthe's mother hid it there before leaving for Berlin, but it was William who told her about it, not Käthe.

"Would you like to see the bedrooms upstairs?"

"No," Anna says. "Thank you so very much." She is beginning to feel uneasy, as if assuming a role she is not entitled to. It's not her home, after all; these are not her memories. "But I would like to see your garden," she asks. "I love gardening," she adds as if to explain her wish. "Your hostas look gorgeous from here."

Magda is pleased. "I'm sorry there isn't that much for you here," she says and suggests that maybe Anna would like to take pictures of the house. Anna nods.

"Go ahead," Yan says, accepting Magda's offer of tea and home-made cake. As she is closing the back door behind her, Anna hears their muffled laughter at the confusion of the first moments. "Come on, do I really look German?" her brother asks.

In the garden the hostas look resplendent, next to big, bushy ferns. They must like the shade of the trees and the acidity of the soil from the needles of the big fir. The hazel bush has been pruned with care. For a split second Anna considers asking Magda if they had found the silver, but it is only a split second. What if it is still there? What if they dig it out now? She doesn't want to put this hospitality to the test of who owns what. She is sure Käthe would not want it. It's better to let things lie buried in the ground.

When she comes back into the house Magda and her brother talk about computers. That might just be a salvation, Magda says. She has been to Taiwan a few times already. Mostly she brought back clothes, but there is more money in electronics. She has managed to sell a few PCs, but what she needs is a store and service. She would have run a business out of here, God knows there is enough space, but it's too far from the downtown.

Anna is asked to join them, for a cup of tea and a slice of plum cake. She is asked which computers are the best in Canada, but her answer — hesitant and cautious, explaining that it depends so much on the individual needs and preferences — is clearly a letdown.

"We can sell the best here, too," Magda says, "Not only hand-me-downs."

Her brother nods. "All sorts of people with money," he says. "Big money."

"You should consider investing here," Magda says. "It's the time, now. Tomorrow may be too late!"

Anna hands Magda a box with maple syrup candy, one of the Canadian gifts she has brought for such encounters.

"We must be on our way," she says. "Thank you so very much for your hospitality."

"That's all right," Magda smiles. "My pleasure. All the way from Canada," she says, still amazed at the turn this day took.

The next morning Anna wakes up late, unwilling to get out of bed, to leave its softness and warmth. As in her childhood, the windows in the room are covered with white lace curtains, freshly starched and ironed. She lies staring at the ceiling, at the plaster ornaments, broken where the cord of the electric lights was added. The wiring was a later addition in this building, and so was the sewage system. Pipes and wires run over the walls. The Germans used to hide them under the wallpaper, her father said, but you can't do that with paint.

She gets out of bed and walks around the room. The floorboards have layers of paint on them, lighter patches show through reddish brown and there is a pattern to their creaks and squeaks, revealing the spots where the nails have loosened. How little has changed, she thinks.

Her parents are up. From another room she can hear her father coughing, a long recurring bout, and her mother's voice telling him to swallow something. "Just take it. For once don't argue with me."

A white shoebox, filled with papers is lying on the table. "Piotr brought it here, after they let him out of the internment camp," her mother said. "He told me he didn't know how he could return this to you."

Piotr brought most of the things that belonged to her here right after the day she called to tell him about William. They are still unpacked, a whole stack of cardboard boxes in her mother's room. Anna will have to go over them in the next few days, get rid of what she doesn't want to keep.

In the shoebox she opens now, lie the smaller, more personal things. Her old notebooks, an autograph book with a mountaineer's head carved on the black, wooden cover, and her letters to him. All of them. The oldest letters are those she used to leave for him at the dorm, and letters from Canada, from the first weeks, when she still didn't know what she would do. These she opens eagerly to read her own words — pleas, it turns out, for Piotr to come to Montreal. *Only now, I see how life could be like,* she wrote then. *Without the daily humiliations we have to go through. You would have no problems finding a job here or in English Canada. I have made many friends already who would like to help.* She is surprised that she was so open in her letters, and so desperate.

I'm afraid, she reads in another letter, *I'm afraid of having to go back, of blaming you for the hopelessness of our lives. I don't want the world to close for me. I know I will only grow bitter with each day spent on these little meaningless victories we have learnt to expect from life, a pair of shoes, a bar of soap. I can't return to life led to a script written by others, always by others, never by ourselves. How can I ever discover who I might become? How could I ever know who I am?*

What did Piotr think when he read it? These incomprehensible, *American* questions? Did he think her spoilt, callous, ridiculous with these newly discovered needs?

Among her old letters she spots a Montreal postcard with a view of St. Joseph's Oratory. On the other side there are two lines of a poem she quoted for Piotr in her own defence: *We don't have history/ We have moments of wasted life,* and a short line she has added underneath: *Maybe because of that past we have hardened our hearts so much, and now we have forgotten how important it is to forgive.*

She wrote the postcard in October of 1981, already thinking of William, already in love. She remembers letting the postcard slide into a red mailbox on Peel Street and then rushing to the small corner bistro across from McGill. William was waiting for her in his tweed jacket and black turtleneck, bent over something she couldn't see.

What else is there in the box? A few photographs of the two of them, together, smiling, locked in an embrace. They both looked so young then, faces smooth, laughing, hands twined. A tiny *samizdat* imprint of Parisian emigré magazine *Kultura*, ideal for smuggling into the country. March 1981: Elena Bonner talks about her dissident husband, Andrei Sacharov, and his life in Gorky where no one but her is allowed to visit him.

The phone rings in the hall. Her mother picks it up, listens for some time and then calls her name. "It's for you," she says and closes the kitchen door.

"Piotr Nowicki," Anna hears in the black receiver, as if she could have forgotten his name.

"It's me," she answers. "Anna." She waits. She doesn't ask him how he is. She doesn't think it appropriate.

"I can see you today," Piotr says. He sounds calm, almost businesslike. "This afternoon."

"Can you hold?" she asks and takes a deep breath, covering the mouth of the receiver. She doesn't want him to hear the uneasiness of her voice. She clears her throat.

"Sorry about that," she says. He doesn't say anything.

She could meet him in a downtown café, on the second floor of *Dwór Wazów*, right near the Town Hall. They could talk there, if that's all right.

"That's fine," he says. His voice is not how she remembers it. But then, maybe she doesn't remember it at all — not anymore.

"At two, then." He puts the receiver down so fast that she hears the click right in her ear.

The truth is that she doesn't quite know how she feels about him. There were times, right after his arrest, when she tormented herself with guilt. Each night, before falling asleep, she prayed for him, negotiated feeble but elaborate deals with fate in which good things would happen to him and erase the memory of her betrayal.

Her hand shakes when she puts on her makeup. The line she draws along her eyelids is too thick, smudgy. She has to wipe if off and start again. In the bathroom mirror her face looks frightened and compliant, and she doesn't like it.

Anna notices Piotr at once, his blond curls, as thick as she remembers. He is sitting with his legs slightly apart, at a low marble table, staring at the floor. She watches when he raises his head and snaps his fingers in the air, summoning a waitress who arrives promptly. He says something to her and turns around to see who is coming in through the door. He looks strikingly handsome in an old-fashioned way — a black woollen jacket, scarf around his neck. Anna watches as he turns around, slowly looking over the faces of the passing women, discounting them one by one.

She has lived without him for so long that sometimes he hasn't seemed altogether real. In Montreal, with William, she began to doubt that she had ever even loved him. It was easier to think of Piotr as part of her that she had outgrown. Now, when he is so close, she has to admit it was a cheap trick. Of course she had loved him once, of course he mattered. He still does.

He cannot see her; she is standing behind the enormous flower arrangement in the window, a high cupola of pale daisies with pink centres, which she, at first, believes artificial. She can't stop herself from touching the pale petals. She lets his eyes wander away from the door and only then walks in. When he looks in her direction again, she waves her hand.

Piotr nods, but doesn't smile. He stands up to greet her, and they shake hands. His hand is strong and dry, hers trembling and cold. He likes that, she can tell from a slight twist of his lips.

"So what, finally, brings you back to this part of the world?" he asks.

"My husband died," she says, and his eyes narrow at the word "husband."

Ten years have passed. Piotr is sitting in front of her, with the signature of another woman written all over him — in his choice of tie, the cut of his jacket. His face is still smooth, but pale. His hands are manicured, cared for, she remarks. A thought, a desire comes over her, to put her hand on his, to feel the warmth of his skin, the soft cushion of hair on his hand.

She says she is back to see the end of Communism.

"I see," he says. "Quite a pilgrimage." His eyes wander away from her, and he leans backward in his chair. It occurs to her that if she had known of Ursula's existence ten years ago, she might have gone back to Poland — to Piotr. This, then, would be her other life.

"You look happy," she says.

He looks at her as if checking that he has heard her right. "Do I?" he answers, his brows raised. So this, too, is the wrong thing to say. She lets it go.

The marble table is cold, and Anna crosses her arms to avoid touching it. In the back of the café, two young women in long black dresses are playing Tchaikovsky on violin and cello. William would have said something about the soulful quality of their bowing, or the accuracy of their intonation. How she loved watching his face when he listened to music, waiting for the moment when his mouth moved from a distant smile to a twitch. It never came quite at the places she expected.

The waitress asks what they would like.

"A glass of red wine," Anna says. Oh, but she will have to choose, the waitress says and brings her a wine list. French, Italian, Spanish or Californian? *Beaujolais Nouveau is here*, a small card on the table informs her.

"Californian," she says.

Piotr orders a beer. *Żywiec.* Polish.

She recalls that Piotr didn't say anything when she mentioned William's death. Not even a token, "I'm sorry to hear that." He is not sorry.

She asks him about his father's Kraków practice, about his mother's health. He takes after her; his mother is still fiercely proud, impetuous, prone to anger, and ready to laugh. In one of the family stories, a party hack told her not to talk to him as if he were her father's lackey. "Then don't behave like one," she shot in his face.

She was lucky. It was the time when people disappeared for lesser reasons. The story was repeated all over Kraków, in hushed, delighted whispers. What saved her from revenge was an event of monumental proportion; the death of Comrade Stalin and the fearful chaos that ensued.

Kraków will have to be restored, Piotr says, after forty-five years of Communism. This vicious, premeditated destruction of Poland. The steelworks of Nowa Huta, the Communist challenge to the bourgeois Kraków, will have to go, he says. The pollution washes away the faces on the monuments, raises the rates of cancer. Anna is not sure where the anger in his voice is directed. Communism? Her?

The waitress arrives with a tray and their drinks. Anna leans back, and sips her wine. "Julio Gallo," the waitress informs her with pride.

"It's fine," Anna says. "Thank you." The wine is slightly sour, but she sips it with pleasure. It gives her something to do. Piotr pours his beer, slowly, into a tall glass and watches the foam rise. His eyes are focussed on the beer glass. She remembers kissing his eyelids, sometime in the distant past, on a sun-baked meadow, on drying moss. A blade of grass in her mouth, she was leaning over him. His fingers brushed her skin when he took the grass away from her lips.

"Do you still hike?" she asks.

"When I have the time," he says and frowns.

Piotr glances at his watch, but Anna can sense he is not really in a hurry. He has assigned this afternoon for her, with his wife's approval. Hanka is probably watching their daughter play, building a tall tower from her Lego blocks or dressing her Barbie in pink jump suits. There is an aura of smoke around him, but he hasn't made any attempts to light a cigarette. He must have thought through his every move, decided what Anna is entitled to, what she should be refused. When she asks to see a photograph of little Wanda, he shows it to her, quickly: a cascade of blond hair, a smiling, mischievous face, on the verge of laughter.

Wanda! Even his daughter's name stings her, the name of a Polish princess who preferred death to marrying a German prince. First made him promise not to seek revenge on her people and then threw herself into the Vistula river. "Follow me, if you wish," she said. A mound to her memory has been raised outside Kraków, high enough to be visible from every part of the city.

"You don't have children?" This sounds like a question, but Piotr knows the answer already. He has been hearing stories, too. Julia, of course, doesn't count. She is William's daughter, not hers.

"Look," she says. "I have no claims. I'll sign whatever you want." That's why she is here, isn't she? To dismiss all obligations. To move on.

"You can't. You own half of the apartment."

"I don't want it."

"How about your parents, your brother?" he asks.

"Silly," she thinks. "Of course." Nothing here is just hers alone. Her parents helped them quite generously with it, and her brother is living there now. She has no right to give up what has been theirs, too.

"So what do you want me to do?" she asks.

She will have to get a lawyer, give the power of attorney to someone she can trust. He wants to do it right. She can buy the apartment off, if she wants. He doesn't mind. It will have to be renovated soon. The old piping is giving way. Communist piping, he says. Communist paint. Communist wooden doors that are now warping and cracking.

"All right," Anna says. She will buy it, for her brother, for Adam. She will pay whatever price he asks. It doesn't matter.

Piotr gives her his business card, from the Ministry of Environmental Protection. *Advisor*, she reads. Polish on the one side, English on the other. His home address is there, too, in the left corner. Pilczyce, a wealthy suburb of white villas with red tile roofs.

"Another glass of wine, Madam?" the waitress asks.

"Yes," Anna says, "Yes, please."

Piotr says that he took Hanka to Bodensee for the holidays. Hanka and little Wanda, who has just turned three. Anna tries to imagine him there, in Lindau, perhaps, with its ridiculous Rapunzel Tower that Wanda would have liked. She remembers her own disappointment. After Canadian lakes, Lake Constance seemed to her tame and manicured. William agreed. They were merely passing it, on the way to the Alps.

Piotr tells her that he now lives in a house with a big garden where Hanka grows flowers.

"Violets are in bloom now." he says, "But the crocuses are all gone."

"So you are happy" she says. "Everything turned out all right."

The struggle is over, she is trying to tell him. *You've done it, Piotr, you have won your revolution. It is a different time now, a time to understand, a time to reconsider. Perhaps even forgive.*

"My, how you've changed," he says. On his lips, this is an accusation — as if only remaining constant mattered. Would she think like that if she had stayed here? Somehow this doesn't seem possible, but she may be deluding herself.

He is finishing his beer, draining the last drops. When the glass is empty, he looks at her. He has been waiting for this moment for a long time. "Everything turned out all right," her words are ringing in the air, less and less convincing with each passing second.

"What did you think?" he says, and his words are meant to hurt. "That I am still mourning your betrayal?"

"No," she says, quickly. "No. That's not what I mean. I've always hoped things would turn out fine for you."

"And if they have?" he asks with a smile she doesn't like, a grimace of a smile, a twist of the upper lip, somewhere on the edge of contempt and indifference. "Why should that make you feel any better?"

"I don't have to feel sorry for you, Piotr," she says.

He hasn't expected it. He was sure she would take it all, in silence. She can see his face change, redden. She has made him angry. He draws the air into his lungs with a hiss.

"I used to feel so guilty," Anna doesn't stop. "So guilty. I thought I should beg you for forgiveness. I knew I couldn't live here, but I could understand you. I believed that one day you would understand me. But you won't. You won't even try, Piotr. You think that because I live in the West nothing I've learned matters. Nothing."

He leans toward her. "War makes a lot of things simpler, Anna," he says. "In prison you lose quite a few illusions. Know who your real friends are. You've made your choice, so don't come here asking for forgiveness."

"I'm not asking for forgiveness, Piotr" she says. "But I thought you might understand."

It occurs to her that once she has agreed that she has betrayed him, little is still possible. Maybe she was too quick with penance, she thinks, but such offerings cannot be taken back easily. She can hear him breathe; she can hear the air pass through his nostrils. She can see the deepening frown on his forehead.

"This is the real end of the war." Piotr says. "We knocked down the Wall, and we will no longer be shoved aside. The West will have to make room for us at the table."

She is watching him as he speaks, but he avoids her eyes.

"Chernobyls were a bit harder for the West to ignore than the Gulags," he continues with a note of satisfaction. "The Iron Curtain could not stop the wind and rain."

She is still silent.

"Soon you may again find yourself on the wrong side of the tracks," he adds. "But, *hey*, you know how to switch sides, don't you. You can always come back."

She thinks: You have won, Piotr. You have been rewarded. What else do you want?

When he stands up, he takes out his wallet from his breast pocket and leaves two banknotes on the white plate, underneath the bill folded inside a white napkin.

"It's my treat," he says and then looks at her. He still needs her eyes to confirm his victory.

Anna watches him disappear behind closing doors. The waitress comes by to pick up the check and the folded bills. "Please, keep the change," Anna says. It is then that she knows she will have to see Ursula, after all.

This is her last evening at home. Yan has taken Basia and Adam back to their apartment, and he will be back in an hour to take her to the station. Alone. It's too late and too chilly for *Tata* to leave home and he would refuse to stay if *Mama* decided to go.

Adam has given her a farewell card he had made, with roses and tulips, red and yellow. *For Ciocia Ania*, it says. Anna detected the straight pencil lines he made and then erased, to make sure the letters stayed even. One of the corners of the card is bent. *Secret* it says. "Open it," Adam whispered, "Open it, *Ciociu*." When she did, she saw a tiny drawing of a space ship and *Come back soon!* written right beside it.

Her mother's skin is loose, too big for her. "It's terrible," she says, and her face takes on a look of disgust. "I've never thought that old age would be so ugly." She pulls on the flabby flesh of her arms. Her hands have grown bony and thin.

The kitchen table is cluttered with jars, bottles, ceramic containers, some empty, some filled with oily liquids Anna cannot identify. Everything in this apartment is odd, mismatched, and haphazard — rickety chairs, sofas that sink with a moan of springs, threadbare rugs. As if another cataclysm were meant to take care of it all, and there was no point in making an effort. They have lived like this for forty-five years.

One of the cupboards, Anna has discovered, is filled with glass jars, washed, stacked one on top of another. A whole cupboard full of empty jars. "What for?" she has asked. "I'll wait until they start recycling again," her mother has said. "We've never wasted anything. This is not right."

The old, broken down refrigerator, Russian "Mir" Anna remembers from childhood, stands in the kitchen next to its successor, a linen tablecloth spread on its top. Inside there are used radio batteries and aluminium cans. Her mother won't throw the batteries into the garbage. "They will leak into the ground," she says. "I know what's in them." In one of the kitchen drawers there is a flat box full of used tramway tickets, neatly arranged in rows.

"You'll soon run out of space, if you carry on like this for too long," Anna jokes, but she is uneasy about this hoarding. In Canada she has heard stories of old women collecting plastic bags and styrofoam trays.

"Not everything old is useless," her mother says. "When I'm gone, you can do whatever you want with it. You can throw it all in the garbage. Then, I won't care."

"*Mamusiu!*" Anna pleads. "Please. Don't say things like that." Her voice is quivering, sore. There is so little time left. Her father has found a dirty cup, and he takes it to the sink to wash it, glad to have something to do, something that lets him hide his face.

Anna's mother looks up. "I can still see her here, by the sink," she says. They all know whom she means. The kitchen was *Babcia's* place. That's where she would sit in the dark, after all the work was done, looking through the window at the ruins across the street. If Anna came in and switched on the light, Babcia would look at her, startled, as if Anna were a ghost.

When Anna is making her bed, folding the old quilt, fluffing up the oversized pillows, her mother knocks at the door. She looks at Anna's suitcases, packed, ready and sits at the edge of the bed.

"When shall we see you again?" she asks.

"Soon," Anna says. "It's not that far, now. A few hours on the plane."

"Yes," her mother says. "But it's not the same. You are not here anymore."

"How is he?" Anna asks. They can both hear how her father is clearing his throat, hacking up phlegm.

"I don't know," her mother says, and Anna can hear fear in her voice. "Maybe this new doctor will tell."

"If you need any help . . ." Anna has already offered to check with her Canadian doctor. Once she knows what it is, there might be drugs she could send.

"I'll let you know," her mother whispers, as if Anna's father could overhear them from the kitchen. "Before you came he told me he would like to be buried here, in Wrocław. He said he knew this land inside out. He didn't want me to take him to Warsaw. Do you think it's all right?"

"Of course it is," Anna says.

Now her mother is smoothing the folded quilt with her fingers. Then, quickly, she takes hold of Anna's hand and closes it on a coral necklace that once belonged to *Babcia*.

"I want you to have it," her mother says. "Now. Not when I'm gone."

The corals are smooth and hard, and Anna presses her fingers on the beads, murmuring her thanks. They are capable of changing colour, *Babcia* always claimed. They know your mood. They grow pale when you get sick, brighten when you get better. But, for that, one had to wear them close to the skin.

"I didn't want to hurt anyone," Anna says, sitting down beside her mother. "I *had* to stay in Canada. I couldn't return. Do you understand?"

Her mother is smiling gently, waving her hand at all these reasons, at the urgency in Anna's voice. This is not what she is here for. "No, I don't understand," she says. "But it doesn't matter, now. I miss you. Every day — I know you are not here."

She is still holding Anna's hand in hers. "Can I ask you something?" she asks.

"Yes," Anna says, "of course."

"Were you happy with William?" This is a question that she must have carried in her for a long time, for her voice is hoarse and slightly uneasy when she says it.

Surprised, Anna stays silent for a while. Her heart speeds up; she can hear blood pounding in her ears.

"You don't have to tell me if you don't want to," her mother is ready to withdraw her question, to let things go unsaid — their old, preferred way.

"I was happy," Anna says, too quickly. "We were happy."

When she begins to cry, her mother takes her in her arms, as she did many years ago. Anna feels the warmth of her hand, gently stroking her hair, but the old childhood comfort is not there.

"You are still a young woman," she hears her mother's voice. "You have to start a new life."

"*Tak, Mamusiu,*" Anna says. The childhood sealing of a promise, the hardest of them all.

PART V

BERLIN 1991

It is almost midnight and the Wrocław Central Station is badly lit, parts of it drowning in darkness. The Plexiglas ceiling over the platforms is yellowed, the colour of nicotine stains. The Berlin Lichtenberg train is waiting already.

Anna is a bit teary after the warm goodbyes, the promises to write, to come back more often, but she is also calmer. As she was leaving, her father turned his head away from her to hide his red eyes.

The train is almost empty, so Yan leaves Anna at the platform with the luggage and scouts the compartments to find one with someone in it, and, as he has stressed, someone who is not going to get off before Berlin and leave her alone, an easy target.

When he waves to her from an open window, he is three cars away. He has found a woman in her late fifties, obviously relieved to have someone in the compartment again. Three gentlemen got off in Wrocław, she says and she was afraid she would be alone. So now there will be two of them, two women travelling together. This is not the best choice, but better than being on her own.

"I'll be all right," Anna says, impatient with all this fuss.

"Your brother is right," the woman says. She is wearing a pair of black pants and a pink angora cardigan. "This is no joke. I have heard they spray sleeping gas into the compartment, and then steal all the luggage."

They have a berth to lie down and stretch their legs, the woman says. It's not too bad. She has been taking this train three times a year, for the last five years. "*Idzie wytrzymać,*" she says. It can be endured.

Before he left, Yan gave Anna a roll of newspapers and magazines to read. *My Style* again, with its glossy photographs.

"Like in the West, see," he tells her, mockingly. The magazine is the creation of General Jaruzelski's daughter who, under the martial law her father imposed, smuggled Solidarity leaflets in her father's chauffered limousine.

"That's real Poland for you," Yan says.

In the train Anna leafs through an interview with a Polish actress, photographed in her mansion outside Warsaw, with her two children, her antiques, treasures salvaged from old barns and restored to their shining selves. "My husband travels a lot," the actress confesses, "and only when he comes back the house is a home again. The children feel it; the dogs feel it. That's when we are a true family."

Anna tosses the magazine away from her. It falls on the floor, but she doesn't pick it up. She opens a newspaper, her eyes stopping on a small note in the corner. *Washington has removed Eastern Europe from its list of possible nuclear targets.* Perhaps she should have left straight for Montreal. Her mother was right; it's time to get on with her life. Time to forget.

Anna's companion clears her throat. Her feet in white nylon slippers look swollen. She stretches them on a brown blanket. Her back hurts, she says. She has been to a few doctors, but they are no good.

"One should not transplant old trees," she says, staring at the ceiling where a lamp protected by a metal grid is dimmed. She is lonely in Berlin, in her nice apartment. "My sister, all my neighbours are in Katowice. I see them only three times a year, now. Before, I saw them every day. In Germany neighbours don't want to know you."

The German route of the Polish exodus, Anna thinks, the hardest of them all. Ethnic Germans returning to their native land, often with just a few words of the *Muttersprache*, desperately searching for a translator, digging up family documents to find proof, any proof of their German origin. In the 70s and 80s even family shame — a father in the Wehrmacht, a grandfather's name on the *Volksdeutsch* list — could become the chance of a lifetime. Old certificates were sewn into underwear or folded and placed inside hollowed heels, hidden from the prying eyes of the Polish border guards.

Volkswagendeutsche, their Polish neighbours called them, but the name had an envious ring to it, a dose of bitter understanding.

"I shouldn't have listened to him," the woman sighs. "To my son," she adds for Anna's benefit.

Anna has heard of weeks spent in German camps, on squeaking beds, six to a room, filling out forms, answering questions, and then, waiting for the verdict on the sufficiency of bloodlines, on the merits of having been born in *Schlesien, Pommern, Ostpreussen, Breslau, Osterode, Katowitz*. All of it amid whispers about Neo-Nazi attacks, Molotov cocktails thrown into the barracks. *Aussiedler aus Polen* killed and wounded to celebrate Hitler's birthday, and to remind them that blood doesn't lie.

The woman on the train is telling Anna a joke she heard in Berlin. "A Norwegian, a Russian, a German, and a Pole are in a train," she begins in a flat monotone. She must have repeated the joke many times. "The Norwegian takes out a piece of smoked salmon, takes two bites, opens the window and throws out the rest. 'Don't be surprised,' he says to his companions. 'It's really good salmon. But in Norway we have too much of it.' The Russian takes out a tin of caviar, eats a few spoonfuls, and throws the rest out of the window. 'It's wonderful, but we have too much of it at home,' he says."

She takes a deep breath and gives Anna a telling look; the ending is coming and Anna would like to shrink, evaporate. "Then," another suspension of voice, a pause, a deep breath for more effect, "the German opens the window and throws the Pole out."

She looks at Anna, waiting for her reaction. Neither of them is meant to laugh, that is easy to tell. A nod of the head will suffice. A few moments of silence.

"Why did you leave?" Anna asks what is expected of her.

"Why?" the woman asks. "Why? I listened to my son. He was the first one to emigrate. Then he came to visit and kept telling me to sell everything and go to Germany. Why live like an animal, he said. Why line up for scraps of meat? You will be like a queen in Berlin. You will walk into a store, get whatever you want. Now he is too busy to see me. Work, work, work.

Everybody works. Nothing else matters." The woman gives another big sigh.

"Why are *you* going to Berlin?" she asks now. It really is an invitation to confess or to explain, but Anna stalls. She says she is only visiting.

"Family?"

"No, a friend."

"That's nice," the woman says, still hopeful that this is just the beginning of a story. She is disappointed when Anna doesn't continue. "A Polish friend?" she tries to prod her, but Anna closes her eyes and listens to the pounding of the wheels.

When Anna wakes up it is six thirty in the morning, and she is already in Berlin. Her companion has woken up, too, and she is stretching her arms. She must have forgiven Anna the disappointment of the evening for she is smiling now, asking if Anna needs any help getting to her friend's apartment. "Oh, no," Anna says, moved by the concern in the woman's voice. "I'll manage. Thank you very much." The woman nods and wishes her a good and safe journey.

Anna has made reservations in an old *Jugendstil* Hotel-Pension near the Tiergarten thinking that she would prefer the marble entrance and the cobblestone street outside over another Marriott. But whatever pleasure the curved lines of the hotel's façade give her, dissipates fast. Yes, she should have gone straight home, to Montreal, she thinks. There is still time to get a few courses to teach for September. A friend at Concordia University urged her to apply. In Wroclaw there were moments, more and more frequent, in which she could see flashes of her new life. Not much yet, an ordinary walk along St. Catherine Street, a dinner party, a drive to the Laurentians. She should go back home, to her classes, her friends. To the trunk filled with emigré stories, her hopeless, unfinished quest for the patterns of escape. No, not the patterns, she corrects herself angrily. Justifications. Redeeming insights, epiphanies of flight.

Why spoil it all now, why scratch at the closing wounds?

"You are *not* running away," she tells herself, in her hotel room with a view of a Berlin street where she could, with great ease, imagine the ruins she has seen in the countless documentaries of the final victory. Soviet tanks rolling through the ruins, a red flag with hammer and sickle perched on the Brandenburg Gate. "Not now, not from here!"

This is the last of Ursula's letters to William: *They were fools, these hard working, silent men from the Sudeten Mountains. The land was poor there, stones and barren soil, and they worked it for centuries, holding to it as they held to their German language. They were fools, for when Hitler came and promised them work and money, paradise on their stony earth, when he told them how they had been abused and neglected, they believed him. "Look at yourselves," he said. "You who have been driven from your Fatherland only to become the germ from which this nation that now tries to claim you has emerged. Without your sweat and blood nothing would grow here. Look at yourselves. You are not like Slavs and Jews! You do not belong to this small, weak country. Not you, not the Giants of the Sudetenland."*

"Your real fight," their Führer told them, "is not for some puny parliamentary rights for the German minority, these monstrous children of barren democracies. You and all Germans who live outside the Reich are now the most important part of the German nation. What I want for you is to conquer the land you live in, to rule it as you were always meant to do. Your loyalty is to your nation, not to the country you live in. Protest, demonstrate, riot. Demand to be returned to Fatherland," he kept saying. "And you will not be forgotten."

The Sudeten Germans listened. They demonstrated against Prague. They broke windows in Jewish stores and fought in the streets. They cheered when, on the Nuremburg dais, Hitler demanded their right to self-determination. And they were rewarded.

On the 29 of September 1938, at the Munich conference applauded by the deluded Europe, Sudetenland became part of the German Reich and Konrad Henlein, the leader of the Sudeten

German Party, its Gauleiter. The Giants of Sudetenland. This was the time of rewards, work and money, slave labour from the conquered lands in the East. A few years of prosperity, until the bodies of their dead started coming back from the front.

In 1945 the Czechs did not even wait for the international treaties to take their revenge. "You have to go," they said. "All of you. You started the war. Your treachery destroyed the Czechoslovak Republic. Why should we allow you to live in a country you helped to kill?"

Revolutionary Guards put on their arm bands and moved into Sudetenland to take their revenge. Well before the allied forces agreed to the expulsion of Germans from the East, "wild deportations" drove away 600,000. The death marches and pogroms that ensued were payment for the delusions of one generation. They were all Germans; they were all guilty; they had to go.

In May of 1945 the people of Sattel gathered in their church for the last mass. It was dark and they lit the candles, but no one was able to say a word. So the priest led their silent prayers and the whole congregation, head touching head, responded in their hearts, without words. A few hours later that priest was killed by the guards; he was trying to smuggle the chalice.

In Weckelsdorf, the guards ordered all Germans to go away. They did. They left their houses, their furniture, their clothes, their china, and went, only to be turned back at the border. Without proper papers, without the international treaties that would give them a place to live, no one wanted them. "Go back where you came from and wait," they were told. But when they got back to Weckelsdorf, now called Teplitz, their houses were already taken; their clothes and silver divided among those who moved in. So embarrassed the new owners were by this unexpected and unwanted return, that the Revolutionary Guard rounded the Germans up and took them away from the town, to the forest. When the guards got back into Weckelsdorf no one asked them what had happened. No one wanted to know. Only when a few months later relatives from Germany began their search, when through Red Cross they started their frantic inquiries, the mass grave in the forest was unearthed. And when the good judges from Nachod looked at the body of a small girl,

crowning the heap of corpses, her stiff hands still raised, still
pleading to be spared, they did not know what to say.

The villages of the Sudeten Germans are empty now. There is
nothing left there but broken fences. Grass is growing through the
floor boards of abandoned houses. Wood, when it is left outside,
becomes grey and brittle from the sun and rain. The graves and
the fields are overgrown with nettle, wild raspberries, and thyme.
Some of the tombstones have crumbled, but you can still make
out some names on them. Pohl, Honig, Navottny.

Anna folds the letter back, carefully. This is the day in which
she will take things easily. A walk in the Tiergarten, a long, hot
bath. She will be kind to herself, gentle. She needs all her
strength now. Ursula is waiting for her.

The lower half of the café window is covered by a white lace
curtain, suspended on a brass rod. Inside, Anna can see a
ceiling fan making its endless rounds, brass lamps on the walls,
and her own pale reflection. It is ten o'clock in the morning.
She is standing in front of the milky glass doors of the *Vamos*
café, waiting for a whiff of courage to take her in. "The waiter
will tell you where I am," Ursula's message read. "Just ask to be
seated at my table."

Anna takes a deep breath of the air still moist from the
morning rain. Walking has made her blood flow faster, but the
residue of a headache is still there, the throbbing pressure in her
forehead. At night she slept badly, waking every hour, dozing,
waking up again. She was screaming at someone in her dream
until her throat hurt. She was pushing at a grey, shapeless body
that gave way under her hands, as if she were trying to move air.

Before coming here, she went through her clothes carefully,
discarding them one by one. The jacket was too formal. The
brown sweater too loose. It angered her that she was taking so
long. "Does it really matter how you look?" she asked herself in
front of the mirror, tossing her hair back, pinning it into a bun.
All I want is to see her, she kept thinking. I know everything I
want to know. I'm not like Piotr. What has happened, happened.
I'll get over it. To Marie, when she called her from Wrocław, she

213

even said that she had forgiven William. "He loved both of us," she said. "At the same time." It sounded very simple then, but words like these don't mean much here.

"Just one look at Ursula," she thinks, "and I'll go home."

Finally, she settled for a black wraparound skirt and a salmon-pink blouse with a black embroidered pattern that added warmth to her skin. And *Babcia's* coral necklace. She let her hair loose again. It did matter, whether she wanted to admit it or not. It mattered to look her best. Now, as she is straightening her skirt, pulling on her blouse to smooth the front, she catches her own reflection in the glass window. The coral necklace coils around her neck, and she touches the smooth surface with the tip of her finger.

"Come this way, please. Frau Herrlich is waiting for you." A waiter has a thin-lipped smile. He is swarthy and well built, and he gives Anna a knowing look, as if he guessed more than he was letting on, a thought that Anna dismisses as utter nonsense. *Frau* Herrlich. A line from one of Ursula's letters flashes in Anna's mind. *I feel married to you in the most profound sense of the word.*

The woman in a red crocheted vest who steps forward to greet her has a bushy mop of greyish curls; her thin face is flushed and drawn. She is rather short, shorter than Anna, even in her high heels. In her late forties, perhaps early fifties. William's age. There is fatigue in the corner of her lips, a tiredness to her skin. Her mouth is too wide, her lipstick too dark.

"It's good you've come," she says in a raspy voice, turning away for an instant, to motion for the waiter. Her English is flawless, but Anna can detect a slight undertone of German. Right there, in the vowels that are a fraction too full, too rounded.

William, darling, you once said that only the extraordinary and the exaggerated interest me. That I have ceased to believe in ordinary human beings. Is this why you love me so much?

"So how do I measure up?" Ursula asks. The irony in her voice stings Anna, makes her take another look. There is a shadow of a smile on Ursula's face, and something else, something intriguing, something that won't be so easily dismissed. "Plain, but striking," Anna's mother would call it, and there would be, in her voice, however strained and reluctant, a layer of admiration for the force that could turn a plain face into a statement. It must be the eyes that do it, Anna thinks, hazel brown, watchful, and slightly haughty. Or the feline intensity that Ursula pours into each of her movements, the self-assured alertness of every turn.

When the waiter comes by, he says something funny, for Ursula laughs, a throaty, warm laugh. Her laughter is a challenge, an overture. The waiter gives her an admiring look. William must have loved that about her, the power to draw looks like his. Anna knows how he liked to have his desires confirmed.

Ursula asks for a coffee and a shot of vodka. "What do *you* want?" she turns to Anna, and Anna asks for a glass of red wine. It really is much too early for a drink, but she might need it. The edges of her eyelids hurt and when she blinks a thin, foggy veil appears between her and Ursula. She keeps blinking until it goes away.

When the waiter leaves them, silence is broken only by the snap of metal against metal. Ursula opens and then closes the shiny brass lock of her purse. She opens it again and this time she takes out a red packet of Dunhills. She holds a cigarette in her hand without lighting it.

The café has booths with soft upholstered seats; high panelling separates them from people sitting at other tables. The voices that reach Anna's ears are sharp, decisive. She would like to be able to understand them, but William had always discouraged her whenever she talked of learning German. "It's French you need here. Look what's happening around you."

"I still can't believe William's dead." Ursula tosses her head backwards, looks at the ceiling. Her voice cracks, softens. She is hot; she takes off the red crocheted vest and sits in her black silk blouse, fanning her neck. "You don't smoke, do you? Do you mind?" she asks, and then lights a cigarette and takes a long, hungry drag, smudging the brown filter with her lipstick.

"No," Anna says. "I don't mind."

The waiter brings a white coffee-pot and a cup on a tray, and makes room for them on the table. Vodka arrives in a short greenish glass, beside a peace of dark pumpernickel bread with butter on a small plate. Ursula drinks her vodka in one gulp and bites into the bread. This is the way men drink in Poland, Anna thinks, with a grimace — a shiver as the burning liquid goes down — followed by a smile of relief. Vodka loosens the tongues, they say. Shows your true nature. The wine Anna ordered has a rich ruby colour, and it slides down her throat with ease she is grateful for.

"I learned to drink vodka in your country," Ursula laughs. She pours cream into the coffee and stirs it fast. There is a paper doily between the cup and the saucer, and Anna watches as it slowly absorbs the drops of coffee that spill from the sides.

A Polish woman and a refugee, Willi? Isn't she another one of your atonements?

"I haven't come here to blame you."

Anna has rehearsed this sentence a hundred times until she could say it smoothly, without hesitation. This is what she decided on, back in Wrocław. Earlier, when she was still bitter, she was to say other things, "I have come to understand. I want to know why he lied to me and why you went along with his lies." But she has changed, now. Unlike Piotr, she has put *her* past behind her, and she is ready to forget.

There are freckles on Ursula's hands, light brown spots Anna stares at. She can feel the shape of the chair imprinting itself on her back as she leans backward. She has an uneasy feeling that Ursula is studying her, that with each glance of her hazel eyes she knows her twice as well as she had a minute before, that soon Anna will have nothing to hide.

She can picture them together, this woman who is sitting in front of her, her eyes reddened by strain, and William, in Berlin, Munich, London, the Alps. William in his tweed jacket with suede patches on the elbows, Ursula's hand brushing hair out of his eyes. They are laughing, drunk on stolen time, on weeks of scheming, imagining what they would say to each other when they meet, going over each precious minute. Weeks brightened by furtive phone calls, notes scribbled fast, lips pressed to pieces of paper before they were slipped into white envelopes. In the Alps Anna can imagine Ursula and William skiing, trying to overtake one another in the powdery plume of snow. Or making love in a wide pine bed, in one of the Bavarian houses with their stained wood balconies, garlands of flowers painted around windows, steep red tiled roofs. William's hand caressing Ursula's breasts, her nipple between his fingers. So long; it went on for so long. Marilyn? What was she doing then? What was she thinking? And Julia?

"Why would you want to blame me?" Ursula asks.

With all her rehearsals, Anna hasn't prepared herself for that. She doesn't quite know what to say. Ursula raises her voice slightly.

"He made his own decisions. Why would I be responsible?"

"So it didn't matter to you that he had to lie?" There is an edge to Anna's voice, now. "First to Marilyn, and then to me."

"He didn't have to lie, Anna." Ursula's fingers tap on the table when she says it. "I certainly never asked him to. He was a coward. I loved him in spite of it."

Now she is extinguishing the cigarette stub, pressing it with her thumb to the bottom of the glass ashtray.

This is another disappointment. Somewhere, however unacknowledged the desire, Anna was expecting a reward for what she considers her magnanimity. She has come here promising herself that there will be no more accusations, and now she is being diverted, led back into the apportioning of blame.

"Listen," Ursula says. "I don't want to keep hurting you. There is no point."

She bends down and takes a manila envelope from a plastic bag that was lying on the seat beside her. "This is what he left behind. I meant to mail it to you, but . . ."

Anna has seen such notebooks before. There are a few of them in William's study. Some black, some navy-blue. Imported from California. William used to buy them in the small stationery store on St. Catherine Street whose limping owner addressed him as Professor Herz*man*, accenting the second syllable, making it float. William's favourite kind for jotting down compositions, notes that mean nothing to her. She can't read music.

The notebook Ursula has brought with her is almost filled, and Anna leafs through it. There are no words in it, apart from a few titles: *Another Dimension, Lament, Sonata for Solo Violin, Foray*. Abstract, enigmatic titles William favoured. She puts the notebook back into the envelope and presses her fingers to her cheeks. The fingers are cool, soothing.

"Are you all right?" Ursula asks, leaning toward her.

"Yes," Anna says, backing away. "I'm fine, perfectly fine," but she doesn't like the sound of her own voice, the plaintive note, the quiver. In the silence that follows, she waits for the time until the heaviness of her body lifts, allowing her to take a fuller breath.

"Why can't you forgive him, Anna?"

This is really too much, Anna thinks. She doesn't have to sit here and take Ursula's fatuous comments. She doesn't need to be preached at.

"And what makes you think I haven't forgiven him?" Anna says.

It must be the abruptness of Anna's movements that gives her away, for Ursula extends her hand as if she wanted to stop Anna from leaving. "Because you haven't," she says. "That's not hard to see."

But Anna has already dug into her purse extracting the plastic bag with Ursula's letters. She is so clumsy. Her wallet and a packet of tissues fall out. She bends to pick them up from the floor.

"Here, take them," she says standing up and puts the letters on the table, next to the empty tray. "They are yours."

She puts a ten-mark note on the table to pay for the wine and rushes out of the café into the street.

"No! Wait, . . . Anna!" She can hear Ursula's voice, trailing after her. "Don't run away like that!"

Only when she is around the corner, Anna slows down and takes a deep breath. She does not go back to the hotel, but walks along the Berlin streets watching her reflection in the shop windows, transparent, ethereal, disappearing when the window ends, reappearing in another one. The walk calms her down, the cool wind soothes her cheeks. It's done, she tells herself. It's over. I can go home, now. I have seen her, and now I can go home.

Back in her hotel room she takes a long, warm shower and runs her hands over her naked body. Her skin is still smooth, still supple, and she no longer wants to be alone. She wants to be stroked, kissed. She wants to feel a man's hot tongue on her thighs, making its way up, leaving a wet trail on her skin. *A man*, she thinks, crouched in the cooling bathtub, her arms over her breasts, and the word soothes her with its vagueness.

"You are not the whole world, William," she murmurs. "You can be replaced."

When the phone rings, she does not move. The phone keeps ringing again and again until it stops at half-ring, like a choke.

Next morning, Anna is out of breath when she reaches the American Express office. The woman behind the counter is trying to help. "Tomorrow is not possible. But I can get you on the one-thirty flight on Saturday. Unless there is a cancellation. Would you like me to call you if there is?"

"Yes," Anna says. "Please."

She has already packed all her things, folded her dresses and skirts, cleared her things out of the bathroom.

"Is it an emergency? Are you all right?" The travel agent has a smudge of lipstick on her teeth, and she is truly concerned. "Do you need any help?"

"I'm fine," Anna says, suddenly embarrassed by the desperation in her voice for which she really has no reason. "No, please, I can wait a few more days. It's not a problem."

"Are you sure?"

"Yes. I'm sure."

She does leave the name and the phone number of her hotel, just in case there is a cancellation, and walks back there to change. All she needs is some loose clothes and a pair of walking shoes. In a small kiosk she buys an English language guidebook to Berlin's sights and a newspaper.

"Too fast," she thinks, forcing herself to slow down. This agitated rush is irrational, she is trying to convince herself. She can stay in Berlin for a few days. It won't change anything, for God's sake. Stop. Take a deep breath, calm down. Another one, she orders herself. The city air carries the whiff of exhaust fumes. She has read somewhere that the first smell here after the Wall came down was the stink of the cheap, leaded gas of East German *Trabbis*.

In a small, outdoor café round the corner from the hotel, Anna sits down to read the morning paper. The *International Herald Tribune* speculates on the content of the Stasi files. Only a year ago the Stasi headquarters in East Berlin were stormed by protesters and rumours abound. The secret police files are so thick that if they were all stacked up they would reach well over a hundred miles. What experts they were! How busy! The Stasi kept an eye on trash dumps and lending libraries; they tapped the booths of Catholic confessionals and monitored public toilets. For years the army of handlers, with their courses in human psychology and their Marxist-Leninist training, was spying on six million East Germans, half the adult population.

Everything was recorded, Anna reads, the size of your shoes, the smell of your underwear, invaluable in sniffing out the author of a pamphlet found in the street. In your file, if you have one, you might find the exact words you whispered to your lover, the colour of the socks you had on when you last took the garbage out. Every graffiti was photographed, every rumour or joke written down.

Soon, she reads, the files will be opened to public scrutiny. Every German citizen will be able to ask for a copy. A hard decision, the commentator writes since, from what is known already, these files contain bitter revelations. A prominent German dissident has just discovered that among a thousand people who informed on her, the most thorough and damaging were the reports of her own husband who had transcribed their daily conversations. Even the most mundane ones, about the kids, the cat, the laundry.

Marie admitted to her once how she thought life behind the Iron Curtain made people's lives richer. "At least you had bonds that didn't easily break," she said. What would she say now?

Germany will have to brace herself for such revelations, Anna reads. Fathers, sons, lovers, no one is above suspicion. All over East Germany with its scaffolding and construction cranes, wives, husbands, and lovers will have to confront each other, asking the same old question. "How could you have done it?"

"They've won the war. I've told you." An insistent whisper from another table catches her attention. A middle-aged American couple talks of the fortunes being made in construction here. The man is wearing an impeccable grey suit, the woman has shoulder-length grey hair. "Shhhh . . . ," the woman says. "Someone might hear you."

Anna folds the newspaper and takes a sip of coffee. It has grown cold and she pushes it away.

There is a note for her at the Pension. The waiter, the one with a short dark moustache, delivers it to her room, on a tray, when she is changing. He smiles at Anna as he extends his hand; she has drawn the attention of the staff and they all fuss over her as if she were not an ordinary guest. It all started with the first of Ursula's messages. With Herr Müller's bow and a telling look.

Ursula's handwriting hasn't changed; it is still hard to decipher. *I've tried to call you, but you were out. I'll come by in the afternoon. I really want to talk to you.*

Anna doesn't wait. She has transformed herself into a tourist, in beige pants and a T-shirt. She slips her guidebook into a canvas bag and leaves.

In 1991 East Berlin looks like a deserted city, its wide streets empty; the giant, pompous buildings along *Unter den Linden* seem abandoned. Grey walls are covered with graffiti: *Stasi murderers. Ausländer raus. German workplaces were taken by foreign workers.*

With the Wall gone, the subway trains criss-cross the city freely. The eastern ones are grey and shabby, with wide plastic-covered seats. The western ones arrive like rare birds, with their red exteriors and seats that are black and sleek. When she leaves the subway station, Anna rushes past the wide stretches of streets, past empty spaces awaiting construction.

She slows down at the sight of the Brandenburg Gate, with its six rows of columns and a stone chariot perched on top. This is no time to hurry. In the past when she came here from the other, Eastern side, she craned her neck for a glimpse of the West. Through the columns she saw some vast, empty space and a few blurry trees in the distance. Nowhere else was the West so close, so tantalisingly close, so very much within reach, but the Wall, crowned with coils of barbed wire, with pieces of broken glass lining its concrete edge, looked unmovable. On *her* side there was none of the jazzy graffiti, the defiant blues, reds, and yellows, no curses or signs of peace. The Wall was guarded by ramrod straight men, their hands resting on polished guns. It was a line that separated all that was ugly from all that was beautiful. On *her* side there was nothing she wanted to keep, and beyond it, everything was worth having. How she longed to cross this line! How overwhelming the thought was, how it surfaced when she would least expect it!

Frantic surges of hope and envy erupted in her every time she heard of someone who scaled the Wall or got smuggled in a car trunk. "They made it," she heard. "Escaped." There was never an official confirmation of success, but all the failed attempts to cross the border were described in the most minute details. For days, the Polish papers glowed over secrets betrayed by best friends, the slip of a hand clinging to a rope, a child's frightened whimper coming from a car trunk. Now, the graves of those who tried and failed are covered with fresh flowers. *Murdered by the Guards,* the inscriptions say.

Anna wishes she were here when the Wall fell, hacking the concrete to pieces and then rolling these pieces in her hands, releasing even the smallest of pebbles inside. Instead she saw it on television, the jubilant crowds, the tears and flowers. "Quick," she called to William, "Hurry up," and they stood in the living room, leaning over the screen, to see better. He took her hand in his, and handed her a Kleenex for she was crying from joy, tears gathering against the rims of her glasses. It was William who drew her attention to the cello player, his chair propped against the Wall, his eyes closed, the hand holding the bow raising and falling gently, like a crest of a wave.

Ursula was here, then. *I know that it won't last, this jubilation,*
she wrote to William, in the letter that Anna remembers only too
well. *I know that we will soon get tired and cynical about it, shrug
our shoulders and ask each other if this, indeed, was such a big deal.
That we will throw our hands up in despair at the people from
there, in their jean shirts, jackets, caps, people from these dark,
shabby, lethargic lands. But tonight there is dancing on the rubble,
there are tears. No one is talking about the bills that will start
coming in. What will we unearth now? What new stories of greed,
deception, and blind obedience?*

The stories keep flowing. Berlin is getting ready for the
trials of the guards who shot at the last two escapees from
East Germany; one of them, Chris Gueffroy, newspaper
headlines remind, was the last man killed at the Wall. *They
say they were following orders,* Anna has read in the
International Herald Tribune, in the chilling echo of the
Nuremberg trials.

Among the pictures that Ursula had sent William there was
a whole package of the shots of the Wall. *These I have taken
specially for you,* she scribbled on the back of one of the pictures.
*The grass on the Death Strip is no longer pristine! Weeds and
rubble have overrun it, as they have taken over the marble steps of
the Zeppelin Field tribune in Nuremberg. By the Reichstag only a
lone watchtower, its roof discarded, has survived. The lamps that
since 1961 have lit the concrete belt have vanished; empty light
poles point into the sky. Did you know, darling, that kilometres of
this concrete have been crushed into gravel that now paves East
German roads?*

The uniforms and insignia of the guards, their medals,
badges and lapels are sold at wooden stalls at Checkpoint
Charlie. For a few dollars Anna can have an East German party
badge, a Soviet star, a medal for the conquest of Berlin. The
young man who sells these treasures is American, a hippie type
with long blond hair, a jean vest. He stoops a bit as he
approaches her with a big smile.

"Ain't it something?" he says. Among the uniforms displayed
in the back Anna spots full regalia of a Soviet general, a green
coat, stars on epaulets, a stiff cap.

"Where have you got it from?" she asks, pointing at the uniform.

"From the General himself," the man smiles. "A bit hard on cash these days. Nice guy, though. Would sell me his nuclear missile if I had enough dough."

"Oh, come on," he says when Anna hesitates. "Buy some of this shit. Anything you want." Pieces of the wall are encased in plastic and have a certificate of authenticity attached. Anna buys a chunk of the wall with a piece of graffiti on it, red, yellow and black lines, mangled, crossing.

"American?" he asks her.

"No," she says, "Canadian."

"Visiting, eh?" He laughs softly as he says it.

"Sure," she smiles, and puts the piece of the Wall into her purse.

As Anna walks slowly toward the Brandenburg Gate, she tries to make out the shapes of the stone sculptures on the top, a horse rushing forward, a robed figure in a chariot. The Gate, her guidebook informs, was designed by a Breslau architect, Carl Gotthard Langhans. It may no longer seem imposing, yet as Anna walks between the stone columns she is moved. For a long while, there is nothing else she wants to do. She just walks underneath the Gate back and forth, unsure if these few steps signify a triumph or just an act of belated defiance.

The thought of Frau Strauss, Käthe's old friend, comes at the last moment; Anna has nothing but a telephone number and a name. But when she calls the apartment, and introduces herself, Frau Strauss's daughter insists that she is delighted and that Anna must come over to visit. "Just for tea," she says, "nothing elaborate. We would so very much like to meet you."

The woman who opens the white door on the fourth floor of Wildestrasse 24, is slim and petite. She must be in her early fifties, the wrinkles around her mouth cut deep into the skin, but she is still attractive. There is a halo of warmth around her, the warmth of pastel colours and red, parted lips. Her long curly hair is kept in place with two wooden combs.

"Come in, come in. *Bitte, bitte,*" Monika waves off Anna's attempt to take off her sandals.

"Doesn't matter. Please. I'm Monika Schneider. *Mutti* has been waiting for you all afternoon."

This is an old Berlin apartment house, with high ceilings, stuccoes, and stoves that are no longer in use but that have never been removed. There is no shortage of space in these rooms. The furniture is old and respectable, a heavy credenza with carved fruit and flowers on the crest, a set of chairs with soft brown cushions, a big leather armchair with head-rests. The dark mahogany table is covered by a lace tablecloth the colour of ivory.

Frau Strauss's apartment is filled with knickknacks. A pair of milky glass doves kisses on the shelf, a marionette — Pierrot holding a birthday cake with five candles on it — hangs in the entrance to the kitchen. Strings of tiny brass bells decorate the walls. Photographs are everywhere, on the walls, on the bookshelves, on the little rosewood table by the window. In one of them, a woman in a white dress is just about to bury her face in a bouquet of white lilies, in another a young man is squatting next to a small aeroplane. There is a set of playing cards pushed aside to the left of the rosewood table. Frau Strauss must have been playing solitaire.

Anna unfolds her gift, a bouquet of pale yellow roses, tied with a green bow, wrapped in cellophane.

"They are lovely, thank you," says Monika, who spoke so warmly to her on the phone, and puts the flowers in the middle of the table next to the old photographs of William and Käthe. "But you shouldn't have bothered."

Frau Strauss is in her late seventies, and she apologizes that her English is not too good. Her daughter, she says, will help to translate if she is short of words. It was lucky that Moni was visiting her right when Anna called, for she lives a few streets away from here.

"Sit down," Frau Strauss says. "Please." A welcoming smile on her broad, wrinkled face.

There is something twinlike about the mother and daughter that goes beyond their kinship, a sense of lightness and the grace of a ballerina. The mother's hair is braided and twined around the back of her head and she moves fast, with surprising agility for her age. Both women wear dresses, not identical, but differing not so much in design as in the colours of the fabric. The mother's dress is dark grey, and has a lace collar around the neck, the daughter prefers light blue.

Anna sits down, carefully, and watches the steam rise from the cups, a tiny whirlpool of warm air, the thin slices of *Apflestrudel* arranged on a Meissen plate, the cotton napkins, pale beige, embroidered in one corner, ironed and impeccably folded. Monika is holding out the plate, waiting for Anna to pick a warm slice of cake. The smell of cinnamon reaches Anna's nostrils, the smell of the apple pie William warmed the day he died.

She must look pale, for both Monika and Frau Strauss are asking her if she is all right. They offer to open the window, and Anna nods, taking a deep breath that brings some colour back to her cheeks.

"I'm sorry," she says. "It must be the travelling. So much is happening. I don't get much sleep." She takes a few sips of tea and a bite of cake.

The photographs on the table are small, with fancy jagged edges. "This here is Käthe. And this, this is Willi." Frau Strauss says. At seven William has short hair and a shy smile. He is wearing knee-high shorts and a knitted vest. In another picture Käthe and Frau Strauss, in berets, their trench coats tightly wrapped around their waists, are standing together, arms linked. Two young, smiling faces.

"You can have these," Monika says. "Please take them. For Käthe. We have doubles."

"Käthe will be very happy," Anna says, "*Danke. Danke schön.*"

"How is she?" Frau Strauss asks. A gift for Käthe is waiting on the armchair. It is carefully wrapped up in red paper and tied with a golden ribbon.

"Frail," Anna says. "But she'll be all right. She doesn't give up."

Frau Strauss nods slowly, with approval, as if she expected nothing less from her friend.

"It's terrible about Willi," she says. "I still can't believe it. He always had so much life in him. He was still so young!" Frau Strauss says, wiping tears off her cheeks. "The last time he was here, he showed us a musical box he had just bought. A really old Austrian one, with bells. My father had a similar one in Breslau. But Willi! It was as if he were a little child again. He wound it up and we all listened. *Lorelei waltz.*"

In one of the photographs on the table William is surrounded by children, two girls and a boy, showing them something, for they all lean forward, enraptured. He is slimmer than Anna has ever seen him and he has no beard. Clean shaven, his face looks younger, but also less familiar. These are Monika's children, Anna learns, and William is showing them a boomerang. Right before the picture was taken he had told them that this bent piece of stick would come back when they learned to throw it the right way. Kurt, Monika's oldest son, wouldn't believe him, so William took them all to the field, threw the boomerang, and it came back.

"You should have seen Kurt's face then," Monika says. "He can still remember it."

"That's Willi," Frau Strauss says, "That's how I remember him."

In the story that Monika sometimes helps to translate in her clear, though accented English, William is still Willi, a little German boy, crying for the red telephone he had to leave behind. When they were told to flee, Frau Strauss explains, the children were only allowed one toy, and Willi took his tambourine. But, choices like that are never final, *nicht wahr?* Here, in Berlin, it was the lost telephone he craved, the ring it made, the shine of its chrome dial. He was so silent and polite, then, a bit frightened, watching people for a long time before he would say anything. He took a long time to decide whom to trust. Frau Strauss remembers giving him cigarette cards that he lined up on the table and arranged in different ways. He could play like that for hours.

"But we mustn't be sad," Frau Strauss says, waving her hand as if she were fighting off an annoying fly. "We must be grateful for what we have."

"Käthe wrote that you were from Breslau, too. I thought it was quite incredible, really, that you and Willi met." It's Monika who says that, shaking her head. The thought seems to please her, like a completed circle, a missing piece of a puzzle.

At the sound of the word *Breslau*, Frau Strauss rises and rushes into another room from which she emerges with albums of old postcards, photographs, and newspaper clippings. "Look," she says, with girlish excitement. "Look here!" She points to the sights Anna can immediately recognise, but only as their later, tarnished and incomplete selves. "*Jahrhundrethalle*," she says, "designed by Max Berg. Bigger than the Pantheon, *Vati* always said. *Blücherplatz*, my father took me there. *Mit Gott, für König und Vaterland*, that's what it said, on the monument . . . *Stadttheater*, a stepping stone to Berlin. Such excellent actors! *Liebichshöhe* with such beautiful flowers and fountains, and the glorietta tower from which you got a view of the whole of Breslau. There was such a fine furniture store on the ground level, *Innen Dekoration W. Quintern & Co.* I remember! We used to go there with Käthe."

"Now, it's called Partisans' Hill," Anna says. She wants to say that the glorietta tower was blown up by the German defence, in 1945, but Frau Strauss is not listening.

Frau Strauss recalls a restaurant on the Oder and a big metal rooster that stood there. With thick black lines where the feathers should be. She used to put a 10 *pfennig* coin into a slot in the rooster's back and a metal egg would fall from the rooster's belly. Inside there were bonbons. Lemon, cherry, strawberry.

"Oh *Mutti*," Monika interrupts, laughing softly. "Now, she will never stop," she says turning to Anna.

"My daughter can never understand," Frau Strauss says with mock exasperation, "But what can be expected? She was born in Berlin."

This must be an old family joke, for Monika smiles and pats her mother's hand.

"Do you know this?" Frau Strauss breaks into a song, a joyful, vivid rhyme, from which Anna can only understand one word, *Liebe*.

"*Silesian lieder*," she says. "You know them, don't you." The song sounds lively, cheeky almost. Frau Strauss's lips twist mischievously, and Anna smiles, amused. Käthe could have sung such songs, but Käthe never speaks of the past. "What's gone is gone," is all she has ever said in response to Anna's curiosity. "I want nothing from there."

Frau Strauss points to the photograph with St. Dorothy's church and the Monopol Hotel, its art nouveau windows gleaming in the sun.

"Here," she says, pointing to the hotel. "I danced. At my wedding. We were married in *Dorotheenkirche*." She is smiling at the memory. "When I tried to talk to Käthe about Breslau, she would call me a silly goose. 'It was just a city,' she said. 'What you miss is your Johann,' she kept teasing me. The way he looked at you then."

"The hotel is still there," Anna says, softly. "You can still see it."

"No," Frau Strauss says, the liveliness in her voice dying away. "I don't want to see how it has changed. What you don't know doesn't hurt you, *nicht wahr*?"

She is silent for a while, before she turns to Anna, fixing her eyes on hers. "You understand?" she asks and waits for Anna to answer.

"Yes," Anna says. "I do."

Frau Strauss smoothes the lace tablecloth, straightening the starched pattern with her hand. Her voice swerves a bit, falters, and she switches back into German, letting Monika translate.

"We were good friends with Käthe. Good, good friends. She — Ulrike, Käthe, and Mitzi. We went to school together, rode horses. My *Vati* was a doctor. He kept such beautiful Arabians in Breslau. 'Look at the curve of their necks,' he kept telling me. He said they moved like dancers, but they were bred for swiftness and endurance of desert treks."

Frau Strauss points to a photograph in a small, leather-bound album. Käthe is there, her hair tied at the back. The frills of her white blouse are freshly ironed. In the corner, in old German script, an inscription Frau Strauss translates: "To my best friend, Ulrike. With loving thoughts, Käthe Herzmann." The photograph was taken in the atelier of the Barasch brothers, the stamp on the back of the picture says.

"We were so silly then. So very young. Käthe and Mitzi were good at German composition and at sports. I was good at mathematics, but sports was more important then. Even the nuns thought so. *Gemeinschaft.* You know that word, *nein*? The feeling of being together. The trips the young people made into the mountains, into the woods, in groups, together, . . . picnics on the meadows. The songs. Having something to live for. Having ideals.

"The three of us, how we laughed. Mitzi's father had a clothing store, on Gartenstrasse, in Breslau. He had a black Chrysler and a driver in uniform who would take us for drives to *Krummhübl*, to the *Scheitniger* Park. We leaned out of the window, to feel the wind in our hair. We liked to skate together, too, on the frozen moat by *Liebichshöhe*. The officers used to come there. So tall and handsome in their uniforms, polished boots. We thought they were like gods.

"How little life means . . . be ready at any hour, they sang. We didn't know any better," Frau Strauss says, softly. "It was still before the war! Before it all went so very, very wrong."

The photographs of Breslau spread on the table may account for the ease with which Anna imagines Käthe and Ulrike together. Young girls dreaming of caresses. Of strong arms that could defy danger. Sneaking glances at the muscular thighs of German heroes, at their stone penises. Giggling at the erect neck of a swan settling between Leda's legs. Walking hand in hand, swinging their purses, aware of admiring looks of passing soldiers.

"Is that when Käthe met William's father?" Anna asks.

"Helmut?" Frau Strauss says and nods.

Helmut. Helmut Rust. In Anna's mind, William's father begins his existence as a shining torso of a demigod, beautiful in his iron, unmoveable presence.

"It was Mitzi's brother, Bernd who brought Helmut over. My Johann was drafted then, and I missed him so much. Helmut and Bernd were both in uniforms. Tall, ramrod straight. So handsome. So very handsome."

In Frau Strauss's story the invasion of Poland is called the Polish Campaign. "The summer before the Polish Campaign," she says. The time when Willi was conceived. "Oh, Mitzi had her eye on Helmut, but she didn't want to stand in Käthe's way. They even broke up for a while, until Mitzi went to the Baltic sea, for her holidays and wrote to Käthe wishing her and Helmut all the best. Wrote such a funny postcard. About sailors who sway their hips when they walk. Asking Käthe if Helmut was everything she had wished for."

The summer of 1939, filled with incessant talk on the radio about the Polish corridor, the indignities suffered by the *Volk*. Such a hot summer, unusually beautiful. Käthe and Helmut together among the yarrow, blue chicory, mugworth, shepherd's purse. It just happened. They were young. They were in love. He was to leave soon.

"Did they have time to get married? Do you have his picture?" Anna asks. She is curious to see if she could spot William's shadow in his father's face. "What did her parents say?"

But Frau Strauss has no pictures of Helmut. None. They all perished. Left in Breslau. No, Käthe did not marry Helmut. There was a quarrel. There was a big, big quarrel. When Willi was born Helmut was no longer in Breslau. He never came back, never even saw his son.

"Why did they quarrel? Was it because of Mitzi? Was Helmut unfaithful to her?" Anna's questions are prompted by her own hurt.

"Who knows what happens between two people," Frau Strauss answers with a question, shaking her head. Käthe didn't want to speak of Helmut so she didn't ask. Maybe it was Mitzi. Maybe not. They were all too young. They didn't know what was coming. This is not what she wants to tell Anna. No, not that part of the story. There are other things Anna should know about. More important. Things about Käthe.

"*Bombenkeller des Reiches*, that's what we called Silesia. Air shelter for the Reich. Rich and blessed, and safe. The fortress of the German East.

"We never stopped to think what it all meant," Frau Strauss continues. Not until the first refugees began coming. 'We are safe here,' women whispered in stores, on park benches, glancing at the skies. The Breslau cellars were filled with food, jars of preserves in even rows. You had to sort out the potatoes, though, cut out the eyes and sprouting leaf-buds, remove the rotting parts. Sift the flour, to keep it free of bugs. Make sure the bags of sugar were dry.

"By 1944 there were food shortages, of course. *Röschen kaffee*, we called our coffee, for the brew was so weak that you could see through it, see the little red roses in the bottom of the cup. But that was nothing. Nothing. You know what we used to say then? Enjoy the war — peace is going to be terrible.

"They lied to us. The Gauleiter Hanke, the papers. They all lied. *Destruction of the Soviet Armies Almost Complete. Combat in East Proceeds According to Plan.* That's what we read in the *Schlesische Tageszeitung.* Even at Christmas time, 1944. People were leaving, if they could find a good reason, for you couldn't just leave. That was called 'spreading defeatism and panic.' Punishable by death. We were sure everyone watched everyone else. Your servants could turn you in, but you didn't dare dismiss them.

"At the street corners the Gauleiter's voice beamed from the loudspeakers: '*Festung Breslau* has sworn its loyalty to the Führer. We will not forget our sacred oath.' The refugees who came from the east sneered at our cellars and preserves and paid in gold coins for sturdy shoes and strong rucksacks. To the Poles and Russians we were nothing but 'Hitlerist cannibals,' they said. There was no mercy for us in the East.

"Mitzi knew she would die. Her mother had bought enough cyanide vials for the entire family, promised to swallow them before the Russians came. All they will find she said, is my stiff body. Mitzi's father would set fire to his store and shoot himself in the mouth before the flames got to him. I asked Mitzi what she would do. She didn't know. "They won't get me, though," she said. She was wearing her cyanide vial in a small pouch, around her neck.

"We stayed in Breslau and waited. Stayed until the rumble of artillery never stopped, closer and closer with each hour. Until heat was scarce and we were shivering all the time. In December 1944, Käthe decided to sign up as a Red Cross nurse. I went along. It was better than sitting at home, worrying. Johann was at the Eastern front. I wondered if I would ever see him again.

"They trained us for twenty hours. *Schwester* Käthe and *Schwester* Ulrike. We had blue striped uniforms. All we were allowed to do was to make beds, bring bed pans, wash the patients. Nothing glorious. Sometimes we were allowed to hold a limb or a bowl for discarded cotton swabs. Most of the wounded were men over fifty or under eighteen. *Volkssturm,* the last hope of the *Reich.*

"Trains were leaving Breslau for the West. Filled, we heard, filled to the brim. At the All Souls Hospital we assisted with the X-rays, took down Dr. Tolk's orders. We had to run after him as he walked, stopping by the beds for a few seconds, writing down his verdict. We wrote it all down, into their records, trying not to look at their faces. It gave them too much hope if we did.

"In the evening there were lectures in the cellar, 'Nursing at the current stage of the war.' We walked down slowly, past the long, tiled corridor with metal lamps, past the laundry with its smell of boiling cotton. 'This is not the time for compassion,' Dr. Tolk said. 'Remember. These soldiers are needed at the front. Our *Gauleiter,* Karl Hanke, said that we will fight to the last man. There will be no surrender!' We were warned to look for signs of marauding, for undue attention drawn to themselves. 'Don't try to save them,' he said. A few days before, a nurse who gave one of the men an injection that kept him from being released was sentenced to ten years by the political tribunal. I prayed that if my Johann were wounded, he would be lucky to find a nurse that brave.

"There were bodies swinging from lampposts, when we were returning home. Hundreds a day. Executed by the SS. We were not to pity them. They were traitors.

Wir werden weiter marschieren
Bis alles in Scherben fällt
Denn heute gehört uns Deutschland
Und morgen die ganze Welt...

"I sang this song," Frau Strauss continues. "So many times, with Käthe, at school. Only when we sang it we didn't really know what it meant."

We will continue marching
Until everything is in pieces
Because today we own Germany
And tomorrow the whole world

Some of the wounded men lay with their eyes closed, breathing hard. Some trailed us with their eyes as we walked through the ward. They begged us for anaesthetics."

Johann Erben. Frau Strauss can still remember his name. Their first serious case. It was obvious by then that there were not enough nurses and even the Red Cross volunteers were allowed to do more than they should have. Two legs crushed, pieces of bones still popping out of his massacred flesh. Tibia and fibula, they had learned the names of the bones only the day before. The matron cast a suspicious glance at their white hands, their breasts that would not flatten under the apron. She, Ulrike, felt faint, but Käthe took a pair of tweezers and began taking the shreds of bone out, piece by piece. The matron thought Käthe, too, would become queasy, that she would not stand it. But Käthe could concentrate on the hard pieces of bones. Her hands deftly picked up the shreds, fast, efficient. When she had finished, the matron didn't say anything, but gave her a long look, and from that time on she would put Käthe on duty with the badly wounded.

"Not me," Frau Strauss says. "I was still emptying bedpans."

So many of the soldiers didn't even know they were dying. They just stared at the ceiling, or at the window. Those who knew it was the end cried for their mothers, girlfriends. They cried for their wives, for God. "We gave them champagne and special food if they requested it — and if we had any."

"Then," Frau Strauss says. "The hospital was bombed. It was still burning when I arrived in the morning, flames shooting out of the windows. I could smell gas everywhere and the air was filled with heavy black smoke. You could hang an axe in this air. "But I work there," I said, stupidly, and the *Kommando* guard shrugged his shoulders. "Not any more."

"We left Breslau together. Käthe, Greta — her nanny — and Willi. For *Hauptbahnhof*. I just closed the door of my house, where I thought I would live with Johann, and put the key under the mat. We all had sturdy rucksacks with wide straps. Willi had one, too. With sweaters and clean underwear. Food, as much as we could carry. Käthe told me to bake cakes with all the flour and eggs I still had. They came out hard, but good to chew on the way. We sewed money and jewellery into the linings of our clothes. Anything that was small and could be sold or exchanged for food and shelter. Willi was so awkward then, in his coat and sweaters. Poor thing. He kept saying he was too hot.

"The *Hauptbahnhof* was so crowded we couldn't even get to the platform. There were people everywhere, spilling into the hall, the side tunnels. People said there would be no more trains. I remember a woman with a baby, screaming, 'Where can we go?' The guard told her to go to Opperau-Kanth. 'Trains are waiting there,' he said. 'There will be enough space for everybody.' He kept saying we should all go there. That it was safer for the trains. 'Mothers don't forget to take *Spiritus* cookers to boil the milk for your children,' that's what we heard from the loudspeakers.

"We didn't go to Kanth. A good thing we didn't. Later, I heard it called 'Kanth Death March.' Eighteen thousand women and children, they said, froze to death. Minus twenty Celsius and icy, bone freezing wind. Babies wrapped up in pillows and blankets. Mothers were afraid to look, afraid to check if the children were still alive. And in the end there were no trains.

"I don't know what happened to Greta. She was separated from us right at the start, swallowed by a wave of refugees. Käthe never found her. She wrote to Red Cross, to refugee camps. Nothing, not a word. Most of the women and children from Breslau went to Dresden we were told. That's where they died, in the bombings. Mitzi went there, too, Käthe found out, from her father's old driver. She just disappeared in the ruins. Burnt to cinders."

Frau Strauss tells Anna of a succession of cold school gyms, peasant barns. Of cabbage soup so hot she could hardly swallow it. A woman let them sleep in her bed. "It's still warm," she said. "Go fast." Of Willi's dirty face streaked with tears. Ditches everywhere were filled with belongings, cast off, too heavy to carry. Books, china, cutlery, plates, Frau Strauss even saw a pair of brass candelabras. Ditches littered with clothes, bundles of clothes. Käthe dug into these bundles like a fiend to find clean underwear for Willi.

"There were so many children. Children with frightened faces, running noses, hands clinging to the handles of sledges and prams. The young and the old always die first, *nein*? The bodies of the dead joined the cast off possessions, frozen until the spring would free them from ice."

Frau Strauss is clearing her throat. She wants Anna to know about Käthe. The way she really was then, in these horrible times. Fate itself willed it that Anna should know everything. "If I don't tell you," she says, "Käthe will take her pain with her, to her grave. Let me tell you about revenge."

"The cellars are dark and damp, and when you huddle in them time stands still. The bodies around you shake, like aspen leaves in the wind. You think of different things. Silly things. How you used to swipe sweet dough from the bowl with your finger in the kitchen. How a mouse hid in a cardboard box and the farmer hit it with a stick and then threw it by the tail into the compost heap. How you heard that the Russians steal watches and wedding rings, and how all will be fine for you don't have any.

"The door of the cellar opens. You can see that the men who stand at the entrance are drunk and they smell of tobacco and vodka and something else, something sharp, acidic, but you don't know what it is. They are Russian, they are Polish. They have bulls-eye lanterns and they cry loud, *Davai suda!* and *Woman come!*

"It all becomes very simple then. You are German or Russian or Polish; you are a man, a woman or a child. There are no other choices. German men are hit in the head with a rifle butt. Children are taken somewhere, but you don't know where.

Women? Women are raped. You have been with them in the same room. You already know their names, Marie, Erika, Ilschen, Frau Neumann. Some of them scream, some cry. What's going to happen to us, they ask. Oh God, Oh God, why is this happening?

"I was taken to a big house and told to wait. I thought I heard Käthe's scream. From another room. Such an unnatural scream. Later, only later, I learned that before these soldiers have been let loose in this village, they have been taken to a concentration camp, to see piles of bodies, heaps of glasses, of hair. That they have been reminded by big white signs on wooden scaffolds. *Soldiers! Auschwitz does not forgive. Take revenge without mercy!*

"The first one gave me vodka to drink from his field flask and then a piece of greasy sausage to eat. He laughed and pinched my cheek and I thought: Thank you, God! He will let me go! Then he hit me. Down, you German whore, he yelled, and I closed my eyes and lay down.

"I stopped counting how many times I was raped. The soldiers lined up. Some spit on me or hit me in the face. I closed my eyes. I didn't care if I lived or died. My throat was swollen, for one of them tried to strangle me, and others pulled him away. Another one pressed a pistol against my chest, and I prayed that he would fire.

"I must have fainted, for when I woke up I had no clothes on. I groped in the dark, in the blood and vomit. There was a wardrobe in the room, and a dress on a hanger. But it was too small. I had to leave the back unfastened, to make it fit. I climbed through the window. There was a church in this village, and I wanted to hide there.

"The church was dark and empty. There was a big cross at the altar. There was a body on the cross. A woman's dead body. Naked, pinned down to the wood by her hands and feet. They had torn away the figure of Christ to make room for her. Her face was swollen and blue, her hair entangled. Her mouth was opened as if she were still trying to say something.

"Käthe, I saw a few hours later. With Willi. Her face and legs were bruised and swollen, but she said she fell down the stairs. 'Nothing happened,' she said. 'Nothing.' I knew she was lying, but it was just as well. I didn't want to hear the truth. I wanted to forget. She said a Russian, Captain Zeneyev, helped her and Willi. 'A good man,' she said. 'Isn't he a good man, Willi?' And Willi said, 'Yes, Mutti.' He was playing with an aeroplane made out of a Russian army bulletin.

"This Russian Captain let us stay in his quarters for a few days. He sent us a Russian nurse. Gave us food. Said he had a boy at home, the same age. Before we left, we saw carts with Polish refugees coming to this village. They moved into empty houses. Their children ran around the yard with hoops, climbed the trees, pretended to shoot at each other with sticks. On Sunday morning, the women, their heads tied in flowery kerchiefs, went to pray in the church.

"Moni, my daughter, she knows all this. I told her all about it, and she says we have to bear our punishment. Perhaps she is right. Johann was a prisoner in Russia, but he was released in 1947. He, too, didn't want to speak about what he had seen. He said we had to be grateful for what we had. Käthe made me promise I would never tell Willi. I never did. But I want you to know. You were his wife, after all. You should know."

"*Mutti*," Monika says, softly. "*Mutti*, it's all right."

Frau Strauss begins to fold the Breslau albums. Her eyes narrow and her lips fold inward.

"It's good Käthe is in Canada," she says slowly. "This is a cursed land. People are afraid of the past here, afraid to love their country, afraid to be proud of it. No matter what the young ones do, the world will never forgive the German people. Käthe was right to go away with Willi. Please, tell Käthe I said that. She will know what I mean."

Frau Strauss shakes her head as she says it and looks up to the stuccoed ceiling, to the rosettes and meanders of white plaster ornaments.

Anna has underestimated Ursula's persistence. Next evening, by the time she is back at the hotel, her feet aching and swollen from the march through the city, Frau Herrlich has already chatted with the proprietor of the pension, and he has brought her cappuccino to the lounge, to the low table by the marble fireplace. He is now motioning to Anna to hurry there, to meet her distinguished guest. "Four times," he says. "Frau Herrlich has been here four times. I saw her on television just a few days ago. But you never left a message for her, did you?"

"No," Anna says. "I didn't."

Ursula rises from her chair, points to the coffee cup, and waves to Herr Müller, a thank-you he acknowledges with a beaming smile. She has tied her hair in the back, straightening the grey curls. Only one unruly strand keeps falling over her eye. Without lipstick her mouth looks smaller and pale, but the lines cutting into her lips are deeper.

"I've been trying to find you," she says.

The anger that seized Anna when she rushed out of the café, ignoring Ursula's plea, has evaporated.

"I've been sightseeing," Anna says. "My flight doesn't leave until Saturday."

"Good," Ursula smiles. "I want to show you something, too."

Anna hesitates.

"Please," Ursula says. "We shouldn't part like this. I want you to see it."

Ursula walks fast, her heels clicking on the pavement, and Anna follows, each step an effort for her swollen feet.

Ursula's car is parked nearby, a red BMW with a black interior, and Anna sits down with relief, stretching her legs as far as they will go.

"You can move the seat all the way back," Ursula says. "It'll give you more room."

She drives fast, taking sharp turns and stopping with a screech of tires, and Anna leans back in the seat. "I know how it must hurt you," Ursula says. "I've thought about it. It was such a terrible time to find out. When you can't grab him by the collar and scream. And William cannot explain, cannot mend anything."

There is so much intensity in Ursula's voice. So much passion. Is she defending William, pleading for him? Her hands are clasped tight on the steering wheel. Anna can see the muscles hardening, stretching under the skin.

"William is dead," she says.

"But he is still hurting you," Ursula says.

"It'll pass. I'll forget."

They drive by the streets, empty but for cleaners who sweep away the discarded fliers, confetti, and cigarette butts.

"When the Wall fell, the longest line-ups were in front of porno shops," Ursula says quietly. "The bouquets of flowers we greeted the *Ossis* with did not last. A few days later you could hear the first jokes: Why should we envy the Chinese? — They still have their wall!"

They drive out of the city, past long rows of one storey prefab buildings, empty at this hour. It is getting dark fast. Anna watches it all, silent.

"You won't forget," Ursula says. "I won't either."

The car pulls up to what seems to Anna like the end of the road, but is only a lowering of the terrain, a big empty lot where she sees a herd of small cars, parked all over the place. When the engine stops, Ursula leaves the lights on and blinks them three times. Slowly, one by one, the little cars light up, doors open, and men come out, disentangling themselves from their sleeping bags. Soon a whole group of them circles the car, and Anna is uneasy. She would have locked the car doors, driven away, but Ursula waves her hand.

"Hi, guys," she says. "Is Andrzej around?"

"Tomorrow," a tall, heavy man says in German. "*Jutro,*" he repeats in Polish. It is only then that Anna realises that all of these men are Polish. She should have guessed it from their faces, broad and tanned, from their moustached lips. Or from the shape of the small Polish Fiats, with their steel shells filled to the brim with soft human bodies.

The men give Ursula quick, suspicious looks, and exchange a few words among themselves. She has opened the doors of the BMW, and is standing up, her foot resting on the chassis. They seem nervous, unsure of themselves, their hands awkwardly looking for something to do. One of them, the heaviest, with short greying hair, lets a load of saliva gather in his mouth and spits it on the ground with a swishing sound. He is calmer than the rest; he has obviously seen Ursula before.

"Your friend," the man asks, pointing at Anna. "She too, looking for workers?"

"You can ask her yourself," Ursula says. "She speaks your language."

The man slowly turns to Anna, and she sees in his look a mixture of embarrassment and anger.

"You speak Polish?" he asks. The question is not a polite inquiry. The man does not call her *Pani*, but uses a direct form, "*Mówisz po polsku?*" Anna does not like his directness, the unwanted familiarity, the underpinning of contempt.

"*Tak*," Anna says. The sound of this one word gives her away, tells him that she does not merely speak the language, but is Polish.

"From Warsaw?" he keeps asking.

"No," she says quickly. "From Wrocław."

He gives her a questioning look. What is she doing here, then, with this German woman in her tight black dress, her red vest, the air of some actress?

"You work with her?"

"No," Anna says. "Just visiting."

"Ah," he says and leans on the BMW, toward her. "Enjoying the sights?" The contempt in his voice makes Anna blush. "Checking us out?" He gives a loud, piercing whistle and Anna, quickly, turns her head away.

"Can we go now?" she asks Ursula.

The men are beginning to leave, one by one. They have already decided that their prospects of getting a job from these two women are slim, not worth giving up a few hours of sleep. Only three of them are still standing around the car, stepping from one foot to another, waiting for something to happen.

Ursula takes out a piece of paper with directions. "I need five for next week," she says. Five, she signals with her palm. The heavy man grabs the paper before she has the time to extend her hand and stuffs it into his pocket.

"*Ya, ya*," he says. "You German whore," he mutters in Polish, loud enough for Anna to hear him. "*Danke schön*. We come."

"*Gut!*" Ursula says, gets into the car and starts the engine. "*Auf Wiedersehen!*"

In the headlights the men seem weightless, dancing in the beams of light, like moths. They look back as they walk away, their white faces distorted and suddenly, Anna notices it now, drawn from exertion.

"They hate your guts," she tells Ursula.

"What else is new," Ursula says. "At least they don't hide it."

"Why are you doing it?"

"What?"

"Coming here, like this, to hire them. It's not legal, is it?"

"Maybe it's my atonement?" Ursula says. The car is speeding again and Anna clutches at the handle above the window. "They need money. I have an assignment. Lots of heavy stuff to drag around. Andrzej tells me they need the money to buy apartments in Poland, to start a business. Their families send them here. That's the only way to end the life of five to a room, or chasing jobs that pay next to nothing and threaten to disappear."

"Andrzej?"

"A guy who brought me here first, a filmmaker from Wroclaw. He used to sleep here with them, in his car. He has a good eye," she laughs. "We might do a film together."

Anna is relieved when they enter the city, when empty suburban streets with their lambent glows are left behind. The car turns into a tree-lined street and stops in front of a heavy, brownish building. Ursula turns her head to Anna, a slight twist, a half-turn.

"Come upstairs, to my place. I don't want you to leave like that."

"Please," she adds, seeing that Anna lingers. "Do come!"

They climb the wide stairs with metal lace in between the steps. The stairs William climbed, Anna reminds herself as she follows Ursula past a spotless landing with its palm tree in a brown terra-cotta pot. But curiosity has already taken over, softened her.

The ceiling in Ursula's apartment is high, stuccoed, like the Wroclaw apartment of Anna's parents; but, here in West Berlin, there was no lack of money to care for it. "You know how Marx's *Capital* got divided?" she remembers her father's old joke, "The West got capital, we got Marx." There are no cracks, no crude coats of paint over hardwood, the passage of time is camouflaged, muted. In Ursula's living room, magazines and papers cover wide leather sofas. Ursula kicks off her shoes and walks into the long, narrow kitchen in which Anna glimpses the brown surface of wood cabinets and black tiles.

"Make us some room on the sofas," Ursula says and Anna folds a newspaper, stacks a few magazines, enough to clear two spots, one for herself and one for Ursula who is moving swiftly, amid the clinking of glass.

This is a large room with walls almost empty but for two enormous photographs placed on the opposite ends of the room. One is a picture of a treetop, its green leaves dappled by the setting sun, its trunk hiding behind a concrete fence, behind the coils of barbed wire. On the opposite wall a carved quotation: *So then because thou art lukewarm, and neither cold nor hot, I will spue thee out of my mouth.*

There is not much of the furniture here apart from two sofas, just a few shelves, a wooden chest of drawers and a big television set — black, taking up the whole corner. Ursula comes in with a tray on which she has placed a green teapot in the shape of a pear, two cups, two glasses and a black bottle of Courvoisier.

"William," Ursula says, "couldn't look at it. I could see he always sat in such a way that he wouldn't have to face it."

"The quote? It is from *Revelations*, isn't it?" Anna asks, looking at the picture of the carving, but even now she is wrong about him.

"The other one." Ursula points to the one of the treetop. "I took it in Auschwitz," she says. "From inside."

Ursula settles cross-legged on the spot Anna has cleared for her, with her feet bare. Her toenails are painted bright red. She pours brandy into big glasses for both of them. A Yoga posture, Anna thinks. The beginning of all moves. She fixes her eyes on Ursula's small frame, muscles stirring under the skin as she bends over to hand Anna the brandy. Gaze like that makes people uncomfortable, but Ursula seems oblivious to it, lighting a cigarette, drawing the smoke in, exhaling. Anna cannot stop thinking about the men in the parking lot, their eyes filled with contempt. One of them had a tiny gap between his two front teeth, just like Ursula's. They still make her uneasy, the way they spat behind them as they walked back to their cars.

"Look here." Leaning over the low coffee table Ursula spreads a pile of photographs that were lying on the side, black and white shots of pale, angry faces, raised fists with chains wound up around them.

"This is Görlitz," Ursula points to the shots of the demonstrators. "And Zgorzelec." She pronounces the Polish name flawlessly, Anna thinks. Andrzej must be a good teacher.

A city split in half she tells Anna, by the post-war borders. When it was divided, the Germans got the town hall, the station, all municipal buildings, the zoo, the theatre, and main churches. The Poles got Oberlausitzer Gedenkhalle and the gas station. Tram tracks that led through bridges were poured over with concrete.

"I got a hint that that's where World War III was brewing. When Poland opened its borders, four thousand ultra-right German youths descended on Görlitz. The plan was to light the German 'fires of warning,' and then cross the border with the flames and light the fires in front of the Gedenkhalle. The German side was blocked with armoured cars and antiterrorist squads. They couldn't get through," Ursula says. "I went there with Andrzej. We filmed the whole scene. I tried to talk to them. It was like talking to ghosts. 'German blood has been spilt into this land,' the guy in a black shirt screamed right into my face. His chin was shaking."

The young men in the photographs have clean-shaven faces and short blond hair.

"William thought I shouldn't have filmed them. I was only giving them free publicity, he said. It was better to let shit like that die out on its own."

She waits until the smoke has formed a curl and vanishes into the air. She sniffs her brandy before taking a sip. William's favourite drink, Anna thinks, the one she has never learned to enjoy. There is a bottle just like it in her living room in Montreal.

"Do you also think I'm obsessed? That I should stop watching?" Ursula has stubbed her cigarette half-finished, but there is still enough smoke in the air; it irritates Anna's eyes.

"No," Anna says. "I don't think you should stop." How could she say anything else? These are her own obsessions, too. Here, in this part of the world, they have all been marked for life.

When Ursula talks, pointing to more faces in the pictures, Anna takes a sip of brandy, and then another one. It burns her throat but it warms her, too. She closes her eyes and thinks that she is tired. She has been chasing her ghosts, hoping for epiphanies. This has been an impossible mission; she has hoped for too much. "It's just round the corner," her father used to coax her on their walks together when she was little and refused to go on. "A few more minutes. We are almost there." That's how he kept her going. You can get a child go a long way on false hopes.

Anna closes her eyes and lets Ursula's voice float. The faces of hatred are all the same, she thinks. Thoughts pulsate in her head, feverish snitches of all the stories she has heard, Polish, German. Käthe's bruised face, her silence. Black spots on *Babcia*'s lips. Ruins.

Her head swims. She has had too much to drink, and the room is circling around her head, sometimes taking off all together. Her eyes sting; Ursula's face and the photograph on the wall split into two separate selves, begin to swirl and rotate, before she wills them to become one again.

"Excuse me," she says and staggers as she walks to the bathroom, trying to keep steady. Inside she washes her face and her eyes with cold water. The pink seashells on the tiles blur and swirl. Ursula's mother chose them, she recalls, and finds it all suddenly hilarious. But the hilarity passes as quickly as it comes. To steady herself, she leans against the cool tiles. The hot, sour lump in her stomach is rising up to her throat, and she begins to vomit, clutching the white toilet seat with her hands, until her stomach feels empty, wrung out from all that lay there. When it's over her throat feels burnt and sore, so she drinks some water from the tap the way she used to do it a long time ago, at school, her fingers interlocking, palms down, to make a trough.

"Are you all right?" she hears Ursula's voice.

"Fine," Anna says. She is feeling better, much better. The

water tastes sweet.

"I'd better make us some coffee," Ursula says.

In the bathroom mirror Anna's eyes are reddened, her skin pale. With a cotton wad she puts on some of Ursula's makeup, a blusher on her cheeks, a dab of powder on her nose. She can hear the music, from behind the bathroom doors, *Tristan und Isolde*, the Furtwängler recording, one of William's favourites. He kept it right beside Beethoven's Fifth. "Auden was right. Wagner was an absolute shit," he would say, finger in the air, "but this is all I care about."

There is a residue in this memory of William. Of disappointment she has learned to stifle. A memory of disappointment. William's grant applications were routinely rejected. "Too abstract," one of the reviewers wrote, "too derivative."

When he stopped applying altogether, she said he was giving up too easily.

"I have all I want, Anna. What is there to fight for?"

"Recognition," she said. "Respect."

"It's so convoluted. It's politics and fashion. I'm tired of it."

Excuses, she thought. But she didn't tell him that. She was there to heal him, not to scratch his wounds. How often did he tell her that he had enough of it from Marilyn. From her, he wanted peace.

"As if it mattered one bit," he would also say. Why would anyone care if he ever wrote another damn note.

"I would."

"Why?"

What could she say to that? That she wanted to see him happy? "I *am* happy," he would say, raising his head over his musical boxes, all their metal parts dismantled, spread in neat rows on a linen tea towel, sanded pieces of wood slowly absorbing the stain. "I'm happy with you. I don't want anything else."

"You must be hungry," Ursula says. "It's getting late." Her bare feet make soft, muted pats on the floor as she moves.

While Anna was in the bathroom, Ursula has warmed up slices of pita bread, and emptied containers from a Mediterranean restaurant — tahini dip, roasted red peppers in oil, eggplant purée — into small ceramic bowls, with their shapes of fish, shells, and seahorses. Yellow, green, blue. The carrots, sliced thinly, are mixed with yoghurt, and Ursula adds a handful of fresh mint that she has chopped up and thrown into the bowl.

Ursula is right. Anna is hungry. She can feel it as soon as her teeth close on the warm slice of pita. The old feeling that Ursula's gaze can read right through her comes back, but it no longer frightens her or makes her uneasy. It may be the brandy or the strange, impossible configuration of fate that does it, the sheer improbability of the two of them sitting across each other at a table. Or it may be something deeper, like the slow but steady pace of a mountain hike that rewards her with a stupendous view of the valley she has already passed.

"Where did you meet William?" she asks Ursula.

Ursula hesitates for a moment, but only for a short moment. "Here, in Berlin, at a concert in the Conservatory," she says quickly, as if speeding through the past could help. "In 1976, at the end of his sabbatical, when he was getting ready to go back home. I walked up to him, asked if I could take his picture. I thought he had an interesting face, something of a sulking child, hungry for attention, but at the same time disgusted with this hunger, above it. I told him that I've always been drawn to contradictions.

"'Go ahead,' he said. 'Shoot!' Her lips twist when she talks about this moment that took place almost fifteen years ago. It still pleases her to remember William's amused consternation.

"The light was rotten and I knew it, but I still took a few shots. I'll have to repeat them, I said. But this will give me an idea, if I'm interested. I called him the next day to get him to come to the studio. I'm still interested, I said and he laughed. He said he was leaving the next day, that he really had no time. So we went out for a drink, instead, and I knew then that we wouldn't let each other alone that easily."

"Why?" Anna asks.

"One of my black hunches," Ursula laughs softly. "He wasn't an easy man to leave. It took him longer to know what was happening," she continues. "He always wanted to believe he could be in charge, that things could be controlled, ordered to stop or to go on. Ours was to be just a passing affair, his last night in Berlin, an unexpected treat. One of those nights when you talk and make love, and then talk some more, happy to be alive. A long night, but not without end.

"He called me two weeks later, from Montreal. He said he saw me everywhere, could not stop thinking about me. 'You are right under my skin,' he said. 'Are you still interested?' I said, 'Yes.' He came back to Berlin a month later."

Anna is listening. She is mesmerised by the soft timbre of Ursula's voice, the warmth of her laughter.

"We always quarrelled. We were too different, too stubborn, but maybe that's what kept us together. We made each other alive," Ursula says.

"You didn't want to live with him!"

"We would've killed each other if we did. I'm not good at compromises. He wasn't, either. It was no use. We both knew it."

The coffee maker is sputtering steam. Anna rises to pour coffee into their cups. She opens the fridge to find milk. Ursula is swinging on her stool, back and forth. She didn't like his latest music, she says, and William knew it. He knew she thought it too abstract, too detached. They were like that with each other. Honest, even if it hurt. He could count on her with criticism like that. "I wouldn't make a good wife," she laughs.

How she still likes talking about him, Anna thinks. How he still excites her.

"How did Marilyn find out about you?"

"He told her. He said she was suspecting something anyway, and he didn't want to lie to her."

"He didn't tell *me*," Anna says.

"Is this really such a surprise?"

Anna takes a sip of coffee. It is so hot that it burns her tongue. No, it is not a surprise.

"Last time I saw William, it was in August," Ursula says. "I took him to Berchtesgaden. I was still filming for the documentary. He kept telling me that I should move on, do other things. That there was no point in this constant blame, in dragging the ghosts out."

In Ursula's story August is rainy and cold in the Alps. "There was a long line-up of cars on the wet, slippery road to Berchtesgaden. The last two kilometres took us twenty minutes," Ursula continues. "We found a small hotel on the hill, with its stuffed grouse, little hats with flower wreaths around them, and painted boxes on the windowsill. *Gemütlich,* we laughed. We wouldn't have it any other way.

"I was there to photograph the ruins of Obersalzberg, with its maze of underground tunnels, the empty lots where once guards kept watch over the Berghof with its giant picture window. I wanted to go to *Kehlsteinhaus,* the Eagle's Nest, a present from Germany for Hitler's 50th birthday, his mountain retreat.

"That's where we drove in the morning, an eerie drive, past walls of old bunkers rotting in the damp air, half hidden under green moss. Past these small villages, churches with black steeples, cascades of red geraniums in all windows. The Alpine meadows. Cows roaming free, brass bells ringing wherever they go.

"By the Hotel Türken, where crowds used to gather for a glimpse of the Führer, there was a sign, "This is a private object. Photography forbidden." I took the picture of the sign. In Obersalzberg we took a bus to *Kehlsteinhaus,* along a steep mountain road. *An engineering marvel, more than five thousand feet above sea level,* a taped voice described the origin of the house and the road, *completed in twelve months in the years 1937/38.* The bus stopped at the feet of the summit, and we took an elevator to the terrace of the Eagle's Nest. On the terrace of *Kehlsteinhaus* waiters offered us beer and tea.

"We hiked the steep loop trail of limestone rocks, caught a sight of the blue waters of Königssee, and the progress of a giant misty cloud, slowly coming our way. I took pictures of the tourists on the trail, the tables shaped like giant *HB Weissbier* bottles, a face of a hooded maiden watching us without a smile, the giant fireplace in the main hall.

"'There is nothing here for you,' William said, 'Let's go.' He was getting impatient, edgy. Fanned his face and frowned. This was an old quarrel over what should be remembered and what should be forgotten. When we got down to the terrace, we found out that we couldn't leave right away. We had to wait for the bus we were registered for. There were too many visitors, the driver explained, they had to keep order.

'He *is* right,' William said, before I had the time to say anything.

"In Berchtesgaden it was raining again, and there were no mountains to be seen, but we decided to go for a walk. On the way we passed a small cemetery. Climbed the low steps and walked by the ivy-covered graves, by long rows of names underneath pale oval photographs with smiling, hopeful faces. *Gefallen 7.7. 1944 bei Stalino, 1943 bei Kursk, im Osten*. I'm just checking the collective pulse, I told him. Someone has to watch all the time.

"William said, '*Therefore thou art inexcusable, O man, whosoever thou art that judgest: for wherein thou judgest another, thou condemnest thyself; for thou that judgest doest the same thing*. St. Paul said that to the Romans. An old priest from around here told me that once.'

'The Church has its own sins to mind,' I snapped. 'They were not exactly without blame.' I hated when he took on a tone like that.

"The rain had stopped and we could see a giant rainbow over the mountains, touching the Eagle's Nest. Eerie, I thought. The shops in Berchtesgaden were closed, but we peeked inside, at the felt hats, the full Bavarian skirts, puffed sleeves, embroidered woollen vests. That's what I want, I said, pointing at a dark green hat with a feather. And you will wear this one, I pointed hat with a *Gamsbart*, a sign of a hunter.

"There was a small *Biergarten* where we took a seat on the wooden chairs under a tree and ordered beer. William was playing with the beer coaster, spinning it on the side. An old man with flaming red cheeks, a few yellowed teeth, a crew cut of grey hair walked in and sat down at an empty table. '*Grüss Gott*,' he chatted us up.

"'*Grüss Gott*,' I said. Asked him about hunting, the weather. I made William buy us a round of beer. I listened to the band, nodded my head in the rhythm of the music.

"'My name is Kurt Macht,' the man said.

"'Ursula Herrlich ,' I said. 'My friend from Breslau,' I introduced William. He was staring at the plastic tablecloth, at a swarm of red ladybugs on a white background.

"Herr Macht took a deep breath. 'Ah! Breslau! Such a beautiful city. It's all lost, now. Damn Commies.' He leaned forward, 'But nobody is blaming them!'

"The *Schnapps* woman passed by with a small wooden barrel hanging over her neck. She poured the yellow *Schnapps* into a tin decanter and offered it to William who drank it all in one gulp. She wiped the decanter with a linen cloth and poured another drink for Herr Macht.

"'You don't believe a word they say do you? You are too young to remember. Wasn't the way they tell you it was,' Herr Macht went on. 'There would be a different song, if we had won.' He nodded his head, staring into the distance.

"'There is too much dirt on this earth, son. Someone has to clean it up.'

"This is when William turned to me and said that he was leaving. He said it in English.

That did it. Herr Macht, red faced, filled with beer, stood up, shaking on his legs. He stared at William, chewing his words, picking them up carefully. 'Traitors like you should be shot,' he said at last, and then he spit. The blob of spit landed at William's feet. 'Put against the wall and shot.'

I laughed. 'See,' I said. 'I'm right after all. The shit is still here.'

"William took me by the hand and dragged me out of the *Biergarten*, before I had the time to say anything else. 'Why don't you say something, William?' I asked. 'Don't you think I'm right?' He let go of my hand and walked away. 'Why don't you quote your priest, now?' I shouted after him. By the time I got to the hotel he was gone. He didn't even leave a note.

Ursula is fanning her face with a napkin. Her cheeks are flushed.

"But he called you in December," Anna says. "Quite a few times. I found the bill."

"Yes," Ursula says, smiling. "We were good at reconciliations. Most of the time. He liked to forgive me. It made him feel good.

But I never saw him again."

She raises to gather the plates, rinse them under the tap before placing them in the dishwasher. Anna scrapes the leftover tahini dip back into the plastic container, covers the rest of the dishes with a plastic wrap. She hands the ceramic bowls to Ursula and they work together, in silence, clearing the kitchen table, wiping its surface, putting things back in the fridge.

"He was better off with you," Ursula says when they are finished. "With you he didn't have to fight. Or forgive."

Anna doesn't say anything, but she is no longer fooled by her own magnanimity. She knows that it is only because William is dead that she can be here and listen to Ursula. It is only because William can never come here again, touch either of them, make love to them, that she can even consider liking Ursula, thinking that this woman who moves with such assurance is anything but a rival.

"How did it happen?" Ursula asks. She means the last moments of William's life, the part of the story she must have wondered about. Julia didn't know enough, then, to answer her questions. "Did he suffer much? Did he know what was happening?"

"He was alone. He was already . . . gone when I came in," Anna begins. "The doctor told me that to him it must have seemed like a stroke of lightning."

This is her William she is talking about, now. The husband she lived with for ten years, the husband who died and whom she will never see again. The husband she misses so badly at times that she wants to bite her hands and howl. It is still January 26, and she is back in her Montreal kitchen, with its scent of a baked apple pie. The door to William's study is still closed and she opens it slowly. She is so slow, so damn slow.

"But why? What did the doctor say?" Ursula has sat down in front of her. She has closed her eyes, but Anna can see that her eyelids are swelling with tears. For a moment, when Anna sees Ursula's tears, for a brief but palpable moment, it seems to her that William might appear, that seeing the two of them, together, would be too much to keep him away.

"Heart failure. The doctor said it could be hereditary.

Asked if I knew how his father died."

On the floor of his study, Anna can see William's body, his grey hair tousled, glued together with sweat. She can see herself, too, bending over him, dropping her purse, feeling if there is still any warmth left in his face. This other Anna still doesn't register what has happened, cannot believe her own eyes. Why isn't she calling the ambulance? What is she waiting for?

"So sudden? Without any warning?" Ursula asks.

"The doctor said it couldn't have been the first one. There was scar tissue on his heart."

"He never said anything? Never complained?"

"No," Anna says, but here she hesitates. "Not to me."

"No, he wouldn't," Ursula says. They both know what they are talking about. He was not willing to admit that his body, this wonderful strong body he was so proud of would fail him. Not William.

Anna can feel the cold panic touching the soles of her feet, making its way up, to her heart. It is the same panic that paralysed her then when she was kneeling beside William, stroking his face, feeling the chill set in. She was always too eager to believe him, to let him dispel her fears. For this she has never forgiven herself.

"I should've known," she tells Ursula, now. "He must have thought the pain would go away. He didn't mention anything to his doctor. There was no record of chest pains in his file . . . But I should've known."

She can see herself talking to him in the morning, still groggy from sleep. William is sitting in bed massaging his left arm. Does it hurt? she asks him. It is a stupid question, he tells her. Of course it hurts. Have you talked to your doctor? she asks. What for? he asks in return. He is already impatient with her, tells her she is always coming up with these thoughts of impending doom. Your murky Polish soul, he laughs and tousles her hair. His left arm hurts and there is a perfectly good reason for it. He has been playing the violin for too long. The last thing he needs now is to have her panic.

"If only I hadn't listened to him," Anna's voice is breaking when she says it. "If I only I insisted . . ."

"NO!"

The bang of steel on the marble tiles startles them both. Ursula must have pushed a knife off the table, as she leaned forward. "No! Anna, don't do that? Don't go this way?"

Anna breathes hard. She mustn't cry, she tells herself. She must stop the choking feeling in her throat.

"Anna, look at me," Ursula says. "He loved you." She takes Anna in her arms and rocks her gently. Her freckled hand is smoothing Anna's hair, gently stroking her forehead, her cheeks.

For a split-second Anna is thinking of beach sand, flowing between her fingers. Ursula's touch is surprisingly soothing, and Anna will remember it for a long time, the touch of her hot, dry hand, and the sound of her own voice, murmuring her consent.

On Saturday morning a telephone ring wakes Anna up. "I'm sorry," Ursula says. "But I've just learned something. It's rather urgent."

It is Anna's last day in Berlin. The day before Ursula promised to take her to Potsdam. *Schloss Sanssouci*, she said. Sounds exactly what we both need.

"My friend, Lothar," Ursula says on the phone, "has been nosing about the Stasi archives. He has just called me. Said I should come right away. It has something to do with Willi's grandfather. Can you be ready in half an hour?"

An hour later they are on Normannenstrasse in the Lichtenberg district, Ursula leading the way among the maze of brown concrete buildings. In the lobby of what used to be Stasi headquarters, still decorated with the statues of Lenin and Felix Dzerzhinski, Lothar is already waiting for them. He is a tall, thin man, with an ascetic face. "You'll have to be quick," he says, shaking Anna's hand and giving Ursula a quick hug. "This is still not quite legal, but someone here owes me a big favour."

Lothar takes them upstairs, into a small room with padded doors. The room is furnished with a shabby table and three hard wooden chairs. The file on the table is an old-fashioned one, with marble coloured cardboard flaps, tied with a grey ribbon. On the white label, in the old German script, a name.

Claus Herzmann.

"Go ahead," Ursula says, when Anna hesitates. "You open it. I'll translate."

Anna's hands tremble slightly when she unties the ribbon. William once said he was relieved to know his grandfather was executed by the Nazis. Not a bad thing to know, he said, if you were German. Inside, pinned to a long typewritten report there are prison shots of a man in his fifties, blank eyes staring into space, stubble on his cheeks.

"That's him," Ursula says, glancing at the report. "Professor Claus Herzmann of the University of Breslau. Executed on May 2, 1945. For high treason."

"What did he do?" Anna asks, overcome by curiosity. She is looking for a shadow of William in his grandfather's face, but it is not there. "Does it say?"

Ursula picks up the documents from the file. Typewritten reports from interrogations, testimony of witnesses. Photographs. From her purse she takes out her reading glasses and begins to translate.

"Professor Herzmann . . . research declared essential for war effort. Address, 7 Gerhart-Hauptmann-Weg, Breslau. Wife, Catholic. One child, Käthe Herzmann, daughter. Member of the National Socialist party from January 1939. Maid, Frieda Gottwald, reported that Professor Herzmann did not purge all the forbidden books from his library and tried to fire her after she became pregnant. She wants it recorded that the father of her child was of pure blood and that she got pregnant in response to the order of her Führer."

Ursula flips through the files, translating what she glances through. "Professor Herzman's wife frequents Jewish businesses. Dated October 1938. The same Frieda says that her mistress told her to lower the radio volume during the Führer's speech. Professor Herzmann is also alleged to have a Swiss bank account."

There is an envelope among the papers and Anna opens it to find a studio portrait of Herr Professor and Frau Professor Herzmann. In this picture William's grandfather's face is handsome and distinguished looking. Clean shaven, hair parted, smoothed with brilliantine. Frau Professor is wearing a small round hat, the muslin veil draped over her forehead.

"Listen to this," Ursula stands up and paces around the table, neatly typed pages in her hands: *I have told Fraulein Herzmann that Germany will be reborn. We have suffered for a long time, but we shall suffer no longer. Our Führer has shown us the way. I told her that we are building autobahns. We are planting trees and forests. We've given men work, and with it we have given them their dignity and their honour. But we are such a tiny part of this earth. We have to work hard to conquer our imperfections. I told her that what stops us in this work are old rules and old morality. We have to forget what we, with our limited minds, think is right. We have to let the strong lead us, be ruthless if need be!*

I have told her that we have to guard the purity of our blood. Bad blood weakens, dilutes the will. The weak are like disease that has to be contained, like a branch that has to be cut off, so that the tree will grow stronger.

I expressed my disapproval of the school she went to; it was run by the nuns. I told her I didn't like to think of my fiancée kneeling in front of this crucified Jew! I pointed out to her that her father, a scientist, a professor at the University of Breslau should not remain blind to the laws of nature.

When we found out that my fiancée was pregnant, I declared my desire to marry her. I went to her father's home the next evening. Professor Herzmann was celebrating his birthday and there were many people in the room. All of them can be asked to bear witness to what has happened.

Professor and Frau Herzmann were in the living room, where my fiancée took me promptly. She had not told her parents about our plans, wishing me to be the one who would break the news to them. It was in front of these witnesses that I asked for the hand of Fraulein Herzmann in marriage.

Here goes a list of names: Herr und Frau Stein. . . Hanemann, Bauer. . . Strauss.

'She will go with you if that's what she wants, but she'll not have our permission.' These are Frau Herzmann's exact words. 'Not that you care for it, not you with your own laws. But whatever you do I want you to know that it is not with my

permission that my daughter will marry a heathen.'

I want to report that I was taken aback by Frau Herzmann's statement but I was also absolutely convinced Professor Herzmann would react to it with the severity it demanded. I was quite prepared to recognize that Frau Herzmann was only a high-strung woman, too weak to withstand such a moment. I want it recorded, however, that Professor Herzmann never said a word to his wife and never offered any apology for what had transpired.

Then I turned to my fiancée and I told her that she knew where to find me. I also made it plain to Fraulein Herzmann that I would marry her, but that I would not stay a minute longer under her father's roof. I had reminded her that the rotten branches have to be cut off. Only sacrifice will bring rebirth. I waited two days. When she didn't contact me, I refused to see her or the child again. Signed: Helmut Rust, SS-Sturmbannführer.

"SS?" Anna asks. "Are you sure?" The chill of the concrete walls makes her shiver.

Ursula shows her the report. Helmut Rust's signature takes an entire line. A strong, determined script, each letter perfectly legible. There can be no doubt.

"*Kadavergehorsam*, cadaver obedience," Ursula says. "They, the SS were above all judgement. In their schools, stripped to the waist, they were taught to fight off attack dogs with their bare hands. If they took flight, they were shot. They tore cats' eyes out, learning not to feel sorrow. They marched in the heat for hours, without a drop of water to drink, crawled through tunnels, ran over obstacle courses, until there was nothing left in them but rage. When they rose from this rage, they believed they were invincible. That they could achieve anything they put their will to. Walk unmoved over corpses, deaf to cries and pleas. Incorruptible."

"She said Helmut Rust was an officer," Anna says, meaning Frau Strauss. "That he and Käthe were in love. That they quarrelled. She never mentioned why." Quickly she tells Ursula of what she had learned that afternoon, just days before. The trek from Breslau. The horrendous story of escape.

Ursula is not surprised. "*Lebenslüge*," she says. "This is what you get here, in this country. A lie you live with for so long that it transforms your life. But also," she adds after a moment, "a lie that enables you to live."

"Käthe didn't lie," Anna says.

"Here is more. Some Wolfgang Hildebrand, the Dean of Chemistry at the University of Breslau, reports" — Ursula keeps translating what she reads — "that Frau Professor Herzmann came to see him. Frau Professor was dressed in black and asked for intercession on her husband's behalf. Which Herr Professor Hildebrand says here he is not going to do. Then some Jürgen Stein reports that Frau Professor Herzmann came to see the rector of the University, asking for his support. The Rector tried to give her money, but she refused to take it. . . Frau Professor's Berlin address. Her letter to her husband, parts of it blackened with ink. A grandson, Wilhelm Herzmann, born in 1940. Claus Herzmann was executed in the yard of Plötzensee prison, April 13, 1945. No last words were recorded. The widow was not allowed to see the body."

Ursula leafs through the last of the documents and leans back on the chair, closing her eyes. They sit silently for a while in this dreary room with its faint reek of cheap cigarette smoke. Lighter rectangular patches on the wall reveal the places from which pictures have been removed. Anna puts the papers and photographs back into the file and carefully ties the grey ribbon. When she is finished, Ursula places her hand on hers and squeezes it gently. Not a sound reaches them through the padded door.

PART VI

MONTREAL 1991

In Käthe's nursing home, the doors to the residents' rooms are left opened, and as always Anna tries not to see what's inside, not to mind their disinfectant and other smells. Waves of recorded television laughter burst out of the rooms, mixing with cries and groans. There are a few Alzheimer's patients here. The nurse who is taking Anna to Käthe's room says that out of all the ways to grow old, this must be the worst. She used to think that not remembering saved them from pain, but it wasn't so. At least for most of them. Memories leave slowly, lingering for months. They cry. They call for their parents, long dead. They think they are being robbed, held captive. One resident, she says, literally walked himself to death. Even when he no longer had the strength to stand up, his feet kept moving.

"Distraction," she says. "We try to distract them. This is all we can do."

In the dining room, the nurse says, a man of seventy has been hitting the arm of his chair incessantly for days. He won't talk with anyone anymore, but speaks to himself. A long string of curses, always the same. His daughter says he has always been such a gentle man. She is surprised he would even know words like that. The doctor ordered a foam pad around the arm of his chair, to soften the blows, but his hand is bruised and bloodied anyway. "Like a piece of raw meat," the nurse says, shaking her head in defeat. "He won't stop."

They walk down the corridor. The door to Käthe's room is closed. Anna knocks.

They can hear the shuffling of feet, and the door opens. Käthe is wearing the same old black dress with white lace collar and the pink angora sweater that softens the paleness of her face.

"Anna," she says, her eyes brightening up. "You are back."

Anna places a terra-cotta pot with a blooming azalea on the table in Käthe's room. Nothing has changed here. The photographs of William, Marilyn, and Julia on the night stand. A music box on the side table. The wicker chair by the window.

There is a small canvas stand right beside Käthe's armchair. The sweater she is knitting is thick and soft, done — Anna thinks — in what *Babcia* used to call a Norwegian pattern, two deer eyeing each other, their heads ready to lock in a fight. Navy blue and white.

"It's for Julia," Käthe says. "It will suit her. I'll make one for you, too, if you like it."

Anna has brought a tin of Turkish Delight, soft fragrant pieces buried in powdered sugar. The tin is decorated with painted figures of elephants, and Anna places it in Käthe's hands. The taste of sugar is one of the few tastes still left to Käthe.

The nurse has brought a tray with juices in small, plastic cups and the pills. Käthe swallows the pills one by one, twisting her mouth in a grimace. Anna watches, half expecting her mother-in-law to argue with the nurse, but Käthe doesn't complain. The nurse must have been bracing herself for some protests too, for she smiles and gives Anna a telling look.

Anna walks toward the window. There is a cluster of wheelchairs outside, on the lawn, beside the oak tree. She might take Käthe for a walk, she thinks. If Käthe gets tired, she will use one of the wheelchairs to push her.

In her purse there is one more letter from Germany, this time addressed to her. At the Berlin airport, Ursula leaned forward to embrace her. It was a long, silent embrace neither of them wanted to break.

Dearest Anna, Forgive me for calling you that, but you have read enough of my letters to know I am not going to stop myself from being rash and impatient. At the airport you said, "Please write to me." I was so moved that I couldn't go back to the apartment. I got into the car and drove to Berchtesgaden. Straight from the airport, like a fool. I asked for the same room at the hotel where I stayed with William last time I saw him. Sat at the same table. Tried to talk to him, but I thought of you, the hesitation in your face, and your pain.

In the morning, in Berchtesgaden, I walked alone in the streets, just walked and thought of how intertwined our lives were. It was beginning to rain, but I could still make out the shapes of the mountains. Then I thought of what you told me about this letter you got from a priest, about the boat ride on Königssee William took many years ago. It was like a sign, a thread I had to follow.

So I took a boat to Königssee, in the rain, past the white foam of waterfalls drowning in the lake. The boat was almost empty and I sat in the back, watching the waves. The young attendant came by, smiling, and asked if I were all right where I was. The drizzle was getting through, he said, and the seat around me was wet already. I said I was fine, but he lowered a see-through plastic cover, to protect me from the rain.

At St. Bartholomä peninsula, I wandered inside the old chapel with its red onion-shaped domes. When I left the chapel the rain got worse, so I decided to go back. I joined the line-up, which wound around a wooden shed, mostly young families with children, joking, trying to keep warm. A little boy in a pointed Bavarian hat, a little troll, tried to charm me. He hid behind his father, and then poked his head out and smiled. "I'm a real mountain climber," he said. "See my tooth," he said and opened his mouth wide to show me the empty space, "I lost it yesterday." Kids in yellow raincoats, rubber boots were running around, screaming and laughing. An elderly woman in front of me was writing her name on the wooden beam of the shed.

The boats arrived, one by one, silently. "Berchtesgaden," "Obersalzberg," "Königssee," filling up quickly. I got a seat across from another family, parents with three children, the youngest around two. The father's hair was wet and curly, and, with his right arm, he was holding the little one who was standing on his lap. The child was leaning backwards and was trying to smack the father over the head, and the father ducked. Every time he missed, the little boy burst out laughing. There was no echo, no flügelhorn . . .

You said you came here looking for an epiphany. Will that do? Urs.

"Julia brought us these," Käthe says, when the nurse leaves closing the door behind her, pointing to a bouquet of yellow daffodils on the table. "She said you would like them, too."

"I have something for you, from Berlin," Anna says and takes out the present Frau Strauss has given her. The parcel contains a beautiful edition of Goethe's *Faust*, leather bound, with gilded pages. Käthe opens it and leafs through it.

"You liked Ulrike, *nein*?" she asks.

"Yes," Anna says. ""I liked her very much."

"We were always good friends, in Breslau and in Berlin," Käthe says. "I don't know what I would have done without her. She helped me a lot."

"I've also brought these," Anna says, handing her the photographs Frau Strauss gave her in Berlin, and the ones she herself took of the Herzmanns' Breslau house. "You and Ulrike, William, Moni, Frau Strauss's daughter," she says as she gives the pictures to Käthe one by one. But it is only when Käthe sees the snapshot of her old house, that Anna can see she is truly moved. She looks at it for a long time, and then points to the sharp endings of spikes in the iron gate.

"The gate," she says. "Willi liked to swing on it. Back and forth. Back and forth. I told him not to, but he wouldn't listen. I was afraid he would hurt himself."

Anna is waiting for Käthe to say more, but her mother-in-law is silent again. So it is Anna who speaks instead. The house is in a good shape, she says, well cared for. She has been inside. Admired the view of the back garden. The evergreens have grown tall — the hostas are especially beautiful. The street couldn't have changed that much, either. Karlovitz was not bombed, like other Breslau districts. There were no empty places, no signs of ruins.

Käthe has closed her eyes. She is listening.

"Frau Strauss asked me to tell you that you did the right thing—leaving. She said that you would know what she meant."

Outside the window another scrawny black squirrel digs into the ground, his whole body shaking from the effort. They are hungry now, rooting for last year's acorns, the ones they buried. Silly, they never know where to dig, ruining the lawn.

Through the window, Anna sees patches of bare earth and tufts of upturned grass.

No echo, no flügelhorn . . . Anna murmurs to herself. No, this is not much of an epiphany. Once, when she first fell in love with William, she prayed that with him she would be better, that she would understand more. Now, she can only wait. Wait for the sound of the elevator stopping at the floor and for the sound of Julia's fast, determined steps along the corridor. Until then she will watch how the darkness gathers outside the window, how the retreating light transfigures the spreading crown of the oak tree in the yard.

Käthe is clearing her throat. The picture of the Breslau house is still in her hand.

"I want to ask you something, Ann*chen*" her hoarse voice breaks the silence. "Willi, he turned out all right, *nein*?"

"Yes," Anna says, softly. "Yes. Willi turned out all right."

THE END

ACKNOWLEDGEMENTS

I would like to thank Canada Council for financial support that assissted me in writing this book.

My specials thanks go to Christopher Reynolds, Shaena Lambert, Barbara Lambert, Lilian Nattel, Ruth Beissel, Jutta Spengemann, Leanore Lieblein, Florence Rosberg, Piotr and Anna Wróbel for their insights and generous comments that kept me going.

I owe personal notes of thanks to my agent, Anne McDermid for her tireless persistence and encouragement, and to my editor at Dundurn, Marc Côté, for his guidance, sensitivity, and advice.

And, as always, to Zbyszek and Szymek.

CPSIA information can be obtained at www.ICGtesting.com
Printed in the USA
LVOW060703130113

315413LV00002B/26/P